MOLL

Alexander Cordell

MOLL

WEIDENFELD AND NICOLSON
LONDON

for Glenys Parry-Williams

ISBN 0 297 84023 1

Typeset by Selectmove Limited, London

Printed by Butler & Tanner Ltd,
Frome and London

Acknowledgements

I wish to thank many librarians, who, as usual, have given me assistance in research for this book; especially Wrexham Library Arts Centre and the Local Studies Department of Shropshire County Library, for information on the life of 'Wild Humphrey Kynaston', the Shropshire highwayman known as The Welsh Robin Hood.

I am also most grateful to Mr Dillon Brooks, the landlord of the *Old Three Pigeons* inn at Nesscliff, near Shrewsbury; now a most respectable establishment, but once – if the depredation of Wild Humphrey is to be believed – the despair of the authorities a century and a half ago.

To Miss Deidre Beddoe I am indebted for her detailed history *Welsh Convict Women* (Stewart Williams Publishers) which has formed the basis of much of my research into 19th century transportation of female convicts.

My thanks, also, to John Murray (Publishers) Ltd for permission to use an extract from Alfred Noyes's famous poem, 'The Highwayman' *Collected Poems* and to W.E. Henley's *Viking Books of Poetry for the English Speaking World*, edited by Richard Aldington, from whose poem 'Echoes' is taken 'Fill a Glass with Golden Wine.'

I thank Marjorie Pickthall for the use of her poem 'Duna' *Home Book of Verse* edited by B.E. Stephenson (and *Magic Casements* by G.S. Carhart) also Mozart's librettist for the words of the song 'When a Maiden Takes your Fancy' (Il Seraglio).

Despite attempts the author has not been able to discover the source of the poems which begin, 'Tonight my Soul is set among the Stars' and 'O, daughter mine, whose future is my prayer.'

My gratitude to the poets who have enhanced the manuscript.

Wales,
1989

Author's note

During his trial for highway robbery, Sir Richard Carling stated that the thefts of which he was accused took place at inns on the road between Hungerford and Reading.

Subsequent evidence disproved this, however: the theft of valuables occurred on the road to Shrewsbury, while Sir Richard was operating from his base at the Old Three Pigeons Inn (and Kynaston's Cave) at Nesscliff.

The perjury increased his sentence, yet knowing this, the man persisted; it can only be assumed that he gave the false evidence in order to avoid implicating the woman in the affair – Madame Le Roy, courtesan and thief; one known to the authorities as the notorious Moll Walbee.

So devoted was the legendary Moll Walbee,
wife of the Norman knight, William de Braose,
that when his castle at Hay was laid waste,
she rebuilt it overnight by carrying the stones
in her apron.

Book I

1839–SHROPSHIRE

One

It was an era of sparkling eyes and snowy bosoms, the latter expressed by the bulging matron in the rumbling, swaying stagecoach, who fixed Moll Walbee with an eagle eye. The lanky lawyer, sitting beside the matron (so soon to be her lover), did likewise. And Moll, beautifully attired in the stolen clothes of her employer, sat beside a portly bishop who dozed in snorts and starts.

Travelling under the title of Madame Le Roy and accepted by everybody as a member of the French aristocracy, Moll was confident that her reputation as a pickpocket was far behind her in the slums of Paris. Dark-haired, she watched the pastoral country of Shropshire fly past through half-closed eyes. Soon the ancient town of Shrewsbury would raise its spires on the horizon; a night there, then on to London where fortune, thought Moll, would surely smile.

All three of her travelling companions showed interest in Moll; her youth and beauty called to them. The bishop did it with artifice, his rheumy eyes tracing the curves of her bodice and the shadowed divide of her breast. The lawyer, risking detection by the matron, peered through his hooded lids, taking in every item of her dress (all of which denoted wealth) from her broad-rimmed black hat to her white leather boots; vaguely, he wondered, having little knowledge of women, if the black hair that tumbled in ringlets was a wig; if it was, thought he, it must have cost a pretty penny. The matron rejected Moll's blatant confidence with repressed explosive piety. And

Moll, suspecting all this and enjoying every moment, sat back in the cushions and listened to the drumming of the hooves on the flinted road. Not even the Chester post-boy's comment diverted her mind from her plans for London.

'Bloody 'ell, Joe – ye don't get many o' those to the pound. If she ties her bootlaces, they'll roll down the hill.'

Dusk and bats were playing in the sky when the stage-coach had left Chester – the Chester to Shrewsbury 'Highflyer' was always slow at an average speed of three miles an hour, for the beery driver stopped at every staging station for ale. Now, near midnight, with the moonlit Severn dancing through Montford Bridge like a capricious Welsh maid, the wind rose in expectant anger; blustering in the lonely hedgerows, it drove its shepherd's fleece across a ghostly moon. Disturbed by the oncoming clatter of hooves and wheels, crows and ravens arose like burned paper in squawking, barelegged quarrels: a bustard, tearing at roadside prey, crouched with a bloody beak, waiting for the monster to pass; from the thickets came shrieks of little things dying. And at a lonely verge emerged a highwayman: long-booted and heavily masked, with his black coat swirling in the wind, he came, and his big mare reared up, her forelegs pawing the air as the stagecoach skidded to a halt.

'*Stand and deliver!*'

Thrown to the floor in a tangle of legs and petticoats, the lawyer was up first and back on his seat with his sallow face well down into his starched collar, while the matron, her plump hands upon her jewels, shrieked hysterically. The bishop sat benignly, crossing himself and praying, while Moll, scrambling free, opened the window of the stagecoach, put out her head and cried in a shrill French accent:

'But *monsieur*, this is wonderful! *C'est magnifique!*'

Ignoring her, the highwayman seized the driver by the leg, somersaulting him down into the road. Then, dismounting, he bowed before the open window and his cockaded hat with its red rose of England swept the road. His eyes glittered behind his mask.

'At your service, *mademoiselle*.' This he said in perfect French, which delighted Moll.

'*Parlez-vous Français, monsieur?*' She fluttered an eye.

'Ah, *oui, mademoiselle!*' And in English added, 'You are truly French?'

'She's French, all right,' said the matron, recovering, then shouted, 'Oh, we shall all be raped!'

'If you are lucky, *madame*,' said Moll, 'so stop the snivelling.'

And the highwayman shouted, 'Out, all of you! Out on to the road – let's see what you've got', and with his horse pistol, waved them into line. There he began to relieve them of money and possessions, dispensing the matron's jewels into a small leather bag at his waist. Now, towering above Moll, his fingers toyed with a pearl necklace at her throat.

'Of paste, *mademoiselle?*'

'Of course,' replied Moll. 'The real ones are at 'ome with me 'usband.'

'You are married, yet wear no ring?'

'That, too, is also at 'ome with me 'usband.'

The moon pulled up her skirts and the country blazed with new light. He asked, 'Then what does a man demand of one so beautiful? A kiss, perhaps?' And his eyes moved over her from the dark hair upon her shoulders to the elegant sweep of her over-skirt of white lace and gold. Scarcely the travelling clothes of a lady of quality, thought he – something the matron had already perceived: possibly the French aristocracy often attired themselves strangely, he considered.

5

The highwayman, knowing many women, had always done his best to leave them contented. Biddy, for instance, the serving maid at the Old Three Pigeons at Nesscliff, had little cause for complaint. Though the lady of royal connections, wife of a Spaniard – she whose amours had forced him to become gentleman of the road – had been unwise to talk at table . . . But the only French woman he had pleasured was a milkmaid aged sixteen in a barn near Arras, a pert, tearful little creature with hayseed upon her breasts. From the humble to the arrogant he had taken them on the road; most had begged tearfully for their lives and their virtue (usually in that order); others had been subject to the vapours, fainting off in the arms of terrified escorts, when a loosening of the stays (which he always insisted upon performing himself) usually revived them. But this particular French girl showed no fear, and her deportment portrayed excellent breeding.

'Then a kiss, perhaps, *madame*, since the pearls are artificial?'

'Why not?' asked Moll, and he took her into his arms, and, bending above her, whispered:

'Actually, I prefer them married. The cheese is that much sweeter when nibbled by another mouse,' and what began as a kiss of quiet formality ended in heat and gusty breathing.

'Why, the *hussy*!' said the matron indignantly.

'It is the French,' explained the lawyer with droll charm. 'Very handy from the waist down – you know what they are.'

The bishop, however, was smiling at the long embrace. For the lips of Moll, by some strange phantasm, seemed pressed upon his own. Long ago, on the banks of the Liffey back home in Ireland, he had kissed a girl like this, and the perfume of her lingered upon his mouth.

'I am obliged to you,' said the highwayman. 'That was delightful.'

'For me too,' answered Moll. 'One day I would like you to meet me 'usband.'

'*Madame*, I'd be charmed.'

'In a duel, per'aps . . .?'

This stilled him, and she added, 'But you can die for two kisses as easily as for one, *monsieur*. You will please kiss me again?'

'It will be a pleasure, milady,' and he bent to her for the second time, which was a mistake, for she bit him. Laughing he pushed her away; still laughing, he swung a leg over his horse while Moll danced like a dervish in the middle of the road, shouting:

'You call me a nibble, eh? I am not a nibbler nor a cheeses, and my man is not a mouse. Next time I come on coaches I bring a gun, like you, and shoot holes in your arses – you 'ear me? *Sacré bleu!* I bloody kill you!' and she picked up stones and flung them after him as, laughing gustily, he galloped away. Now, with her hat off and her hair down, she raced after him in the moonlight, shouting:

'Bastard! One day we meet again, *monsieur*. Bastard!'

'My dear woman,' protested the lawyer, 'the man has gone, pray compose yourself.'

'And shoot holes in your arses, too,' cried Moll, and got back into her seat.

The coach rumbled on again, and the smiling moon, full and yellow, was sitting on top of Wrekin Hill like a gypsy's tambourine.

Two

The highwayman, more interested in Moll than profit, reined in his black mare (which now had its forelegs painted white to prevent identification) and tethered her at the Severn Arms, Montford Bridge, where the stagecoach, after shedding a wheel, was being repaired.

Elegantly attired in a gray frock coat and silken breeches, and no longer wearing the mask of a highwayman, Sir Richard Carling (recently cashiered from the 38th Regiment of Foot) knew he was taking a calculated risk. Any of the three old fools in that stagecoach, quite apart from the French girl, might recognize him, he knew, but women and gold, he reasoned, often demanded risk. Also Biddy Boddy, of the Old Three Pigeons at Nesscliff, had gone down with adolescent spots, which had seriously perturbed him; so this delightful French piece had arrived at precisely the right time. Twisting the ear of a passing pot-boy (whose name was Tommy Ructions) he entered the tap-room of the Arms and thumped the bar for ale.

Sir Richard's entry coincided with the arrival of another coach from Chester, and through the open door of the tap-room he saw the Quality coming in: the elders and their bewhiskered sons of muscular virility, square chins and barks; while their shagged out, nasal wives implored the servants to control the scurrying children. And through this assembly came the inn landlord, his fat arms outflung like a herald of Caesar, crying for passage:

'Room, please, ladies and gentlemen—allow entry for our foreign guest!' And Moll, looking gorgeous under a pink parasol, inclined her head courteously this way and that to the bows of the men and bobbed curtsies of the servants.

'By God,' whispered Richard into his pewter, 'have they many more like you in France?' Reaching out, he got the same Tommy Ructions by the ear again, drew him close and whispered, 'Her name? *Quick* – her name?'

'Who, sir? What, sir?'

'Her name – the French one – I didn't catch her name.'

'Not allowed to give names, your honour!'

'Her name. I also want her room number.'

'Oh, Jesus,' said the pot-boy, wriggling, and Richard said softly into the ear he held, 'You have been to my room, small one?'

'Aye, sir. Took your bag up, sir, didn't I, sir?'

'Then you probably noticed what would appear to be a jar of pickled onions standing on my dressing table?'

'No, sir!'

'Next time, look. They are, in fact, not pickled onions, but the little goolies which pot-boys like you normally keep in their trews – they who have refused to give me ladies' room numbers.'

'Room number four, ground floor, sir,'.

'Excellent,' replied Richard. 'Here's a penny, and there's more where it came from. Now her name?'

'Madame Le Roy,' said Tommy Ructions.

Wondering where the next guinea was coming from – having already spent her entire fortune on the coach fare from Chester to London – Moll, now bathed and changed into a clean set of her mistress's beautiful underclothes (the petticoats were of Chinese silk edged with Alençon needle-point lace, the drawers with ruffles of pink) now sat at her dressing table in bedroom number three and with bright red garters at the knee combed her hair in what was afterwards known as the chignon style. Later, with her parasol at a jaunty angle, Moll sauntered out to the river bank where the stalls were being set for the *Calan Mai* market, it being the first day of summer.

All here was sun and gold, with burly auctioneers shouting their wares and farmers' wives, starch-aproned and busty, duffing up butter pats and fishing out golden hot bread from outdoor ovens.

There were cheese stalls, trinket stalls, fruit and vegetable stalls laid out in rows, with apples polished like the cheeks of cherubs; wine from Spain, parrots, perfumes from the East and handbags of the finest Moroccan leather. And, although the market was packed with humanity from gentry to slum beggars, Richard Carling knew, without turning, the nearness of Moll behind him with the instinct of the hunting male. Therefore he held higher the leather bag he was examining, as if for her inspection, and asked:

'Two shillings? Is it fair, you think?'

Moll replied coldly, 'It is of real Moroccan leather, *monsieur*. A man would be a skinflint to pay so little.'

'You know eastern prices?'

'Perhaps not, but I know a bargain when I see one,' and the stall-holder bawled from a toothless mouth:

'It is indeed, lady. Made from young goat leather tanned in our village in Algiers with imported divi-divi, the dried seed-pods of South America – none other – and decorated by the needles of our wisest people.'

'That is good,' answered Moll, 'but if you stop lying, we will know that they come from England and are tanned with bark.' She turned to Richard. 'You are going to buy it?'

'On your recommendation. You called it a bargain.'

Richard took the bag and paid his two shillings.

'One for me also,' said Moll. 'Sixpence?' She rummaged in her handbag.

'Two shillings!' cried the stall-holder affronted. 'It was agreed.'

'He agreed it,' replied Moll, 'not I. Argue more and I will demand ten per cent off for cash.' She gave him sixpence and took the bag.

'Call the policeman!'

'Yes, call him, for I know you long-nosed thieves. This leather is stolen, is it not?' And the hawker moaned at the sky:

'Foreign lady, do not talk of theft, I beg you!' And he took the coin, spun it up, and bit it in his teeth, saying:

'It is always a pleasure to do business with the French. Please come again,' and Richard protested:

'What about me? Hers was sixpence and I paid two shillings!'

'That is the difference between us,' said Moll. 'The English may 'ave the Colonies, but one day we will 'ave the world.'

'It is a topic for discussion,' said Richard, and they walked off together, each with their Moroccan bag.

Later, Moll put on a nightdress of such exquisite silk that it could only have been afforded by an Eastern princess. Then, opening a bottle of lavender oil, she rubbed some into her small, white hands, especially the left one. For this hand, said she, had to be especially cherished: it was one that could lift a matelot's wallet from under his nose without the bat of his eye. Now, as she did every night, Moll wrapped this left hand in muslin to keep it tender, and, sitting at the desk in her room, picked up a plume pen and wrote on notepaper, in French. This, being translated into English, read:

> My darling Chantelle,
> This is the first opportunity I have had to write since leaving Paris, but I cannot allow your eighth birthday to pass without sending you a kiss – here then is a large one from your ever-loving sister.

From Le Havre I came across the sea to a place in England called Dover, and from there journeyed to Wales. Here I worked as a parlour maid in a rich house and, through industry and loyalty, was shown great kindness; I left there after only a month with a purse nearly empty, but with half my generous mistress's wardrobe. Now I am on my way to London where, without doubt, I shall be shown equal consideration by people richer than I: so rich, indeed, that given good fortune I may soon be able to ask our Uncle Maurice to put you on a ship to England, where we will be reunited. That we will soon meet again is the loving wish of Francesca,

Your devoted sister.

1st May 1839.

PS: it would be unwise to tell you my whereabouts.

Now, before retiring for the night, Moll sat by the French doors (which were level with the garden) and looked out upon the lawns of the inn. The night was black in a gusty blustering of distant trees; beyond lay the quicksilver brilliance of the lovely Severn, the river that had been ploughed by the boats of invading Phoenicians and heard the tramping of the sandalled feet of Rome on their way to Vericonium, for history was Moll's favourite subject once . . . during the time of her father's wealth.

Now, however, she began to wonder how she was going to pay the landlord's bill when the stagecoach set off in the morning, for once she had taken the role of a French aristocrat the die was cast and she would have to play the drama to the end. Should her plan fail then it would be back to the justice of France, or languish in a stinking English prison such as the infamous Newgate.

She studied her face in the bedroom mirror, turning it this way and that, and said:

'You are Francesca Le Roy, the wife of the first secretary to the French ambassador in London. Moll Walbee, the pickpocket of the Paris streets who killed her lover, the thief Jean Pierre, is dead, you 'ear me? *Dead.*'

These words she repeated in French, savouring every syllable the better to understand it.

From bedroom number four, next door to hers, Moll listened to the petulant complaints of the matron who had lost her jewels, and a serving maid's consoling replies. Somewhere beyond the lawns an owl hooted dismally, its cry increasing Moll's sudden sense of foreboding, and her thoughts turned again to the handsome young man she had met in the market – it being important for her to find someone with whom to form an alliance necessary to the future plans she had in mind. And best if such a partner was a male, thought Moll, for a man could prove handy in a world of violence.

Of all the men she had yet seen, this one was the most impressive; but strangely, Moll could not banish the impression that she had seen him somewhere earlier . . . perhaps in the inborn arrogance with which he held himself? she wondered.

Meanwhile the matron in the room next door sat up in her bed awaiting a visitation from her lover-to-be, the lawyer. Earlier, she had arranged her wig to fall upon her great bosom like two sets of curly black candles. And now, with the French windows unlocked to facilitate his entry, she closed her eyes and breathed with mounting desire.

Somewhere in the inn a clock struck midnight and in the tap-room the lawyer, the prospective lover, obliterated the thought with another swill at his brandy.

'Reckon you've 'ad enough, ain't you, sir?' asked the landlord. 'It's time you was abed wi' your handsome wife.'

Richard, having slipped out into the stable yard to water and feed his horse, returned to the tap-room to finish his second tankard of ale, and the lawyer, now three sheets in the wind, surveyed him with a glassy stare. In the deep recesses of his befuddled brain, he cursed not only the landlord, the inn itself and the matron awaiting him, but also the highwayman who had relieved her of her jewels on the road – jewels he had planned to acquire for himself, being a lawyer.

Further, he cursed the legal circumstances that had brought him to this pass, for lawyers who absconded with their clients' money were the legitimate victims of those who shared their deadly secrets. And with over ten thousand pounds of the matron's capital stacked away where she couldn't find it, he now had to dance to the jig of her desires, since, if anyone was likely to smell a rat, it was this accursed matron.

Now marriage to a lifetime of her gluttonous obesity faced the lawyer as an alternative to arrest for breach of promise; to say nothing of a gaggle of honking bloody relatives and seven obnoxious brats by previous husbands all deceased through biological deficiencies.

The outcome of his criminality faced the lawyer. Imminently the necessity to prove his virility would be upon him, for the matron, he suspected, would not take kindly to a wilting lover.

Inexpert in the business of copulation with anyone, including large matrons, the lawyer had only the faintest idea of how to set about it. Indeed, his sole experiences in this connection went back nearly fifty years when, enticed into the woodshed by Dirty Girtie, the girl next door, he had stood, aged seven, on a pile of bricks in an attempt to reach her lips in a game she called 'Mothers and Fathers'. Later, this descended into an exercise named 'Hunt the Wren'. He never knew if he'd got the wren or not, but discovered that she wore orange-box rope for garters. Therefore, armed only with this primitive knowledge, and with a large lover awaiting him, the lawyer yearned for Girtie's lisped instructions like a drowning man clutches at straws.

Richard, with his own particular business in mind and anxious to be rid of him, assisted him through the door and halfway along the passageway. But the instant Richard left him, the lawyer, like a man on his way to his execution, shuffled out into the garden and sought concealment in a clump of rhododendron bushes. There he awaited the courage to enter the matron's room through the French windows.

Richard, in his nightshirt, now tiptoed along the corridors in search of what he thought was Moll's bed-room and was disappointed to find it locked. But, knowing that women admire persistence, he now entered the garden and, searching until he found the French window, was overjoyed when it opened to a touch. So was the matron, who, believing him to be the lawyer, opened fat arms to him. Meanwhile, the lawyer, concealed in the garden, rubbed his eyes in disbelief, for nothing like this had been described in Blackstone's *Commentaries on the Laws of England.*

And, while the lawyer stared with drunken incredulity, Richard, his caution banished by such a warm reception, now indulged himself in a rapture so careless that it was a full minute before he realized he was with the wrong lover. Leaping out, still unrecognized, he fled.

The matron screamed long and loud which, as Moll explained later, all hell broke loose at the inn.

Out into the garden came the aristocracy, the men in nightshirts, the ladies carrying shrieking children, with maids yelling, cats being booted and dogs barking all over Montford.

Which gave Moll the opportunity to drift like a ghost around the vacated rooms, lifting a ring here, a necklace there, and shovelling into her little Moroccan bag loose change usually deposited by males when removing trousers. Then she drifted back to her own room, unseen, unsuspected.

And Tommy Ructions, sitting in a broom cupboard under the stairs and listening to the commotion, smiled his toothless smile.

Three

The next morning was bright with sun, but doleful at the breakfast table where long faces complained about the thieving antics of the younger generation, for Moll's nocturnal expedition had gone well. She, for her part, ate heartily of devilled kidneys and bacon, bowing this way and that in harmony with the morning, with Richard at the next table down in the mouth.

Later, with her luggage aboard the repaired stagecoach, Moll patted the head of Tommy Ructions in the hall and, kissing his angelic face, took her leave of landlord and servants in grandiloquent style. And then, with Richard and she travelling inside, two traders and their wives outside, and Richard's black mare tethered behind, the postilion awakened the village with his post-horn and the coach clattered over Montford Bridge for Shrewsbury.

'*Monsieur,*' Moll asked Richard, 'did I not understand that his grace the bishop was to accompany us?'

This occurred half a mile up the road and Richard looked through the back window.

'You're right,' he answered. 'Here he is now.'

The stagecoach halted, and the bishop, red-faced, staggered up, shouting at the driver:

'Would ye leave me behind, you idiot? And me guaranteed a safe passage to the Ecclesiastical Commissioners in Shrewsbury?', and with the help of Richard climbed aboard. Easing his great shining backside on to the seat beside Moll, he added:

'Beggin' ye pardon for the affront to ye dignity, milady, but I'd just left the yard to perform a natural function when away to hell this thing went carryin' all me personals,' and he leaned out of the window and shook a red fist, bawling, 'Ye'll get no tip off me, ye spalpeen, indeed, I'll beat the asses reins off ye when you get me into town.' Then he stood up and bowed to Moll, saying:

'In all the world, have ye met a place like that blitherin' inn, lady? Sleep? I never closed me eyes, for there was a fella next door slandering the night wi' wheezing and snorin', and then there comes a screeching tumult wi' folks in nightclothes scamperin' crazy!'

'Thieves were about, your grace,' announced Richard gently, and shot a lingering look at Moll and the little Moroccan bag lying upon her lap.

All the guests, including himself, had been interrogated by the Montford special constable brought in by the landlord; only Moll had been granted immunity from this, with fervent hopes that the French aristocracy hadn't been too inconvenienced.

'Thieves, did ye say?' cried the bishop. 'And other shenanigans too, son, take it from me; for some plump, hardy wenches were takin' the midnight air an' all – saw one as clear as me eye, bumming up her skirts across the lawns, with a quare fella after her in his nightshirt, and me a celibate.'

'Did he catch her?' asked Moll.

'Oh, Allanah, I hope not, darling, for she was a woman o' plume and beauty, and twenty years younger I'd have opened me door to her.

'"*Cead mille falteagh!*" I'd have called to her – "Welcome, kindly welcome", for I don't object to hanky-panky if I'm a party to it. Is there money missing?'

'About ten in gold, I understand, but also jewels, *n'est ce pas?*'

'Lifted by somebody who knew exactly what they were doing,' added Richard. 'And the village constable was useless – it takes a thief to catch a thief.'

'You can say that again, son! There's swindlers, card-sharpers and fly-pockets, to say nothin' o' Dick Turpins and suchlike lurkin' on the roads. We'll be lucky to get to Shrewsbury in one piece.'

'It looks as if trouble's already here,' said Richard.

He was right. Mounted horsemen surrounded the coach. It skidded to a halt, and the landlord of the Severn Arms shouted, pulling open the coach door:

'Gotcha! Thought you'd got away wiv it, did you?' He felt the bishop's collar and heaved him out on to the road. 'Rapacity and kleptomania – I can smell one a mile off. Come easy, fella, come simple,' cried he, 'for the last bugger I had wiv a collar back to front was a bloody footpad,' and he shook away the bishop's protests. 'Come on, we'll soon 'ave you safe and happy in the Montford clink, my lovely,' and Richard, intervening, said:

'Are you sure you've got the right person, landlord?' The little man bowed, his moleskin cap sweeping the road.

'Your honour, how could a fine gent wiv your deport-ment know a buccaneer done up in the rig o' a bishop? Don't you realize that, within another mile, you and your fair creature' (and here he bowed to Moll) 'could 'ave been dished, diddled, done brown and abducted to foreign parts? – you in a den o' thieves, sir, and your lady in a whorehouse, beggin' your pardon, madam.' Moll sat back in the cushions while the bishop sobbed:

'I am innocent! By the nails of the holy Cross, ma'am, I am innocent. Mercy, in the name of God!'

'Shake him proper, mind,' said the village constable coming up, 'and he'll be tinkling out the swag,' and they upended the bishop and shook him to rattle his bones.

19

'Get 'is luggage, landlord. Doubtless the loot's in there,' and Moll said with great sincerity:

'*Messieurs*, you are perfectly certain you 'ave got the right man? As my friend here would agree, thieves come in many different shapes and sizes . . .'

'Leave it to me, lady,' said the landlord. 'Bill Bottom o' the Severn Arms is a very good judge o' character,' and with the bishop howling, they dragged him away. The horses were whipped up; the coach clattered on through Shelton Roughs for Shrewsbury.

A fair was at its height around the Welsh Bridge as the coach threaded a path through the crowds of hawkers and vendors packed around the Shrewsbury Hotel.

The country folk had flooded in with their farm produce and their stalls were end to end on both banks of the river, while along the roads the sunlit morning was filled with the squawks of hens, the shrieks of sacrificial pigs and the baa-baaings of sheep on their way to slaughter. Fat upland cows, their chops plastered with the gold dross of buttercups, munched greetings to the summer, and the balmy air, gentle with promise, was perfumed with udder-milk and honey: from a shine of blackbirds came the songs of coloratura sopranos.

Leaning out of the coach window, Moll shouted excited greetings in French to scampering children, and blew kisses to their buxom mothers: these, bunned up in their starched linen aprons, waved welcoming hands as the coach went past, meanwhile stirring up huge vats of steaming tripe and onions and tended sizzling pans of faggots and peas, and the air was filled with the cries of packmen and hawkers and the rumbling of gigs and carts.

On, on, and Market Square was packed with people like herrings in a brine-barrel, with clusters of children around the Punch and Judy shows. There were dancing bears, monkeys climbing sticks to the music of hurdy-gurdies, tramps dressed like sailors dancing the hornpipe, and the old girls from the Workhouse Outing kicking up their black-stockinged legs to Irish fiddles. Urchins, ragged and sallow-faced, drifted among the people for easy pickings; professional pickpockets – instantly identified by Moll – worked serenely amid the shoulders of fustian cloth or lace.

Now the coach gathered speed and swung into the entrance of the Talbot, the hotel from which stagecoaches radiated to London and the provinces, mainly carrying the very best people.

Some of the very best people were already in residence, which was why Moll had travelled to it all the way from Chester. The newspapers being full of talk about Sir Roger Martin and Lady Thora, the rage of Thespian London.

These famous actors, with their travelling company, had been touring with *The Tempest*, Shakespeare's epic, and enjoying large audiences; and Lady Thora, it was reported, was spending most of her income upon jewellery, a fact Moll had noted. These two were enjoying morning coffee in the great hall when Moll arrived.

Sir Roger adjusted his monocle, the better to view the apparition in white, which, followed by Richard, appeared to float into the hotel hall. 'By gad, milady,' said he to his wife, 'just give an eye to that!' And Lady Thora, once a courtesan of low degree but now a lady of quality, whispered back:

'And here my duck – in Salop! You want to get on to that, you never know what'll come of it. You 'ave her, I'll take her escort.'

'Shall we make their acquaintance?'

'Lead me to it,' replied Lady Thora.

Curtsies and bows now, the overborne pomp of staged greetings, but Moll's eyes were upon the ropes of pearls on

21

Lady Thora's wrinkled breast . . . and the chunky gold bracelets that rattled at her wrists.

'Charmed, I'm sure!'

'Foreign, are you?'

'French, milady.'

'Your husband, ma'am . . .?' Lady Thora's baggy eyes twinkled out of her long-lost youth.

'A travelling companion only, I fear,' replied Richard, gallantly. 'They're a pair of queer old birds,' he added to Moll when they got clear. 'I suspect we're likely to see more of them.'

Moll did not reply. If the hand of fortune played her kindly here, she reflected as she unpacked her travelling trunk (taking care to put the little Moroccan bag safely under the mattress of her big four-poster . . .), she could clear enough with a good fence, and in one good lift, to put the future of Chantelle beyond doubt.

Chantelle . . . *Chantelle* . . . Moll saw two bright eyes, incredibly blue, against the pastoral beauty of a French village.

At dinner in the Talbot that evening, Moll ate duck and green peas – she always consumed exactly what she liked; it made no difference to her figure – in the knowledge that this time she need not be afraid of the bill: the ten guineas in gold from the guests in the Severn Arms had seen to that, though the jewellery had yet to be fenced.

'May I join you?' asked Richard, suddenly arriving.

He really was the most handsome man in evening dress. Moll replied:

'If I do not 'ave to pay for your dinner.'

Grinning, he took a seat opposite her.

'On the coach you said you was a poet, *monsieur*. All poets is 'ungry and 'ave little money to pay.'

'Actually, I had the intention of paying for yours.'

Voilà! thought Moll. 'Ere we go! All the same, these men. They buy the dinner and think they buy the body;

they spend six months on the bosom and the rest of their lives trying to climb back on to it. The nearest this one would get to a breast was the chicken he was ordering now. Besides, he was attractive; this made her wary.

The duck and peas finished, Moll belched, pardoned, patted her chest, made big eyes at him – 'Oh, la – la!' and began to pick her teeth with gusto. With one eyebrow slightly raised, Richard watched her, allowances having to be made for French cousins, of course; yes, thought he, she needed watching, but this one he could watch all night.

Soon, given reasonable luck, he would make love to her. In the last few hours, attendant upon his growing suspicions regarding her, a small intriguing affection for her was stirring. Her brash charm vied with her astonishing beauty, in pink (and it was surely the most expensive dress on a woman he had ever seen) she looked ravishing.

'Get on with your chicken, *monsieur*,' said Moll.

This man's presence was having a frightening effect upon her. He had arrived at a time when she had set her mind upon relieving Lady Thora of her jewels, and this was disturbing.

Even his nearness across the table – and this, she told herself was pure adolescence – brought a dryness to her throat that the wine did not banish. Moll watched him, her expression unchanging over the rim of her glass; it was a long time since Jean Pierre had made love to her.

No man, she reasoned, had the right to affect her thus without her permission, and sitting there she wished him to hell and back. Now she raised her eyes and watched him while he ate. This he did with excellent manners; in all his movement dignity and good breeding persisted. Clearly, too, he was beautifully educated.

'You will call me Richard, please?' he asked, smiling up.

'No,' replied Moll.

The dining room was filling to capacity, mainly by the frock-coated, mutton-chopped elders of the town with their dumpy, commonplace wives; most of the men, Moll noticed, were bald. Wealth and fat living (while the poor starved relentlessly), seemed to remove hair quicker than scissors.

Such as these she had seen in Paris, while she roamed the slums with Chantelle in search of food. These she had seen behind the windows of fine Parisian restaurants – a sea of bloated faces and piquant profiles, mainly of female adolescents out for the night with lecherous uncles. In the dining room now were the boozy actors of Sir Roger's travelling players: flamboyant and exuberant, they stuffed smoked salmon and pâté into their choleric faces and washed it down with iced champagne, meanwhile quoting aloud from Aristotle to Racine and the obscenities of an unrefined Chaucer. Lady Thora, for instance, her hair down, flushed with wine, and most of her bosom spilling over her laced-up corselet, declared to the room in a harsh contralto:

'"And, like this unsubstantial pageant faded, leave not a rack behind. We are such stuff as dreams are made on; and our little life is rounded with a sleep . . ."'

'Talking of sleep, I'll be early to bed tonight,' said Moll, 'if only to be rid of this lot.'

'You dislike them?' asked Richard.

She emptied her hands at him. 'They are not real!'

'Of course not. They are actors.'

'Are poets real?'

Richard shrugged. 'Some – those who are worthy to be called poets.'

'And you are not?'

For reply, he leaned towards her, and filling both their glasses, held up his between them, saying:

'If poetry is tonight the main topic, would you like to hear a little of mine?'

24

'Of course!' And Richard quoted:

'"Fill a glass with golden wine, and awhile your lips are wet, press their perfume unto mine, and forget that every kiss we take and give, leaves us less of life to live . . ."' and he touched her glass with his, adding:

'"Then again your whim and mine, in a little while have met. All your sweets to me resign, nor regret that we press with every breath, sighing, singing, sighing, singing . . . nearer death . . .?"'

There came a silence between them. Moll said:

'*Mon Dieu*! How beautiful . . .!'

'You like it?'

'It astonishes me. When did you compose it? Last night while with the matron?'

'Touché,' he answered. 'Last night I was outwitted.'

'So was she, by the noise she made. Did she not enjoy it?'

He watched her again, his eyes narrowed. Vaguely, Moll wondered where she had seen those eyes before; they glittered now with a magnetic fascination.

It was cooler in the garden.

Here, amid flowering azaleas they wandered together under a fractured, opal moon. A little wind stirred a tracery of branches; the earth was vibrant with new summer smells. And Moll, who had a nose for a scurrying mouse, named to herself the long dead meadowsweet and celandine. Once here, she thought, bloomed the vermilion haze of Californian poppy, as they did back home in Brittany; here, also, the moon was hoarding up shadows in her cupboard of night, buttresses that loomed about them as they walked. Searching the darkness, she could not see the face of Richard beside her.

If he made a move Moll knew she would reject him, although her body called. The worst thing that could

25

happen to her at this moment would be to fall in love with a poet, all of whom were usually penniless. And, as the affair with the brutal Jean Pierre had taught her, romance must play no part during the collecting of other people's property: when the fox fell in love with the rooster, farmyard commotion was stilled into a deathly silence.

'How soft is your hand,' said Richard.

Oh God, thought Moll, 'ere he goes.

'It is a hand for lacing up a lady's bodice,' he added.

'And doing up me boots,' said Moll.

He smiled down at her. 'You trifle with me!'

'Lest you forget me 'usband.'

The thing to do, Moll reminded herself, was to get him talking. While the quickest way to a male heart was through the stomach, safety also lay in quickening his tongue, for men were boasters long before they acquired the art of deception. And if, in the end, she landed in bed under this one, let it be upon her terms, not his. More – and here lay an unfathomable presentiment of disaster – somewhere she had met this man before . . . or somebody distinctly like him . . .

Now the path through flowers in this tiny garden led to a rustic seat, and here they sat.

Richard said, taking off her accent, 'Would that 'usband of yours forbid you sitting 'ere with me?'

'Per'aps.'

'Would he dislike even a request to know your full name and title?'

'I am Francesca Le Roy, the Marchioness de Hauteville, which is my 'usband's country seat in the village of Avenses le Compte. You know it?'

'No.'

Thank God for that, thought Moll. 'Your name now, please?'

26

'Richard Carling.'

'You will tell me about yourself?' And Richard began:

'I was born in a great room within a manor house standing in a thousand acres of the finest land in Shropshire. My mother was Scottish, my father a wealthy farmer whose family went to the Crusades, relieved the Turks of much of their treasure, and brought it home to England.' He looked at the moon,

'Indeed, one of the first things I can remember was a large mahogany box decorated in the Romanesque style, its lid supported by golden Grecian dancers. This box was filled with sovereigns. When I went into town I used to take a handful.

'In due course I was sent to Eton, where I learned Latin and resisted the sexual advances of older boys; thence to Sandhurst, after which my father bought me a commission in the Indian Army, my grandfather having had connections with Clive during his plundering there. You know of this?'

Moll shook her head.

'And so in places like Poona I hunted wild boar with fellow officers and killed my fellow men in the name of England – Pathans, Dervishes and fanatical Afghans, who objected to us looting in their country. My life was filled with deeds of gallantry, mostly performed by foot-slogging British soldiers, for which medals were pinned upon my breast at garden parties.'

'You must have been a marvellous soldier!'

'Oh yes, they approved of me. My life was the gaiety of ballrooms; we officers in scarlet uniforms with epaulets upon our shoulders to make us look broader and busbies upon our heads to make us appear taller. I became a social gadabout – one assignation after another with high-class whores called debutantes.'

'*Pardonnez-moi!*'

'It doesn't matter,' replied Richard. 'Suffice to say that one day, during a drunken brawl, I realized that eventually I'd stand before St Peter and answer for my sins, so I bought myself out of the army and took the Cloth.'

'Took the Cloth?'

'Became a monk.'

'*Non!*'

'Ah, *oui*! As an apprentice to the Ancient Order of the Disciples of Pachomius, I rejected all worldly wealth, wine and women,' and Moll cried:

'But the great lands in Shropshire and the box filled with gold?'

'Made over by legal bequest to the Disciples of Pachomius.'

Richard was watching the effect upon her, and added, 'After which I became a poet, as you see me now. You like the story of my life?'

'Charming, but I do not believe it.'

'Francesca, I swear to it – every word! But now tell me about you. – Men's lives are so dull.'

'The French have a word for it – *non!*'

'But that is unfair!'

'Privacy is a woman's prerogative, do not you English say?'

Owls were shouting their heads off all over Shrewsbury; ringdoves were cooing from their cotes in the hotel yard, and here, when Moll and Richard arrived back from their walk, they came upon a scene more reminiscent of a Roman orgy at Viriconium than respectable Salopia. For if there was one drunk sprawling on the cobbles of the yard, there were fifty: in an alcoholic mist Sir Roger's company of Thespians were snoring away the night in costumes ranging from Desdemona to Prospero and King Lear to Othello. With clothing disarranged in the last clutches of sensual pleasure, all had given themselves up to licence; women moved their naked limbs like disjointed puppets, their lovers too drunk to perform the role of Cupid.

'They've been having a time of it,' observed Richard.

'This, my dear friends, is the dance of life!' cried Sir Roger, emerging from the ballroom with a tipsy Lady Thora upon his arm. 'Thespians all – most intimate of friends – welcome to this last provincial stop before we besiege London with our art. Tonight, on the boards of the Royal Theatre, you produced a performance of *The Tempest* that reduced me to tears! There was not a dry eye in the house . . .'

But Moll scarcely heard the old actor; she was hypnotized by the glittering array of jewels upon Lady Thora's scarlet gown.

'King Lear,' shouted Sir Roger, 'calls upon Nature to enlarge the evil and crooked passions of a mad king. Othello inspires jealousy in tragic form – all these you have interpreted beautifully under my guidance. But in your recent performances of *The Tempest* you have entered realms of true poetic vision . . .' And Moll looked bored.

Neither was Richard listening; he was remembering, instead, the coincidence of her absence during those vital minutes at the Severn Arms when the guest rooms had been vacated after the matron's shrieks.

Lady Thora now joined in the applause for her husband's speech, which caused her jewellery to dance and tinkle with alluring enchantment, and Moll's eyes shone.

'There must be a hundred pounds on that bosom,' Richard said jovially.

'Twice as much!'

This one, thought Richard, needed careful watching,.

Moll was thinking that it was all very well planning to lift Lady Thora's jewels, but one must have a constructive plan for getting the loot away instantly; or, as with the unfortunate bishop, allow the blame to fall upon another . . .

At the moment, the only person Moll had in mind was Richard. Which was a pity, but necessity was the mother of invention.

Sir Roger was speaking to his actors again, so, taking Moll's hand in his, Richard led her to a little bower of roses.

Richard asked, 'When were you married, Francesca?'

'But three months ago.'

'Really? Then you're practically still on your honeymoon!'

'We started our 'oneymoon in France, but my 'usband was called to London, so I am killing time until we meet again.'

'And you are on your way to join him now?'

'At the Charing Cross Hotel. I am leaving on the morning coach.'

He said, 'How brief our meeting! Were I your husband I would not allow you to travel alone.'

She spread her fingers in an empty gesture. 'One cannot 'ave a 'oneymoon without an 'usband.'

Unexpectedly, Richard hooked his arm around her waist and drew Moll hard against him.

'I do not want to leave you, Francesca.'

His kiss, not his embrace, had an astonishing effect upon her.

For while a man can change his identity by growing a beard, wear different clothes – invoke every known trick to change his appearance in the eyes of an astute woman . . . his kiss, even to a careless one, is his signature.

Moll had known this kiss before.

This man, unmistakably, was the highwayman.

It made his betrayal a great deal easier.

Four

On this particular *Calan Mai*, Shrewsbury (later known as 'The Town of Flowers') was suffering from the activities of a miscreant known as 'The Ditherington Rapist'. Moll had reason to look upon him as a beneficiary – he was more; he was her saviour.

The depredations of this character extended from the Welsh Bridge to the English one, proof that he didn't discriminate on grounds of nationality.

Many an unsuspecting Welsh spinster had commiserated with a Welsh neighbour upon her deflowering in an unguarded moment, and, give a dog a bad name, Alehouse Jones (this was his name) was known to be at the bottom of it.

Only once had he been apprehended for unusual behaviour; when he stood in the dock of the Quarter Sessions (a pathetic little figure in a tattered hunting jacket) and pleaded guilty to indecent exposure after somebody had hit it with her handbag while going down Dogpole, a street in the town.

The defence counsel being brilliant, the case of Rakes versus Regis was quoted, and, under cross-examination Alehouse declared, 'I only 'ad it out, your worship, for the urinary process, like. Being caught short on Pride Hill.' Which the magistrate, being over eighty, naturally understood. Thus was the prisoner discharged without a stain upon his character, while the woman with the handbag got a month for assault and battery.

Thereafter, Alehouse enjoyed the confidence of the

community, and with this in mind resolved upon his next victim, one he had long coveted – Primrose, the large wife of Albert, the landlord of the Talbot Hotel. Inflated by nature to exactly the right proportions, but taking up most of the bed, Primrose, hand in hand with her spouse, was asleep in a unison of snores in the next room to Moll's when the Ditherington Rapist struck.

With the town clocks chiming two in the morning, some in the inn were still awake: Sir Roger, for one, was sleepless, having set eyes upon the exquisite Madame Le Roy.

'Where you off to, Flower?' asked Lady Thora, as he eased himself out of the sheets.

'Answering a call of nature, my love,' replied Sir Roger, and with his nightshirt held up around matchstick legs, tiptoed out on to the landing and there fixed a bulbous eye at the keyhole of Moll's door. She, combing out her hair, was awaiting the inn's silence before committing her next burglary.

Alehouse, having climbed the wall of the Labour in Vain Inn (its sign portrayed a white woman bathing a black baby) had slunk along Butcher's Row to the Talbot Hotel. Entering the stable yard, he tiptoed over the scene of last night's bacchanalia, where the cast of *The Tempest* again lay four sheets in the wind. Now, gripping the ivy-clad walls of the inn, he went up hand over hand like an ape, and his little fat bottom gleamed ominously in the moonlight as he reached Primrose's bedroom window and noiselessly slid up the slash. Primrose, within, opened one fluttering black-lashed eye, and whispered:

'Well done, my duck, I thought you was never coming. I've given our Bert a run o' the laudanum, so he ought to sleep sound,' at which moment Moll saw Sir Roger's roving eye at her keyhole and pushed a feather into it.

So, whether it was the antics of the lovers or the howls of Sir Roger will never be known, but in seconds all the sleepers were out on to the landing, when Primrose took the opportunity to faint right off.

'Blood and hounds!' cried Albert, supporting her. 'I 'ave been cuckolded in me own bed and within a foot o' me missus. It's the Ditherington Rapist, gents – after 'im, after 'im!'

During this commotion, which had come as a Godsend, Moll did her rounds of the vacated rooms: like a ghost in white she drifted; and on the bedside table of Lady Thora was all her heart's desire – jewels enough to keep Chantelle in luxury for a lifetime.

It was then she noticed a pair of little paste earrings, and took these, too, dropping them into her small Moroccan bag . . .

And, while most of the guests were racing in pursuit of the rapist, Moll was on her way back to her own room when, astonishingly, she met Richard.

'History repeating itself, it appears,' said he, in his nightshirt. 'The events in the Severn Arms happening all over again!'

'And why, may I ask, are you not pursuing the intruder?' asked Moll.

'Because, dear lady, I would rather pursue you.'

'Look!' said Moll to change the subject, and flung open the landing window.

With the Moroccan bag concealed in the folds of her nightdress, Moll and Richard peered out.

Leaning on the sill they watched as Alehouse, initially cornered, went round the stable yard at speed, pursued by guests with riding crops and brooms. In and out of the haltered horses, gigs and traps he went, then disappeared through the yard gate followed by the infuriated landlord with a blunderbuss, which exploded, sending its contents after his small, retreating figure.

'Mind you,' said the landlord, returning, 'don't get the wrong idea about this fine establishment, for it don't 'appen all the time, do it, my love?' And Primrose, broken by the experience, hung sobbing upon his arm. 'It's just that he do tend to come randy round about springtime, don't he?'

'Yes, Bert,' sobbed Primrose, damp.

'He be difficult to stamp out, really speakin',' continued her husband. 'For he do slip through a window wi' a happy knack, and he's got a wife's nightie up afore she can say Jack Robinson, ain't that so, my beauty?'

'Yes Bert,' said Primrose.

'And the trouble is that he ain't like a normal fella, for he's in with him and out with him like jack rabbit. But we'll bloody 'ave him, beggin' ye pardon for the language, ladies – and 'is pecker'll come off an' all, or me name's not Albert.' He shook a hairy fist.

All agreed in a nodding of heads.

'So now, I suggest we retire back to our rooms, with the request that members of the fair sex do lock their doors unless accompanied by known male companions.'

On the landing, Richard repeated the landlord's words into Moll's ear:

'Unless accompanied by known male companions. Would you put me into such a category?'

'Try it in French,' said Moll, all ears, and Richard did so.

'I'll give it some thought,' she replied, and walked away, it being necessary to get her Moroccan bag into a place of safety before discovery of the theft.

Richard was thinking what a fool he had been not to have realized her game earlier. Clearly, she was working the inns of England while he was working its roads.

Two birds with one stone? he wondered. Perhaps they ought to collaborate.

Richard found the idea appealing. Also, it was the duty of a virile young Englishman to leave contented the wife of an absent Frenchman. Now, at her bedroom door, Moll said, 'Oh this is a terrible 'ouse! If I get frightened in the night and knock upon your door, you promise to 'ave me?'

'You can bank on it,' said Richard.

Five

Moll was thinking that this particular English mouse was a sly one; so the trap must be baited with care.

Richard (with his Moroccan bag safely under his pillow) was thinking that, in order to kill both birds with the same stone – take over all assets which this Frenchie possessed – he would have to use cunning, for if you wanted to find a fool in Britain, you didn't bring him from Brittany. Nor were French women lax, apparently, when it came to protecting their virtue.

Wondering how he could achieve both theft and seduction with a minimum of effort, he was still pondering this near dawn, when a low tapping came upon his bedroom door. Opening it, he saw Moll in the fading moonlight.

Her dark hair hung in waves over her shoulders and the nightdress he had seen before reached to her feet; but had since acquired the lowest neckline he had seen on a woman. But Richard noticed something else, and with even greater interest: under Moll's arm was her small Moroccan bag, which, he was now assured, carried the loot of at least two inns, and she said in a plaintive voice loaded with a French accent:

'Richard, I cannot sleep. Always I awake to imagine that dreadful rapist bending over me, and I am terrified.' She smiled appealingly up into his face. 'May I also bring my valuables and come in?'

But she was already in, and the door behind the captive closed; Richard said, 'I told you that I was at your service, Francesca, and I count your trust as a tremendous privilege,' and he gestured with magnanimous grace. 'You shall have my bed, my friend, I shall sleep in a chair.'

'Oh no, I will not 'ear of it!'

'Nor I any protest, for I am an English gentleman. Look – you can keep your valuable bag under your pillow, in the way I safeguard mine.' He patted the bed.

Moll made a pretty face of protest. '*Monsieur*, we are grown up people. Would it not be possible for us both to 'ave the bed – you on one side, me on the other, with the bolster down the middle?'

'Like the Walls of Jericho? Would this guarantee your virtue in France?' And he chuckled softly.

'It would go a long way towards it.'

'Then so it shall be!' said Richard; and he put the bolster down the middle of the bed and climbed in, while Moll, with the regal dignity of a princess, gathered up the folds of her nightdress (during which she managed to show both legs) and got in on the other side of the bolster.

Momentarily, they lay there, their hands folded upon their stomachs with official decorum, and each one's Moroccan bag firmly under the pillows.

'Now,' said Richard, 'if thieves and rapists arrive in the night, they will have us both to contend with.'

'What is left of the night,' replied Moll, and added: 'You understand, don't you, that I would not be in this bed with you unless you enjoyed my total trust?'

'Of course, Francesca.'

'Indeed there are many French girls like me who take marriage very seriously.'

'Naturally, you can't tar everybody with the same brush.'

'Besides, my 'usband is a very jealous man. If he saw me in 'ere with you, he would probably kill us.'

'Who would blame him?'

Moll asked from the darkness, 'You believe in the sanctity of marriage?'

'Yes, although I happen to be a bachelor. Mark you, the longer I lie here, the harder it becomes.'

'You . . . you mean that you might even take advantage of a lonely wife like me if the opportunity ever arose?'

'Quite possibly. It's my ambition to be shot by a jealous husband at the age of eighty.'

'*Monsieur*,' said she indignantly, ''ad I known you to be so unprincipled, I would never have got myself into this ridiculous position. Surely you would not take a woman against her will?'

'Ma'am,' said Richard, 'yes, if needs be.'

'Then I shall get up and run for the door. I thought I 'ad met you before, sir, but could not put my finger on it.'

'*Madame*,' said Richard, 'you will now be given every opportunity . . .' and his arms went about her hard and strong.

And in their tempestuous breathing, Richard changed over the Moroccan bags; in the stuttering of their gasped enchantment, the change was made. And Moll, though realizing the move, made no sign of it but clung to Richard, while he, in an outpouring of his long celibacy (he hadn't been home for a fortnight) covered Moll's face with kisses. And in his embrace Moll called his name loud and clear while fighting the temptation to giggle at such perambulations.

'*Richard!*'

She was now the lost one and lived again, within his strength, the red-walled room of brilliant tapestries which once was her room at home; the brass-knobbed beds of squalid attics where the crazy roofs of Paris wounded the sunset: chintz curtains she saw now; the ebony thighs of Montmartre negresses, and the black-stockinged wanderings of the Stinkerque harlots. She heard again the accordion dancers of Jean Pierre's sleazy human circus; felt the exotic sleight of hand that lifted a duke's wallet or the contents of a sailor's pocket. All this returned in a blaze of unconscious thought – all this returned as Richard made her one with him. But this was not the tiger's lair of the lusts; Richard was strangely gentle with her for one so strong.

'Jean Pierre . . .' Moll's lips said, but not her heart.

'Who . . .?' Richard now, instantly aware.

'It do not matter,' said Moll and immersed her being into the blinding darkness when Time is obliterated – when steel is forged in loins that melt in tumult. This is the tiger's cry when no words sound and the night speeds on in unheard chimes of distant clocks and fractured dreams . . . the dreams in which the male is lost, the female dominant. And in that brief disarming when a man is alone in the joy, Moll's fine left hand, nurtured and bred for such occasions, moved beneath the pillows and exchanged . . . one Moroccan bag for another; so that hers was again beneath her pillow, and Richard's was returned.

Oh, these men of boastful pride, she thought – how does any man know what a woman feels? There he goes, thought she again, as his leg slid out on to the floor: and the bag goes next, thought she, as Richard deftly pulled his own Moroccan bag from under his pillow, and serve him right.

Now so feigned was her sleeping that Richard wondered if she had died, so silently she lay, as in a repose of death . . . meanwhile watching all beneath her half-closed lashes: saw Richard's stealthy creep to his clothes, the silent haste as he pulled on his breeches. Up goes the shirt; wave the arms, tuck in the flaps, down on the bum. Now pull on riding boots . . . with insidious little peeps at the bed to ensure that the one about to be betrayed is out to the wide – a satisfied wench if ever there was one, eh, lads?

Somewhere in the dawn a cock crowed, and Moll saw Richard stiffen.

The cock crowed again and, crouching by the window, he listened as another had listened two thousand years ago.

For the third time the cock crowed . . . as the window casement opened. One leg out now, his coat in one hand and his Moroccan bag in the other. Moll heard him land with a thud on the cobbles below.

Then only did she stir, leaving the bed for one last glimpse of Judas; watching him lead the mare, already saddled, out through the stable gates and on to the road. And still Moll watched as Richard's lonely figure, riding the dawn, galloped like a man demented down Wyle Cop . . . and took the road to Chester.

'Son of a bitch!' she cried, her fist up. 'I hope they hang you! For now it is my turn.'

Then Moll went back to bed and, smiling, slept with the confidence of a job well done.

And smiled again, a woman's smile, one that is never seen by men; and sighed and laid her head upon the pillow where Richard's head had lain, and whispered to the dawn in her mother tongue:

'I'll say one thing for him, he's a hell of a man to sleep with . . .' and sighed contentedly as the dawn came up over Salopia.

Six

'Thieves! Murder!'

Lady Thora was first out on to the landing with Sir Roger in pursuit. 'Oh, my jewels, my *jewels!*' And she swooned off in lamentation, with Sir Roger patting her cheeks and slapping the backs on her hands, and his shouts brought the guests running in expectation of another rapist. And when Moll arrived at a carefully judged moment, one old girl got an attack of the vapours, then another; soon the landing was littered with inert bodies.

'For Gawd's sake, what's 'appened now?' shouted the landlord arriving in a nightshirt.

'Oh,' shouted Moll, adding to the confusion, 'what a terrible 'ouse! First rapists, now thieves – and all me money and jewellery gone – 'ow shall I pay me bill?'

'And my old man's wallet!' called another.

'And my loose change,' shouted a third. 'Damnit, sir, I'm taking this to court!'

'Now, quiet, everybody, quiet!' bawled the landlord with authority. 'We'll 'ave a roll call to see who's missing, for I reckon I 'eard the thief making a getaway. Who 'eard hoofbeats round about cock-time?'

'I did!'

'And me!' shouted a choleric ex-major. 'By gad, I know a rascal when I see one,' he said to Moll. 'Too handsome by far, that friend of yours, milady!'

'Where is he?' asked the landlord, counting the guests.

'Where's his mare gone?' asked another.

'It's in the stables,' and someone ran to look.

41

'Oh, no it bloody isn't!'

'By Jesus,' said the landlord, 'you're right, the bugger's gone!' And he seized his blunderbuss hanging on the wall, shouting hoarsely, 'After 'im, gents!'

'After who?'

'After the thief and varmint!'

'Call the redcoats!' – everybody after 'im.'

'And the best of luck,' whispered Moll at the landing window, watching as they galloped out of the stable yard.

Lithe and shining with sweat, Richard's horse galloped full stretch to the north-west and home, which, in case her master was ever wounded, she had been trained to do.

For the first twenty minutes Richard made good time; keeping clear of the roads he took the little streams and culverts in his stride; ducking under overhanging branches and leaping little crags and boulders. But to the west of Montford Bridge and within sight of the Severn Arms the mare shed a shoe, and this called for a blacksmith. Therefore he dismounted and began to walk with the horse to Nesscliff. Soon he could hear sounds of pursuit.

The landlord of the Talbot, galloping from Shrewsbury with a troop of dragoons, put up a hand and halted them.

'What was that, mister?' said he, and reined in his horse.

'Somebody coming through the trees,' said the captain of the dragoons.

'Some mad fella laughin' too, ain't it?'

And so it was that while many villains are caught in tears, Richard was caught in laughter. Indeed, he was still holding his stomach when the redcoats closed around him; he having stopped to check the jewels, and found them vanished.

'Ye'll soon be laughing on the other side of ye face, young fella,' said the landlord, and the horse raised her head and stared at the stupidity of humans as the soldiers seized Richard and hauled him, still laughing, to his feet.

'So, what 'ave we here?' asked the landlord, snatching at the Moroccan bag and emptying it.

Out came soap, a little towel, a shaving brush and a razor. All stared and the captain then said, peering down:

'There's something shining at the bottom.'

The landlord shook the bag again and two small artificial earrings dropped out, shining in the early sun.

'Scoundrel and reptile!' roared the landlord. 'And to think ye led that innocent French lady a dance, an' all!'

At which Richard began to laugh again.

Said the dragoon captain loftily, 'To be a common thief is one thing, but to deceive such virtue puts you beyond redemption. You, sir, are a wretch and a cad! It is no laughing matter.'

'Mind you, we anna managed to catch 'im with the jewels – well, not all of 'em, sir,' suggested a soldier.

'But this,' said the dragoon captain holding up the earrings, 'is enough. Clearly, the property of Lady Thora for use on the stage. Anything of real value would have been fenced by now – these villains get rid of it sharper than monkeys. But the rope is certainly around this thief's neck.' And he held up an earring to the sun.

Meanwhile, suitably chastened by her supposed losses, Moll, sitting at the breakfast table in the dining room of the Talbot, dabbed at her eyes with a little lace handkerchief, ate two eggs and bacon and finished it off with buttered toast, marmalade and black coffee . . .

She was surprised when a waiter handed her an envelope, whispering secretly into her ear:

'Found it in the hall, milady; it is addressed to you.'
Moll opened the envelope, took out a single sheet of
notepaper and read:

ODE TO A LADY AT BREAKFAST
Tonight my soul is set among the stars.
These fetters fall, and I, at last, am free.
Tonight my soul has burst its prison bars
I enter to the light of love, with thee.
What if the dawn brings grief again to me?
Tonight, I live, and nought my rapture mars.
At love's high altar, I am crowned with thee.
Tonight my soul is set among the stars.

Seven

With the London guests' departure delayed until official testimony was taken, Moll watched, now sadly, when the redcoat dragoons returned to the Talbot, leading Richard's mare for auction. The dragoon captain clicked his heels and bowed to her.

'Captain of the dragoons, at your service, milady.'

Moll rose from her chair. 'You 'ave caught him?'

'Red-handed, *madame*, thanks to your excellent intelligence. He had disposed of all but two small items of the stolen property, and is now incarcerated in the local lock-up to await the Quarter Sessions. He's a slippery customer, and I'll be glad to get him in front of the circuit judge.' The captain paused sufficiently to appear impressive. 'You arrived here with him, I understand.'

Moll shrugged. 'We travelled from Montford Bridge together, if that is what you mean.'

The captain nodded. 'You realize, I take it, that he is Richard Carling, the notorious highwayman? Indeed, the man who actually held up your coach?'

'I do now, *monsieur*'.

'He took the valuables from three out of the four passengers, but from you he took only a kiss?'

''Ow could I stop 'im?'

'Later, in this very inn, you dined with him and were seen walking with him, yet at no time did you suspect his true identity?'

'I did not!' And Moll added angrily, 'You have got 'im, what else do you want?'

45

'Enough evidence to remand him in custody.'

'I 'ave told you everything I know.'

'We would like it in writing.'

'When?'

'By tonight.'

'You shall have it, captain. I too, 'ave lost money – so I cannot pay my bill. Perhaps you would explain this to the stupid landlord. I would do anything to see this thief behind bars.'

'Then perhaps you would delay your departure to London until after the magistrate's sitting.'

'Delay?' Moll was appalled. 'My 'usband is awaiting me at Charing Cross.'

'*Madame,*' answered the captain with suave charm, 'I took the liberty, not an hour ago, of despatching a messenger to London to advise your husband that you might be a little late – first secretary to the French Embassy, is he not?'

Oh God, thought Moll, but said lightly, '*Monsieur le Capitan*, you think of everything.'

'Not everything, *madame*, otherwise we would not be in this predicament. But with your help and Lady Thora's identification of the earrings, we'll likely have this rascal dancing on his toes a week after the Quarter Sessions. Good day to you, Madame Le Roy.'

After the dragoon had left, Moll paced her bedroom floor.

For the first time, flight appeared a necessity. Standing at her window she watched the travelling players setting up their tables for yet another day of drinking. All was activity: lace-hatted serving maids were scurrying with buckets and brooms, ostlers carrying feed, farriers hammering, and she saw Richard's mare, captive and morose, being re-shod in a cloud of steam and smoke: this, more than anything that had happened so far, brought home her betrayal with strickening intensity.

46

What had earlier appeared mere risky entertainment, a contest of wiles, had now been set in its proper context, and her sense of triumph was being sullied by contrition.

Momentarily, she put her hands over her face; full realization of her act now upon her. This man might suffer a long imprisonment; indeed, if the dragoon captain was right, he might even hang. The possibility appalled her.

That afternoon Moll went down to Mardol Head. Nearby, in Market Hall, the hucksters and street criers were shouting their wares in a symphony of rush and bustle; this ancient town, rich in picturesque half-timbered houses, dated through the elegance of the Queen Anne and Georgian periods to the blood baths of Roman Viriconium.

From the mediaeval Grope Lane (where it was said no woman trod without the disarranging of her petticoats) to the ancient square, the stalls were packed with traders; drunkards and tipsies staggered in rowdy chorus out of the inns from Pig Trough to Wyle Cop and Shoplatch to Pride Hill, their songs a descant to the bellowing of cattle. Ladies delicately lifted the hems of their garments over the oozing sewage of the gutters; donkeys and mules, their forelegs deep in rutted mud, dragged impossible loads from Cutler's Row to Frankwell. And over the cacophony of human bedlam the afternoon sun burned down.

Here Moll bought a pair of buckskin breeches, black leather riding boots from the saddler and a riding cloak; a broad hat of gray completed the outfit and a bag of food and a bottle of wine for the journey she had in mind, which was almost anywhere from the Talbot Inn. Carrying these in parcels she returned to her room there, and was not surprised to find a solider on guard outside her door. He sprang to attention.

'Captain's orders, ma'am, in case the varmint escapes and tries to molest your ladyship.'

Moll entered her room. 'You are saying that this rascal might attack me?'

'If he made a bunk for it, like, ma'am, for we've 'ad 'im under lock and key before; he's a slippery customer if ever there was one. After all, it was you who put the finger on him, weren't it?'

'I never thought of that,' answered Moll.

She locked her bedroom door, realizing that when a reply was received from London she would be under arrest.

Night came, with much coming and going of soldiers. Moll dined alone, aware of the interest cast in her direction. Men spoke in gruff monosyllables, women whispered behind their fans, and the waiter, a bruiser with an inborn arrogance, served her with cold impartiality.

Returning to her room after the meal, Moll lay upon the bed fully dressed; then, when all was quiet save for the riotous drinking from the tap-room (where beards were being parted and ale going down necks like lift-and-force pumps) Moll got up and listened at her door.

The soldier behind it grunted like a man in a doze; her inactivity now quickened into silent haste.

Flinging off her dress, Moll changed swiftly into the breeches she had bought and pulled on the long boots. Stuffing her hair under the broad hat with its little rose cockade, she linked the riding cloak at her throat and silently opened the casement window. Only a few Thespians were in the yard, either flat upon their backs or slumped over tables. St Julian's struck the hour of four as she went down the ivy-clad walls hand under hand; and the black mare, almost as if expecting her, whinnied softly as Moll approached her.

The yard door creaked ominously as it opened, the narrow road beyond faced them. And Moll heard, in the instant she mounted the horse, a man's shrill cry come from the rooms above her. This was followed by a mad stampede as others were called from sleep; now men were stumbling down the inn stairs, but these sounds died into the racing hooves of the horse beneath her, as Moll gave the mare full rein.

And the soldier on guard outside her door, smashing his way into her room with the butt of his musket, got to the open casement in time to see the black mare, with the cloak of its rider flowing out behind her, go clattering down Wyle Cop, and take the road to Chester.

It was a long time since Moll had had a horse between her knees, but the sunlit rides with her father along the Bois de Boulogne in happier days returned to her. The mare, as if demented by the sudden freedom, raced madcap as one pursued; to the west she went, ignoring any attempt by Moll to rein her in.

Only when she had covered miles at full gallop did she respond to the bridle, then broke into a trot. Dismounting, Moll tethered her in the clearing of a sombre wood; there, with the mare grazing contentedly nearby, she flung herself down beside a stream for sleep.

Later, the evening sun began her business of making shadows; sun-shafts, brilliant in coloured beams, sent darts of fire into the gloom. It was a paradise of rare periwinkle and early flowering clematis, its coloured trumpets heavy with bee-hum: coltsfoot and bluebells stretched in small seas here, vying with bittersweet and foxglove for colour on the gold of a thousand autumns. Here Moll slept, yet did not sleep. For now the old awareness of an enemy was upon her again, as in the old days of the Paris pickpocketing.

Through half-closed eyes and ears she listened to a world of sound; the boastful song of a distant cuckoo, the grinding wheels of a coach and the noisy clattering of hooves along a flinted road nearby; and within such sounds the evening dozed in a heavy somnolence, and a scented mist arose to greet the coming dusk. Somewhere in the wood a ring dove called to her mate, the sound contralto on the colder air: a nightjar hummed its plaintive tones. In the melancholy vacuum between day and darkness, uneasy cockerels jarred the silence with alarms to humans about slinking runs of fur and claw. And in the last moments before returning consciousness a vixen called to her cubs in furious anger, screeching into Moll's slow wakefulness.

Upon her feet again, she remounted the mare, with one intention only – that now darkness had come it was necessary to put as many miles as possible between herself and Shrewsbury; and the black mare, as if with the same accord, galloped again with new strength under a rising moon – as straight as the flight of an arrow – to the place of oats and water which she called home. Through Montford they went, taking the bridge at speed, and faint moonlight glinted on the blind windows of the Wingfield Arms as they thundered along and then, with Great Ness upon their right, the mare slacked speed and dropped again into a canter, then a trot; to stop near a roadside verge.

Faintly above her came a creaking, and Moll looked up. In the light of a misted moon she saw a sign above her, gently swaying in the wind.

The Old Three Pigeons Inn.

Moll, with only a faint memory of passing this inn earlier, wondered where it was.

But Richard's mare knew that she was home.

Eight

Moll was about to dismount from the horse when yellow light shot the road and a girl came out of the inn; she was busty, with white lace on the hem of her long black dress and a frothy lace cap upon her head, and she cried in a thick Irish brogue:

'Is that you, Dicko, me darlin'? And you, Meg Mare?'

The horse entered an opening in the hedgerow, its hooves silent on a bridle path; over her shoulder Moll now saw the girl, framed against light. Music came, the hefty pumping of a melodeon, the bass shouts of men and the shrieks of women; the girl added harshly:

'Ach, please ye'self, then! But I've lit peat in the grate for ye, and Meg's fodder's by the steps. Give me an hour and I'll be up to warm ye bed.'

Her voice then faded in the gentle thumping of the mare's hooves.

Here a path through overhanging branches was shot with moonbeams, a black tracery cutting fingers in the starlit sky. The path curved to the right; silver light blazed – an unimpeded view over a landscape of astonishing beauty.

The horse climbed now, turning its back on the moon. Reaching a dense wood, Moll entered almost total blackness, leaving it to the horse to feel for a path it clearly knew well. A blank stone redness reared before them; the mare stopped and grazed; Moll dismounted.

★　★　★

Behind her was a forest; before her a sandstone wall that halted progress. And then, as her eyes became accustomed to the darkness, Moll saw before her a flight of steps leading upward, cut into the sheer rock face.

Astonishingly, Meg Mare, as the Irish girl called her, began to mount these, climbing them as casually as a human climbs stairs. Higher, higher went the horse as Moll watched, then it paused and deliberately looked back, as if expecting Moll to follow; and she did so, coming to a stout, nail-studded door of massive thickness. The horse nosed this, swinging it open, and entered what was clearly a small stable; water was standing in a sunk manger, the remains of oats were scattered over the floor. Next door to this, in an adjoining chamber, the contours of the cave made shape in the glow of a peat fire below a chimney carved out of the rock; beside this was a little open-air window.

Smiling Moll looked about her.

Warmth and comfort were here. Smells of food pervaded; she saw a neat row of cooking utensils; a little fly-proof box displayed the remains of bread and cheese; salted bacon hung from a hook in the ceiling. Deeper within, near the smouldering fire, a broad trestle bed had its blankets, and even a pair of sheets, neatly folded in soldierly fashion. Lying on the blankets was a tiny two-barrelled flintlock pistol; above the bed, on the wall, hung a big horse pistol, one of a brace, thought Moll, for surely she recognized it as one seen in the hand of Richard Carling when he held up her coach.

Now she did not smile; this was clearly his home. A home, she reminded herself, to which he might never return, now that she had so successfully betrayed him. Faintly, Moll wondered if he would have done the same to her . . . yet now it seemed that he was offering her this place as a haven of safety; the thought was bitter, and ironic.

At the little window, Moll looked down on to a small forest clearing some fifteen feet below; a bold drop for a man if trapped, let alone a woman . . . It was then that she noticed, near the cave entrance (and Meg Mare looked suspiciously over her shoulder at the intrusion), a deep-cut engraving of the initials:

H.K.

This in itself was a mystery.

There came the scuffle of feet in the forest below; standing clear of the window, Moll peered down.

A little man, shrivelled and bewhiskered, had arrived. Wearing a moleskin cap and in rags, cranked with age, he lowered a bundle he was carrying and called up to the window:

'Are ye there, me boy?'

Moll drew back from the window.

'Are ye awake or sleepin', Dicko?'

Moll put a hand through the opening and gestured a reply; the man shouted:

'There's been a "fightin" at the Pigeons, says Biddy, so she didn't call for the fodder till bat-time, and I'm late. Big Meg'll be playin' hell wi' me. Are ye well?'

Hands on hips at the delay, the old man stared up, so Moll waved her hand again. Grunting, he limped off, then turned, shouting:

'They tell me ye got the Chester stage, so I hope we'll be eating proper this week, for there's another mouth to feed in the village – Saul's missus breached a son. Say, can ye hear me up there, Dicko, or are your ears gone loose?'

Suddenly, the horse barged the cave door open and began to descend the steps, neighing shrilly; the old man opened his arms to her, then stooped, ripped at the fodder bag, and fed her.

Moll watched. Talking softly to himself, he took off the mare's saddle and bridle, then waved briefly up to the cave window.

'Sleep easy then, for I'm first watch. I'll have Joe Fence around to ye in the mornin'.'

The significance of the situation wasn't lost upon Moll, but the moment she stretched herself on the bed and pulled the blankets over her aching body (this had been the first gallop in years) weariness swept over her in waves of increasing intensity.

Meg Mare came up the steps again and entered the adjoining stable; even this did not awaken Moll from the depth of her slumber.

Biddy Boddy, one of the two serving maids at the Pigeons (as the locals called the inn) eased the last drunk through the tap-room door with the assistance of Snap, the dancing dog, and went back to the business of swabbing down the counter, with the help of Rosie, a part-timer.

Rosie, compared with Biddy was a shinbone in stays: the long and the short of it, the drinkers said, for Biddy Boddy, still with puppy fat was a boiling joint. Now, with her large breasts cuddling and cavorting above her bodice, she scrubbed, swabbed and polished, while singing bawdy Irish doggerels in a high-pitched, cracked soprano that turned up the toes of the churchyard corpses, said Saul Clay, the Nesscliff undertaker; and if I woke up in the morning with that beside me I'd decapitate her, added Eli Rumbletum, the landlady's lover.

A happy little community had Nesscliff in the year 1839 with the Old Three Pigeons the centre of activity whereby curates obtained their brandy, gentlemen their rum and perfume for their ladies; to say nothing of night frolics supplied by Biddy and Rosie.

Indeed, it was claimed by the Nesscliff villagers that all the needs of visiting dignitaries could be supplied 'off the peg'. This the true ambition of Shaun Casey, the tavern's highly unrespected landlord.

And, like a lambent flame around which fluttered every moth in Nesscliff, Richard Carling had become its nineteenth-century Phoenix: he to whom all gave respect and affection was a fleecer extraordinary; something more than the Shropshire Robin Hood who took from the rich and gave it to the needy Welsh, he was Nesscliff's beating heart. And his absence for a few days running was always viewed with consternation; his return being celebrated with feasts of steak-and-kidney and plum-and-apple pie, all prepared with loving care by Blodwen, the landlord's wife (who came from Swansea). Proof of her affection was clearly given – she always ironed the tails of Richard's shirts, but never did her husband's. While Biddy and Rosie, out of respect, did their best to stay celibate for at least a couple of days before Richard's expected return.

Richard Carling was wanted in three counties for highway robbery, to say nothing of reported seduction of ladies of grace and favour in the backs of coaches while their unhappy escorts walked home barefooted.

Village guards were set outside the entrance to the cave to prevent disturbance of his sleeping hours or improper entry by the forces of law and order.

The Nesscliff villagers were not fools. Richard was their queen bee; it paid them to keep him alive. Nearly three hundred years before, their ancestors had protected Humphrey Kynaston in the interests of the village constitution, so Richard, in performing his appointed role, was but one in a sequence of many. Thus down the generations did Nesscliff prosper and the centre of the activity, wherein the loot was received, stored and fenced was the Old Three Pigeons Inn. This being run by Irish Shaun Casey, whose administration often took him on journeys to the Welsh coast (when kegs of brandy had been known to float in from the Irish Sea). During such sojourns, Blodwen, his Welsh rose and the darling of his heart (because she couldn't get her hands on Richard) would throw handfuls of gravel at the window of Eli Rumbletum, the Celtic way of enticing fornicators.

So, the Pigeons was a sanctuary to any passing trickster, smuggler, highwayman or tart; the border refuge of vagabonds and saints; a Rabelaisian equivalent of the wit and laughter of François, a criminal friend of friars. 'I,' Richard claimed, 'go in search, like Rabelais, of a great "Perhaps" and discover it better in the tap-room of this warm and homely inn than when kneeling before the scarlet of a popish altars.'

Biddy Boddy, for her part, was now going in search of Richard, and, creeping into his cave near dawn, removed her clothes and inserted a plump, bare leg under Moll's blankets; then, snuggling down deeper into her warmth, whispered:

'Arrah, me lad – shift over, so I can come in,' and put an arm around Moll's waist . . . who opened wide startled eyes in the darkness.

'Oh, me duck,' said Bid, 'I ain't 'alf missed you – wake up and give old Bid a treat, there's a good boy,' and planted a wet kiss on the back of the neck before her.

Up went the bedclothes.

'What the 'ell is 'appening?' said Moll.

Nine

Shaun Casey ran a good tavern; even his sworn enemies granted him this. He had a still in the cellar for the brewing of Irish poteen and casked his own cider on the premises, too – dropping a couple of dead rats in the swill to give taste to the body.

For the comfort of passing travellers he kept a bed with a warming pan under the sheets and serving maids of generous proportions ready to oblige. Indeed, there wasn't a tavern to compare with him in the county in terms of lavish hospitality, and with ale at a farthing a pint his prices were unbeatable.

Rumour had it that The Pigeons was haunted by the ghost of Humphrey Kynaston (the fifteenth century highwayman) – a rumour made fact by Emmie O'Hara, a fat cook brought in by Casey from Connemara. For one stormy night Humphrey appeared with a sword through his heart and asked for a pint, and she lifted her skirts and nobody saw her for months.

The oil lamps in the tap-room were now turned low, so that nobody there, said Moll later, could see the shame of his neighbour's face.

The flickering light cast shadows upon people lining the walls: sallow, thin faces; others fat, well fed and already flushed with wine, though the night's business had not begun. But hunger stained the withered cheeks of Tip Topsy, the village idiot, and his stumpy teeth rolled in his dribbling smile.

Beside him sat Justin Slaughterer, his shirt stained with blood from the day's killing. Ben Pullet, the chicken farmer was there with cockerel feathers in his moleskin cap, eyes skinned for profit. Boyo Bad Thing (who kept dirty pictures pinned to the walls of his forest shack and had the face of an ingratiating pup) was present in the hope of seeing a woman hanged. Many men he had seen strangled up on Gallows Holt, but never a woman.

There was Long Fella and Short Chap, the ostlers, and the farrier Pincers (temporarily freed from his chain in the barn), a mad deaf mute who conversed in piggish grunts.

Rum-Bum-Baccy, the sailor smuggler down from Anglesey was sitting beside Tom Cakebread, rat-catcher and spare time baker; and in a corner, with both eyes open for trade, sat Saul Clay, the undertaker who was once a monk.

Altogether they were a most respectable gathering, as Moll told Chantelle when she wrote again to France, and in the middle of them was Landlord Casey.

Moll, her hands tied behind her back, faced him and her accusers. For these were now her judges and jurors, with Eli Rumbletum, the local hangman, fingering his rope in hope of a killing.

'Untie her hands,' commanded Casey. 'Frogs speak mainly with their fingers,' and someone shouted in a shrill falsetto:

'She be a real Frenchy, mind, so watch her!'

'Untie her, I said,' repeated the landlord, and Biddy Boddy reluctantly obeyed. Moll flexed her cramped fingers. Casey asked:

'What's your name for a start, my beauty?'

'Francesca Le Roy,' she said and he shouted, moving angrily:

'Ach, don't give us that bloody stuff, or we'll burn the truth out of ye! Eli, put the poker in the fire.'

Moll looked around their faces. 'Moll Walbee.'

'That's better. Foreign, eh?'

'French, I 'ave told you.'

'Right, now tell us how ye came about stealing Meg Mare, our Dicko's horse,' he said and added: 'Look, missus, I'll make it easy for ye. He held up your coach east of here and took trinkets off an old girl, a lawyer and a cleric,' and here he crossed himself. 'But nothin' off you. Then your coach sheds a wheel and you land in the Wingfield Arms, up by Montford, am I right?'

'If you know, why do you tell me?'

'I didn't. It was an educated guess. And then?'

'Then your man Richard Carling joined me there.'

'At the Severn Arms? Tell me why?' And somebody bawled with bawdy laughter:

'I'll tell ye why, Frenchy – he were after your tail!'

Rosie, breasting up with a pewter of ale cried, 'Ach, Mr Casey, there's too much gas, so there is. I say get her toes dancing, and ask questions after. Who's on?'

The room clattered with shouts of agreement and stamping; Casey held up his hand for silence.

'We'll do it my way, or not at all, me darlin's,' and turned to Blodwen, his wife: she, who sat like a great motivated corpse, silent in her obesity; now her great dark eyes fluttered open.

'I say give 'er to Pincers. It's time he was mated again, mind!'

'Ach no, that would be a terrible waste!' shouted Casey.

'She's a gorgeous piece, so she is, and there's good money in her,' said another.

'Then get on wi' it, or we'll be losing the customers. Let's have her history.'

Moll said, her attitude defiant, 'In Paris I was one of many pickpockets. But the *gendarmes* come after me, so I go to England. In Chester I 'ear of travelling actors carrying jewels; in Shrewsbury they was playing, and I decided to steal them. They were staying at the Talbot Inn, so I went there.'

'And so did Dicko?'

'It was at the Talbot that I recognized 'im. Earlier, at Montford market he bought a little leather bag; I bought one, also.'

'And then?' interjected Casey.

'Then I robbed the actors. I put the jewels in my leather bag and that night Carling exchanged the bags. But I exchanged them back again, and he went galloping off, believing he 'ad got the profits.'

All were intent; Moll could see their expressions in the red light of the fire; craning necks and nervous expectation. It was a tale of deceit and cunning, so it intrigued them; and now she was talking to save her life. One said, and she thought it was the slaughterer:

'Our Dicko runs off with an empty bag. Pull the other!'

Moll smiled. 'Except for his shaving brush and razor.'

'No!' Casey exploded with bass laughter, slapping his thigh.

'Are ye tellin' us ye diddled him?'

Moll nodded.

'That he did the legging and left you with the loot?'

'Mark, Mary and Joseph!'

The tap-room was a bedlam of merriment and hoarse oaths.

'You? You put one over our Dicko?'

'She's lyin', Casey,' said Biddy Boddy. 'Our Dicko anna that daft!'

Then came silence; Tom Cakebread, the baker, asked, 'But who put the finger on Carling after the bunk?'

'The bunk?' asked Moll. 'What you mean?'

'After he'd run off.'

It was all or nothing now, and Moll knew it. Friendships meant little here, knavery and guile alone were respected in this devil's kitchen.

She said, 'Somebody 'ad to be blamed for the theft, yes? And it was not goin' to be me, for I am a professional. You?' She stared loftily from face to face. 'You are only footpads and bandits, and so was he. But I 'ave been trained in the best French School.' Her accent thickened as her confidence grew, for some were now showing admiration. 'To be a thief in Paris, *mes amis,* you first 'ave to stay alive. And know it with every breath you take. Your man Carling thought he was dealing with a fool – that was a big mistake. And his second?' Moll awaited total silence. 'His next mistake was thinking that his leather bag 'eld the goods I stole. It did – a pair of paste earrings belonging to one of the actors; it takes a thief to catch a thief.'

Casey asked, 'Ye planted 'em?'

'I did more. I informed on him, and the soldiers arrested 'im.'

Casey rose to his full height and glared down at her. 'Son o' the Father, deliver us,' he whispered. 'Me heart's scalded for the loss of a decent fella, but you're a marvellous creature for all your wickedness, so ye are, and I'm proud to be sharin' the same roof. Don't you agree, Blod?' And his wife said huskily:

'*Diawch!* If she can stick it up our Dicko she's too good for me.'

But Biddy Boddy said, 'Aye, well that's all right, see? But if ye want the truth of all that, let's see the jewels.'

'Ach, indeed. Have you got them, Frenchy?'

Moll nodded, and Biddy shouted:

'Then give us the proof, for I hunted high and low in Dicko's cave and found no more'n a stick o' rhubarb,' and Moll replied:

'Do you think I would put them where you could find them, *chérie?*' and here she took off Bid's thick Irish accent:

'I put 'em safe before you arrived last night, and me spending me time easing ye out o' the blankets – for as fast as I got her one leg out she was puttin' in the other!' And waving down the laughter with both hands, added, 'And her puttin' kisses on the back of me neck and callin' me her dear little duck Dicko, and beggin' me for treats!'

'But we still haven't seen the loot!' This from Tom Cakebread amid hooted laughter, while Biddy Boddy scowled.

'No.'

'Then for all we know, you've told a pack of lies.'

Again silence came to the room. The fire glowed red on their faces; the rough features of those stained with drink; the smooth profiles of Bid and Rosie; the slobbering Tip Topsy, the bearded Justin Slaughterer, and the fatted cheeks of Eli Rumbletum.

'But meanwhile, *messieurs, mesdames,*' said Moll, ''ere is something on account eh?' And took from her pocket a diamond ring. This she tossed up. Casey snatched it in midair and held it up to the lamp.

'Ach, t'is solid gold,' he breathed. 'Rouse yourself, woman – just look at that!' He gave it to Blodwen.

'It is worth the fortune of a prince,' said Moll.

The ring went from hand to hand, with oohs and aahs on everybody's lips. 'And there's more where that came from – if you trust me,' said Moll. Then she moved among them, easing herself through the crush, and Rosie cried:

'Where's the thing gone for God's sake?'

'Sure I handed it to ye, woman,' said Biddy.

'You did not!'

Argument now, with voices raising in accusations because the ring had vanished; men were patting their pockets and women looking down their bodices. And the babble rose in threats of violence.

'Don't tell me you've lost it!' boomed Casey.

'I tell ye – a moment ago I had it on me finger!' cried Bid.

People were crawling on the floor now, lamps being lit and everybody quarrelling with more suspicions than teeth, and Casey bawled, 'I tell ye, I had it and bit the gold, and it's somewhere in the room. So if I find the woman who's got it up her skirts, I'll make her scream, ye hear me, you thieving lot?'

'Eli had it last, Shaun!'

'Jesus, no – I gave it to Blod.'

'And I gave it to Saul – didn't you see him with it?'

Casey whispered malevolently. 'Now, I'm givin' you bastards one last chance, for that ring was fourteen carat . . .' He took the poker out of the fire.

'Look in your back pocket, Mr Casey,' said Moll, and it stilled him; motionless he stood with the poker glowing before him. Then his hand moved to his pocket and the ring was in his fingers.

'In the name o' the Pope!'

All eyes turned to Moll.

'This is what I'm sayin',' said she. 'You are amateurs, all of you. Handled properly, I could turn this place into a fortune. But the way you 'ave treated me, I shall leave here now,' and Casey begged, his hands together:

'Stay Frenchy. I'll lay quart bottles on the alter of heaven for ye, and treat ye splendid. I tell ye – ye'll never rue the day ye threw your lot in with Shaun Casey, the landlord o' the Pigeons. Are you on?'

'What about Richard Carling?'

He opened his arms to the room in vacant surprise. 'Richard Carling, did ye say? Who's that bloody fella?'

The tavern exploded in oaths and laughter, and he shouted:

'Sure, the King's dead, so long live the Queen! I'm all for Frenchy! Who's with me?'

Slowly, the cheering died and all eyes turned to Moll.

I'll give it some thinkin',' said she, and shouldered her way out of the inn to Meg Mare, who was tethered outside. Biddy was waiting there too, and said:

'Don't count me in with that lot, Frenchie. I'm all for my Dicko and I'll stay that way – and one day get even with you an' all, so remember it!'

'As you wish,' said Moll, mounting the horse. 'I do not want your man.'

'Then why hang around here?'

'Because I owe him one, as the English say. Meanwhile, you continue to love him. That is 'ow it should be.'

Ten

'*Attention!*'

Moll spurred Meg Mare; came out of a roadside thicket and barred the way of the London coach. Up reared the leading horses as the driver braked; the coach wheels skidded, bringing it to a halt.

'*Vite! Vite!*' Reining in, with the mare's forelegs pawing air, Moll bent and opened the coach door, shouting 'Out of it all of you! Line up!'

But the driver, Old Sam Hayward, who had been pounding the Shrewsbury to London run for over fifteen years, reached for his blunderbuss, and Moll's horse pistol shattered the night. The ball took Old Sam's hat, drilling it and sending it flying. Afterwards, in bad dreams, Moll wondered how she had missed taking his head off; so did Sam.

'*Vite!* Come on quickly!'

And there trooped out on to the road five of the Quality; they came shivering; females led by a small boy; Moll judged his age at eight.

'Are you going to kill us, sir?' His small face was pale in a rush of the moon.

'Not if you give me money, *garçon!*' Moll dismounted, ruffling his hair in the moment before his mother, a woman of height and dignity, snatched him against her. The other children were presumably daughters, all shivering with terror, wearied by travel and their own sickly adolescence.

On top of the coach, chained hand and foot, sat a

prisoner, and there was a dignity in him that his rags did not diminish. This, thought Moll, but for a chance of fate, could have been Richard on his way to prison.

From his high perch, the prisoner smiled down, saying 'Sure, you're the finest sight I've laid eyes on since leaving home, sir.'

Moll ignored him. Now facing the mother of the children, she was also watching the driver, for she had heard of Old Sam Hayward while at the Talbot. He was a legend; a man who had left more than one highwayman dying in the road. But the mother's eyes never left Moll's, and she said:

'"*Attention*" – did I hear correctly? You people are nothing but scum! Isn't it enough to have our roads infected, without shipping in foreigners?' And she broke into a volume of insulting French.

Moll bowed to her, relieving her of an emerald ring, a gold necklace and a tiny Pelayo brooch.

'You will hang for this, *monsieur*!'

'*C'est possible.*'

'I shall make a point of remembering every feature of your face – an effeminate male if ever I saw one,' she said, and the prisoner shouted down:

'Lady he can be the sister o' Dick Turpin, so long as he shakes me padlocks.' And the woman cried:

'That I should have to talk with such filth!' She glared at Old Sam. 'If it's the last thing I do, coachman, my brother will make you pay.'

'D'ye know who her brother is?' asked the prisoner lightly.

Moll said, ignoring them both. 'Right, everybody back into the coach,' and the woman asked:

'You've heard of Mr Bosanky, the circuit judge? One day you will make his acquaintance.'

'I will look forward to it,' said Moll, and called up to the driver. 'You – down here!'

Unruffled, Old Sam alighted.

'The keys,' said Moll.

'The keys?' He played for time, looking up and down the moonlit road.

'The keys to free 'im.' Moll jerked her head at the prisoner, and the woman shouted, now from the coach window:

'Are you mad? Just look at the size of him! He's a murderer. He'll kill us all if you release him!'

Moll snatched the keys from Old Sam and tossed them up to the prisoner; the padlocks clicked, his chains fell into the road, and next moment he had vaulted down beside her saying gruffly:

'Ay ay, mun! One day I do good for you, eh?' And the woman shrieked:

'For this my brother will hang you, you criminal!'

'You are the criminal, *madame*,' said Moll. 'You take everything and give back nothing. Long ago, in France, you would have been sent to the razor.' She waved the released man back with the pistol. 'You away out of it!'

There was a wood where moonlight filtered down through trees, and an overhanging bluff of rock that sheltered sight from the road.

With the stagecoach gone, Moll took Meg soft-footed through the moonbeams and, reaching the bluff, there rested. Once sure that she had not been followed, she knelt, scraping at the earth.

Beneath her scratching fingers a little silk bag emerged; untying the top, Moll put into it everything she had taken on the road that week, but the necklace, ring and brooch she had removed from the lady and a few other trinkets she kept in her pocket, such evidence being necessary to show to Casey. Securing the bag, she returned it to its hiding place.

Remounting Meg, she took a lonely path back to the Pigeons. And the moment she was out of sight a figure emerged from the shadows and, approaching the hiding place, knelt. A man's hands searched the disturbed ground, delved, and drew out the silken bag. Opening it, he shook out its contents: a tiny silver tiara studded with diamonds and trinkets of jewellery lying among a dozen sovereigns. The gems sparkled, sending light coursing over the man's bearded face.

Returning the little hoard, he reburied the bag, leaving all as securely as Moll had left it.

Six miles away, Shaun Casey sat alone in the Pigeons, watching the tap-room door. When he heard hoofbeats in the stable yard, he stiffened, his hand moving to the flintlock pistol beside him; then Meg Mare neighed, and Casey smiled.

He had had a profitable three days.

Earlier, he had returned from Holyhead, where down on the beach he had taken aboard his cart two casks of brandy, a stone of best tobacco from the West Indies, and a small barrel of whiskey shipped in from County Wicklow; for all of which he had paid in sovereigns. Then, with his mule clip-clopping back to Nesscliff, he had thrown a handful of gravel at the window of Maisie Mooney, the Irish piece who lived in Llanstir.

After a night of debauch with Maisie, Casey then dozed in a drunken stupor on the footboard of his cart, leaving it to the mule to take him home to the Pigeons.

Now with a quart of brandy and a pound of tobacco as a bribe for Justice Bosanky, he awaited the return of Moll from the road.

Shaun Casey didn't go a lot on women, he said; their place was in the kitchen and the bed. Also, his volatile Irish nature rebelled against being dependent upon a female for the payment of his smuggling dues, since his debtors were after him. Yet, he told himself, there was something to be said for one who could outwit a man like Richard

Carling; and one, withall, who could match him in loot from the road: indeed, to be fair, the Frenchy had done better, and a man wasn't in a thieves' Exchange and Mart for the benefit of his health. Now Casey raised his hoary head as the taproom door came open and Moll entered.

'How you done?' he asked.

Moll shrugged, approaching. 'It is good.'

'You got the Shrewsbury to London?'

For reply, she tossed a miscellaneous collection of jewels and gold on to the table before him. Casey rubbed the gems against his coat and held some up to the lamp.

Moll said, 'The ring, necklace and brooch I took from a woman who said she was the sister of Judge Bosanky . . .' and Casey's expression changed from benign enjoyment to a sudden malevolence, and he raised a pale face, whispering:

'By the Holy Grail! A fat piece with five kids and a face like a chopper?'

'She said she was Bosanky's sister,' Moll repeated.

'And ye took from her? Ye bloody French idiot!'

'You did not tell me otherwise – you told me to take from the Shrewsbury to London run, the Hayward coach.'

Casey rose. 'God help us, ye useless gunk! Jesus, we're walking on hallowed water now! Bosanky will have the skin from me bum, and yours too.' Then he subsided, and a slow smile spread across his countenance. 'And yet,' he whispered to himself, 'we could turn it to the good.' He glared at Moll. 'You swear on your grave that this is the lot ye took off his sister?'

'I do.'

'Then here's three guineas for your week's work.'

'You are a damn thief, Mr Casey. What you call a dirty bugger.'

'Aye, that's the generally accepted opinion, but one with both eyes open, girl. So I'll tell ye somethin' else.

You might be a dab hand at lifting gentry's jewels, but I know every sparkler the Quality unloads when it undresses for the night – from the ruby on the hand of a duchess to the diamond on her old man's snuff box. So, if you're after rookin' the fiddlers and he finds out, you'll go six foot down without a funeral service – ye hear me?'

They stared at each other and Casey added, 'For the villagers are not that gladdened by you, don't ye know? They were right fond o' Dicko Carling, and you got shot of him.'

Moll nodded.

'Right, so we'll get down to the real business.' He turned his head and roared, 'Biddy Boddy!'

Rubbing sleep from her eyes, Bid entered.

Casey said, 'The Quarter Sessions are upon us, and Mr Justice Bosanky is on the road . . .'

'Aw, no, Shaun!' Bid wailed.

'He's on the road wi' his coach and six, with his postilions and his footmen, on his way to Shrewsbury Sessions, and he'll be callin' here at the Pigeons for refreshers, so we'll be treating him decent, won't we, Bid?', and he patted her.

'I want nothin' to do wi' the old soak!' Biddy protested. 'He's a dirty old faggot!'

'No doubt, but you'll dress yourself tidy, for we've all got to do our bit in the name of the nobility.' He slapped his leg and roared obscene laughter. 'Sure, it's not askin' for your life, Bid, not even your virginity!'

Moll said, 'He is comin' – the magistrate?' and Casey replied:

'The big fella himself, God bless the Pope. Have you ever stopped to consider why the constables pass here on the gallop? And never a query to its landlord about the rights and wrongs o' a bit of liquor and baccy on the side? Have you asked why the carts come and go between here and Llangefni and ne'er a customs fella within a mile o' me sitting on the footboard? With enough fire water in me rum casks to start an Indian war, and not even a tarpaulin coverin' 'em? It's because o' the benign indifference o' Justice Bosanky, that's what. And you rob his own sister, Moll, bless your heart!' He shouted laughter.

Moll asked, 'You bribe him with drink and tobacco?'

'Ay ay, and a little bit o' Biddy thrown in,' and Bid cried:

'I ain't staying the night wi' him, Mr Casey. I'm telling you, I anna staying the night no more!'

'Aw, girl, come off it,' said Casey. 'What's a wee bit o' hanky-panky between maids and their customers? I tell ye, Bid, it's the least a foine looking bit like you can do for a Quality gentleman, and him that grateful he'll likely drop ye a sixpence.'

'Ach, no, Mr Casey,' whispered Bid, 'for these days he do act awful queer.'

'Aye well, the Quality do things different to us, so you've got to make allowances.'

'That don't mean he's got to dance with me bare in the middle o' June.'

'Do it to please ye uncle.'

'You anna me uncle!'

'That's true, girl, but remember the gallows up on Wolf's Head? For that's where we'll all land if we don't please his worship. Up there swinging in chains with the crows peckin' your eyes out, do you want that?'

'Whoo! No, Shaun Casey!' said Biddy, shivering.

'Ay ay – on Gibbet Holt in the Gallows Wood, that's where you'll end if you don't play polite with the very nice gent, bless him.'

Moll asked, 'When is he coming?'

'A week next Sunday, the day before the Sessions.'

'Where does he lodge?' Moll noticed the gigantic Pincers watching her through the tap-room window.

71

'At the Judges' Lodgings, down in Belmont, Shrewsbury – what's it to you?'

Moll shrugged. 'I just wondered,' and Casey snapped:

'You wonder about the next stagecoach, milady. Meanwhile, I've got two traders in gigs and a merchant bound
for Birmingham the day after tomorrow, so you've
enough to keep ye busy. Are ye fretful?'

'No, that is what I am 'ere for.'

Biddy said tearfully, 'I ain't all that keen on it, ye know,
Mr Casey,' and he reached out, caught her by the bodice
and shook her to rattle her bones. 'I keeps you here to tarty
up the gents, my girl, and ye can't pick and choose.'

'If my Dicko was here, he'd see to it . . .' Biddy
faltered.

'Well he ain't. They've got him in the Shrewsbury Clink
and he can rot there for all I care, for we're doing foine,
aren't we, flower?', and he kissed the air at Moll. 'And
I'll tell you somethin' more. I'm paying off that Rosie
this weekend, for I'm cutting down on the overheads and
jugging up the profits,' and Rosie, hearing this, came to
him with her hands beseeching.

'Mr Casey, for the love of God . . .!'

'You're sacked,' said he, 'for you're spending more
time with ye sick brood than entertaining the clients,
and now Moll's here we can do without ye.' He put a
big arm around Moll's waist and drew her against him.
She asked:

'Is it a highwayman you want, or a bed–mate?'

'Both, me darling.'

Biddy whispered between her teeth as she went out
with Rosie. 'You'm a bitch, Frenchy – a damn bitch!
And I'll get even!'

When the house was quiet, Moll went up the stairs to
Biddy's room and tapped on the door; it opened and the
girl peered with tear-stained eyes.

'What you want?'

'To speak with you, please.'

'You bugger off, ye've caused enough trouble,' Biddy said and added: 'You done up my poor Dicko, and we ain't talkin'.'

Moll asked, 'Do you want 'im back?'

Biddy stared at her in the dim light of the landing, and Moll said, 'Because I can arrange it. But first, let me come in, so we can talk.'

Later, Moll went into the yard where Meg was tethered; mounting her, she galloped up to the cave, this being the safest bed in Nesscliff, she thought, with Shaun Casey getting ideas.

She did not see Pincers, the giant farrier, watching her from the shadows of his forge; nor see him drop to his knees beside the glow of his fire and put his great hands in his yellow hair, and scream. Three times he screamed, did Pincers, his mouth wide open in his bearded face . . . yet made no sound. Not a whisper he made in those screams, but furiously rattled his chains.

'Dear me,' whispered Blodwen Casey around midnight, going under the sheets. 'Just hark at the palaver old Pincers' makin'!'

'Aye. It's the full moon on him.'

'He's telling us it's time he was mated again.'

Eleven

Folklore is alive in Floreat Salopia; like the lady ghost of Fitz Manor, who sighs and sobs around dark corridors; or Mad Mytton of the Mytton and Mermaid Inn on the London Road, who set fire to his celluloid collar because he couldn't remove it; the wraiths of Fulk Fitz Warine and Roger de Powis (whom he slew at the foot of Nesscliff Hill) . . . still walk the dark shrouds of night and peer through kitchen windows at times of storm. Jenny Greenteeth still haunts Bomere Pool, waiting to pull children down into its murky depths, and scores of Little People drink the clear water of Roman Well that cascades down to fill Meg's trough in Kynaston's Cave.

Only forty years before Moll came to Nesscliff, the words of Shaun Casey were true: Gibbet Holt dangled from its gibbet the bodies of felons in chains, their faces painted with tar, food for flocks of long-beaked crows who fattened on human flesh in Gallows Wood. On the eve of May, Biddy Boddy always cut birch and rowan and pinned them over the entrance of the Pigeons to keep out wandering witches . . . any passing young ones like Moll Walbee being welcome, said Shaun Casey.

'As welcome as the flowers in May,' said he. 'English, Italiano or French,' and he bowed to Moll as she came through the door. 'For I'll say this for ye, I've yet to set eyes on a beauty such as you, and I'd give the fingers o' me right hand for a minute of joy in ye, me little titmouse, for me missus is as frigid as a penn'orth o' starch.'

'Please?' asked Moll, not understanding.

'Ach, me darlin', you don't have to beg me, for now you're out o' those breeches and into a maid's skirt, I'm dyin' the death for ye. Are ye on? I'm a wonderful big fella and I'd pleasure ye foine, little woman.'

Said Moll, 'We do not go by size in France, or a cow would catch a hare,' and Shaun Casey laughed bassly, slapping his pads, and the drinking customers – the wizened old labourers of another era, with their snuff stains on their stomachs and their mouths yellow with cider – these nodded their hoary heads together and said it were only a matter of time: Shaun Casey, they said, would bed the Empress of Russia if she bided round here too long.

'Where are ye off to now, then?' asked Casey.

'Nesscliff market,' said Biddy, coming up with the sun on her face. 'I'm after trinkets and beads for me ma's birthday, and Moll's coming with me.'

'Oh aye? Not the pair of you gallivanting, for I need one here,' and Bid protested:

'Och, it's me half day, Mr Casey!'

'Right, get off, but Moll stays.'

'I do not,' said Moll. 'We will start the way I am going on, Casey. I work at night, so do when I please by day,' and she slammed the inn door behind her.

Casey stood by the window of the tap and watched Moll and Biddy, with baskets on their arms, going to Nesscliff market, and the belly on him was soiled by the wish for her and he drank deep of the Llangefni brandy, staring in his lust.

'Give me three guesses,' said his wife behind him, and this turned him, saying:

'I give you Eli, missus. What's good for the goose is right for the gander.'

'That's a goose who'll baste you proper.'

'Don't bank on it,' said Casey.

The May afternoon was girt with brilliance and there was a shine of starlings along the hedgerows as they walked, Moll and Biddy, now friends.

With their bonnet streamers flying in the wind they went, all their cares vanished, for the curlews were shouting demented at the sun, and he, big in the belly in expectation of autumn, snoozed like a ball of molten brass and rolled his rear over the sunlit Wrekin: that great mass of earth that a giant dropped on his way to bury Shrewsbury, said Biddy.

'You were born 'ere?' asked Moll, as they walked.

'Hatched, I was, not born,' said she, 'for me hair came as soft and yellow as a duck's belly, though we've real Irish blood. Me great grandfer had a hand cut off for wandering east o' the Liffey river, where all us Boddys were born and bred. They was bad times. Then we come here.'

'They are bad times now,' said Moll.

Tail-buttoned rabbits bunnied before them as they walked, and down from Ness Hill the warm air sipped and kissed their faces in a scent of milking and a rattling of milkmaids' pails coming from the farms. Biddy said:

'It were good for me when my Dicko was ridin' the roads and bringing home loot, like Humphrey Kynaston did way back in the ancient times. Two gents, ye know, aye – robbers, true, but good fancy chaps, who know how to treat a woman. Time was, before you sent him off, he'd come back cold from the rides; and I'd hear him galloping up Nesscliff Hill to the cave . . .' and Bid stopped and patted a nearby bank of green moss, saying, 'Put yeself down here, Moll Walbee, and hear me out, for you done a terrible thing to me, putting my man away.'

Biddy smiled at the sun. 'We've always had what they call Welsh Robin Hoods feeding our village. One after another since Wild Humphrey Kynaston killed John Hughes three hundred years back. T'is Nesscliff's history, see?

'They rode the roads and beggared the stage coaches, taking money off the merchants and giving it to the villagers; so in return, we guarded 'em and fed 'em, shod, groomed, baled and watered their horses and fenced their loot in Oswestry market.

'And one after the other we've had wicked old sods o' landlords in the Pigeons, though the fella we got now is the wickedest sod of all. But I'll say this for him – he played fair and square with my Richard.' She smiled again, dimpling, in deep reflections. 'You know what my boy used to say? "You ain't much to look at, Bid Boddy; Bid you come and Bid you go, for I canna stand females who hang around, see?"'

Tears came into her eyes now. 'So I'd lie abed in the Pigeons and wait to hear old Meg a-coming. And there was always feed and water for her and a greeting fire for him, with a rabbit stew or somethin' sizzling in his pot, for the nights come cold round these parts.

'And then, when the inn was quiet, I'd slip up there in me cloak and nightie to see if he wanted me. And if the cave door were locked against me, I'd know he had a tiredness on him; but if it were open I'd know he had a wish, and when he had a wish for a woman, only Bid would do, he used to say.' She looked at Moll. 'You think he meant it?'

'I am certain of it.'

'I mean . . . he did a job with you, didn't he? Helped you to steal at the Talbot Inn – but . . .' She faltered . . . 'but he didn't try no funny business, did he?'

'No.' Moll lowered her face.

'Like knocking on your door, or romping, or kissin' pretty with the moon – not even that?'

'He do not do that,' said Moll.

Biddy sighed, holding herself. 'I ache a lot and burn my breasts – but only for him, ye understand? Time was I used to do what Shaun Casey told me; you get a gentleman off the road, well, it's natural, ain't it? But not since my Dicko loved me, oh no. Since he fancied me I kept myself decent.'

'I understand.'

Now Bid rose, smoothed down her dress and said, 'Really speakin', I should hate you, Moll Walbee, for you clinked my fella. And I'd put me hand in the fire if it would get him back. I should hate you, but I don't. You see, he's my chap for always, now I'm goin' to have his baby . . . I know, 'cause I checked the date.'

The words took Moll's breath. Biddy continued, 'Time was I came frit to death at the thought, especially when he went to prison. But he'll come looking for this Bid the moment he's out, he wouldn't have done it lest he loved me, would he?' She made a wry face. 'Oh, I know, I've had gents off the road – he's a right old bugger to me is Shaun Casey – but I only loved my Dicko.'

Moll said, 'He might be in the prison for years . . .!'

'All right, I'll wait for him.'

'And meanwhile?'

'I'll manage. Other girls have.' Biddy laughed, clapping her hands together. '*Jawch*! He'll 'ave a real old bouncer by the time he gets out, won't he?' And then her joyful expression changed. 'But now I got to think about that old soak, Judge Bosanky. Casey says I got to sleep wi' him again, or the beggar'll hang me.'

They sat in momentary silence, listening to the summer; Moll said quietly:

'Bid, listen carefully to me please. What if I were to take your place?'

'Sleep with that old crow? What you sayin'?'

'If you can, I can.' But Biddy shook away her hand, saying indignantly:

'You can't! It's all right for me because I'm nobody, but you – you're Quality. Why, anyway?'

'Because he's going to sentence your Dick to death. Do you not realize that?'

'Of course I do – that's why I'm going to beg him, see?'

'You do not beg men like Bosanky. Biddy, I can save Richard, and you cannot.'

'How?'

'By releasing him from the prison. Could you do that?'

Biddy said, her voice low, 'You can try, missus, but you don't know what you're in for – shannikin with that bloody old Bosanky. For a start, he anna like a normal fella. He do get up to some mighty queer things for an old 'un. You'm a lady, Moll Walbee – you just don't know!', and Moll said earnestly:

'I am not the lady you think I am. Leave me to do this, and I'll set your Dicko free, but if you interfere with what I am planning, then you can watch him come in the hangman's cart up Wolf's Head on Cranberry Moss.'

Biddy shuddered. 'Tell me what you're going to do then.'

'First, we have got to talk to Rosie, and obtain some help from her,' said Moll.

Later, in the cave, Moll wrote three letters, the first, to Richard Carling, the second for the use of Mr Justice Bosanky of the Judges' Lodgings, Belmont, Shrewsbury. These two letters she wrote in English; the third, and last, was written in French:

Ma Petite Chantelle,
I am now in London, for my affairs have flourished since last you heard from me. Indeed – and this will delight you, Small One – I have also fallen in love with an English gentleman. He is a man of wealth, and we are soon to be married.

His name, dear heart, I will tell you later, but you will be interested to know that he is a titled gentleman. Meanwhile, now he has escorted me to London, I live in great luxury in a big hotel (not with my lover, you understand, for the salons here would not approve of that). But he takes me almost every evening to receptions and balls where I wear the most lovely clothes – Chantelle, you should just see the clothes and jewellery I wear in London! Can you not see me in the old minuets and quadrilles, dancing with young gentlemen? Oh my love, the music and the dancing! It has to be seen to be believed!

I pray nightly that your illness has passed and that you are again strong and healthy. Let Uncle Maurice read this letter, and when he does he will learn of my great difficulty in sending money to him from England, which is necessary for your keep. Also, since it would be difficult for Uncle to change sovereigns for francs, I have adopted a simple plan to repay him for his kindness to us – I shall send jewellery, of which I possess a great amount; presents, my darling, from the man who loves me. I write this dressed in a gown of pink satin that reaches to the ground. Roped pearls I am wearing at my throat, white satin shoes are upon my feet. Upon my head (and I wear my hair down over my shoulders) is a diamond tiara – the same as Mama used to wear, remember? So be of good heart, Chantelle; the evening star is our secret rendezvous – and we will one day look at it together. This is the prayer of your devoted sister,

Francesca
London. 9th May 1839

Folding the letter and putting it into a safe place, Moll then descended the cave steps, and whistled up Meg Mare.

★　★　★

With the reins loose in her hands, Moll rode slowly through the forest to the place where she hid her treasures. Sombre moonlight filtered down upon her through overhead branches, and the horse was at times hock deep in the refuse of autumns.

At a rocky bluff, Moll dismounted, knelt, and drew from the earth her little silken bag, not knowing that eyes were watching her from a nearby thicket. And yet, deep within her woman's intuition there was growing an unease.

Kneeling in the dark, Moll looked about her; every shadow, every filtering moonbeam seemed to threaten; the smallest movement of restless bird or scampering vole became emphasized into violence; sweat sprang to her forehead and she wiped it into her hair. Then rising to her feet, she smiled: carry on like this, she thought, and she'd end as mad as Tip Topsy, or worse . . . and here Moll straightened . . . like a lunatic in the mould of Pincers, the giant farrier whom Casey kept chained up like a dog.

Moll did not know that he was watching her now.

Ragged, heavily bearded, the farrier crouched motionless, for in Pincer's mad head there roved the cunning of the fox. When the woman moved among the trees, she who sometimes rode and sometimes led the horse, so Pincers moved; when she stopped, he stopped, which is the manner of the animal in the hunt. And now in the thicket he watched as Moll stared about her.

Time was, as Blodwen's half-brother, Shaun and Blodwen had taken Pincers in to save him from the jeers and taunts heaped upon the mad; and keeping him on a roving chain within the farrier's shop, had him taught the rougher tasks of the blacksmith's trade.

As time passed and he grew to manhood, there formed within his decaying brain a lust for freedom, so Casey lengthened the chain and thickened it. And Pincers, the ragged captive of a giant's size and strength, slept in straw; seeing beyond the heat and blaze of the forge beautiful panoramas of greenness and space, and liberty called him. With this call came licence – the wish to hunt and kill; to follow his lust for a mate. Realizing this, Casey found a female of Pincers' kind; and she was given to him.

It was a mistake, for now the animal in Pincers flourished.

On the night of a full moon he broke his chain and went up Nesscliff Hill.

Moll, returning, climbed the steps leading to the cave, opened the door and went within.

Pincers watched.

For weeks Moll had lived here without fear of being followed; with such unconcern did she enjoy this haven that she often did not bother to shut the massive door.

Pincers meanwhile, still following, raised his great head to the steps, and his eyes, their pupils strangely whitened by his cataracts, stared opaquely as his bare feet felt for the treads; finding them, his squat body rose grotesquely, his ragged arms steadying himself for balance; thus he ascended while Meg Mare, grazing below, whinnied soft disapproval. Upwards he went and reached the door: already he had seen the soft light of Moll's oil lamp that framed the cave window; now this light struck his bearded face as the door rasped open.

He peered within.

Moll was kneeling, preparing for bed, and her back was to the door.

A few moments earlier she had heard the mare's soft warning, but only when it was repeated did she come upon her guard. Also the air had moved within the confining walls, bringing the stink of sweat and tattered

82

clothes; a strange putrescence amid the forest perfumes . . . and Moll stiffened.

She knelt motionless, now aware of an invading presence; and with her ears tuned to the breathing behind her, in panic sought escape . . . cursing her stupidity for not locking the door.

The lamp was flickering, casting distorted shadows upon the red walls, and Moll saw, in the moment before the flame was doused, the pearl handle of the little flintlock pistol projecting from under her pillow. In the moment before the lamp smoked, bringing the darkness that saved her, Moll leaped. But her fingers missed and the little gun went tumbling away . . . as Pincers, roaring like an animal, bore her down on to the bed. Instantly beneath him, next moment she was free, twisting sideways as the fist that would have clubbed her senseless struck the floor, and Pincers howled with pain and rage. Now in darkness, they faced each other, and Moll saw, outlined against the window sky, the shaggy head of her attacker.

Pincers lunged, caught her and swung her aloft; Moll made no sound: he, gasping and bellowing, sought to pin her beneath him, but her speed matched his animal strength; so in the darkness Moll eluded him, slipping this way and that to avoid his arms. Finally, in a supreme effort, she made a dash for the door, but slipped and fell behind it, and Pincers' big hands hauled her upward. Struggling in his embrace, Moll screamed, and the scream echoed along the wooded tracks. Now he pinned her down; she screamed again as his hands clawed at her. And Shaun Casey stiffened in the bed at the Pigeons Inn. Opening one eye at the second scream, he sat upright. Leaping out, upending Blod in the process, he snatched a horse whip as he ran to the farrier's shop next door; there he saw the broken chain.

'*Pincers!*'

'What the hell is happenin'?' cried Blodwen, halfway out of the bedroom window, her hair in crackers.

'It's Pincers!' shouted Casey. 'The thing's away!'

'*Uffern dan!*'

Half the occupants of the Pigeons then went streaming up to Kynaston's Cave like a gaggle of hags in the French Revolution.

Moll, now biting and scratching at the face above her in the dark, made fists of her hands; and flinging one outward, struck the little pistol; her fingers closed on its butt.

Using it as a weapon she crashed it down upon Pincers' head. Howling, he slackened his hold. In a moment Moll slipped sideways, and while the man floundered after her, drew back the hammer of the weapon and fired. Light blazed; the detonation was thunderous, and the ball took him in the shoulder. She saw his mouth drop open in surprise and pain; and like a wounded elephant he ploughed around bellowing, hauling his great body away for escape. Now, teetering at the top of the cave steps, his feet slipped on the sandstone grit, and he pitched forward; to go tumbling, his arms and legs flying, down the whole flight to the bottom. There he lay at the feet of Meg Mare as Casey and the others came running up.

'Right, you!' cried Casey, and the whip went high while Pincers howled, protecting his face.

'Are you all right, me darlin'?' called Casey, resting with the whip.

Moll nodded. 'For God's sake stop beating him, the man is mad.'

They led Pincers, chained, back to the inn.

Moll did not know then that her brush with Pincers would change the course of her life.

Twelve

'See ye on Resurrection Day, me darlin'!' bawled Shaun Casey as Rosie got her belongings together on her two-wheeled dog cart, and started out for mother and home.

'Sure to God,' said she, as Moll met her on the road to Shrewsbury, 'that won't be likely, for that fella's forfeited membership of the human race. And what do you want with me, ye bloody French nincompoop?' Big, rangy, she struck a hostile attitude.

'A word in your ear please.'

'Ain't you done enough damage?'

Moll said, reigning in the mare, 'Do you want to get revenge upon Shaun Casey?'

'Revenge?' cried Rosie, and she held up a big fist. 'I'll fill his gob wi' dust. On me father's grave, I'll not rest till he's got a stone on his head.'

Moll had always felt sorry for Rosie, who, from morn till dusk (with little brothers at home and a dying mother) babied and bottled and comforted; struggling to make ends meet on the three shillings a week Casey paid her for days of sweat and toil. 'But I needs the money,' said Rosie. 'God 'elp us if I lose this job.'

Now Moll said, dismounting from the horse:

'All right, you hate Casey? Then listen, and you'll do Dick Carling a good turn and Casey a bad one.'

The moon, beamed down with a broken-faced malignancy.

'Is that the lot?' asked Rosie, after listening.

85

'That is all,' replied Moll, and took from her pocket three sovereigns. 'These are to comfort your mother. Do what I ask, and when Carling is free, there's more where it come from.'

'God bless you for the sweet wee thing that you are,' said Rosie. 'You can rely on me,' and the gold leaped in her hand.

Now, with moonlight filtering through the trees of Nesscliff Hill, Moll went back to the cave and primed and loaded Richard's tiny flintlock pistol.

There was more going on in the Old Three Pigeons Inn that dusk than a Tipperary bun fight, everybody being well oiled with the fruits of St Patrick.

Blodwen, two sheets in the wind, was doing a fan dance with bottles; Shinbone was arming Saul Clay around, their clogs stamping in the spit and sawdust; Tom Cakebread had Belinda Porridge, a new arrival, in a wrestler's half-nelson, and Rum-Bum-Baccy was prancing like a bullfighter with Short Chap acting as the bull.

'All in all, it's a marvellous, disgusting exhibition,' shouted Shaun Casey, clapping the time.

Ben Pullet and his new niece, one breast bare, were kicking up their legs to the music of Irish fiddles, while Justin Slaughterer was in a corner looking at Boyo Bad Thing's dirty pictures.

It was a palace of sorcerers with ale and porter going down and cider swilling under the doors, and they've never heard such a palaver, said Blodwen since Beelzebub and the Pope got together on raw gin.

Everything female between nine and ninety had their skirts above their knees to the music of the Irish reels; bosoms were bouncing, knees and arms akimbo in time with fiddlers' elbows.

On the edge of the dancers, flattened against the walls, the male population of Nesscliff was hooting and shrieking like Cherokee Indians in a hugger-mugger confusion.

'Mind you, my special guest, Mr Justice Bosanky, do like to see the place behavin' with its usual sensitive decorum,' said Casey, 'so round and round we go, me darlin's, and you've never heard such a palaver since the Irish climbed the Tower of Babel.'

Now the inn door slammed on the revelry. Silence fell on Nesscliff Hill like the lid of a coffin.

A mile away Moll sat astride Meg, the black mare.

Silhouetted, as something carved from stone, she sat against a lanterned sky, and the moon was as big as a Dutch cheese, lighting the Roman road to Oswestry into a purple ribbon. And this was the road that Moll was watching. On little blusters of the night wind about her came faintly the bawdy revelry of the Pigeons as a strange and terrifying irreverence; it stained, for her, the beauty of the night.

Along this road, within a few hours, Moll reflected, would come the ornate stagecoach of Mr Justice Bosanky, continuing a journey that had begun in Chester.

With six horses drawing his carriage, three postilions riding them and two footmen standing behind, he would arrive in his capacity as circuit judge, there to pronounce sentences upon prisoners in the relevant towns, leaving behind him a trail of felons to suffer imprisonment, transportation, or death.

Not since the infamous Judge Jeffreys, notorious for his sadism at the 'Bloody Assizes' following Monmouth's insurrection, had a more terrifying name been bandied from mouth to mouth.

Ruthless in his repression of theft, Bosanky, according to Shaun Casey, was himself corrupt, for this same judge hypocritically allowed total licence to the Pigeons of crimes ranging from customs duty avoidance to keeping a disorderly house; largely for the benefit of Justice Bosanky.

Although himself immoral, this judge would give short shrift to Richard, now in Shrewsbury lock-up awaiting trial for highway robbery. And it was she herself, Moll remembered bitterly, who had put him into this man's hands.

Later, on sighting Bosanky's coach, Moll returned to the cave. Here, with careful haste, she changed into the clothes of a serving maid: brushing out her hair, she tied it in plaits with red ribbons, the style which Bosanky preferred it was said. Her black worsted stockings she held up with red garters; her red flannel drawers reached to her knees, and her black woollen skirt just revealed her brightly buckled shoes. With a lace cap pinned to her hair, her bodice laced tightly and her bosom pushed high, Moll looked at herself in Richard's cracked shaving mirror and decided she was better than most.

Now, with Meg Mare installed in the cave for the night, and carrying a bag in case of eventualities, Moll took the bridle path that led to the carousing in the Pigeons.

She had timed it well. Coming around the bend in the London Road were the leading horses of the judge's coach. Light and smoke hit her as she opened the tap-room door, and following Moll in came one of the footmen. Gorgeous in his three-cornered hat and suit of silver brocade, his presence snatched the room into silence: with an arm upraised, he shouted commandingly:

'Pray silence for his honour, Mr Justice Bosanky!'

The tap-room door went back upon its hinges, and Bosanky was in.

Moll judged his age at fifty. Of medium height and choleric countenance, Bosanky's features betrayed his irascible nature. For this was the face which had stared into those of a thousand men condemned; the baggy eyes that betrayed their inner calculation were compassionless, these were the eyes that had seen public hangings, wailing orphans and prostrate widows. Light blue and cold, they momentarily met Moll's the moment Bosanky entered. Then the eyes moved slowly to Biddy who, also arriving, draped herself in a curtsy upon the floor like a dying swan.

Moll, with her fist on her hips and her chin tilted up, did not move, save for her eyes which roamed over Justice Bosanky with cold indifference . . . from the crown of his balding head to the white silk stock and bulging satin waistcoast; to his breeches and riding boots of black calf leather.

'A word with you, landlord,' said he, and his voice, like a cinder under a door, belied his portentous appearance; Casey leaped to his side in fawning obeisance.

'At your service, ye honour!'

'The anteroom would be my pleasure.'

'Of course, sir.' Casey led the way, leaving the room in an eerie, suspended silence.

Biddy was shivering. 'I tell ye again', she whispered into Moll's ear, 'he be a queer old beggar . . .'

'Ten pounds of tobacco – the usual?' commanded the judge.

'Ready and packed, ye honour! Shaun Casey's always at your service, don't you know,' and he wheedled and cajoled. 'Likewise the brandy, sire, if I may be so bold – the best, as befits ye station – straight from the vineyards o' France and it cost me a pretty penny, not that you're interested.'

'Not in the least. Whisky?'

'Now, there ye have me, me darlin'. Your honour will be the first to appreciate . . .'

'Whisky, I said.'

'Ay ay,' and Casey bowed low, sweeping up the floor with his cap, and thought, Och, the mean ould sod, and him on twenty thousand. Sure, he'll have me scratching a tramp's arse, so he will, but said:

'May the saints preserve ye for the foine man ye are, Justice Bosanky – faith, hope and charity, say I, and a wee drop o' the hard stuff, beggin' your pardon. How many bottles did ye wish?'

'Twenty, and make it sharp,' and Bosanky stared around the room with open disdain, adding, 'All this is against my better judgement, Casey. If an ill mood ever takes me I'll shut this devil's kitchen and have the lot of you on ropes.' His voice lowered and he snatched at Casey with a bejewelled hand and drew him closer. 'Listen, you dregs of the licensing trade, you scum of the victuallers! Magna Carta says that justice shall not be denied, sold, nor delayed. To discuss with you the manifold absurdities of our legal system I shall make no pretension, for you, fool that you are, would only understand one word in three. But consider, Casey, the augmentation in wealth and population were I to advise the government to employ sufficiently of law enforcement officers to keep you and your kind under proper control! There were only twelve apostles to preach the Gospel – it would need five thousand and twelve custom officials to stop your riotous living and infamous progress along the roads to Llangefni. Ay, I know – Llangefni is the receiving home of your iniquitous brew . . . is it not?'

'Oh, my Gawd!' said Casey.

'But more, much more. Here in this hovel you harbour highwaymen and thieves, do you not? Footpads and brain-thudders are your legitimate customers. Indeed, Casey, I go further. It is a bawdy house, a brothel, a bordello, a haven, for which I could have you and your broad-beamed spouse whipped at the back of a cart from here to Shrewsbury Guildhall.' The judge was livid, and he pulled the landlord's face to within an inch of his own. 'Not a month back, my good sister was waylaid and relieved of a ring, a brooch and an excellent golden necklace – one which I myself gave her, Casey! And you have the confounded audacity to offer me in recompense a few bottles of brandy?' He shook Casey to rattle his change, saying, 'Produce these articles, my friend – every item of jewellery in pristine condition, or I swear that you'll be cooling your heels in Shrewsbury lock-up.'

'Och dear,' croaked Casey, shivering. 'By the tears of the Holy Mother . . .!'

'Blasphemy now, is it? By the living God, I'll have your life – produce them!'

And Casey, with trembling hands, drew out of his pocket the ring and gold necklace Moll had stolen, and dropped them into the judge's hand. 'Here all ready an' waitin', sir!'

'And the prisoner your effeminate thug released, no doubt for some further immoral and predatory intention, where is he now, Casey? I have one villain awaiting my justice – your infamous Dick Carling who kept this cesspit in luxury – but where is the notorious dandy who now operates from this devil's kitchen under your protection?'

'Jesus alive and reigning, don't go on!'

Bosanky pushed Casey down into a chair and stood over him, adding softly, 'I have informed you of the danger in which you find yourself. And there is but one way by which you can cool my anger, and it is this . . . You'll recall that on other occasions I have sought the company of one of your serving maids – an obese little creature who goes under the name of Biddy Boddy. I seek her company again, for the innocent have always attracted my devotion. We talk philosophy late into the night, you know.'

'Kind sir, she's ready and willin'!'

'But this evening, upon entry here,' added the judge, 'I noticed a woman of very different proportions. One who did not kow-tow like the others, and this pleased me.'

'Your worship,' said Casey, 'ye have only to lift a hand.' Gaining confidence, he said, 'She's a French beauty, over here to get experience of the victualling trade, and she'd take pretty to a man of o' your foine proportions.'

'Arrange it,' commanded the judge curtly. 'She's to come to my lodgings in Belmont, Shrewsbury, on the evening of the fifteenth. I'll send a coachman for her.'

'Yes, your highness.'

'Fail in this and I will not only remove this Satan's parlour from under your feet, I will rope your neck!'

And Casey, the moment the coach and six moved off, seized Moll's hand and drew her secretly into the anteroom, whispering:

'Frenchy, I've got a marvellous surprise for ye – you'll never believe your luck! The judge fancies ye. He's going to take ye into his lodgings and discuss your credentials. You never know what might come of it . . .'

'Don't tell me, let me guess,' said Moll.

Thirteen

Perfumed, powered, curled and in the uniform of a serving maid, Moll awaited the arrival of the carriage sent by Bosanky in the anteroom of the Pigeons, listening to the bawdy laughter from the tap-room where Snap, Tip Topsy's little terrier, was dancing for the customers. For this was ratting night and Snap Ratter was at his best after a pint of old and mild.

So as Moll peeped around the tap-room door, Snap Ratter danced with his forelegs beating the time. The customers clapped and roared in chorus. The oil lamps glowed from the beams; tobacco smoke swirled; the flames of a peat fire danced in grotesque shadows, and the language going up was enough to stain the soul of Satan. This, thought Moll, was Richard's life. These his friends, from the innocent yokels of the surrounding farms to crooks like Eli Rumbletum, Tom Cakebread, Tip Topsy and Justin Slaughterer, the dregs of society.

It was a concoction of all the worst in life – and Moll had known some prime examples in the slums of Montmartre. Was Richard Carling, therefore, really worth saving? In terms of the swaggering brawlers, the ruffians and desperadoes she was watching now, he wasn't . . . Or did he live on Nesscliff Hill removed from this jubilant immorality? . . . When a village harpy could be breeched on the floor by a passing traveller, and a clog dance performed by a fool with his trousers off?

And this, her attempt to release him from prison . . . was he worth the effort, perhaps in exchange for her own life? Had she got contrition out of context? Moll wondered. Would he do as much for her? – he who kept his door unlocked when he fancied a woman, and locked it against her when he wanted sleep?

And was Biddy Boddy, the pathetic young serving maid so hopelessly in love with him, just another listed in his book of conquests?

So much for Biddy, but how did Moll Walbee stand?

The music from the tap-room rose to a higher note; an insubstantial pageant that beat upon Moll's mind as she moved away from the door; and then, on the highest point of its crescendo, the tawdry discord ceased. And in the following pin-drop silence she heard Shaun Casey shout:

'Ah yes, fellow. Wait outside in the cab and I'll give the filly a shout!' And the door of the anteroom went back on its hinges and he stood there, did Casey, rocking upon his heels.

Bowing in mock ceremony, slopping his ale, he said bassly, 'Milady, your coach awaits ye!'

Moll, going through the tap-room, ignored him and the clients lining the walls drooped over their jugs with boozy intent. Casey cried after her:

'Don't forget ye glass slipper at midnight, either, tho' it'll need more'n a pumpkin coach to save your fancy man! The judge will be topping him a week come Michaelmas!'

Shouts of laughter greeted this, and Blod Casey said with her hands on her hips at the door, 'Shall I tell you what's expected of ye, Frenchy? For he knows more tricks than a conjurer's tom cat,' and she fisted the air, her great bosom shaking with laughter.

The horse and carriage were standing on the road, the moonlight beamed. Wayside trees shrank like crouching hunchbacks; somewhere in the village a dog was barking dismally. The driver, top-hatted and beautifully turned out, bowed.

'Miss Walbee?' he said, and opened the cab door. The whip cracked; the hooves beat on the flinted road to Shrewsbury.

So far so good, thought Moll; if Rosie played her part there was a good chance that the plan she had prepared might succeed.

Near the Severn Arms the driver leaned down and called:

'My employer, Mr Justice Bosanky, greets you with the hope that you have a pleasant journey. Also, I am instructed to call for you at the Judge's Lodging House when St Julian's strikes the hour of six in the morning. Kindly be ready, for it is imperative that you be off the premises before the townspeople are about.'

Though of impeccable manners and a man of good education, one probably with a daughter of her own age at home, he would never understand the role he was playing – that of a pimp. Such as he, in the pay of a corrupt aristocracy, served their foppish masters unquestioningly.

'I shall be there, make no mistake, *monsieur.*'

She was being sickened by men, and now this one in particular.

'This is the first time you have visited the judge in his lodgings, *mademoiselle?*' His grinning face again appeared upon the glass.

'Get on with your driving.'

Through Shelton Roughs and Frankwell they went, the half-timbered buildings of Tudor Shrewsbury with their windows leaning over them as if in blessing. Now over the newly completed Welsh Bridge, and on to Claremont. Faint music came from the Shrewsbury Hotel where carriages were clustered for an evening of gentry revelry.

On to Town Walls now, where Moll caught a glimpse of the river, surpassingly beautiful in the light of the moon.

95

The carriage slowed on reaching Belmont, then stopped outside a beautiful Queen Anne building. All the elegance of sumptuous surroundings swept into her again as the driver rang a bell: a door opened, exposing a beautifully decorated hall laid with soft-footed carpets. A footman in livery stood silently before her.

'Pray enter, ma'am,' and he bowed, closing the door the moment she was within.

'You have an audience arranged with Justice Bosanky, I believe.'

The butler was undersized; his hose was of silk, his tunic and knee-length trews beautifully woven and braided; silk ruffles were at his throat and wrists, but his eyes were those of a cod in a face that had died. Indeed, the room itself into which Moll was shown, though ornately lovely, was as cold as a mausoleum. The Chinese carpets spoke of wealth and luxury, but it was the decoration of ceremony and privilege; its beauty stank.

'Where is the judge?' asked Moll.

The butler stared with injured eyes. 'Where is the judge you ask? How dare you! You will kindly sit and await his arrival. He will come in his good time.'

'Then inform him, *monsieur*, that I am about other business, apart from his,' and the reply came instantly:

'You are above yourself, young woman! Sit and wait,' and he swept away with fine pomposity.

This, thought Moll, was the epitome of the arrogance once experienced by France; a disdain for the 'lower orders' – who, in France, set about collecting bloodstained heads in baskets.

'His honour will receive you now,' said another flunkey.

Moll nodded.

'Follow me.'

With his stockinged legs rising before her up a scarlet staircase, she followed this one, a valet, to a first floor

96

landing; Moll entered a room dominated by a big four-poster bed. She saw the moon hanging in a window, and heard a whispered consultation, the unmistakable voice of Justice Bosanky:

'Go to bed – you and all the servants. And ensure the woman is out of here before six of the clock, you understand?'

For the first time Moll experienced fear.

Silence.

The old house was talking to itself in creaks; the moon in the window suddenly brightened, then sank behind purple clouds, bringing the room to total blackness.

It was akin to an entombment.

Minutes past; the intensity of the darkness was playing upon Moll's nerves. Then another door opened and light lanced the carpet. Bosanky, with a lamp held high, whispered through the opening:

'*Mademoiselle* . . .?'

'Yes?'

'I will be with you in a moment. Meanwhile, remove your clothes,' and the sudden dazzling light subsided into a glow: Moll moved silently towards it, peering around the door into a small red chamber.

Here the judge was undressing in gasping haste, flinging his clothes about carelessly, as a man might do before his final copulation. Now down upon a chair he was tearing off his boots; on his feet, now approaching nakedness, he stooped to a travelling trunk and from this drew female underclothes.

Moll watched through the crack of the door.

The man before her, waving hairy arms into a petticoat, looked ludicrous; he pulled upon each fat leg a woman's stocking, crowning the absurdity with bright red garters at the thigh. Women's buckled shoes came next; upon his head he laid a golden wig that trailed its locks either side of his face; a face suddenly aged by its life of the perverted – a transvestite, the basis of his corruption.

Yet, this same person had jurisdiction over his fellows and sentenced them to punishments in the name of justice and morality. Now he was squatting at a little dressing table, smearing rouge upon his cheeks and carmine on his mouth, giving himself the appearance of a clown.

But now Moll was also undressing.

Beneath the cloak that covered her was the riding tunic she wore for the road. The skirt she unfastened and dropped to the floor revealed her riding trews and boots; within seconds, with her hat upon her head and her hair pushed up into it, she was no longer the serving maid from the Pigeons, but a youth ready for the road. With the flintlock pistol in her hand she awaited Judge Bosanky.

The door of his dressing room opened wide, illuminating with sudden brilliance, the bed, furniture, the deep-piled carpet.

'*Mademoiselle . . .?*' Bosanky crouched like a hunchback in his flimsy colours; now he entered the bedroom peering about it.

'*Mademoiselle!*' he repeated.

And the moment he was in, Moll, behind the door, kicked it shut.

'Where are you?' demanded Bosanky, turning swiftly.

Astonishingly, the voice was that of a woman.

'Turn up the lamp!'

Brightness obliterating the darkness, exposing Moll with the pistol in her hand and Bosanky in all his comic absurdity before her. It was the tragic comedy of his life exposed, and the disbelief upon his features contorted the scene into drollery; the final act of his pantomimic hypocrisy.

Bosanky made no sound. His mouth dropped open with incredulity; speechless, he stared at the pistol, then straightened as realization dawned; now he opened his mouth for the cry, but the pistol rose to his face.

'One word and I will blow your 'ead off.'

So they stood, the flimsily attired *doppelganger* of the woman . . . and the woman dressed as a man. But now the former's senses were returning.

'Ah yes!' Bosanky said softly. 'The Old Three Pigeons Inn! I might have expected it – Shaun Casey at work!'

'It is not.'

'Then why . . .?'

'Sign this,' commanded Moll, and tossed a paper at his feet.

'I will sign nothing.'

Despite the preposterous situation in which he found himself, the man's command returned. Stooping he picked up the paper, read it, and said:

'This is a document granting the release of a prisoner.'

'Yes, Richard Carling, who is being held for your judgement.'

The paper was trembling in Bosanky's hand, the pistol in Moll's was firm. Bosanky said drolly:

'He must be of trifling importance. With nineteen cases awaiting my judgement, I haven't even heard of him.'

'Then sign the paper.'

'And if I do not?'

Moll said, 'My life is nothing with him in prison, Bosanky. I'd think less of killing you than puttin' my boot on a beetle,' and he replied suavely:

'An effeminate highwayman, according to my sister . . .' His baggy eyes drifted over her. 'The scum of the roads! It is only a question of time before we hang the lot of you . . .' He paused. 'Meanwhile, if I sign this release, of what use is it to you?'

'None.'

'Exactly. Do you really think such a letter – even with my signature – could obtain a prisoner's freedom without an accompanying magistrate?'

'Of course not.'

'Then how do you intend to effect it?'

She saw his eyes: they were measuring the leap for the pistol; if he reached it and disarmed her, he would prove the stronger, and Moll said, tightening her finger on the trigger:

'You will come with me, you will act for the magistrate.'

His voice rose. 'Stupid woman dressed as a man! Do you think I'd agree to that?'

'If you do not, I will kill you – stupid man dressed as a woman!'

Bosanky's panic suddenly became apparent.

'You will let me dress properly? Please, for God's sake!'

'No. You are coming like that, but you can cover yourself with your cloak. The lock-up is in Gullet Passage.'

'How informed you are! You realize that this will cost you your life? An affront to one of Her Majesty's judges is a crime no less than an attack upon her person.'

'Sign the letter,' said Moll and, going to a little bedside table, he did so.

'Now get your cloak.'

'It is down in the hall. Mademoiselle, I beg you – let me dress decently.'

'Of course not. I am not a fool.' She waved him away with the pistol. 'One sound, Bosanky – just one shout for the servants and you are dead.'

'You are a fool if you think you can get away with this,' he said, and he preceded her down the stairs to the hall.

At the front door he turned; tears were suddenly upon his face.

'Have you thought of what this means to me? The shame, the disgrace will be worse than death.'

'You should have thought of that before.'

The stars were big in the Milky Way: together they walked the deserted streets to the lock-up in Gullet Lane.

Again, so far so good, thought Moll; but, even if she succeeded in releasing Richard, nothing would be gained unless Rosie played her part . . .

'You swear you will let me keep my cloak on?'

'If you let me have Richard Carling, or I will strip it off you in front of them all. Get on!' And she prodded him with the pistol.

Fourteen

Gullet Passage lived up to its name.

In its day, in plague or in health, it harboured tattered beggars who rattled their plaintive bowls at every passing tradesman and felt the collars of swaying drunks. But Gullet's more loathsome claim to posterity was the housing of people awaiting the mercy of men like Justice Bosanky.

Thousands of unfortunate felons had left its damp lock-up (known as the 'Clink') for the Assizes and transportation to the Colonies or death by ritual strangulation up on Gallows Hill.

Richard Carling, doubtless entitled to the latter, now shared a cell with two others – a swindler and a murderer. All were lying on the straw-covered floor when, of a sudden, a white envelope came sliding through their bars.

'What's that?' asked somebody and picked it up.

'It is for me,' said Richard, tearing open the envelope; he read:

> When the door opens, run to the Golden Cross where Meg Mare will be waiting. I will meet you later, at the usual place.
>
> Francesca

Richard said to his companions, 'You're in luck. When that door opens, make a bolt for it – all in different directions.'

They stared with disbelief.

★ ★ ★

Still prodding Bosanky with the pistol, Moll whispered:

'Right. Your gaoler has delivered the first letter. Now show him the one you have signed for Carling's release.'

'You recognize me, gaoler?' the judge called.

Bearded, swarthy, the man peered back at him. Bosanky said:

'You recognize me as Justice Bosanky, the circuit judge come here for the Assizes?'

'Aye, your honour!'

'Then open the door so I can enter – come, be sharp,' and the man said, dolefully:

'By ye leave, your honour, t'is more'n me life be worth without the order signed and sealed by a magistrate . . .' and he winced and munched at his whiskers.

Bosanky said brutally, 'It will be more than your life is worth if I do not gain entry to my own premises. Open up! I am not a twopenny magistrate, man, I am your judge!'

'Holy Mary, Mother o' God!' breathed the gaoler, rattling his keys.

The cell door grated open on its hinges. Yellow light banished .the shadows of Gullet Passage and as three famished humans raced to freedom, Moll, with her pistol in Bosanky's back, pushed him and the gaoler into the cell, crying:

'The keys, Richard, the keys!'

Richard snatched them from the gaoler and locked the cell door.

And Moll, Richard and the others clattered down Gullet Passage, while Bosanky and the gaoler, now locked in the cell, raised enough commotion to wake churchyard corpses.

Rosie, astride the filly she had borrowed and holding the reins of Meg Mare, waited with growing agitation in the shadows of the Golden Cross Hotel. And heard, as St Julian's clock struck the hour, two sounds: the first was Old Sam Hayward and his coach clattering down Wyle Cop on his way to London; the second was a hullabaloo from Gullet Passage where Bosanky and the gaoler were coming to blows.

Then she heard the sound of footsteps: Richard and Moll, hand in hand, came running out of the darkness. Now they were up in the saddles – Moll on the filly, Richard on Meg Mare.

Along Fish Street and Butcher Row they went at a gallop, and over the fields to Mardol. The Severn flashed its tide swim at the moon as they cantered down Frankwell, and Moll saw, a hundred yards before she reached the Welsh bridge, Richard go racing over it full pelt. She stopped, letting him get clear.

There came to her as she listened to the gasping of the filly, the thought that he was galloping out of her life, that this imprisonment, from which she had snatched him, had led them not to their freedom, but into an unnamed confinement.

It was as if this man was now lost to her. The knowledge restricted her breath, and a knifing pain grew within her. She sat there, fighting the vacuum that had suddenly possessed her. At the very moment of release when he had so briefly greeted her, Richard seemed to have gone forever.

The moon, as if relenting, beamed over the town in a magical splendour; lighting the crisis-cross, crazy roofs and glinting along the streets and alleys as in repentance. Yet surely, she reasoned, in granting this man his freedom she had made a personal act of atonement. And perhaps, for the first time since their meeting, she knew in this fulfilment a sense of belonging that she had known with no other man. No coquetry was here, no sentimental romancing. For the first time in Moll's life her inner charlatan had gone, reducing all her former affairs to pillow talk and Bohemian ill-taste.

'What about you, then?' she asked and stroked the filly's ears. 'What will you do about it, when you discover you are in love?'

Then she kicked with her heels and ran for the Welsh bridge; to Nesscliff she went, with the left hand of dawn touching the eastern sky.

Jinny Oolerts, who called themselves barn owls, were singing to the moon as Moll galloped past a deserted Pigeons: shriek owls, their shrill sisters, were telling that it was the end of the earth as she reined in the filly and took the bridle path that led to Kynaston's cave.

Richard, already within, was awaiting her, and Moll ran into his arms.

What began as a kiss of greeting ended in heat and strident breathing.

Forgiveness and explanation were unspoken.

At their first love making, there had been about Richard a mood of contrary indifference; this was now exchanged for a growing intensity, as if the parting had enriched his desire. And in the haven of the cave the intimacy of their presence bridged the strangeness of reality.

Earlier, Biddy had been into it to clean, and lay the peat fire where an iron pot filled with Welsh *cawl* now bubbled its greeting. Meg's manger had been filled with fresh oats; her trough at the bottom of the steps with fresh water. Even the white shirt Richard was wearing now – worn after a wash and change before Moll had arrived to join him – had been ironed to greet his homecoming. And now, squatting on the floor beside Moll, he spooned up the stew, and tore at Bid's freshly baked bread with strong white teeth. Prison, Moll reflected, seemed to have affected him mainly through appetite.

'My God, you took a chance,' he said.

Moll shrugged. 'Most betrayals demand retribution.'

There grew upon his face a boyish simplicity. 'Don't tell me I didn't ask for it – I'd have had you if you hadn't had me, but highway robbery's nothing compared to the abduction of a judge.'

She smiled. 'An English rope to match the French one?'

A nightjar sang in the following silence.

'What do you mean by that?'

'What I say.'

He grunted audibly, breaking bread. 'The wives of first secretaries don't usually do business with highwaymen.'

Moll laughed joyously. 'Did I say I was the wife of a first secretary?'

'During the course of conversation.'

'During the course of conversation, my friend, I likely said many things. I fear you made the mistake of taking me too seriously.'

'Based on sincerity, it's a mistake we English make.'

Moll made a face, putting down her bowl and moving to the window where stars stood like eyes of fire. 'And this is where you English are stupid. Some would say that you got what you deserved. One day, perhaps, you will learn about women.'

'I'm learning every moment.'

'And do not like what you discover?'

Richard rose and took her into his arms.

'On the contrary. In the business of two-timing I know little about the French, but in the business of love I'm halfway to Paris.'

'Not now.' Moll held him away.

Then later:

'Damn you, Richard! Here we are within an inch of a rope and all you can think of is lovemaking. If you need someone that quickly, my friend, don't choose me.' Moll threw up her hands. 'The first thing I want is to get out 'ere; if the dragoons come we'll be caught like rats.' She paused. 'Also . . .'

'Something else is worrying you?'

'Yes. What will become of Biddy?'

'Biddy? She threw in her lot with Casey. She'll have to take what's coming.'

The coldness had returned; perhaps it was the usual male weakness of self-preservation. She said, now, kneeling and warming her hands at the fire:

'She also threw in her lot with you.'

'Oh, so that's it! And what was I supposed to do? – Set up house with her?'

'You did that – here.'

In the forest silence of little barks and screeches, Richard sat morosely.

It was not enough, thought Moll, to have him returned to her; it was also necessary for him to face his responsibility: like most men he was strangely childlike. She asked:

'Supposing she has a baby?'

'What?'

'You heard what I said. Supposing Biddy has a baby?'

'What makes you think it would be mine? – you're taking a lot for granted.'

'That's what you did when you seduced her. She was under sixteen.'

'Aha! The girls have been exchanging confidences!'

'Of course. If women didn't get together sometimes, men would have it even better! You leave here, Biddy could have your baby.'

He gasped with indignation. 'Listen to it! At a time when the law's doing its best to hang the father, you talk about an improbable baby. Biddy's been around, and she didn't need any persuading.'

'She was a child!'

'She's a woman!'

'You know what will happen to her, don't you?'

He raised his dark eyes to her face.

Moll said: 'She goes to church you know. They'll beat her up the mountain with Bibles and brooms . . .'

He replied, uncertainly, 'What . . . what are you trying to tell me?'

'That she has conceived.'

A vein in his temple was suddenly pulsating. 'God Almighty,' he whispered.

'And what are you going to do about it?'

'Go down there.'

'Wait until daylight – we'll go together.'

'Oh no we won't. I'm going now. You stay here.'

'How will you handle it?'

'Give her money. I've got some tucked away.'

'She'll just love that.'

'Christ, what else can I do?'

'Promise you will come back to 'er when the child arrives. That's the standard behaviour, isn't it, even if you don't.'

'Damn me, you're cynical!'

'Aren't I! Cynicism is the gift men breed in women.'

At the door, he said, 'It strikes me you've had some bad experiences.'

'That's right. Now say goodbye to the girl you 'ave seduced, and we'll all be 'appy ever after. You men are all the damn same.'

Smiling, Richard said, 'The trouble is that you 'ave discovered there was somebody around before you!' (He was mimicking her accent.)

'Not in the least. I've managed passably, all things considered.'

'Then stop playing the virgin. I don't ask for your history; don't put your nose into mine.'

Seeing him about to leave, she knew a sudden panic – possibly he may not return. After all, what had they in common save betrayal? And clearly, like all men, one woman was as good as another – everything resolved into the material. Had she allowed him to make love to her, perhaps he wouldn't be going now . . . and yet it was she herself who had begun this talk of Biddy.

Now a chasm of coldness had formed between them which nothing could bridge; indeed, what was happening now was challenge and bitterness: nothing of this had she planned. In her dreams of reunion, warmth and light were promised; this had now vanished into the illusion of a brief unsustainable affair.

Moll thought: If he leaves me now, I shall die . . . and the sound of Richard's voice returned her to reality.

'Ah well, I'll be off,' said he, and she cried within herself: Stay, please stay. It doesn't matter about Biddy, it doesn't matter about anyone.

'Perhaps I won't come back. You realize that? You're so bloody keen I do the right thing.'

She thought: If you leave me after all these dreams, I shall not exist . . .

'Please yourself,' Moll heard herself say.

'Goodbye then.'

And the moment he was through the door, a shot clattered and echoed in the forest.

Moll raised her face.

'That came from the Pigeons.'

Fifteen

With news that a troop of redcoat dragoons was coming, great was the panic at the Old Three Pigeons Inn and Shaun Casey, possessing his own intelligence about troop movements in the vicinity, was soon packed and ready and with his mule and cart, bound for an indeterminate stay in the arms of Maisie Mooney.

Justin made a bed down in his slaughterhouse, to be near the clients; Rum-Bum-Baccy took off for Shelton Roughs and Tom Cakebread returned to the village and his legitimate business of baking for the community. Indeed all, including Tip Topsy, turned over new leaves with the exception of Boyo Bad Thing who pasted more nude ladies on the walls of his forest hut. Blodwen fought the temptation to follow Shaun, but 'You anna gettin' me within a mile o' that old tart,' said she, and set up house in 'Cupid's Abode', the one-up-two-down cottage of Eli Rumbletum, now a sidesman in the village church.

Indeed, such was the mass evacuation, that the only people left in the Pigeons were Long Fella, Short Chap, and Pincers; these first being required by law to serve the staging post. And one other . . . who could have made her way to safety, but did not – Biddy Boddy.

'You three, away out of it,' commanded the lieutenant of the dragoons, dismounting, and the ostlers moved fast. 'You,' said he, catching Biddy by the arm and hurrying her along before him – 'upstairs!'

'What for, sir?' asked Biddy.

'Does not your bedroom overlook the road?'

'Why, yes, sir.'

And a sergeant, barging into the tap-room called up the stairs, 'I knows it, sir. The maid's bedroom covers the road. We'll get a ranging shot in 'afore he arrives.' And the redcoats thudded up the stairs to Biddy's room, driving her before them.

'No ranging shot, sergeant,' said the officer. 'A musket shot would echo miles up the road to Shrewsbury.'

'What have you come for?' cried Biddy.

'You'll know soon enough, my beauty,' said the sergeant. 'Tie her up and gag her, for she's a shout on her like an Irish tinker. Remember me, Bid Boddy?'

Over a century later, a poet wrote:

> They tied her up to attention, with many a sniggering jest,
> And they bound a musket beside her, with the barrel beneath her breast.
> 'Now keep good watch,' and they kissed her . . .*

And the moment before they gagged her, Biddy Boddy asked:

'Why you doin' this, mister? What 'ave I done to you?'

'T'is a little matter o' Sir Richard Carling who habits round these parts, see? You've been a naughty girl wi' him, haven't you? And, since he's managed to cook himself out o' Shrewsbury lock-up, it's our guess that the first place he'll call at is 'ere.'

Kneeling at the single window overlooking the Shrewsbury Road, the redcoats loaded and primed their muskets.

In the darkness they waited – the officer, the sergeant, the redcoats and Bid Boddy, for Richard to come.

'Later, if you're lucky, darlin',' said the sergeant, 'you can see him dangling his footwear up on Gallows Hill. You can 'ave a front seat, too – I'll see to it particular.'

* Extract from 'The Highwayman', by Alfred Noyes.

Biddy closed her eyes and bowed her head over the musket.

Somewhere downstairs in the deserted rooms a clock struck the hours . . . Distantly on the night air came the sound of oncoming hoof beats.

'Here he comes, lads,' said the sergeant. 'Hold your fire and we'll collect the bugger alive,' and Biddy, hearing the hoof beats, straightened on the musket, her fingers writhing in search of its trigger . . . and found it . . .

Moll and Richard, at the door of the cave, stood listening to an echoing musket shot. 'I tell you,' she repeated, 'it came from the Pigeons.'

'If it did, trouble is getting too close for comfort. Biddy or otherwise – I'll see her one day – we ought to get going.'

'Where to?' asked Moll, picking up an envelope. Richard asked:

'You are posting a letter at a time like this? To whom, may I ask?' He was standing at the top of the cave steps now. Meg Mare and the filly were tethered below, grazing in sleepy content.

'To my sister.'

'I didn't know you had a sister.'

Moll smiled up. 'I told you before, there's a lot you do not know about me or young Biddy, come to that.'

Packing up their belongings, they locked the door and rode off together, Richard on Meg Mare, Moll on the filly.

The dawn came up in magnificent splendour, red over the distant hills; stars were fainting out of the sky over the distant Wrekin, where lovers take the highest kiss in Shropshire.

And Bid Boddy drooped over the musket, with her hair hanging loose, standing in a pool of blood: it being necessary for a magistrate to see her before we cut her

112

away, said the lieutenant. The hoof beats she had heard
were those of a passing traveller.

One place being as good as another, Moll and Richard took
the road to Chester.

As they rode, Moll a little behind him, as befits a lesser
human, she thought, she surveyed Sir Richard Carling.

Outlined against the sun of morning, his was almost
a princely dignity, for he sat Meg Mare with a male
arrogance. Wide of shoulder, with a head of black curls,
his was a Byronic masculinity. 'A curled darling of the
gods,' quoted Moll to herself, 'whose outward seeming
doth suggest true manliness within.'

Never in her life had she seen so handsome a fellow . . .
one who, with a cavalier carelessness was walking out on
Biddy without a backward glance.

Moll loved him. Her heart, her loins ached for him.
But had she been granted one word to describe his
character, which evinced charm and good breeding, she
could have found it in a single adjective.

Bastard.

Reaching a little clearing in the roadside near Oswestry,
they rested on the bank of the River Perry.

Here Richard snared a rabbit, gutted, skinned it and
pegged it over a hot-stone fire; a manner of cooking he
had learned from travelling tinkers, said he. This they ate
with their fingers, stripping the flesh off the bones and
dangling it into their mouths, and the relief and pleasure
of the escape to freedom brought companionship.

'What now?' asked Moll, and Richard stretched himself
full length on the grassy bank and stared at the peaceful
swim of the river.

'Now we will do our best to stay alive by travelling.
Once the dragoons get on your tail, you move. The nest

we've rooked around this vicinity is fouled, but there's good pickings still to be had around Chester.'

'You expect me to share the life of a vagrant?'

'You've got no option. You're in this up to your ears.'

'I could think of easier ways to earn a living.' It sat him up on an elbow, and he said:

'Really? Haven't you done pretty well on the road?'

The moon now made a glow, rippling faintly on the ruffled sheen of the river; the afternoon of travel had been hot and now a night mist was rising over the autumn country.

So much, Moll thought, for her plans to enter high society and live by sleight of hand; so much for the high-flown letters to Chantelle telling of her gentleman lover and social successes. She said wearily, watching Richard through drooping eyelids, ''Olding up stagecoaches and sleeping rough may suit you, but it doesn't appeal to me.'

'Then why spring me out of gaol?'

'To save your neck.' It intrigued him, for he moved closer and regarded her, saying softly:

'You are strange and beautiful, but, like all your sex, totally incomprehensible. First, you set me up, then betray me; but instead of making off with the loot, you concoct this elaborate plan for my escape. Why?'

'Because I relented.'

'My dear girl, in this business you mustn't do that.'

'Unlike men, women are governed by conscience – that is something you will not understand.'

He grinned down at her. 'A nobler breed, eh? Then you enjoy it, girl. I'd not have done the same for you. I may exhibit all the aspects of a gentleman – my title confirms it – but I'm a thief and a philanderer. Also, unlike you, I possess no conscience. Had I been in your shoes, I'd have stood on Gallows Hill and watched you dangle.'

'No doubt. Now let me go to sleep.'

'Did you hear what I said?'

'Word for word. It is good to know that I risked my life for one of such high principles. Sleep . . .'

'At a time like this? Now's the time to celebrate success! Lie still, little French girl, and sleep if you will while I make love to you.'

'Not 'ere you don't. I demand a bed.'

'Beds cost money. Here it is free.'

'I 'ave money. Even a sovereign would put us in the feathers at the first tavern we come across.'

The moon was in her eyes; Moll heard Richard's voice as if in dreams.

'You have never slept in the open before?' he asked, now kissing her face.

'Once, in a barn in Brittany, but that was nearer June . . . Sleep in the name of God.'

'This is getting me nowhere,' said Richard. 'I'd know where I stood with an English girl.'

'Make the best of it,' said Moll, 'this one's French.'

Meg Mare and the filly were tethered in trees nearby, away from prying eyes. And, while the mist made phantom shapes on the river, Richard undid the top of Moll's coat and her body was warm beneath his hand, and he saw the whiteness of her under the moon, and his hand was a brown stain upon this whiteness, and her hair, falling over it, was a shining blackness. Moll knew this, and did not prevent it, because although through tiredness she had no heed of him, there was an enduring safety in his arms and comfort in the nearness of him.

Also, it had come to her that he had a wish for a man's comfort, not for mere fancy: that he had been long without Biddy, and despite her pert replies and refusals, she pitied him; so what was at first contrition now became laughter, and a new and piquant vitality surged in her and induced a sudden wish that she should be one with him. Therefore, when his hands touched her, she knew this, and was aware. The wild flowers became heavy with scent after the day's heat; Moll smelled them, and it became part of the sweetness of his touching; the dampness of the grass was warm beneath her head, as Richard was warm upon her in the loving.

This, thought Moll, is a cleansing; it is like washing clothes on the bank of the river at home, when whiteness comes to stained things, blowing on the line; it was a cleaning of all that had happened before in the ribaldry of the Pigeons, the vulgar banter and dirty talk of its tap-room, the bawdy antics of Blodwen, the hoarse shrieks of Pincers; yes, a washing of the house that is the mind; for Richard was gentle with her, and affectionate despite his strength. Now he said to her:

'When I take you to London we will go into the great houses. I will buy you wine – good French wine – you will like that?'

'After a glass of the red stuff I am delirious,' said Moll. 'Give me another and I am a fool.'

Now Richard was enjoying her, and there was a great pleasure in her now that she possessed him.

'Lie still,' commanded Richard.

'I 'ave no alternative.'

'That is right. Lie still until I let you go.'

The moon pulled down her petticoats over her brightness, enveloping the world in darkness; they lay clasped together and did not move.

'*Mon Dieu*,' said Moll later, sitting up. 'That was a step in the wrong direction. I thought we was going to a tavern.'

Richard did not answer; it was he who was sleeping now.

In a distant lane, when the stars rode high, there arose a squawking in the rushes and the gossiping of disturbed moorhens; the melancholy moon saw in its silver wake a soldier standing alone; and the soldier, a redcoat, held

116

a spy-glass to his eye. Framed in the circle of glass, in a sudden explosion of moonlight, two figures lay together; and this was Moll and Richard.

Then the redcoat beckoned and more of his kind came out of the forest, bringing with them a man haltered on the end of a rope like a slave being sold at market, and this was Pincers, the farrier.

A lieutenant said, 'This fool is right, for all his madness. It is the prisoner and the one who forced Bosanky to release him; the judge wants them both alive.' He raised his hand and more redcoats followed him into the forest; all silently made their way to the place where Richard and Moll were lying.

Now, leaning above him as he slept and unaware of being watched, Moll kissed Richard's face. And knew, even as she did this, that she would follow him to the ends of the earth despite his faults: to death, if needs be.

The latter now, appeared a possibility.

'On your feet, the pair of you,' said the dragoon lieutenant as his redcoat troop, with drawn sabres, closed in around them.

'I'll say one thing for you,' said Richard, awakening. 'You didn't waste much time.'

'No need to,' said the lieutenant. 'Justice Bosanky gave us a free hand to comb you scum out of Nesscliff – the tavern, Kynaston Cave and all. Casey turned Queen's Evidence and this big chap gibbered and pointed about you and the woman leaving the village. Dumb as he is, it seems he owes her one.'

The soldiers laughed with surly contempt.

'So what happens now?'

'The gallows for the pair of you, if Justice Bosanky has anything to do with it,' said the lieutenant.

Haltered by the neck and prodded by bayonets, Moll and Richard took the road to Chester.

117

Sixteen

January had come in like a withered spinster with a long blue nose and a wig of icicles, sweeping up the hedgerows with skirts of snow and dancing in clogs with her skinny legs bandy. And Moll, in a thin blouse, held about her the standard hessian sacking handed out to prisoners in transit, and shivered to have her bones out on top of the Chester to Shrewsbury stagecoach.

With one wrist manacled to the prisoner's rail, she braced her body against the bumping, swaying ride, for the horses were under the whip at full gallop for Shrewsbury, from where Moll would be taken to London and Newgate Gaol. And either through some ironic twist of fate, or possibly by arrangement, thought Moll, a passenger travelling beneath her was none other than the ugly sister of Justice Bosanky; she whom Moll had robbed at pistol point months earlier.

Now, also journeying from Chester to Shrewsbury, the woman was relishing her moral victory by thrusting her head out of the window at intervals, calling up:

'Enjoying yourself, my poppet?'

Moll stared through the sleeting rain, ignoring her.

'Only another fifteen hours or so! You'd have weathered it better in a frock coat and breeches!' And she cackled like a hen.

The wind was sweeping the sodden fields with needles of pain that stung Moll's face; earlier, she had been almost encased in snow that rimed her lashes. An hour after leaving Chester an icy numbness had possessed her; it now seemed to contain her soul, and the prospect of three years in the infamous Newgate Gaol in London appeared to Moll but a distant threat: she expected to be frozen to death long before then.

With a staging point at every seven miles or so she would stand up, rubbing her frozen legs to obtain circulation.

Such suffering was the accepted hardship of felons so transported. If some perished on the journey then it was one less to imprison and feed. If the stagecoach crashed and the prisoner 'upstairs' was killed, then 'death by drowning or other fatal injury' was a legal verdict, and a pauper's grave dug; few prisoners carried burial money, and, if they did, were soon relieved of it by gaolers.

'Do you think you'll survive, thief?' Other passengers trooped into the hall of the Wynnstay Arms, Oswestry, and Bosanky's sister, again recklessly attired in a jewelled necklace and her fingers cosseted with rings, smiled up from the entrance, adding:

'Not so good now, is it, since you lent your name to highway robbery. I said my brother would give you your just desserts!' She spat the words and disappeared into the inn.

A pot-boy came from the kitchens; clambering up to Moll's perch, he gave her a piece of stale bread and a mug of water.

'There ye are, missus,' he whispered, and pressed her icy hands.

Moll opened her fingers to find a toffee, and bowed her head as the wind again swept into her.

Now the coach lurched along rutted Watling Street; past the Old Three Pigeons Inn it clattered, which was as empty as a coffin without a corpse, for its windows were boarded up and its doors barred against wandering vagrants.

Midday saw them crossing the Welsh Bridge at Shrewsbury, where Moll would spend the night in the lock-up, in a cell near the one she had released Richard from. Shrewsbury was the great stagecoach centre in 1840; no fewer than twenty coaches radiated from half a dozen different inns.

The 'Wonder' driven by Sam Hayward, for instance, left the Bull and Mouth at five o'clock in the morning and arrived at the Peacock in Islington, London, at the same time next day. A hundred and fifty horses each ran for one hour, usually at a slow gallop, in the twenty-four; and were seldom worked for more than four years before retirement or slaughter. In the day's journeying the 'Wonder'– on which Moll would travel – lost some eighty minutes in horse changes in the twenty-four hours of travel, and the fare was a guinea for 'inside' seats and ten shillings for 'upstairs'.

Moll, being a guest of Victoria Regina, naturally travelled free, if inconvenienced.

The dangers of being manacled to the coach were apparent since flood water often forced the inside travellers to stand upon their seats. When coaches were actually swept away by rivers in flood, those upstairs had small chance of survival.

Later, in competition with the Talbot Hotel, the Lion of Wyle Cop introduced a faster coach called the 'Stag', which did the London run in under fifteen hours, but here the whips were used so lavishly that many horses died of heart attacks which proved dangerous to the gentry travellers . . . Stage hotels would wager on the time taken, and one inn lost £1500 once in competition with 'Nimrod', the quickest stagecoach running to London.

Later, Moll sent to Chantelle a description of the 'Wonder' leaving the Lion; this letter has been saved for posterity:

Before St Julian's church clock struck five in the morning, all luggage had to be safely packed into place. Then Dickie Ash, the coachman (who was succeeded by Sam Hayward) took his seat on the box and, with a last warning to male passengers, 'Now gentlemen, if you please, time for drinking is up – I am now in charge,' and at the crack of a whip the four well-groomed steeds would prance forward under the Lion archway, and immediately the skid was applied as we went down Wyle Cop at fourteen miles an hour. Just think of it, Chantelle, such speed! There were at least four poor people 'upstairs' with the luggage, but naturally, your sister, most beautifully dressed in furs and with rugs for the long journey to London, sat inside with my hand on my gentleman's arm. The first stop was about ten miles away at the Haygate Inn, Wellington, and later at the Jerningham Arms at Shifnal in time for breakfast where, served by waiters in silken hose and liveried tunics, I ate eggs and bacon and buttered my toast with farm butter to a height you would never believe! Hot punch to warm us at the next stop then, and on, on to beautiful London. My darling girl, you just cannot imagine the life I am having . . .!

'Hey you, up there – you 'ad some'ut to eat?' somebody shouted.

Moll put her blue hands together. 'I 'ad some bread and water last night.'

'Then that's your lot, till ye get to Islington.'

The hunger sickened her; ice seemed to form between her brain and skull. In a daze of weakness, she clung on as the coach thundered over the English bridge and along the Roman road to London.

East of Shifnal, at a place called White Ladies' Priory when the sun was rising, Dickie Ash, the coachman, hauled in the four horses to a trot and a highwayman came head on to meet them, levelling a blunderbuss. Discretion always being the better part of Ash's valour, he dropped the reins and raised his hands.

The highwayman, heavily cloaked and masked, dismounted; with his weapon at the ready, he approached the coach window; the coach guard, until now well down into the luggage, slowly rose, his hands held high.

'The prisoner's keys, damn ye eyes!' shouted the highwayman, and Moll thought she'd heard that voice elsewhere.

Gathering courage, Dickie Ash cried, falsetto, 'It's a hangin' offence to release a prisoner, mind!'

'Then you don't mind, mister, if I kill the bloody coachman, for I've nothin' to lose,' and reaching up, the highwayman, a man of great size, snatched at the keys and tossed them up to Moll. Bowing, he said:

'Release ye'self, milady,' then opened the coach door, bellowing, 'Now out, the lot of ye – your money or your lives.' And the unfortunate passengers, led by Bosanky's sister, lined up at the roadside. There they were relieved of their valuables.

With the help of the guard, Moll climbed down to the road and seizing her by the wrist, the highwayman drew her beside him. As the coach started away at speed, he took off his cloak and fastened it about her.

'Remember me?' he removed his mask, adding:

'Tom Sprogg, ma'am, and at your service,' and he bowed low again.

'Young Tom never forgets a service – neither good nor bad, he don't forget. What's ye wishes?'

This was the man who, as a prisoner, she had released from this same stagecoach, when first she had taken to the road.

Moll staggered against him. 'Food and warmth, in the name of the Mother!'

'Missus, ye've come to the right place,' said Tom.

★　★　★

There was a little dark arbour in the forest, near a lake called 'The Pool'; here the sun made no entry. Tom Sprogg, dismounting from his big shire horse (no other could carry him, he explained) blew on a charcoal fire, fanning the flames into redness.

'Is it warm wi' you now, little woman?'

He was a giant of strength and purpose, breaking off huge branches to feed the fire. 'God help us, the way they treat us,' said he, 'and us poor gentle folk goin' about our lawful business. Now eat and fill your belly, the steaks are good round these parts.' In minutes he had a bag open, a frying pan out and meat sizzling in the pan.

Later, Moll said between starving mouthfuls, 'You knew I was on the coach for London?'

'London and Newgate,' said Tom, double bass, 'because, from the time your chap was took I've been following ye. "Tom Sprogg," says I, "ye owe that little vixen one – and she's a lady, in or out o' breeches, or I anna seen one a'fore." And believe me, missus, I seen women in plenty. I'd 'ave been swingin' up on Cranberry long ago if it hadn't been for you, so I've been followin' your progress, like – from the time you took up wi' the Pigeons, to the night you sprung your chap outta Gullet.'

'For a man your size you go very quietly, *monsieur*.'

'Ay ay, girl, but I gets the gold in the end, see? Slow but quiet, that's Tom Sprogg,' and he grinned wide at her, his white teeth shining in his smooth brown face, for he had shaved off the stubbled beard: no oil painting, this one, thought Moll, but passable for a woman to wake up to in the morning.

'And I always gets me woman in the end, an' all,' he added.

'But not this one,' said Moll. 'Let us make it clear – not this woman, *comprenez-vous*?

'Ach! That's sad,' he grumbled like an overgrown boy. 'Since I've been followin' mad for ye in all weathers. I

123

even had me eye on that beggar Shaun Casey too, lest he wronged you, for he's lower than a snake's bum. And when they clinked your fella, good riddance, said I, for here comes Big Tom, and he'll catch this old girl bending. He's in clink an' you're out, Tom Sprogg, says I – get in, son, now's your chance.'

Moll did not reply and Tom said, 'Sad about that little Bid Boddy at the Pigeons, weren't it?'

'No man is worth that.'

'And Casey and his lot got clean away with it!'

In her mind's eye Moll saw the Pigeons shuttered and barred. But it wouldn't be long before new management took it over and the same thing happened again. Tom Sprogg said:

'Your Dick Carling got off light, too. Hanging's too vulgar for a member of the aristocracy, I suppose. Seven years for armed robbery! They'd have topped me, but then I'm workin' class.'

'His knighthood didn't save him. The judge was too tied up in the scandal,' said Moll.

She could have told him the detail of it, but she was too weary. The whole business was a whitewash to save Judge Bosanky; they had sent her to Chester Assizes for the single crime of stealing from her mistress there. Moll knew they dared not put her on trial in Shrewsbury, for the whole sordid business would have come out. Tom said:

'You got off light, too if you ask me!'

'The only one who did not was Biddy.'

Moll rolled herself up in a horse blanket and lay on the ground. And she slept but did not sleep, fearing Tom Sprogg for all his charm, and now he said:

'If I could trap a pretty little woman like you, I'd hie me down to the little cottage in Gloucester, which was me home. There I'd go into her and fetch out sons. Me ma had eight, an' I'm the youngest, so when I see the right pair o' childbirth hips, I'm mating for ten. Ay ay, missus . . .' and he sighed and folded his hands behind his head.

'You will need two women for ten sons,' said Moll dreamily.

'Ay ay, and I nearly had 'em once. Since I'm six-foot-six in me socks, I decided on a pair – the daughters of old Abraham Shonko, the Christian Jew livin' down Appleby.

'Miriam and Magdala were their names – identical twins – and they topped six foot. I tell ye, you've never seen two such pieces o' female horse-flesh to brighten a man's heart. "Going for two guineas each," said Abe, "for they're eating me outta house and home." "Let's look 'em over." Says I, "where are they?" "Upstairs between the sheets," says Abe and bawls up the stairs, "Miriam, Magdala, get your clouts off; there's a suitor coming up to look ye over," and I followed old Abe up to the bedroom and there, sure enough, were the terrible twins giggling and blushing, with only their heads sticking out, and I tell ye, they had faces for chopping firewood. "Let's have a look at 'em," I says, and pulled down the top sheet, and those two females, were possessed of all the joys of Israel; but the moment I did that they turned over on to their tums. "For the love of heaven buy one of 'em," pleaded Abe. "Just smack the rear o' the one ye fancy!' "I'll take the pair of 'em off ye hands for a guinea each, and no more argument", says I, and smacked the bums of both. "Done", says Abe, and shouts down the stairs, "They're away, missus. We'll start eating the moment they're off the premises."'

'Where are they now?'

'Back with Abe and his missus,' said Tom. 'Two months and a week I had 'em in finery, for the thieving was good 'afore I got nicked. And every day for nine weeks solid I pleasured 'em once and twice on Sundays. But if their bellies were larger after that hard work, it was only because they were eating their heads off.

'Not a sign, I tell ye, of being in the family way. The only fella calling regular at the house was the monkey man, and ye know who he is. This 'as got to stop, Tom Sprogg, I told myself, they're doin' the same to you as they did to Abe.'

'So what 'appened?'

'I raided another coach, took them back to Appleby and sold 'em back to him for five bob apiece.'

'And not a son in sight?'

'Not a dicky, until I comes across the right lady, I suppose. You ain't interested, you say? For I'm finished with the large pieces now, and I'm after the little ones like you. You only got to ask, remember.'

'I told you before, Tom, I 'ave got me own man.'

'And him off to Botany Bay for the next seven years? I could breed six boys in ye before then, for I could look the world over and never find a woman firmer in the haunch and bosom than you. Ach, come on, give the lad a chance.'

'Goodbye, Tom.' Moll unwrapped the blanket and rose.

'Are you away? God, I've only just found ye!'

'Goodbye,' repeated Moll, and he answered:

'All right, but one good turn deserves another, you realize? So I dug this up for you, to keep it safe.' He threw her the little bag of jewels she had buried months ago.

Moll tossed them up, caught them, and on tiptoe, kissed his face. 'God go with you, Tom Sprogg, and grant you sons. Meanwhile, I 'ave got a debt to pay.'

Strangely, he didn't ask her what . . . but said:

'There's a few more bits o' gold in your bag as well – to see you on your way.'

He looked gigantic standing there in the Forest.

126

'Any time, remember, if ever you become broody, let me know.'

Days later they got him on the highway, though it took six redcoats to shackle him. And they sent him, haltered, to the Old Bailey and hanged him, but the rope broke on the first drop.

'Jesus,' said Tom Sprogg, 'that were a bloody tight neck-tie. Don't they spin good hemp in London?'

So they tied him better and dropped him again, and while he was strangling, a woman with a French accent cried from the crowd:

'Die hard, Tom Sprogg! All your friends are here – Miriam, Magdala, Abe, Missus and me. *Die hard*, Tom Sprogg!'

And people wondered who she was.

Book II

1840–PORTSMOUTH

Seventeen

Mufflered and buttoned up against the frosty February night, bearded Captain Zachary of the convict ship, the *Lady Juliana* shouldered his way into the bar of the Six Oysters and thumped the counter for ale.

For the past half century he had been drinking here when, as a cabin boy, he had arrived on a tea clipper on the China run. Unknown, unwanted, he had scrubbed the floor for sixpence and the landlady took him in. As boy and man he had been coming ever since.

'Three fingers of the Red Eye,' he said now, and the barmaid batted a mascara eye at him, but he didn't spare her a look. Normally he'd be after a woman, but not tonight. In a day's time, when the *Lady Juliana* set sail with two hundred female convicts aboard, he could take his pick.

As Captain Zach took his drink and sat down at a table, Moll Walbee came in.

Earlier, arriving in Portsmouth, Moll had spent the night in the Six Oysters. Attired in warm clothes and with money to spend, she had sent some of her jewels by ferry courier to Uncle Maurice, Chantelle's guardian in France. Come night, with a fair wig to cover her dark hair (she was aware that her description might be circulating in the towns) she came downstairs from her attic bedroom and entered the bar; here she sat among half a dozen harlots until she caught the barmaid's eye, and asked:

'Do the captains of convict ships come in 'ere?'

'Half a dozen of 'em. Which one you after?'

'The captain of the *Mandarin*.'

The barmaid made a face. 'Until last week you'd have needed Captain Zachary, but he's handed the *Mandarin* over to Captain Muddle and he's commanding the *Lady Juliana* these days. What ye want?'

'A voyage to Australia.'

'You'll be lucky! But you'll get nowhere wi' old Muddle, the sod. Take it from me, girl, you want a favour done, steer clear of Muddle; besides, he couldn't take you if he wanted to – no women aboard the *Mandarin* this trip.'

'And Captain Zachary?'

The barmaid shrugged. 'You can try, but I can't speak for 'im. He's already got two hundred convict women.'

The customers laughed with bawdy gusto, and the barmaid added:

'Hang on, he'll be here any minute, but he don't take virgins, mind. Foreign are you?'

A man drinking nearby asked, 'Why pester old Zach? Won't I do, Frenchy?'

'Leave 'er alone,' shouted the barmaid, and added confidentially to Moll, 'Mind, you've gotta watch old Zach – he's fathered more brats than Abraham's uncle.' She came from behind the counter. 'You after a voyage, ye say?'

'Yes.'

'Zachary might still take ye – they'll do most things for cash. But if you take my tip you'll run for cover; a woman never knows where she is wi' him. He's up and down like a bride's nightie. On the run, are ye?'

'No.'

The woman twisted her scarlet lips into a wry smile. 'They never are,' she said, and went back to her counter. 'I'll give ye the nod when Zach arrives. All right?'

By the year 1700 the rotting prison hulks on Britain's south coast were becoming overcrowded; disease and squalor in the fetid air of their cells brought death quicker than the foul prisons of Newgate and the Fleet, at a time when a child could be hanged for stealing a loaf.

Following Cook's landing at Point Hicks seventeen years before, the British government saw in Botany Bay, Australia, an opportunity to dispose of felons to a distant part of the Empire with little chance of their returning. So in the year 1787 the First Fleet under the command of a Captain Arthur Phillip set sail with his flagship, *Sirius*, and support ships carrying over a thousand personnel, to colonize the new territory.

Transportation to the American colonies had carried on earlier, but with the British aristocracy fearful of revolution at home penal laws became even stricter, and the Insurrection Act laid an even heavier burden upon transportation – thousands of Irish patriots were chained for shipment.

Between the years 1788 and 1840 over 120,000 men, women and children were sent to Australia, forming for the new colony an ancestry of the worst and best of human kind, from the degraded criminal to the finest and best in patriotic ideals and intellectual vigour.

Captain Zachary (of tremendous height and girth) was undertaking his last shipment of prisoners to Van Diemen's Land. An American by birth, he was now enjoying a last look at England, his adopted country, before boarding the *Lady Juliana*.

As he sat drinking, he was wondering if he would ever see Britain again, for he was contemplating a happy retirement as a provisioning administrator on the Tasman Peninsula.

Therefore he now looked round the crowded bar of the Six Oysters with some nostalgia. Little had changed, he thought, in fifty years: the same odorous conviviality that sailors exude, the same smells of ale, sweat and sawdust;

the same bright-eyed seamen in dark jerseys, their faces tanned by sea-wind; the same oaths and raucous laughter.

Soon they would be contemplating their last night ashore. There would come the usual sailor's farewell to wives, or the amorous embraces of painted harlots; and after that the 'shipboard weddings' on the deck of the *Lady Juliana*, where every member of the crew was provided with a woman to comfort his voyage – the women being nothing loathe and the supply plentiful. And it was sea custom that the captain of the ship should take first pick of the talent. Captain Zach had done it before, he would do it again, though to date he'd seen nothing aboard to take his fancy.

Now he frowned, his glass suspended, as his first mate stood swaying before him.

'How ye doing, cap'n?'

'Fair to middlin'.' Zachary frowned up.

'Mind you, outta this cargo I ain't seen one I'd lay for tuppence.'

Zachary drank steadily, not replying. His blue eyes surveyed the smaller man, who said thickly:

'The Irish are the best wi' their long black hair to lead ye a dance, but they'll have a knife in your ribs before ye can say Killarney. Drink up, sir!'

Zachary said, 'Hell's a blazing, Mr Bishop, so drink the tavern dry. But stagger wind'ard of me in the mornin' and there'll be hell to pay. You've had enough, man, and so have I,' he added, and he made to go, but Moll suddenly appeared before him.

'Captain Zachary?' She paused at his table.

'At your service, lady,' rising, he bowed. 'French, are you?'

Moll smiled assent. 'You are the capt'in of the *Lady Juliana*?'

'Yes.'

'And are you sailing to Australia tomorrow?'

His wrinkled eyes showed mischievous delight. 'Unfortunately, now I've met you.' He paused. 'But you were wanting Captain Muddle, they said.'

'Yes, *monsieur*. His ship, the *Mandarin*, was the first one I 'eard about. Any ship for me, so long as it is goin' to Australia.'

'Australia's a big place. What part?'

'Van Diemen's Land.'

'Why not go by passenger ship? They're out of Falmouth twice a month.'

'Too long to wait.'

'Which means, since you won't travel passenger, that you've got no papers, I suppose.'

Moll nodded.

'Why not?'

'It is a long story, *monsieur*.'

'I bet. Next you'll be tellin' me you've got no money.'

'Money I 'ave and I pay well.'

Zachary's eyes twinkled with veiled humour, and, sitting back, he regarded her and said, 'You women beat me. Tomorrow I'm shipping out two hundred females who are just beggin' to be left behind. It's love as usual, I suppose.'

'What do you mean by that?'

'It's love, lady. The old man gets nicked and transported and his girl can't live without him.'

'It is not like that! It is my brother.'

Zachary sipped his whisky. The bedlam of the bar-room beat about them, battering on the low ceiling; somewhere in a corner men were making a ring for a cock-fight and bets were being called amid the shrieking of the birds. Ignoring Moll's reply, Zachary asked:

'Look, just tell me what he's been up to, eh?'

'He stole jewellery.'

'Did he now! He was lucky not to be topped. How long did he get?'

'Seven years. You are right, *monsieur*, he was lucky not to be hanged. My family is disgusted with him.' Moll's voice rose. 'But he is still of the family, and we will not desert 'im!'

Zachary pulled out an evil-looking pipe, filled it from a pigtail of shag tobacco, lit it and blew out a cloud of acrid smoke. 'What makes you think you can help if you go there?'

Per'aps if I spake for 'is good conduct he could obtain a ticket of leave.'

'Jesus, he'd be lucky!'

'My father insists that I try, sir.'

Zachary sat back, smoking and watching her. 'You know, I've listened to some tales in my time, but never to such a load of bloody codswallop as this one. You've got no papers and it's all a pack of lies. I'm too old in the tooth to be hoodwinked by a squirt less than half me age. But if you tell me the truth – that you're on the run and you've got a lover out there needing feminine assistance – more, that you've got passage money, then I'm your man. But with one stipulation.'

'Please . . .?'

'Don't be too eager, lady. First listen to the proposition, for I don't beat about the bush when I'm after a lay.

'I'm out on tomorrow's night tide with two hundred females aboard, and you're welcome to share me cabin. I'm knocking sixty, but I'm not beyond the charms of women, and I've never had a French piece accordin' to my recollections, though I've taken 'em all colours in me time, with or without permission. So that's it. A five-month voyage with all the captain's privileges – good food, cheap wine, and enough love for a Turkish harem. Are ye on?'

Moll replied, 'Do you always make such improper suggestions to women?'

'Invariably.'

'You must get your face slapped many times.'

'Aye, but you'd be surprised how many I sleep with.'

He watched her with a wry smile; her eyes were slanted up at the light, her expression distant, and he thought she was beautiful.

'What about the authorities?'

'Authorities?'

'The people aboard. I told you I have no papers. Are there not certain regulations . . .?'

'Stone the crows, woman! I'm the regulations and the authority. Once we slip moorings off Portsmouth, I'm God almighty.'

'I will give it consideration.'

'You won't, you'll answer now.'

'It is agreeable.'

'I should bloody think so. Most women would jump at it!' and he beckoned Moll to follow him. At the door she caught the barmaid's eye.

'Good luck,' said the woman. 'You ship aboard with Captain Zach, girl, you're going to need it.'

'*Merci*,' replied Moll.

Eighteen

For fourteen long years I am sentenced
For fourteen long years and a day
For meeting a bloke down the docks
And sneaking his ticker away.

With Moll aboard as the guest of Captain Zachary, and over two hundred convict women battened down below hatches, the prospect of a comfortable voyage opened up before her, for the *Lady Juliana* was as spic and span as any leaving Portsmouth. She was sharing the cabin with a man she rarely saw except on deck, for the traffic in the Channel was thick, said Zachary. He spent the first night up at the wheel with the pilot, leaving Moll the luxury of being alone.

But on the second day in the Channel the sky threatened; mist began rolling over a grey, forbidding sea and the wind rose in sudden, tumultuous fury. The silence of below decks was broken by a constant, high-pitched wailing from the chained wretches in their cells below.

Now a stiff north-westerly struck the *Lady Juliana* and the crew of twenty scampered over her wet decks.

'Shorten top-s'ls!' Zachary's voice rang out from the wheelhouse. 'All hands to the sheets, bosun! Starboard ye helm – that's it, fella – handsomely, handsomely! Steady as ye go!'

Seeking shelter behind the wheelhouse, Moll stared out on to a bucking, pea-green sea where white-topped rollers, driven by a storming nor'-wester, came crashing down upon the ship and shivering her planks. Now came Zachary's shout, 'I'm goin' below for a spell, Mr Bishop.'

'Can't keep her on course, cap'n!' cried the mate.

'Then steady her two points to port and hold her there. I'll be back!'

Moll shouted as she clung to everything handy on a staggering journey aft, 'Is this a bad day?'

He was drenched with rain and spindrift, his beard loaded with water, and he beat the rain from his sou' wester before he entered the tiny cabin.

'Jesus, no! This is average around these parts!' The ship suddenly heeled to a gust; the rollers thundered as they beat her off course, and she yawed sluggishly; Zachary went to the door, held it open and bawled, 'Steer small, helmsman. Keep her prow on, damn ye!'

Moll watched him as she wiped rain from his face. There was about him a giant nobility; one raised and spewed up by the sea, which was his home; a different Captain Zachary to the one ashore. Now there was a fine, sturdy beauty about him.

'How you doin'?' he asked her.

'I will be better when it is calmer.'

'Settle ye down, woman. You've a fine bunk and a clean vest on you, which is more'n some. I pity the poor bitches battened below. And another fifty or so comin' aboard at Falmouth.'

Later, the wind dropped to a sigh, the sea calmed and the sun came out. The *Lady Juliana* with her topsails filled, heeled to a gentle tack and was warped by rowers up to the wharf at Falmouth. The hatches were opened and the female convicts, soaked with bilgewater and vomit, straggled up on deck to the banter of the crew.

★ ★ ★

139

Here was the riffraff of a debased community, a refuse of womanhood. Misshappen, many of them, most of them in the rags and tatters of land-based prisons, where the best of their clothes had been stolen by their gaolers.

Old hags were chained to bright-faced girls, some as yet untainted by the demands of the great industrial towns, where drunkenness and vice flourished openly in pace with landlords' profits.

In Cardiff alone, from whence many of these women had come, over a 150 whorehouses employed more than five hundred prostitutes and scores more operated in the maze of criss-crossing courts and alleys. Some were farm girls, possessed of the dark hair and prominent cheeks of their Celtic origins, their complexions ruddy with outdoor living. Others, quiet of disposition, seemed broken by their fate; their feet bare, their hair tangled, and of sallow appearance.

Moll watched them. Clear of them in the body, but close enough to distinguish their misery after their battering by the sea, she saw in their wasted countenances the tragedy of her generation. These same she had seen in France, a degeneration of her sex by uncaring men. Later, she read:

> The lawless vices and rude habits of the men are communicated to the women. Even in offences against property, often committed with extreme violence, the women more largely participate: this is, in some degree, owing to the masculine pursuits in the mills and coal pits, where women are so employed; this degrades them to the habits and brutalities of the men.

And yet, examining some of the 'crimes' for which these women were being transported, it was clear that the government was more concerned with the colonization of

Australia than common justice. Alone again in Zachary's cabin, Moll read the list of some of their names and offences.

Fanny Bennet of Montgomeryshire, aged 13 – no offence indicted.
Ann Thomas of Glamorgan, aged 17, theft of a wine glass.
Elizabeth Lewis of Monmouth, aged 18, theft of a piece of bacon.
Sarah Rees of Haverfordwest, aged 20, theft of a shift.
Elizabeth Hughson of Brecon, housebreaking.
Catherine Lewis aged 42, stealing wood.
Mary Burns aged 47 of Pembroke, stealing chicks.
Mary Williams of Carmarthen, theft of clothes.

With the ship moored at the Falmouth wharf, some unchained women paused in their deck wanderings to stare up at Moll on the poop-deck, their expressions truculent. Some with children at their skirts – Charlotte Williams of Carmarthenshire had nine (three were pestering her for food; the other six she had left behind in the workhouse). What Charlotte's fate would be in Australia, Moll could only guess.

Now the live snouters (pigs) and sheep were being hauled aboard in a prodding of sticks and bellowing protests. Cranes hauled the more obstinate sky high and landed them in a scramble of hooves and shrieks; here the crew roped and tied the victims and dragged them below to slaughter pens in the prow. Hens arrived upside down in batches, in a clucking, squawking chorus.

There were casks of fresh water in barrels, nets of branbread and carcasses of salted beef. But this activity was not confined to the *Lady Juliana*, it was going on at half a dozen ships right down the wharves, including the male convict ship, the *Mandarin*. China tea-clippers were being loaded along with great men o' war bound for Canton on the China run, in support of the coming Opium War where Britain was about to soak China in the blood of the poppy, despite the appeals of the Chinese Emperor to Queen Victoria. And the wide expanse of Falmouth harbour was criss-crossed with row boats, day boats and steam pinnacles, all engaged in the business of ferrying and provisioning.

'Come, Francesca,' said Zachary, 'we'll take a turn ashore,' and he cried, 'When loaded, kindly stand off, Mr Bishop. I'll be back for tomorrow's tide.' The first mate, now resplendent in blue, saluted.

'You see, ma'am,' said Zachary, as he armed Moll down the gangplank, 'I've a proposition to put to ye.'

'I thought you had already done that.'

'Aye, but you'll need to hear this one on a full stomach.'

'Evening, Cap'n Zach, what's your pleasure?'

A foreign waiter of saturnine countenance looked Moll over amid the usual rampant activity of a dockside inn. Here doubtful sea-going characters of large stomachs and larger appetites filled their capacious jowls with steaming forkfuls of steak and kidney, jabbering meanwhile in every tongue, from Escobar to Peru: dusky Caribbean waitresses (of all people in Falmouth) balanced trays of luscious foods and eyed the male customers with duskier glances.

'Right now,' said Zachary, 'a good dinner, whisky and a fine cigar; and after that the best double bed in the house for the lady and me – and I said the best, or you'll never hear the end of it,' and he waved the man away.

'The proposition first,' said Moll, and Zachary took the cigar, lit it and blew out smoke, saying:

'I propositioned you before like you said, ma'am, but I wasn't sober then. But I've been sober for over twenty-four hours, and old Zach's been thinkin'.

'I've been thinking that I've been at sea for nigh on half a century, and never had a woman to call me own. So I've taken a soft old job as a provisioning administrator in Van Diemen's Land, with the intention of picking myself a missus to warm me bones come old age.' He glanced around the room. 'Can ye hear me above this bloody palaver?'

Moll nodded, and he continued, 'So this is my last trip, see, and it struck me that when it comes to a pillow wife, I need look no further than you . . .' Moll made to interject, but he silenced her with a gesture. 'Yesterday I offered you the acrobatics o' a single man's cabin, but now I'm offering decency. Are you listening?'

'Have I any alternative?'

'Tomorrow, when we're at sea again, the crew will want their Monkey Parade. Do ye know what that is?'

'I 'ave the feeling you are going to tell me.'

'Well, they'll drink their mornin' grog, then call for the women. We'll clink them free of their irons and bring 'em up on deck. There the men will take their pick – one woman each to comfort the voyage. This is the unwritten law. Not even I can break that law, lest I want a mutiny.'

'And you also take your pick?'

'That's it! The captain takes first shuffle!'

'First shuffle?'

'Like cutting cards – ace high.'

Moll laughed, but not with humour; he continued, 'Then first mate takes his, then b'sun, then the quarter-master, and so on, down to the cabin boy, if he's capable.'

'And how do the convict women feel about that?'

'They're keener than us.'

They laughed together in a new companionship. Zach-ary said, 'That's how it's been wi' me for six voyages, but not no more. Right now, like I said, I want a pillow wife.'

Pressing her hand against his lips, he added:

'See, I've been thinkin' about you. I'd be doing no service to a decent woman to bed and bunk you. I've had me fill o' the harlots and want to start clean. So, this is my new proposition. I'll sail you free like I said. When we get to the Tasman Peninsula you'll have your own rooms, with a servant to scrub and clean, and I'll not begrudge you your woman's whims. More, I'll do me best to get this . . . this brother o' yours under me roof and pull the strings to set him free.

'I'll give him to you, if you set up house with me. And it just could be, girl, that I won't last all that long.' He smiled at her. 'The sea has a way of taking the heart out of a man. Two years perhaps . . .?'

'Don't tell me you're proposing!'

'No, no clerics and no altars, no ring – just your promise. And when Davey Jones puts me in his locker, all I've got is yours.'

Later, the meal finished, they went upstairs to their tavern room.

This was not the smothering strength of a man with no regard for sensitivity; nor was it the fussing ardour of the aged. Instead, Zachary cleaved to his lover at first like a young man, and, but for his bass whispers and the male outrage of his bearded face, Moll could have imagined a dearer in the loving . . . the caresses of Richard and the wondrous intonations of his voice.

And now, in the thick arms of Zachary and the knowledge of him in the dark, Moll saw beyond the leaded casement the myriad silver of a moonlit sea where other tragedies of life and love were being enacted; the gorging shark and the victim mackerel, the deep, dark places where the ocean had stains, the scarlet counterpane of a billion sacrifices. How small in comparison, she thought, this little sacrifice for a lonely human.

Later, when Moll needed him, Zachary rose up in the bed and left her; as a man approaching death, he left her, and paced the room, looking up at the window stars; there being neither rank nor ruler in the business of love, save the strongest. And when the dawn came up, blooming on the walls of the little tavern room in the unpitying daylight of love's reckoning, Zachary returned and held Moll in his arms. And he who could stand at the helm of a great ship and rule the waves, could not possess one as small as Moll Walbee.

Knowing this, he wept, and Moll held him.

'I am sorry.'

'Zachary, it does not matter! I tell you, it does not matter!'

And she held him closer while the sun rose in splendour out of the sea and brought the dawn.

After breakfast, Zach and Moll went with their bags down to the wharf, and abroad a waiting pinnace, a sailing boat of blue-jerseyed sailors and polished brass.

With Zach talking to the helmsman, Moll stood on the prow facing the wind as the little craft ploughed towards the convict ship standing off-shore.

On their way out it passed row-barges carrying female prisoners who were making up Zachary's compliment aboard the *Lady Juliana*. Moll watched as they sped past: fifty-one women chained together in degraded desolation, while lusty sailors rowed them out to the prison ship.

All were carrying a blanket, a straw palliasse and a pot of oil and tar for the killing of shipboard lice and cockroaches; emaciated, most of them, and all in rags, they yet raised a cheer towards the *Mandarin*, the male convict ship. A few of the crew returned the faint greeting with the usual bawdy banter: isolated bare arms waved from the *Mandarin*'s portholes or stuck like amputated limbs up through the hatches.

Unknown to Moll then, this was the convict ship carrying John Frost, the leader of the Chartist Rebellion, to his fate in Van Diemen's Land.

Unknown to her, too, Richard Carling, also aboard the *Mandarin* and chained like the rest, was staring in disbelief at the little pinnace as she tacked across the bucking harbour, now leaving the convict barges astern as she ran for the anchored *Lady Juliana*.

Like the Queen of Sheba looked Moll: bright silk was her cloak, a present from Zachary; her bodice was of yellow, her gown green, and her golden wig was flying out behind her in the wind.

'By Jesus, she be some woman!' said someone else, rattling his chains beside Richard for a better view through the porthole.

Said a third, 'One thing's sure, mister, she ain't a doxy.'

'The mistress of the captain of the *Lady Juliana*,' said the doctor, and a fourth, seeing Richard's staring disbelief, asked:

'You know her?'

'No!' said Richard.

But still he stared until the pinnace was lost from view.

And Moll went on her way, not knowing of his nearness.

Strangely, when Zachary joined her at the prow he saw tears upon her face, but he, being Captain Zach, thought it was spindrift.

Nineteen

My true love she were beautiful
My true love she were young
Her eyes was like bright diamonds
And silver was 'er tongue
But she's took a trip on a Government ship
And she's ten thousand miles away

The *Lady Juliana,* sister to the giant three-master of the 'First Fleet' to Australia, clipped merrily along in the arms of a stiff sou'wester: a watery sun shone with new vigour, instantly vaporizing the northerly storm clouds.

Once clear of the Channel and tacking south for the coast of Portugal, February flung away her shroud of winter; the clouds shed their lowering frowns; a new and astonishing brilliance poured over the wasteful sea. And when Moll came up on deck, she saw a faint dot on the horizon.

'The *Mandarin* comin' up starboard,' said Zachary with a telescope to his eye. 'Reckon come midday we'll be fore-reachin' her; Cap'n Muddle's goin' to love it!'

They stood together, braced to the pitch and roll of the ship, and he added:

'You realize that brother of yours – the fella you mentioned – might even be aboard that old rust-bucket?'

He was clearly allowing her the lie.

'When was he sentenced?' he asked.

The sails thundered, the booms swung to a new tack, and Moll momentarily clung to him. 'Two months ago.'

147

'Where?'

'Chester Assizes.'

Zachary pondered this amid the scurrying of barefooted sailors as sheets were tightened in a lull of the wind.

'If he took the December Assizes like you said, he'd likely be aboard that old tub after waiting in the Portsmouth hulks. And if he's there wi' Cap'n Muddle, he's sailing with revolutionaries. Have ye heard of John Frost?'

'Who?'

'Dear God, have you not heard of the famous Chartist leader?'

'No.'

'The fellas who took a leaf out o' your French Revolution to tip our Queen off her throne?'

Moll shook her head, and he laughed. 'Then your education's been sadly neglected so, I'll tell ye somethin' more, Francesca. With Muddle seein' to your future, you'll never lift him on a ticket of leave without his personal recommendation.'

'What has he to do with it, once my brother is ashore?'

'Nothing, usually, but Muddle's retiring to Tasmania like me. He don't carry a prisoner to see 'em stolen from under his nose.' Turning Moll into his arms, he held her against the pitching of the ship. 'So maybe you'd find it best to throw your lot in with Zach, and we'll try to kill the goose together.'

Moll did not reply, for the prisoners were streaming up from the cells below.

Zachary added, 'You see, now I've got ye I'm reluctant to lose you.' He turned to the commands of Mr Bishop, who bellowed:

'Right girls, line up, and we'll see what you're made of!' And the crew, their duties suspended, gathered around some twenty selected prisoners. 'And if this is the best ye can muster out o' two hundred and fifty, I'm settling for me pension next time ashore. Come on, look lively!'

148

'What is happening?' asked Moll.

'I told ye, didn't I? The Monkey Parade,' said Zachary. 'They're what made me look like this – long service, bad ports, good ale and wicked women.'

In their tattered clothes, some holding their rags together to cover their near nakedness, the women stood disconsolately. So much for Zachary's talk that these were keener than the men, thought Moll; apart from one or two who were clearly harlots, none raised their heads as the crew gathered prospectingly about them.

The mate cried, his voice shrill above the thundering sails:

'Right you, the skipper takes first pick o' the brood. Cap'n Zach?'

Zachary laughed, holding up a hand. 'I got mine, Mr Bishop. Carry on, if you please,' and the mate bawled:

'And I got mine sorted out last night as well, didn't I?' He pulled out a woman and settled her beside him, adding, 'I'm tellin ye, messmates, she's got more tricks in her than a Jamaican monkey, ain't you, my lovely?' And the woman, obviously a prostitute, lifted up her skirts and did a light fantastic, showing her legs to roars of approval.

'Next up. Dr. Gedding, ship's surgeon.'

Cheers and laughter at this, with burly sailors stamping the deck and falsetto cheers going up. All heads turned to an old man's face peeping above the officer's companionway: Dr Gedding, as undersized as an Irish leprechaun and drunk, waved his skinny hands in fervent disapproval.

'Come out, sir,' called Bishop, 'join in the fun, for I've got just the boiling joint for you.' And he pulled out of the line a portly matron with her hair done up in crackers and wearing a sack apron. 'She'll have ye gold ticker off you before ye can say abracadabra – she's some woman! Are ye on?'

Moll looked around the faces of the men.

Here was the brooding lust of hunting males; bearded faces, scrubby countenances; the riffraff of Britain's sea ports, for only the unwanted sailed these convict ships, and as a last resort. The wizened visages of the old, she saw; long-term, seafarers who lived on women and rum; the coarse, brutalized, foul-mouthed and depraved.

These the dregs of the dockside taverns and dives, where women were only pawns for their appetite; who between ships lived like animals in the doss-houses of London Docks and Pier Road, Portsmouth, sleeping in lice-infested beds that never grew cold . . . the louts and mudlarks, the rowdies, ruffians and vagabonds, mostly diseased; the pot-wallopers of a dozen ports from here to the brothels of Asia, where the cheapest commodity in the East was women.

'Roll up, roll up, me lucky lads!' shouted Bishop, and Zachary, Moll noticed, joined in the applause of his mate's obscene antics. 'Here's another one.' He pulled a young girl to the front. 'A princess if ever there was one and a few years back you'd 'ave snatched her from her cradle. How old are you, my lovely?'

The girl – Moll guessed her age at twelve – was weeping; with her hair down and her hands clamped to her face she was swaying to and fro, snatching away Bishop's attempts to touch her. 'What am I bid for this beauty?' And a voice cried:

'Bid nowt, Mr Bishop, I'm the quartermaster here, so I'm next up; give her here!' And there came from the mast, pipe in mouth, a shrivelled shrew of a man with a naval cap on the back of his head and a beard like Absalom's goat. No more than five feet high, this one, his features ingrained with dirt and loose living.

Moll turned away, isolating herself from the shrieks of the girl as the quartermaster dragged her off; and knew a sense of self-abasement, being powerless to intervene in this mad circus. And when, in humiliation, Moll turned to him, she saw upon Zachary's face total resignation. Smiling down, he shook his head saying:

'I told you before you came – shipboard law. Break it, and I'd have a mutiny. Captains are cast adrift for less.'

'It is scandalous and disgusting.'

'You've led a sheltered life, I see. She's probably less innocent than she looks, you know.'

'She is a child, Zachary, a child!'

From below decks came a shrieking.

Pale-faced Moll stared at him, and he emptied big hands at her.

'What do ye take me for, woman? An ogre? And if ye want that little chicken's history so bad, you can bloody have it.'

Crossing the deck, Zachary snatched the paper from the mate's hand, and read softly from it:

'"May Davies, aged fifteen; Liverpool Assizes, 1839" – which means she's sixteen now, remember. "Charged with theft and prostitution; dram-drinking, gin . . ." Listen to this. "Having sprung from beings rank and noxious in a bed of vice, is now a juvenile harlot of the Liverpool docks. Sentence – fifteen years in Her Majesty's penal colony of Van Diemen's Land. NB. This person is a product of the perishing classes who has lived notoriously by plunder, and is now considered of the dangerous order!"' Zachary held the paper out of the wind. 'Does that suit you?'

Moll said, 'I do not believe it!'

Zachary slapped the paper in his hand. 'Believe it or not, it's all down here. Look for yourself. God! The virgin purity league! These are facts, so don't waste sympathy on a guttersnipe, for that's all May Davies is. The quartermaster's doing her a favour. Pull yourself together for the men are watching. They'll be thinking it's a dolly-mop I've brought aboard.'

Above the hissing foam and the thundering sails as the ship blundered on, Moll could still hear the shrieks coming up the companionway from the quartermaster's cabin.

And while the cheering and hurrahs continued as the Monkey Parade went on, vaguely Moll wondered if Queen Victoria, now in Europe called 'The Royal Pimp', knew of these things; and, if knowing, would have cared about the child being raped below.

Twenty

There's the captain as is our commander
There's the bosun and all the ship's crew
There's the first and second class passengers
Knows what we convicts go through.

As if the *Lady Juliana* had tired of her winter clothes, she now filled her sails with a warm southern wind and heeled hell-bent for the tropics. Under a burning sun, she tacked down the coast of Portugal in a tumultuous song of wind and spindrift. With the sea repentant after a night of storm, the crew opened the hatches, and the prisoners stumbled up on deck; chained together, they shielded their eyes from the glare of the sea.

In batches of fifty they came, their spirits quelled into obedience by hardships already endured and threats of worse to come. For the crew made talk of Atlantic gales awaiting them in the Southern Ocean when Cape Town came up on the port prow, saying that to date the voyage had been a rest cure.

So they stood placidly together on the slanting deck while the marines in their scarlet uniforms stood guard on the poop: the crew, with threatening banter, released them from their chains.

Young girls shared company with aged grandmothers; family mothers, the matrons of the industrial towns, stood side by side with ruddy-faced farm women or bawdy London tarts.

From a respectable distance, outside the door of Zachary's cabin, Moll watched.

Many of these women had come from Millbank prison, a fortress-like structure on the Thames estuary, where conditions were harsh enough; but nothing so harsh as the appalling Newgate gaol in London (where Moll would have been but for Tom Sprogg) which Elizabeth Fry, the prison reformer, described when entering, 'like going into a den of wild beasts . . . Shuddering when the door was closed behind me . . . for I was locked in with a herd of desperate companions . . .'

Miss Fry continued, 'There were no uniforms provided, many wore rags, and the begging, swearing, gaming, fighting, singing, dancing and dressing up in men's clothes were scenes too bad for me to describe.' She added:

'Millbank, an improvement upon Newgate (where prisoners could starve to death if they lacked money for food or bribes for the gaolers) was soulless and bare of the smallest human comforts, yet was feared by women prisoners for another reason: the matron there recording that,

> With a woman new to the rules, the business of hair cutting is rarely performed without remonstrance. Women whose hearts have not quaked at murder, clasp their hands in horror at the prospect of losing their hair: they weep, beg, pray and even assume a defiant attitude; resisting to the last until overcome by force . . .

The matron, a Mrs Robinson, goes on to recount the case of an old gaolbird who was as vain as a young girl, saying, when the scissors approached, 'I am married now, mum, so this hair belongs to me husband; so you dare not touch it, according to the law, for all my possessions are his. Not even the Queen of England can lay a finger on this hair.' But the matron records that she lost it just the same.

These unfortunates, the product of Victorian moralizing, lived in an era of total hypocrisy; pregnancy, like poverty, was considered a crime.

Mrs Robinson (clearly a humanist) tells how Jane Ellis, a young Welsh girl who took to the streets to feed her baby, was sitting in her Millbank cell, head bowed and shameful, when a prison visitor – the very man who had seduced her – passed her by with all the trappings of haughty piety and disdain.

Indeed, in the year before Moll set sail on the *Lady Juliana*, the Royal Commission on the Constabulary Force categorically dismissed poverty as the cause of crime, stating:

'The notion that any considerable portion of the crimes against property is caused by blameless poverty or destitution, we find disapproved at every step.' Yet, the examination of the *reasons* for sentencing such prisoners on the *Lady Juliana* that morning is repeatedly exhibited.

Charlotte Davies, for instance (that moment on the deck of the *Lady Juliana*) at her trial for trying to sell an apron she had stolen, stated, 'I was just famished with hunger, your honour', and Jane Griffiths, standing next to her, said when caught selling stolen goods, 'I am in want of meat'.

Both these young women were being transported for life.

Speaking to these two later, Moll learned the facts of what had brought them to the *Lady Juliana*: of the hunger of their homes, the brutality of their husbands and the

155

gaolers who had taken their clothes, leaving them in rags in the middle of December; of how, waiting for the *Lady Juliana* at Portsmouth, they had spent whole days killing bugs and cockroaches with the standard oil and tar in the prison ship, rotting and leaking, that once was a man o' war in Britain's prideful Navy.

Vain attempts to purify the air below decks where they languished in their tiny cells included smoking out the vermin by lighting fires; and setting off minor gunpowder explosions hopefully to drive the pests up on deck where the rats could be clubbed and the crawlers squashed. Bread and potato soup had been their diet, and fierce beatings by their warders for the smallest misdemeanours.

Later, in Van Diemen's Land, Moll recorded the tales of aged prisoners who had been transported in the First Fleet over fifty years before.

One, Simmie Lipson, a Latvian immigrant to Britain sentenced to life transportation for housebreaking (she stole items to the value of eight shillings) was transported on the *Lady Penrhyn*, a leaky old tub soon due to act as a prison hulk at Portsmouth.

Simmie said that she had left Falmouth in December, 'in bitter cold and when hail was falling': her only covering when she was taken aboard in chains was hessian sacking, and of this she had made herself a vest and skirt. Added to this was a regulation blanket. 'And missus,' said she, 'I'm telling ye, I nearly perished of the cold that winter, for the seas rushed along the decks above and poured down the hatches and washed us out o' the straw. We thought our last day 'ad come.' A story confirmed by the surgeon aboard the *Lady Penrhyn*, who later recorded for posterity:

> The convict women were so terrified that most were on their knees in prayer, but in less than an hour after

the storm had abated were uttering the most horrid oaths and imprecations that could proceed out of the mouths of such abandoned prostitutes.

Certainly, little doubt exists as to the dissolute and degraded majority of the classes transported, particularly in Victoria's reign, but the injustices perpetrated on the comparatively innocent among them stain the annals of British history. Instances of incessant and terrifying brutality are recorded.

Aboard the *Friendship*, for instance, a ship of the First Fleet, four women were put into irons for fighting, a sore punishment since the ship then lay in the frightening heat of Tenerife. Later women consorted with members of the crew who had managed to break into their quarters and upon discovery the women were ironed and the sailors flogged. And it was on this ship – and not all such occasions have been recorded – that a woman abusive to the captain was tied to a grating and flogged like a man; a ship's officer stating happily that 'the corporal did not play with her, but laid it on'.

Shipboard punishments were ferocious: aboard the *Lady Penrhyn* bad language and thieving meant the torture of the thumb screw, flogging with the 'cat' or a shaving of the head.

Not all the women were hardened cases. A sailor aboard this ship wrote:

There was a young Scottish girl whom I have never got out of my mind. She was young and beautiful even in convict clothes, but as pale as death and her eyes red with weeping. She never spoke or came up on deck, but sat constantly in the same corner; even meal times roused her not. At length she sank into her grave – of no disease; she died of a broken heart.

★　★　★

157

This was the ship that has been described as a floating brothel where drink flowed as freely as in the lowest tavern; such were the conditions in which this young girl died.

Yet the voyage of the First Fleet does not compare, in terms of horror, with what convicts, male and female, endured aboard the Second Fleet; one writer stating, that 'the Slave Trade is bountiful compared to what I have seen aboard the *Surprise*, the *Scarborough* and the *Neptune*'.

This small fleet was run by contractors who kept the prisoners, male and female, in fetters for the entire voyage. Often up to their middles in water, many died emaciated and in chains. The Reverend Richard Johnson, visiting one of these ships when it tied up in Sydney Harbour, wrote:

> I beheld a truly shocking sight . . . a great number lying naked without bedding, and unable even to turn themselves; the smell was so offensive I could scarcely bear it. The landing of these convicts was shocking, being slung over the side by ropes. On reaching air, many fainted, others died, more died in the boats before reaching shore. Here they were unable to stand, but crept on their hands and knees. All were indescribably filthy, being covered in their own nastiness; their heads, bodies and rags were full of filth and lice.

It is worth recording that Captain Trail, one of the Second Fleet Commanders, clearly guilty of murder (out of a thousand convicts he transported, a quarter died) was later appointed to a high government post in South Africa.

Twenty-one

Oh, Maggie, Maggie May, they have taken you away
To slave upon cold Van Diemen's shore!
For you've robbed so many sailors and dosed so many whalers,
You'll not cruise down Lime Street any more!

'Ship *ahoy!*'

For the last few days the *Mandarin* had been on a marvellous sou'-easterly tack and shown the *Lady Juliana* clean heels. But now, with a softening wind and calmer sea, the lighter ship found speed and hauled the *Mandarin* back. From a faint topsail on the bright horizon, she slowly grew into shape, and Captain Zach, his thick legs braced to the heaving deck, cried:

'How does she call, crow?'

And the man in the crow's nest bawled down; 'The *Mandarin*, like ye said, sir!'

'You sure?'

'Certain sure, cap'n – I can smell the bugger from here!'

'All hands shorten sail!'

Men scampered along the decks and leaped to the ratlines, racing upwards; others, barging away convict women, flung their weight against ropes. A windlass churned in creaks, whining above a sudden squally wind.

'Stand by lads, let her pay off!' Zachary's voice pierced a sudden commotion of thundering sails and confused water as the boom came over with a crash and the ship settled to a new tack.

159

'Steady as she goes, helmsman – what the hell you up to?' And Zachary put his telescope to an eye. 'Hard a starboard, *hard* I say!' The *Lady Juliana* plunged sluggishly as the rollers washed hard against her beam; then, as her mainsails filled again, she was up and heeling away like an unleashed hound.

'Hold her off, quartermaster! Port now, port! Keep her at that!' And Moll saw the *Mandarin* a mile ahead, floundering about in irons.

Zachary, grinning wide, joined her behind the poop-deck shelter, crying:

'We run her down, eh?' Triumphant, he slapped water from his cap.

The ship yawed suddenly and Moll clung to him so that his wetness was upon her face and the strength of him contained her; a man of the sea, she thought, if ever there was one.

Yet within his massive strength there was a blatant sensitivity; Byron's *The Bride of Abydos*, beautifully bound in calf leather, was upon his cabin table. Here trinkets from Asia and darkest Africa abounded in agreeable confusion; paintings of Tahitian maidens decorated its walls with sensuous flowering scenes of jungle dances, virile and beautiful; now came contrasting English cricket scenes of Victorian moral rigidity; the languid, brilliant and the profane typified Zachary's sensibilities: only last night, holding Moll in his arms in the narrow bunk of the cabin, he had informed her, with intimate belief, upon the existence of fairies on the Isle of Man, whom, he claimed, he had talked with on the sands of Peel; the sands of Peel, said he, where the Vikings had landed and performed their sacred rites of the Blood Eagle upon the unhappy villagers. Darkly conspiratorial was his mind; one moment gentle and uncontriving, next enrobed in a devilish shroud.

'Can I help with the women?' Moll asked, for now the ship was on an even tack came the business of dressing

160

them in official clothing; which, since the horror of near nakedness aboard the early fleets, was now a government issue. And so, as the crew heaved the canvas-packed bales up on deck, Moll helped in opening them and distributing garments to the convict women: they unfettered so they could change, located her presence at the head of the queue with unbridled contempt as she handed out the items:

> One woollen gown
> One cotton jacket
> Two pairs of shoes
> Two flannel petticoats
> Three shifts
> Two handkerchiefs
> Three pairs of stockings
> One cotton petticoat
> One linen cap
> One hessian apron
> One container bag

One old lag, bent, worn, and looking more like a hag of the French Revolution, screeched in a cracked soprano:

'Like as not, missus, I'm a gettin' more this mornin' than ever I 'ad in me life, *lookee!*' She held up a cotton petticoat.

Now a big canvas bath was filled with sea water, and one by one the women stripped and climbed up steps into it; their rags and tatters being gathered and thrown overboard.

Above the bath with a broom stands Mr Bishop, the mate. The grating opens, a woman plunges into the water; the grating closes and the mate lends to, scrubbing the woman's back and any other part he can get his broom to, while shrieks and curses float up from the bath and the surgeon peers down for visible signs of infection.

'Next one up! Come on, girls, look lively!'

Naked as when with the midwife, pathetically trying to cover themselves against the vulgar blandishments of the watching crew, one by one, from aged grandmothers to comely wives and fat or spindly girls, they filed into the bath like sheep being dipped, and Moll watched, appalled.

'Does this really 'ave to happen?' she asked Zachary, who pushed his cap on to the back of his head and shouted boisterously:

'Scurvy, fever, flux, boils, spots, rashes, clap, to say nothin' of fleas and lice! And you ask why? This ain't a health resort, girl, this is a convict ship!' All this within a shrieking of foul oaths and vicious imprecations that Moll never thought she would hear from the lips of women.

'Right you, next lot up – the children!' yelled Bishop.

Jesus alive and reigning, thought Moll, and for the first time aboard the *Lady Juliana* she crossed herself. She had almost forgotten that children were also aboard, despite the cacophony of their howling from the decks below.

'All right for you, ye poxy God-botherer,' whispered a woman, passing. 'I been an old man's darlin', too, but at least I got paid for it, ye cow.'

Mandarin comin' up on starboard prow!'

It was an ocean of white water now, with the rollers foam-crested and roaring, and the *Lady Juliana* took it full along her timbers: raking her masts over the sky, she bellowed her displeasure as she heeled and went about.

'Comin' up cannon-shot, cap'n!' wailed a voice from the prow, and the ship slid parallel to her quarry, then shot forward in a slump of the sea.

The crew of the *Mandarin* and prisoners lined her rail, waving and cheering as the *Lady Juliana* came abreast.

Now the women rattled their fetters and whirled them around their heads, and the *Mandarin*'s convicts did likewise so that the waves flung back the sound in an orchestra of metallic, hissing swell. It was a sudden and uncouth symphony of joy; and the women, pulling up their skirts, waltzed around the deck while the convicts of the *Mandarin* dropped their trousers, till the crew got among them with rope's ends.

Almost instantly, the two ships slid apart; the *Mandarin* plunging in the *Lady Juliana*'s wake: windless suddenly, she lay to, rolling sluggishly in the swell, then the lighter craft, caught in a quick blow, settled head down and sped away in billowing sails.

A stupendous sight, said Richard Carling later.

He had not seen Moll standing in the shelter of the companionway.

Five weeks later, tacking in heavy weather against the South Equatorial Current and a thousand miles from land, scurvy struck.

With the spices of Africa borne on the warm winds of the Cape Basin, it blew in the face of an expectant mother in the fetid air of the bunks and killed her and her unborn baby in hours. It crept on germ-ridden air into the cabin of the stalwart marine guards, and the sergeant, his body nearly covered in the puffy patches (where bleeding occurs under the skin) lay stiff in his bunk in terror of moving; movement inducing terrifying pain.

One by one the women went down with it, the creeping inertness of the body that is confused with paralysis, the patient being frightened to move. It came up on deck and attacked the helmsman, then the quartermaster (despite their antidotes) and the girl he had made his reluctant mistress.

Zachary said in the cabin, 'This has been coming on gradually; these women were on a restricted diet before I even got 'em.'

'There is no cure?'

'Oh aye, there's a cure – fresh meat, vegetables and tomato juice.'

Moll said, 'But we and the rest of the crew have been drinking lemon juice.'

He made a droll face. 'Lemon, orange juice, it helps – but not for prisoners. Government funds don't run to it.'

'So they just allow them to die on these long voyages?'

'Francesca, you've much to learn, for all you've been around. The more who die getting to Australia, the less it will cost when the ships arrive. Transportation wastage!'

'I think that is scandalous!'

'Tell that to the quartermaster; Dr Gedding says he's on his last legs.'

'I am more concerned with the girl in 'is cabin,' said Moll. 'I have been down to see her. Is there no 'ope at all?'

'Grapefruit when we get to the Cape, perhaps.'

'How long?'

'Another three weeks.'

'She will not last that long.'

Within a week of reaching the Cape of Good Hope, cholera struck.

With the *Lady Juliana* clipping along at a merry rate now, safe within the promise of the West Wind Drift, she left St Helena on the starboard prow where Zachary had considered landing for fresh vegetables.

'Why not?' asked Moll. She was kneeling at the bunk of the girl called the Quartermaster's Piece by the crew; a pale and now sickly adolescent in the last stages of scurvy, and Zachary had called in to see her progress.

'The quartermaster just died,' he whispered, and gestured up to the deck above. 'Fit and healthy, we thought, but he had a fall ashore before we left, apparently, and the

164

scurvy attacked the injury.' He bent over the sleeping girl.
'How's she doing?'

'Perhaps she is better.' Moll was cooling the girl's
forehead with cold compresses. Zachary said:

'Queer, ain't it? A tough old quartermaster snuffs it and
she, half his size, hangs on.'

'It was not the scurvy that killed the quartermaster,'
said Moll.

'What then?'

'The cholera.'

'Ach, don't be daft!'

'I 'ave seen it before. It is the cholera.'

'So you know better than the ship's surgeon?'

'The ship's surgeon is a drunken fool. He is not a
doctor, he is an undertaker.'

Zachary said with quiet heat, 'Then keep your opinions
to yourself. Talk cholera now, and we'll have a mutiny on
our hands!'

'From two hundred women in chains?' Moll rose. 'I
have seen the cholera. In Paris I 'ave lived in the sewers.
In sewers, you 'ear me? If you had lived in sewers, my
friend, you would know the difference between scurvy
and cholera. You can die from both, but scurvy takes
longer. Cholera is quick. This is why you 'ave a dead
quartermaster, and good riddance also.'

Zachary's eyes weighed her with quiet indecision,
'You're a deep one. Are there any more at home like
you?'

'Fortunately, no. Too wise, all of them, to put a foot
aboard this floating hell,' Moll said, and the girl in the
bunk moaned in her sleep.

Moll straightened. 'Just now I called the doctor a
drunken fool, but perhaps he cannot be blamed for what
'appens on this ship.

'But you, Zach, are sober, so you are the real fool.' Her
voice rose to a harsher note. 'A criminal fool, perhaps,

for sailing this graveyard with its load of corpses.' Moll suddenly screwed up her hands and beat them upon his chest, while he held her in her onslaught of fury.

'What kind of a man are you, and who are the animals who pay you for this filthy trade?' She paused for breath, her eyes bright. 'The only decent people here are the ones lying in filth. Why do you hate us women so? You beat and revile us, make us into receptacles for your lusts, chastise us, say prayers over us for the people we 'ave become . . .' She thumped herself. 'Then chain us like animals and send us to the other end of the earth to cleanse what you call your society . . .'

'Your English is improving,' said Zachary, with droll charm.

'Also my intelligence! For I 'ave come to my senses. You call us prostitutes, tarts, harlots and trollops, so I call you men lechers, whoremongers and seducers who have only one intention – yes, I've heard something from the women aboard – to serve the brothels of Melbourne and Hobart. The whorehouses built by English money, profit for an aristocracy as corrupt in London as it was in Paris. But we put an end to them, by God!'

'By God,' echoed Zachary suavely, 'at last we're hearing some home truths!'

'You will hear more, Captain Zachary, for I have only just started.' and she jerked her thumb. 'Now get out of here for I want to strip and cool this girl.'

'And what if she has the cholera?'

'She has,' said Moll. 'I told you.'

The *Lady Juliana*'s bell dismally tolled the hour of midnight, across a silent, sullen sea. With her sails hanging like dishrags in the hot, tropical air, the convict ship rolled impotently, its booms and spars creaking, and the women battened down below decks sweated and groaned, for women suffer more than men when closely confined.

Time was, only three decades before, that male and female convicts shared the same bunks; side by side, in chains or out of them, when a woman giving birth could be chained to a man already dead. It has been recorded:

> There was no draught through the barred hatches; the convicts were so packed together that free movement was not possible: they could only sit on their palliasses and suffer in patience. Above them (in the tropics) the pitch boiled in the seams of the hot deck and dropped upon them, burning their flesh as it fell, in sleep or wakefulness. Day in and day out the terrible calm went on, and the consuming heat and airlessness sapped the lives of the spent-up convicts. Hideous incidents filled the weeks as the ship sailed on with its burden of disease and death. Weakened by the continuous heat and shortage of water, the women succumbed in the poisonous atmosphere and to fever in its various stages.

Moll, with her bowl of cooling water and rags, entered the stinking air below deck and stopped from time to time to wash the faces of those still awake; women who once belligerently challenged her presence now accepted her ministrations with faint gratitude, their spirits broken by privation and sea sickness. Earlier, fo'rard, a child was born to a woman from Hull; she, a lusty, bright-eyed creature of fancy manners and worse language, now lay in an apathetic quiet while Moll drew the child from her – a boy; an amazingly large, sprightly creature who bellowed lustily in chorus with the sobs and groans about him.

'Thank's, mum,' said the mother.

'It is a boy.'

'God tend ye, missus.'

'What is your name?'

'Becky Hansom – hansom like the cab, ye know. Handsome is as 'andsome does, my chap used to say.'

'Your husband?'

'Gawd no, never married 'im. He couldn't settle, see? Ants in 'is pants. Ye won't understand that bein' French . . . up and down – a bum-fizz we calls him, like a bloody jack-in-the-box. But he were good to me, mind, never laid boot nor finger on me. He's the seventh, ye know.'

'The boy, 'ere? The seventh? Where are the others now?'

The woman wiped stray hairs from her sweating face. 'Gawd knows. My Alf won't keep 'em – he'll be orf for his pints. In the workhouse, I suppose, poor little buggers. Mind, the eldest is a girl. She's ten, so she'll likely see to 'em.'

She was as hard to look at as the rising sun. Aged thirty, she looked sixty; yet, withall, she had kept her woman's dignity. Not a sound she made during the birth. 'Pop 'em out like rabbits, don't I?' said she. 'I never 'ad no trouble after me first. "You can 'ave the next half dozen," I told my Alf.'

The women, some resentful at the intrusion into their personal calamity, turned away their shining faces as Moll stepped among them, pausing beside some, kneeling to others. It was against the rules, but she gave them sweet, cold water from the captain's cabin, not the bilge-water of the daily canisters (two pints a person) half putrid and warm, served out by the marines – one pouring it while the other stood on guard: water, the vital commodity, always in short supply.

Then the tropical becalming ceased and the rain suddenly teemed down and soaked them as they laid there. Later, when they trooped up upon deck, they stood facing the wind, letting it blow against their hot bodies. The sky was all over blue now, the ship plunging along, breasting the great green billows rolling down the coast of Africa;

also the wind held perfumes of the mango plantations and coconut glades.

Seeing Moll, the women gathered excitedly about her with their rough banter.

'Mornin', frog! How ye doing?'

'I am well.'

'Oh, Jesus, listen to it! Bleedin' hoity-toity!'

'Leave her alone, she's a lady.'

'More'n you are!'

'The only one aboard, I reckon.'

'Morning, miss!'

'*Bonjour, madame!*'

'Chinese now, are we?' They touched her; one caressed her hair.

Zachary said, 'You done more in a few weeks wi' that lot than I've done in years. I don't know how you put up with 'em.'

'They are people, and many of them are charming, which is what men do not understand. The Cape of Good Hope tomorrow, is it?'

'If the wind stands free – afternoon, latest.'

'You will take me ashore?'

Unseen, Zachary kissed her. 'I'll do more than that, missus. Tonight, God willing, I'll make love to ye.'

'What has God to do with it?'

'You'd be surprised! They tell me the legs go first, but it's a lie, poor old Zach!'

'That is a pity. I would like you to make love to me.'

'Though I'm an ogre?'

'It was no more than you deserve. Men! *Vous êtes terribles!*'

'Lady, tonight you'll see how terrible I can be.'

On the night before they ran into the Cape harbour, the girl in the quartermaster's cabin died.

Moll was sitting by her bunk; the pale, smooth profile, as cold as alabaster, was on the pillow.

It could, thought Moll, have been Chantelle: the aristocratic features, the tumbling black hair, the scarlet lips of fever . . . and the lustrous blue eyes that Moll closed gently with her fingers.

On her knees now, saying:

'Holy Mary, Mother of God, receive the soul of May Davies.'

At that moment Zachary entered.

'Leave us, Zach.'

He bowed to her, saying, 'Tears dry quickest of all, Francesca,' and closed the cabin door.

Hearing this, Moll saw in the dead girl's face the face of another, and clasping her hands, wept, saying:

'Chantelle! My sweet, my precious . . .'

Twenty-two

You lads and lasses attend to me
While I relate this misery.
My hopeless love was once betrayed
And now I am a convict maid.

The *Lady Juliana* stood offshore in Cape waters, awaiting her turn at the landing wharf. Most of the women were up on deck, lining the rail and staring up at the phenomenon of Table Mountain; before them a small forest of masts speared the evening sky. The calm lagoon-like waters of the harbour were a ruffled sheen of cobalt blue. Tiny carry-crafts seemed to dance on the sea like delirious fireflies.

Moll, in the cabin, wrote by the light of an oil lamp:

Cape Town, South Africa.
6th May 1840.

My darling Chantelle,
You will be quite astonished to receive a letter from a country so far away from England, and it is a marvellous story I have to tell you.

You will remember the rich English gentleman called Richard who was my escort in London? Well, prepare yourself for a great surprise – we are married!

Yes, Chantelle, I am married and gloriously happy. More! At this very moment I am on my honeymoon, for he has brought me to this lovely place . . . where, let me tell you, he owns *diamond* mines!

Can you imagine such wealth? Indeed, *chérie,* I am writing this in my cabin aboard one of his ships, for his family's money lies in trade between Africa and India, to which he promises I shall one day go (if, as he puts it, I behave myself!).

Meanwhile, Richard's business takes him to a place called Hobart, in Tasmania – Uncle Maurice will show you where that is on the map; I am to accompany him there for a little while, before voyaging back home to England.

Oh, Chantelle, you should see my man! This is a real man, my girl, not the animal called Jean Pierre. So tall and handsome is he that sometimes I think I will die of joy. But more than that, he is a Knight of the Realm – *Sir Richard,* if you please! And now I am called Lady Carling – you understand? All the women are after him, of course, but they do not stand a chance, for it is only me he loves.

Did you get the packet of valuables which I sent to Uncle Maurice before leaving England? Beautiful are they not? – and believe me, come about most honestly, through the business. But they are nothing to the jewels I now possess; and those I will put upon you when we meet.

Meanwhile, until that time comes, think lovingly of your big sister although we are so far apart. I keep telling Richard how beautiful you are; I am quite certain he does believe me!

I beg you, do everything that Uncle Maurice instructs. Learn your lessons, pay attention to your teachers, also, be obedient. And dream, as I do, of the moment when we will again be in each others' arms, for I love you better than life. *Je t'adore, je t'adore,* as Papa used to say to us when we went riding in the Bois de Boulogne, remember? And we used to claim that he was talking to his horse!

Every night I pray to the Holy Mother that one day
I will return to you.
Your devoted sister,
Francesca.

Night fell over Table Mountain, a blessed maiden of shadows
and dreams for the affluent ashore. But here, in the oppressive hold of the *Lady Juliana,* the women, chained against
escape, lay in stinks of brimming buckets of urine and
faeces while their companions in tribulation, the rats, sat
rubbing their forelegs like dwarf anthropoids, pondering
their own escape from a dungeon of human destruction.

The ship, like a restless child, rolled and creaked in
the quarantine of cholera; a passionless surrender after its
long journey, its red and green navigation lights burning
wounds in the ebony waters of Walvis Ridge.

Here in phosphorescent loveliness, the little sea urchins
danced in darting splendour; while on the other side of the
Lady Juliana's rotting walls, the honour of a generation
died in the grip of bestiality.

For the last three weeks of the voyage shipboard
funeral rites had been performed, something new to
Moll, and terrifying: corpse after corpse, after a brief
sojourn beneath the Union Jack, had slid into the deep
to Zachary's muttered prayers . . . while the *Lady Juliana,*
who had seen it all before, wandered like a drunk across a
sun-blazing sea and in her wake exposed the sea predators
which, for the last thousand miles had followed the ship
in expectation of a meat harvest.

Vaguely, Moll wondered how sharks knew when death
occurred aboard ship; and, if knowing, then died of
cholera.

'Are you writing a letter?' Zachary entered the cabin, his
immensity dominating the tiny room; he began to throw
off his clothes. Moll answered:

'To my sister,' and the scarlet wax flared as she sealed the envelope.

'I didn't know you had a sister.'

Moll, head on one side, reflected on the words. 'That's what everybody seems to say.'

'Can you blame them? You are an enigma, Francesca. Just when I think I know all about you, I realize I know nothing.' He sat down, removing his trousers in grunts and wheezes. 'Do ye realize I don't even know your surname?'

'That's because I haven't told you.' Moll rose 'Are you changing to go ashore, or are you coming to bed?'

'Bed preferably. It's been a hard day and I've got to be up in the morning.'

'Then you will need a good sleep.'

'Actually, honey, that weren't ma immediate intention.' He mimicked Negro talk.

'Zach, it is too 'ot!'

He gave her a wry smile and rolled into his bunk, while Moll climbed into the one above him. Momentarily, they listened to the old ship's creaks and groans. Then Zachary said, 'Tell me about this sister.'

'There is little to tell. Her name is Chantelle. She is nine years old and is cared for by our Uncle Maurice in France.'

'You left her in his charge when you came to England?'

There was a silence. Moll said, 'Are you asking this in an official capacity?'

'As your husband – by mutual agreement, remember?'

'The truth then,' and she took breath. 'When my mother was with us – she left my father after an affair with a military officer – we lived in a small cottage in the village of Avesnes le Compte, near Arras. But after my mother left, my father moved the family to Paris. He was a banker and there was no shortage of money. Indeed, we lived in great style in a 'ouse overlooking the Bois de

174

Boulogne. It was nothing for Chantelle – then aged five – and I, to rein in our horses and bow to ministers of state riding by.'

'An enviable childhood.'

'Unfortunately, the days of idle riches did not last,' continued Moll. 'An embezzlement at the bank brought my father to trial, the threat of prison, and suicide. At the age of sixteen I was left with an empty 'ouse, a small dependent sister, and possessions distrained.'

'Distrained?'

'Owing to creditors, who forced us out on to the street. It was winter. The very clothes we stood up in belonged to others and they showed no charity. Even the contents of the food cupboards were rationed out to us . . .

'Friends, overnight, became enemies; the only person I could turn to was our Uncle Maurice, my mother's brother, but he was away in the East. I was penniless in December. To be aged sixteen and penniless in Paris is bad enough, but worse in December. We starved, Chantelle and me. In the end we were scavenging in the refuse bins where I picked out the best bits for her. Vagrants and prostitutes were our only friends; each gave small gifts to us – a loaf here, a night's shelter there.'

'Good God!'

Moll said, 'I shall never forget those slum women. If I ever become rich, I shall return to Paris and repay them. But, more than feeding and sheltering us, they showed respect for my position. Many would have expected me to sell myself.'

'Honour among thieves . . . ?'

'Something nobler. I was of the so-called gentry class.'

In silence now they lay, listening to wave-lap and faint groans and sighs emanating from amidships where the convicts suffered the stifling heat.

'And then?'

Moll took a breath of deep reminiscence. 'But it could not last, and I fell in with a man called Jean Pierre Lamont, a pickpocket who lived by his wits.'

'He seduced you? The usual tale?'

''Ow did you guess?' Moll said bitterly. 'It was necessary; not for the first time has the vagina fed the stomach, so do not look so pious.' She waved away his protest. 'But Jean Pierre did more than that: he taught me the trade of the light-fingered gentry, the curse of the Paris boulevards.' She smiled in reflection. 'I proved excellent at sleight of hand . . .' Moll turned in her bunk and looked out of the porthole at the gem-stained harbour of Table Mountain.

'Indeed, so good was I that I became his source of wealth and pleasure – his income by day, his delight by night. In return, he protected me and my little sister from thieves not doing so well. I was good, I tell you.' He noticed the sudden excitement in her voice. 'One night at the opera I brought Jean home a fortune. You know something? I could pluck a hair from the 'ead of a duchess while shaking 'ands with her duke!' And they laughed together.

'And then?'

'Do you really want to know? You will not sleep so well, if you do . . .'

'I'll chance it.'

'I killed 'im' said Moll.

'Jesus, Mary and Joseph! Ye what?'

'I killed 'im,' Moll repeated. 'One night I returned early from the streets and found him naked, in the attic with my Chantelle, so I killed 'im.'

'He had raped the child?'

'I was too late by a minute. My little sister bled much, but Jean Pierre, he bled more. I always carried a knife for street protection and I got 'im as he tried to get away through the window. He fell through the glass

– I 'elped him with my boot – into the courtyard fifty feet below.'

'Dead?'

'*Monsieur*, 'e was dead from the time I came through the door.'

Zachary rose from his bunk and helped Moll down from hers. 'Does anybody else know about this?'

'The police.'

'They came after you?'

'Of course, but it was a *crime passionelle* so their 'earts were not in it.' Moll shrugged. 'In France we make allowances for the palaver of love; Jean Pierre was no loss to anybody; they were probably 'appy to be rid of him – it was the money they was after.'

'The money you earned as a pickpocket, you mean?'

'Of course. And they got it all. But I 'ad to leave France, you understand? To stay would have meant arrest, and perhaps imprisonment – I was not worried about that but . . .'

'Chantelle . . . ?'

'Of course. She was the one valuable thing in my life. She was screaming – you know 'ow children can shriek? Also her blood had stained her clothes. I . . . I just picked her up and ran.

'It was near midnight and Paris was singing its enjoyment, for this was Montmartre – the Rue Caulaincourt, near the cemetery. Covering Chantelle with a shawl I hid among the graves, and when the city was quiet I crept out, and we ran down Chevalier to Sacré Coeur. I made her kneel and pray with me. I must 'ave been mad.'

'And then?'

'Then I took 'er along Rue de Rustique until we got to the Bois de Boulogne where my Uncle Maurice lived. He 'ad been away in the East for months.'

Moll took Zachary's hand. 'Even when things are dark, Zach, never forget God, for you will not believe this. I had prayed to the Holy Mother and my prayers were answered. For, standing outside my uncle's door was the cab that had brought him from the railway station; he 'ad returned home minutes earlier.'

'He took you in?'

'I did not ask for myself. 'E took Chantelle in, with the promise to bring 'er up as his own daughter. With money Uncle Maurice gave me, I took a boat down the Seine to Le Havre, and from there went by ferry to England.'

'Where you became Madame Le Roy?'

'*Mon Dieu!* 'Ow did you know that?'

'Easy. You see, I commanded the *Mandarin* until a few months ago, when I signed it over to Captain Muddle and became skipper of this old crate, remember?'

'This happened because the government was transporting Chartist revolutionaries and they wanted a disciplinarian aboard. But I had read up on the prisoners. The most important fella aboard, apart from the Chartists, was one called Sir Richard Carling, so I studied his trial . . .'

'And learned about Madame Le Roy?'

'Hook, line and sinker – from the moment you come across him to the moment you fixed him – God! You dished, diddled him and tied him up!'

'I am not proud of it.'

'He should have kept his eyes open, shouldn't he?' Zachary slapped his thigh and shouted laughter.

'It was unforgivable . . .'

Reaching out, he lifted her chin. 'Aw come off it, lass! You beat him at his own game. If ye hadn't done him, he'd have done you!' But Moll turned away, saying softly:

'He's been sent into hell. I will never forgive myself.'

'Meanwhile, so much for the wayward brother who needs saving for the devoted family, eh?' He made a wry face.

Moll said, 'If I had not lied to you, you would not have taken me.'

'You're bloody right I wouldn't.' He poured himself a drink. 'There's me heading off to be provisioning administrator in the Colony and find meself carrying a wanted prisoner. You realize you cooked the goose of Justice Bosanky, too, I suppose? Premature retirement!' He drank deep, gasping. 'Let's hope the same don't happen to me.'

'Justice Bosanky – retired?'

'For gettin' his gaols mixed up with you, my petal . . . Come on, darlin', let's have the rest of the story while we're at it!'

There was nothing for it now but to tell it; and Moll explained her role in the trickery of Richard at the Talbot Hotel; of how she had tried to redress her betrayal by releasing him from Bosanky, only to have them both arrested.

'And then you did a bunk, eh?' Zachary groaned. 'Well, one thing's certain, he treated you better than you treated him, for nothin' of your yarn ties up with his trial. According to Carling, everything happened in Hungerford and Reading – Shropshire don't even come into it.'

'I know. He perjured himself trying to protect me.'

'Ah, what's a little betrayal between friends, girl? Aren't we all gagged, bound and executed at birth, anyway – Carling along with the rest of us?' And he added jocularly, 'So what happens now, my beauty? You'll hang around with me, I suppose, till lover-boy gets his ticket?' Moll said quietly:

'When I betrayed Richard, I thought myself very clever. But I played dirty, and Richard played clean. But I tell you

179

this, Captain Zachary: I never dreamed I'd be sending him into untold misery; the sin of it is my last thought at night and my first every morning. Do you understand?'

'That,' answered Zachary evenly, 'is because you're in love with him. Meanwhile, he's in the clink and I'm as free as air – so where do I come into it?'

Moll walked into the little cabin. There was no sound but the slapping of the sea against the ship's side; the lights of the Cape shore slid up and down the porthole glass. The decision would be irrevocable. She replied:

'I'll be your woman till we get to Port Arthur; after that, you are on your own again.'

'Christ, ye don't wrap things up, do ye?'

'That was the bargain, and I will keep to it. But the moment I'm ashore I belong to Richard Carling.' He smiled blandly at her and opened his big hands in a gesture of resignation, saying:

'Meanwhile, this lover fella's in chains in the *Mandarin* and I'm here, so let's make the best of it while we can, eh?'

For reply, Moll unbuttoned the top of her nightdress and dropped it to her feet.

'Dear God, don't tell me all that's really for me,' said Zachary.

Book III

1841 – AUSTRALIA

Twenty-three

Cascades. The Tasman Peninsula,
Van Diemen's Land.

Cascades did not properly develop into an approved
convict outstation until two years after the *Lady Juliana*
anchored in Storm Bay in July 1840.

New probation centres (centres of convict labour) were
proliferating – Saltwater River and Sloping Island having
already been established; but beautiful Cascades on the
Tasman Peninsula, still sat like an unspoiled diamond
against the blue of the Tasman Sea.

Disappointingly, it was over a year before Zachary got his
appointment confirmed as provisioning administrator at
Cascades; so he and Moll had to kick their heels, he said,
in an outlandish place called Maria Island, a practically
defunct convict settlement off the Forestier mainland.

Here Moll learned the need for patience, passing her
wakeful hours in planning for Richard's escape; rejecting
one scheme after another, until came the joyous day of
Zachary's appointment and his posting to Cascades.

Then, and only then, came the promise of turning
each hare-brained escape scheme into one of fundamental
reality.

Cascades was a panorama of Elysian loveliness under the
vaulting eternity of the sky.

Here conspiratorial caves were lit by flooding moonlight, so far untouched by the savage hand of Man.

Surrounded by great tropical forests, ancient hunters here stalked their prey in ritual stealth; great shoals of fish rubbed off their fins in plenty; the undersea coral reaches blazed; bright festoons of heliotrope and mother-of-pearl glimmered in refracted loveliness beneath the crashing breakers, where played the minnow, manta and shark-fish. Here swam the turtle, the watersnake.

This was the home of the dolphin and the albatross, that wandering giant of the Tasman Sea; here lived in their groups the primitive native of the most unflattering kind, the Aborigine, of whom a visiting Dutchman wrote three hundred years ago:

> These differ little from brutes . . . they have great bottle noses, full lips, wide mouths: the two fore-teeth of the upper jaw are wanting in all of them . . . they are of a very unpleasing aspect, being black-haired, woolly and curled of coal-black visage, they go naked, save for a handful of grass and rind. The earth is their bed, heaven their canopy.

But the coming of the White Savage had long dispelled the black one from his ancestral homeland, and now, upon the arrival of Moll in Cascades, all the bounteous goodness of the place lay before her; the long, sweeping fields whose dying mango groves, once flourishing, were filled with the most astonishing butterflies of every conceivable colour and description. Parakeets and parrots flew abundantly in jabbering choruses; cranes and cocka-toos screeched and whistled and the beach was thronged with pelicans, bustards and a score of differing sea-birds.

'Well here it is,' said Zachary, and mopped his sweating face.

With three convict porters carrying their luggage – all of dissolute and starved appearance – he and Moll went

184

hand in hand up the steps of an ivy-clad log building of two-storey construction, upon which, painted in large white letters stood the name:

DUNA

It was set in a wilderness of isolation flanked with overgrown banksia, the Australian honeysuckle, its foliage of bright green contrasting with a silver whiteness that flourished in every rush of the wind. In startling clarity stood the house, facing the blue of the ocean; each wave-lap drifting shoreward in surging foam, to the dunes beyond the garden.

'Get the luggage in,' ordered Zachary, and the convicts obeyed; their eyes, half-closed to the light, were hooded and veiled; with beards speckled with sweat, they moved in their ill-fitting uniforms of brown and black with the lethargy of men half dead, and Moll pitied them, seeing in their apathy a vision of young men full in strength before the coming of the avenging State. And saw further, to the youthful, unlined face of Richard, now their comrade in this charade of crime and punishment.

'Come on, get a move on!' bawled Zachary, and hastened one along with his boot.

And Moll saw, in an effort at self-removal, a small black dot upon the azure sea. Focusing her eyes against the glare, she made out a little raft on the breast of the waves, now high on a crest, now hidden in a trough; and Zachary, beside her on the verandah, followed her interest, for a lad was fishing from it.

'Ubara,' Zachary grunted, nodding seaward.

'Who?'

'Ubara, the Aborigine – fishing for our supper. A lazy good-for-nothing, accordin' to what they tell me,' and he entered the house as if he had said nothing out of the ordinary.

Two of the convicts exchanged meaningful glances.

★   ★   ★

185

Within the spacious living room, Moll asked, 'A provisioning administrator, are you? Why didn't you tell me? It sounds most important.'

'I did tell you, but as usual you weren't listening,' answered Zachary, and the bearers hauled a tea-chest past them and clattered upstairs to Moll's indicating finger.

Ignoring this reply, she asked:

'You not going to sea again, Zach?'

For answer, he snatched a little melodeon from the hand of a passing convict and, sitting, began to play a plaintive tune. In delight, Moll sat also, clapping her hands together. Against his accompaniment, Zachary sang in a rough, tuneless voice:

When I was a little lad, with folly on me lips
Feign was I for journeying all the sea in ships.
But now across the southern swell, every morn I hear,
The little streams of Duna runnin' clear . . .

'Excellent! *Magnifique!*' cried Moll, stamping her heels on the floor, her legs akimbo, and the three convicts paused in their labours to listen, as Zachary sang again:

When I was a young man before my beard was gray,
All to ships and sailor-men I gave my heart away.
But I'm weary of the sea-wind now, I'm weary of the foam
And the little streams of Duna call me home . . .
The little streams of Duna call me home.

There was no sound in the room save the crashing of distant surf and the hissing of the swell. But Ubara, the Aboriginal boy, paddling homeward on his raft, had heard the voice of Zachary whispering across the sea and raised his woolly head with its snub profile.

186

He wiped brine from his blunted features, did Ubara, aged seventeen, for he had never heard a white man sing before in this accursed place where men shrieked commands and wielded whips for the smallest indiscretion. And the melody, faint though it was, stirred memories of his tribe, which was far away in the dreamtime of an Aborigine's world, where spirits walked and stones talked: a world of prehistoric kangaroos where men and women danced to excite their passions by the light of the moon, whirling around the *Kobong* (in his case the totem of the Stoney Creek tribe to which he belonged).

Somewhere, panting within this strange and plaintive foreign sound, thought Ubara, was the weeping of his race . . . a tragic sobbing.

But now, with Zachary's song ended, Ubara sat motionless on the bamboo raft and was sorry that the noise had finished; for surely, thought he, it was not reality which he had heard – a white man singing – but some barbaric sea spirit in a cavern beneath him and, thinking this, he was afraid.

Therefore, seeing the sun-glittering fish at his feet (which he had caught by swimming despite the sharks), he snatched them up and flung them overboard to appease the sea spirit, and, with the song-noises ended, paddled slowly back to the little wharf that served Duna, the provisioning administrator's white house in Cascades. For to this house he was an apprenticed servant, and as such he must be obedient, for the sun was high: to return home either in sea mist or when the sun was tiring could mean the whip.

And, as he paddled to the tune of his own tribal humming, which was a grunting, bumbling apology for a song, Ubara vaguely wondered as to what manner of man this new boss would prove: the whip or not the whip?

187

– this was the only question. And he eased his body to the wrack of his torn shoulders as he paddled homeward.

Moll, meanwhile, was exultant. 'But Zach, you did not tell me! How beautiful is your voice!' She threw her arms about him as he sat there with the melodeon, and the convicts, still labouring in with tea-chests, bundles of clothing and cabin boxes, adopted an air of placid removal, neither looking nor hearing, though observing all, which was the safest policy with a new arrival. For many brutal predecessors had lived in Duna; little could be said for administrators of the executive class, the white-duck civil servants over from Hobart. They, without even tryin', lads, could be bastards . . . But less, surely, could be said for the captain of a convict ship, most of whom would flog a man on a whim.

Yet one thing was certain sure, they thought – he had brought with him a flighty piece of womanhood if ever there was one. The beauty of her, the very perfume of her presence betrayed their manhood's longings by their show of cold disassociation, since even a glance in her direction could end on the bloodstained triangle. Superintendents, overseers, foremen, warders and javelin men – the prisoner trustees who were worse than most – were very pernickety when it came to their women.

And while they laboured, transferring Zachary's possessions – Moll herself possessed little, apart from her clothes – from their handcart to the house (one quite tastefully furnished in cane and leather) Moll watched these men; and saw in them the man that perhaps Richard Carling had become because of her.

Yet knowing also a new and exciting sense of fulfilment, that, after coming so far she was now almost within Richard's presence, breathing the same air. This knowledge obliterated the obscenity . . . that the game with Zachary must be played to the end.

188

Twenty-four

Ubara, the Aborigine, came up to the house where Moll was unpacking Zachary's cases, he having gone to report to the Convict Railway at the Norfolk Bay Station. Seeing the Aborigine coming fearfully, Moll waited on Duna's verandah, and there met him.

'Good afternoon, Miss Lady,' said Ubara, and bowed.

'Good afternoon. You are Ubara, the fisher boy?' asked Moll, and Ubara saw her whiteness, and to him her ugliness, for she was unlike the blackness of his mother and sister in the Stoney Creek tribe beyond Eaglehawk Neck. The blackness of his relatives' faces and bodies was beautiful, unlike this woman's; yet for all her ugliness, this white stranger was gentle in the voice,

'I am Ubara, Miss Lady,' said he.

'You have brought fish for me to eat?'

'I have not brought fishes, Miss Lady.'

Moll tried desperately not to show humour. 'Why not? Did I not see you out there fishing?'

'Yes, Miss Lady.'

'Did you not catch fish?'

'I caught them, Miss Lady, but put them back into the sea.'

'Why?' Moll came closer and Ubara's bedsheet eyes rolled in fear.

'Because I heard strange sounds, and the sea spirit spoke to me and called them back, so I returned them.'

'Oh dear,' said Moll, and sat down upon the verandah steps, regarding him. 'Then tonight we do not eat.'

189

'Tomorrow would be better, Miss Lady,' and his thick lips broke into a smile, exposing two missing teeth, which, when his loins had told him his maturity had been reached, he had knocked out with a stone, thus making himself amiable to females. Certainly no Aborigine female would have entertained a lover to mutual advantage when possessed of all his front teeth.

Ubara added, 'I am not allowed to fish in darkness, Miss Lady, nor when the mist is sad on the sea, lest I travel to Eaglehawk Neck and sail home to Flinders Island. But tomorrow, if the morning is good, I will bring back many fishes for you.'

'And now?'

'Now I have come to work outside the house. Also to sweep and clean for you, and perhaps make shine the knives with sand and paper. I bring water from the well, too for Miss Lady to drink.'

'That will be satisfactory,' replied Moll, taking him off. 'Who taught Ubara to speak such beautiful English?'

'One Miss Lady in the mission school; she taught me, but I cannot read and write.'

'You come from Van Diemen's Land?'

'I do not.'

'From where, then?'

Turning, the boy pointed north, saying, 'From beyond Eaglehawk I come, even across the sea to Geelong, for I am of the Stoney Creek tribe who now live on Flinders Island.'

'Then what are you doing here?' Moll made to ask this, but the question was stilled in her throat, for she had seen his back; the flesh was split deep and encrusted in the healing where a whip had cut.

'Who did this to you, Ubara?'

'It was he who has gone and travelled far, not to come back. He did it to me.'

'Why?'

'Because I fish late near Eaglehawk, which is against the law. I deserved it, the Miss Lady in the white mission said. All those who fish late or in sea mist get the whip, you understand?'

'By Jesus,' said Moll beneath her breath, 'not now I am 'ere,' and she put out her hand to him and beckoned him to follow her.

Later, in dusk, but before Zachary returned from the Norfolk Bay Station, she bathed Ubara's back and anointed the wounds. When Zachary returned, Moll said:

'I think it is disgraceful. Have you seen that boy's back?'

'Ach, to hell!' came the reply. 'You don't know these people, I do. He broke the rules, didn't he? In my book he deserved it.'

'Not that! It was barbaric!' And Moll flung herself round to him, red-faced. 'He's a human being. You wouldn't do it to a dog.'

'Human, did you say?' Zachary chuckled bass laughter. 'You want to remember the way we won this accursed country. It was a shooting gallery. You go hunting? All right, you get yourself a wallaby. And if there weren't no kangaroos around, you got yourself an Aborigine.'

'You are proud of this?'

He eased his body down into the nearest cane chair and slopped whisky into a glass. 'Tell you the truth, I haven't given it a lot o' thought. What's for supper?'

They ate in mutual silence with the white cloth between them.

The next day Moll was in the kitchen cooking a supper of fish caught by Ubara: fine big bass that swam in teeming millions through the Bass Strait between King and Flinders Isles, some finding their way south, past Triabunna, into Storm Bay. And Ubara, rolling overboard from his raft despite the sharks, speared them as they floundered by, holding each victim aloft, treading water in laughing exuberance while the cooler, sunlit day rained diadems of light. And Moll, in her kitchen in Duna, had heard this laughter and, raising the rattan blinds against sun glare, looked seaward, smiling.

Later, Ubara, paddling homeward to Duna's yellow sand-shore, laid each fish upon a stone; and there with his gutting knife had made them ready for table. Placing them upon a rush platter he carried them up to the verandah where Moll was waiting, and laid them at her feet as a savage lays before his gods the fruits of sacrifice.

'For your bowels, Miss Lady.'

'Thank you. For the captain's bowels, also.'

And Ubara had shrugged with the native disregard for objectionable subjects; Aboriginals being expert in the art of the insult without really trying.

Said Zachary, chewing lustily, 'This morning, at the Signal Station, I was received in audience by Sir John Franklin, the governor of the Colony. I thought, it was the Pope.'

'You did not like 'im?' asked Moll.

'On the contrary, he's a charming man.' He gave her a sideways glance. 'Incidentally, he was interested in you.'

'I cannot think why.'

'Paternalism, I suppose. When sea captains become administrators at my great age, and marry, the boss-man is usually interested. He wants to meet you.'

'That could be dangerous.'

Zachary shrugged it away. 'Why? You're over ten thousand miles away from the Chester Assizes. Nobody could possibly confuse Mrs Zachary with Madame Le Roy or even Moll Walbee, thank God.'

'Let us 'ope you are right.'

'Unless, of course, you give them reason.'

'What do you mean by that?'

Zachary pushed away his plate, gulped at his wine, and said with audacious frankness, 'Just what I say. As my wife you're like Caesar's – above suspicion. But if you give them a single instance that engages their interest in you . . . God knows where it'll end.'

Moll said, 'Are you trying to say something?'

He lowered his wine and fixed her with a cold stare. 'All right. You came here for a reason – Richard Carling. I know it, you know it, but link your name with him and you'll end in prison.'

'One word from you, you mean?'

He made a face. 'It sounds brutal, but yes, if you like. You're hostage to fortune.'

The moon was round and full, hanging in the glass of the verandah window; Zachary rose and slid back the door; a cool sea wind entered the room, bringing with it a perfume of spices. Moll said:

'You'd hand me over, you mean?' She followed him out on to the verandah.

'If pushed to it.'

'But you'll wait until I give you a reason, I hope.'

Turning, he faced her. 'I'll give you one now. We've been over a year together, but totally apart. I could snap my fingers and a dozen women would come running. Here we live as strangers.'

'It was our agreement.'

Somewhere out in the banksia foliage a kookaburra laughed; the sound an ironic accompaniment to the situation.

'It is an agreement I want to break, Francesca. Separate rooms! My God! The moment the servants arrive it'll be all over the Colony.'

'I've told you before, there is no need for servants. With Ubara here for the outside work, I can handle the house myself.'

He grunted dismay. 'You know, you women astonish me. Aware that your silk-fringed purse is your major possession, you're always so bloody loathe to part with it, yet it's a commodity that goes ten to the pound around here.'

'If they're that available I suggest you find one.'

Zachary put his big hands upon her shoulders; his sea-bitten face above her, decorated as it was with the bright curls of beard and head, obliterated the stars. He said:

'Now that, me love, is exactly what I've done. Her name is Dilly, a convict charmer I used to hunt before; so unless you and I share the conjugal bed with better grace than now, she'll arrive first thing in the mornin'.'

'If she does, she'll sleep in the henhouse.'

It was cool on the beach beyond the sands of Duna. A shepherding wind was driving billows of white fleece across the breast of a patient sea; sheep most beautiful to watch under the plate-broken moon.

With her hands linked behind her back, Moll wandered, argument and counter-argument competing within her.

The situation here was untenable, she thought: it was all right playing the sacrificial victim, but a reluctance to provide Zachary with nightly enjoyment could lead to a whisper in high places. A mere hint from him that he had been hoodwinked could lead her into the woman's prison at Paramatta, a greater misery than that which she was enduring now. Every woman was supposed to have her price; this, it appeared, was one demanded of her. The answer was to arrange Richard's escape, and her own, as soon as possible.

Returning she walked up the sloping beach to Duna, seeing Zachary as she raised her eyes to the house. Against a gigantic and lovely frame of convolvulus Moll saw him, and mounted the broad steps to the verandah, there to

194

pause as Zachary came out of the shadows. In a brief obscuring of the moon she saw his face in grotesque shadows, an undertaker: now his fine looks gone, his jowls appeared to sag; a man aged; the heavy brows she saw, the visage of an ape. It was not, she thought, the same man she had met eighteen months ago, but one in whom she had awakened the instincts of the primate.

He said, smiling. 'Does lover-girl come tomorrow, or not, then?'

It was a moment of decision; to have another woman in the house could mean the end of everything she had planned.

'No,' she replied. 'One woman at a time in a kitchen, Zach.'

'Come then,' he said, and took her hand.

When the outrage was over and Zachary had gone, Moll lay there in pain, thinking of Richard.

Twenty-five

Petticoat Boy, Timbo Weller (the thief with the contorted jaw) and their comrade, Sole Bungy, all stripped to the waist, laid their weight against the bogie-flat of the Convict Railway, and heaved with the lethargy of men under the lash.

For the past fortnight, with three other convicts, they had been so employed; propelling the railway wagon along its five-mile route between the Norfolk Bay and the Long Bay Stations.

With no draught animals available in the Convict Colony (all labour being dependent upon human strength) Captain O'Hara Booth, the commandant of Port Arthur, devised this convict-hauled railway for the carriage of goods and passengers.

Pulled by relays of convicts, the single wagon ran five journeys a day: this considerably shortened the distance between Port Arthur and Hobart, a fact that had not escaped Moll during her planning for Richard's escape.

So far, however, she had failed even to locate him, but all in good time, thought she. Putting first things first, the priority was to obtain Zachary's confidence, the second was to devise a fool-proof route. Escape from the peninsula was nothing new; many in the past had achieved it. Some, however, had been found drowned on the rocky promontories from Eddystone Point to Southeast Cape . . . while others had ended in the stomachs of the voracious Storm Bay sharks.

Now Moll sat upon the front of the flat wagon with a javelin man (a trustee convict – usually the worst of bullies) sitting before her and another squatting behind, both with their pointed sticks (hence the term 'javelin men') at the ready, when the stick would flash out and goad the hauliers to greater effort.

The six convicts, three hauling in front while three more pushed from behind, grunted and groaned. There were no other sounds but the grating of the iron-shod wheels on the rails and the singing and squawking of a myriad of coloured birds . . . in a hell that should have been a paradise. And while Moll sat in trembling apprehension of the cruelty, the rest of the travellers – eight in all (from local signalling station superintendents to their fat complacent wives) – dozed and juddered under the glow of a raging sun.

Timbo Weller, a Cockney pickpocket whose pitch was once the London East End, was perhaps the most intelligent of the three convicts pulling the wagon in front.

According to Richard Carling, their comrade in Hut Five at Impression Bay (three miles west of Duna), all three were behind the door when brains were handed out.

Petticoat Boy, for instance, had put his trust in a woman, which had landed him, said Richard, in Van Diemen's Land for the term of his natural life; while Sole Bungy, a small-time forger, had broken the rule that while you can outrage the wives of gentry at some cost you must never touch their money . . . fifteen years' hard labour. People of this intelligence, added Richard, deserved all they got.

'Then how about you, Sir Richard bloody Carling?' one of them had said. 'Didn't you put your trust in a woman?'

'Wrong,' replied Richard, 'I fell in love with her, which means that I'm the bigger idiot.'

* * *

Timbo's fame as a pickpocket had already spread among the convict huts, he having been known to relieve a warder of his cell keys, which, for safety, the man kept locked around his waist (it was fifty lashes for the loss of the keys) and then, when the warder was on the verge of a heart attack, return them to him without disarranging his waistcoat.

Indeed, so expert was Timbo in the art of light-fingered theft that he would give to his comrades manifestations of his skill: all present losing their possessions one moment and getting them back the next. John Frost himself, for instance, the leader of the Chartist Rebellion (also in Hut Five) once lost his wedding ring and found it on one of Richard's fingers.

And so, on that day, Timbo, the king of the London slums, found himself, without knowing it, in close proximity with the nimble left hand of the queen of the Paris gutters. But now the wagon slowed on a gradient and all six convicts, including Timbo, heaved and strained to keep it going.

'Come on, come on! Put your backs into it!' bawled the front javelin man, and raised his pointed stick for a jab at the nearest man.

'Damn pig! How dare you?' cried Moll, now upon her feet.

And Timbo, looking over his skinny shoulder with frightened eyes, saw a vision of beauty he had not seen earlier: a woman of bright fair curls shouting with fury, one who wore upon her breast a silver brooch.

Now Timbo wondered where he had seen this woman before; despite his attempts, he could not place her. But then Petticoat Boy, an expert in womanhood, whispered into his ear:

'You know who she is, don't ye? She's the piece we saw coming aboard the *Lady Juliana* when we was berthed in Falmouth.'

'Gawd, so it is!' whispered Timbo.

It was a long time since Timbo had been in the company of such gentility; and longer since he had seen an emblem made so available upon such an enticing breast: the temptation that assailed him now was one borne of a career of theft. And Petticoat Boy, his mate, seeing Timbo's backward glances at Moll (who was now sitting in demure and defenceless loveliness) whispered as they heaved together on the ropes, 'Don't you bloody dare, Timbo, ye hear me?'

'She's a fine set-up,' whispered Timbo in reply. 'I could lift it wi' me eyes closed . . .'

'What you want it for, anyway?' replied Sole Bungy, who now guessed what was happening. 'If ye got it, you couldn't fence it. Give over.'

Meanwhile Moll, accepting a helping hand as she stepped off the wagon, smiled at the world as the brakes went on at Port Arthur; turned herself sideways to avoid the offensive smell of Timbo, who had managed to impede her progress, lift the brooch and slip it into his trouser pocket, leaving Moll to go on her way.

'Hell's bells, that were neat!' said Sole Bungy, admiringly.

'Let's 'ave a look at it then,' said Petticoat Boy.

'Not 'ere, ye bloody idiot,' answered Timbo. 'It shows you're jist amateurs, don't it? Once you've stacked the loot, lads, ye don't show it ag'in until you're safely back 'ome.'

'I swear by the bones of me ancestors! *Marvellous!*' said Sole.

'Me, too,' added Petticoat. 'I reckon he's a genius – hey up, lads, she's a comin' back . . .!'

And Moll, smiling apologetically, returned to them, saying;

'What a head I 'ave on me! I 'ave forgotten my parasol,' and passing them, retrieved it from the wagon. Opening it, she whirled it gaily about her head, and was off again.

'Jeez,' said Petticoat, 'she do smell as sweet as a nut!'

'I'd rather be in 'er than in the Navy,' said Timbo. 'But I tell ye what, fellas – I'd give a quid to see 'er face when she misses that brooch!'

Few amenities existed in Port Arthur in 1841: a small military barracks, a distant loading wharf, the elegant commandant's residence, its spacious grounds dominated by a steepled church. But – and this was the reason for Moll's visit that day – outside the commandant's administration hut, near the Commissariat Stores, stood a notice board of which she had heard: a board that daily gave the names and location of all Port Arthur's prisoners. She little knew that when she laid down her head to sleep in Cascades, Richard, in Hut Five at Impression Bay, was within three miles of her . . .

Indeed, unknown to either of them, they were, at that very moment, even closer. For while Moll stood looking for Richard's name, he, with his back to her, was working in chains on the loading wharf not a hundred yards away.

Such, said he, when he learned of this later, being the irony of a convict's life. In this world, he added, when one dog is getting the worst of it, all the other dogs start upon him too.

Now the evening sun shone in magical splendour, and Moll, having identified Richard as a prisoner at Impression, found herself wandering aimlessly in the grounds of the commandant's house. She became aware that she was an intruder upon private property when a most handsome man in an immaculate uniform of blue and gold came swiftly towards her.

'Madam?' He had no difficulty in discerning Moll's wedding ring, for his dark eyes were everywhere, tracing every line of her from her white summer hat to her lace overlay coatee of white and silver.

'Yes?' Moll glanced idly about her.

He clicked his heels lightly. 'Captain O'Hara Booth, ma'am, at your service,' and he bowed with gracious charm. The day flooded about them in a benefaction of sun; cooler now, the trees nearby were exultant in a sudden wind.

Rarely had Moll seen so handsome a man; never had Booth met so beautiful a woman. He saw Moll against the roseate light of threatening dusk, with the sun sinking into the distant harbour. And Moll, but for the bulk of his presence, would have seen, had she raised an eye, a troop of chained convicts marching wearily from the loading wharf to the head of the Convict Railway, and one of these prisoners was Richard.

Moll said 'I 'ope I 'ave not been trespassing?'

'If this is trespass, ma'am, I approve of it. Your name, may I ask?'

'I am the wife of Captain Zachary.' Moll curtsied with studied grace, realizing that if ever she required cunning, it was now: this, she knew, was no mere official, but the commandant of Port Arthur, a man answerable only to the governor. And a vicious man withal, one whose name rang in the halls of Europe for sadism. A word in the wrong place here could put her behind bars. Booth said with native Irish charm:

'Women are at a premium here – the right sort, anyway,' and he bent towards Moll. 'And sure to God, will ye tell Captain Zach that he has the congratulations of the entire community upon his choice of a wife?' He added, inquiringly, 'You have come down from Cascades?'

'On the railway.' Moll held her parasol at a jaunty angle.

'To inspect our amenities here?' He sounded droll.

Faintly on a southern wind came the sound of a man screaming; it came and went in quick warm flushes, then died into the silence of song birds and a feathering rush of wings. Captain Booth, Moll noticed, didn't appear to hear this, but added:

'You realize, Mrs Zachary, that it's your husband's intention to cocoon you in Cascades? So far he has turned down every request to meet you.'

The man screamed again. They walked together. The bile rose to Moll's throat and she swallowed it down. Booth said:

'Unfortunately, my wife is away in New Zealand, so I am unable to entertain you properly at home. But I can see to one aspect of ye visit, ma'am – that you return home in greater comfort than coming down in my chaise and pair.'

'Thank you.'

'Meanwhile, will you also accept an invitation to a party aboard the governor's yacht? For our sins we've got a prison commissioner arriving soon from England, and it is necessary to make a good impression upon him. Pledge it now, dear lady, for we're dyin' to entertain you.'

Dying is the word, thought Moll, for the man had screamed again.

Captain Booth bowed to her acceptance, adding, 'Then your husband will receive the invitation in due course.'

Now they had arrived outside the main entrance of his ornate and beautiful dwelling. A shouted command raised a chorus of anxious voices, and within a minute a chaise and pair of fine horses clattered to a stop before them.

'*Merci*, Captain Booth.'

'Madam, this pleasure is mine.' Booth kissed Moll's hand and assisted her into the carriage. 'Until we meet again.' His dark eyes shone with pleasure.

Not if I see you first, thought Moll.

★ ★ ★

The occupants of Hut Five, on the outskirts of the convict station at Impression Bay, laid upon their straw mattresses in the exhaustion of men being worked to death.

They came from the chain gangs who built the roads on the Tasman Peninsula, from the hewers and hauliers in the log-rolling centres, from the working parties employed on wharf-loading where the ships unloaded provisions from a world that cared little about their fate, from the relays of men who heaved on the wagons of the Convict Railway.

Not only the refuse from the slum kitchens of Britain were imprisoned on Van Diemen's Land, but from almost every other country and nationality in the world; the government in Whitehall taking little heed of international protest.

From the revolutions of Ireland came the scallywags and gentle intellectuals; the felon who had missed the noose for murder lay side by side, chained or sleeping, with the peasant farm lad transported for the theft of a bag of turnips. French prisoners of war, the Bagues, and sailors from the ships of Spain, shared with English or Chinese the brutality of warders and javelin men. Here, in Hut Five, for instance, when all returned from their daily labours in the working gangs, ruffians and vagrants squatted on the hut floor and dipped their wooden spoons into a communal cook-pot of rice and skilly, the watered soup which formed the staple diet . . . sharing company with men like John Frost, the leader of the Chartist Rebellion in Britain. This man, and Richard Carling, were lying side by side when Timbo, Petticoat Boy and Sole Bungy entered the hut with noisy banter.

'Have we got some'ut to tell you!' cried Timbo, shaking the end of Richard's mattress, and Richard, still chained (until the hut javelin came later to release his fetters) rose on his pillow.

'Give me three guesses,' said he.

'The piece we saw comin' aboard the *Lady Juliana* in Falmouth, remember?'

'Who?' asked Richard, sitting higher.

'Come on, come on, shiver up ye roes, man – the Captain's bit o'stuff – you said ye knew her . . .'

'I said no such thing.'

'Whether ye did, or not, she's here, Sir Dick, and I've got some'ut to prove it,' Timbo fished vigorously in his pocket.

'He's got three certificates to say he's sane, remember' commented Richard, and settled back on the mattress again.

'But I tell you it's true!' cried Timbo. 'You told us ye gave her a Pelayo brooch? Well, she came down to Port Arthur this mornin' on the railway, and I see'd it on her, didn't I? So I had it off her to show to you,' and he continued to rummage in his pockets.

'What was the colour of her hair?' asked Richard.

'The colour o' gold, me darlin',' said Petticoat Boy. 'I never saw the likes o' that piece in a week o' Sundays.'

'Wrong one,' announced Richard. 'Madame le Roy's hair was black . . . anyway, where's the brooch?'

'I got it here somewhere – I had it didn't I, Petticoat?'

'As clear as me eye, for I saw'd it, comrade.'

'Let's see it then,' said Richard.

And the other occupants gathered in a circle around Richard's bed-space while Timbo, exasperated, fought to find it, turning out his pockets.

Richard said, 'You mean you had it, but you haven't got it now?'

'Someone lifted it orf me!' cried Timbo, now distressed.

Richard said, 'Let's be clear about this. You took a brooch off a woman, you say?'

'As neat as you like. I saw it 'appen,' said Bungy.

'And having stolen it, where did you put it?'

'In me pocket!'

Richard persisted, 'You say you took it off her on the down journey. Was she anywhere near you on the return run?'

'She didn't do the return run.'

'So you didn't see her again after you put the brooch into your pocket?'

'Hell, only for a second or two . . .'

'So, you *did* see her again.'

'Only when she come back for 'er parasol.'

'Her parasol?'

'Aye, she forgot it, see. Left it in the wagon.'

'And she returned to collect it?'

'Oh aye,' said Timbo, 'but that don't mean nothin', do it?'

Richard linked his hands behind his head, sank back upon the mattress, and chuckled at the ceiling.

'It do,' said he, taking Timbo off, and began to laugh, softly at first, then louder; and the others looked askance at him, until Timbo cried, 'All right, I must 'ave dropped it somewhere, but I tell you, it were her – for I never forget a woman.'

'It was her all right,' said Richard.

Twenty-six

Moll, wearing the brooch, waited at the end of the little wharf at Cascades for Zachary to bring the *Sea Witch*, his provisioning sloop, in from the sea.

She was a neat twenty-two footer, three tons weight unladen. Repainted at Zachary's insistence, she was as bright as a new pin. Resplendent in his blue uniform of provisioning administrator, with direct access to Captain Booth, Zachary leaped ashore with all the euphoria of a skipper with a new important command.

'Well, what do you think of her?' He stood back admiringly.

'She is beautiful,' replied Moll and thought: there are tremendous possibilities here! Until this moment I had imagined, in terms of escape, the vagrant life of the bushranger; nomad wanderers of the Forestier region, seeking opportunities of stowing away on something sailing out of Hobart. But this . . . a sea-going boat . . . Now Zachary cried enthusiastically:

'Ain't she as fine a little lady as ever put to sea? She's been provisioning the semaphore garrisons for the past ten years, but she's never been so fit – her timbers copper-nailed, her shiplap recaulked, and now she's debarnacled she's got a fine turn of speed!'

Moll stood watching as Zachary's crew, an evil-looking javelin man in the uniform of a convict, gave her a final covetous look and disappeared below deck. Zachary, taking Moll's arm, led her up the sloping beach to Duna. Moll said:

'Now that the boat is 'ere, I suppose you will be away even more?'

'Not likely. I'm getting rid o' that good-for-nothin' javelin, and teaching you to crew for me.'

'You mean you will take me with you? Even teach me navigation?'

'Why not? It's a safer bet than leaving you here in Duna gettin' fancy ideas. For there's always another fella idling around a pretty woman.' And he flung back his head and sang as they walked:

> When the nights are warm and shiny,
> Then beware of evil men.
> If you're not at home to mind her,
> Then some fancy fop will find her
> Where's your charmin' creature then?

'Unfair! I am in love with you!'

'I should think so,' said Zachary 'So might there be time to give the proof o' that on a bed before ye start the dinner?'

'No! I am starvin'!'

'For I could sink ye twice with me boots on, and again between courses before I set ye up for the night.'

'Dinner,' said Moll, with finality, and pushed him away in gusty laughter as he smothered her with kisses. She, fighting down the loathing that possessed her, thought: this is the man who once wept because of his impotence. If this is the effect I have upon them, I'll have to watch it in future.

Laughing together, arm in arm now, they climbed through the sandy hillocks to the house; and Duna, sparkling white in the dying sunlight, rose like a goddess to meet them. There, on the verandah, Moll's laughter died in Zachary's kisses, and Ubara, the Aborigine, watched furtively, wondering at the stupidity of the white-bellied people. Zachary said, entering the house:

207

'I was with Captain Booth this morning. He tells me he met ye in Port Arthur Wednesday.' And Moll replied:

'Yes, I got bored, and went down on the Convict Railway.'

'Ach, that in itself's a filthy experience! But you'll not be alone in future, I can promise. What did ye think of the handsome fella? And why didn't you mention you met him?'

''andsome, yes – but that's about all.'

Zachary bellowed with laughter, and filling a glass, gulped down whisky like a man parched. 'Didn't ye fall for him? Every other skirt in the peninsula has. And did he mention he was inviting us to the governor's party?'

'Yes. The invitation's on the table.'

'Is there anything else on the bloody table? For I'm hungry enough to eat an Aborigine.'

'Steak and kidney pudding, and a spotted dick afterwards. Your favourites.'

'Dear me!' cried he, and hugged her to him. 'You're a broth of a girl, Francesca. Lead me to it.'

This one, thought Moll, is an enigma. Now that he was at sea again, he appeared revitalized, reborn.

While they were eating, Moll said, 'I still do not understand this provisioning job you are doing.'

In fact she did; but needed time to think. Zachary replied:

'Jesus, I've told ye twice, woman! They've commissioned *Sea Witch* to sail between Cascades and Port Arthur. I pick up stores at the marine department and provision the new signalling stations as they come on stream. From Eaglehawk Neck to the coal mines on the nor'-westerly tip right down south to Port Puer, the Boys' Prison. Everything east of the railway is already provisioned by rail.' He ate greedily, adding:

'Sure, this is a marvellous steak and kidney,' and with his mouth full and pushing more in, snapped at his fork like a dog snapping at flies.

Moll closed her eyes.

After dinner, sitting in a cane chaise longue on the verandah, Moll looked up at the stars, and the moon, an orb in a sky of fleecy clouds, seemed to drip silver light over the earth.

Impression Bay, not three miles distant, was a faint glow pulsating in the darkness. It was amazing that Moll and Richard were now almost within touching distance. Zachary said with mumbling discontent, 'You've gone very quiet . . .'

'I was thinking.'

'About what?'

'The governor's invitation card says it includes a sea trip up to Eaglehawk Neck. Where's that?'

Zachary yawned vacuously, his demeanour depicting a wish for bed, and said, impatiently, 'I mentioned it earlier, the most nor'-easterly point on the peninsula.'

'What makes it so important?'

'Ach don't bother ye head.'

'Tell me, Zach.'

He drained his glass. 'Being a peninsula, Van Diemen's Land is joined to Tasmania by a stretch of land – a strip about two hundred yards long and forty feet wide at its narrowest point. So that strip has to be guarded . . . this is a convict colony.'

'So that it cannot be used as an escape route?'

'You've got it. Therefore, to cut off escape on to the Tasman mainland – and once a convict got there he'd be hard to find – Booth has it protected by dogs.'

'Dogs?'

'Chained dogs – some say mad dogs – about fifty of 'em stationed facing each other. Dogs that are always half starved, howling to get at each other. Try getting past that lot.'

'How terrible!'

'Why so? It's security like this that allows us to sleep, though the chance would be a fine thing.' He yawned again, lugubriously impatient.

Moll said, 'So no convict can escape over Eaglehawk Neck?'

'Nobody's done it to date. Satisfied?'

'No. Why are we being taken to see it?'

'Because it's Sir John Franklin's pride and joy, the *pièce de résistance* of every party he throws. I've been there six bloody times.'

'Perhaps he has a warped sense of duty.'

'Ma'am,' said Zachary 'the same could be said of you. Give a man a break, in the name of God. I'll go and warm the bed.'

Soon, *soon* . . . thought Moll, and smiled up at him. And she heard Richard's voice as if it were from yesterday. '. . . press their perfume unto mine, and forget that every kiss we take and give, leaves us less of life to live . . .'

'*Francesca!*'

Now it was a bellow from the bedroom.

'For Christ's sake come on!'

This, because of what she had done, had also to be endured.

Having watched Zachary slip moorings and take the *Sea Witch* out into the bay, Moll walked barefooted along the Duna sands.

The early morning reflected splintering light; a damp heat told the advent of another glorious day. Old golden mists of dawn barged across the canyons of the sky. Petrified by the threat of heat to come, a million tiny crabs, of varying and brilliant colours, spiked the wavelets about Moll's feet.

210

For here a thousand varieties of sea creatures lived out their lives in primeval seclusion; sea-snails and tiny octopuses, frog-fish, cow-fish and turtle, which Ubara often brought in from the sea (at first praying over them before the gutting). Here went the sea horses, chitons, slugs, stingrays and starfish; these, the deadly enemy of the delicious scallop, were killed on sight by all Tasmanians.

Moll paused opposite Sunset Caves and looked seaward; seeing the white sail of the *Sea Witch* now as a dot on an emblazoned horizon; all was peace and dedicated isolation in a world as yet untainted by Man: loveliness not yet emasculated by the creeping cancer of O'Hara Booth's empire, the onset of a hell on earth. Within a year, said Zachary, the bark huts of convict grief would be constructed here, their long straight lines punctuated by the flogging triangles of a distant queen in an England gone mad.

Standing there, watching the disappearing *Sea Witch* there came a need to Moll that she should cleanse herself of the occupying dreams of Richard's escape. Certainly, if this was to be successfully achieved, it must be planned soon, and with meticulous respect for details, and these now concerned all her wakeful moments.

The sea and its crashing breakers called to her as a relieving purity, so stripping off her clothes, she ran as naked as a sea sprite into its embrace.

Wading up to her waist – forgetting the threat of sharks – she dived and swam along hummocky sea-sands where gleamed ancient coral reefs of glistening mother-o'-pearl. Breaking surface, she sprayed from her hair a myriad diamonds of light, like a child of the sun: and did not see, in this playing with water, a figure emerge from Sunset Caves.

Ubara, the Aborigine, walked slowly down the beach into the tide-swim, and stood like a statue of a primitive man, watching Moll splashing in the sea; and he was naked as her. There was beauty in it – naked man, naked woman: one watching, the other unaware.

At Ubara's feet lay Moll's clothes, also the wig of golden curls. Seeing this, Ubara picked it up and held it up to the sun in a long and consuming wonder; thinking how strange it was that a woman should take off her hair before going to wash in the sea.

Stranger, too, that she should use such a bauble to decorate her head; such ugliness, thought Ubara – she who did not possess the beautiful, woolly hair of the women of his tribe. But then, white people, he had learned, possessed many strange tribal voodoos, unlike his people who were quite uncomplicated. Nothing, for instance, could explain the comic devotions of those who knelt before a bloodstained man nailed to a wooden cross, and eat pieces of bread which they said was his body; drink wine which they said was his blood.

Moll, having finished bathing, came out of the sea and saw Ubara. And seeing him, paused, not because of her nakedness, but because of his; then realized that this meant little to Ubara, either. Did not the women of his clan, like the men, go naked on the earth, she reasoned: on certain occasions only, out of dignity, covering their pubic hair with a leaf or a prickly scallop shell?

And so, ignoring the situation, Moll waded out of the sea and, raising an arm, called in greeting to Ubara, and he called back.

Seeing Moll coming, Ubara danced for her as the cock parakeet dances before its hen, flinging his arms and legs about and crowing harshly; hearing this, Moll wondered what would happen next, for this was a sexual ritual dance.

Ubara for his part, thought how strange it was that this Miss Lady wore no clothes, for the mission women who educated him were always stuffed up with petticoats and drawers, from ears to ankles. This he knew, because he had seen one of them sitting on a well that gurgled water, and it had become clear to him that she was doing her toilet, which was a strange place – on a well from which he had often drawn drinking water for their afternoon tea; this the women of his clan did also, but squatting on the ground. The sight had astonished him, because until then he had not realized that white ladies went to the toilet.

Furthermore, this Miss Lady coming now – the one who decorated her head with golden curls – was unlike the women of Stoney Creek; not so beautiful, of course, because they were black, and she was white, but the wetness of the sea upon her made her body shine so that she appeared like a goddess of the sun. Also, unless he was very much mistaken, she was possessed of all the items necessary to a woman, including breasts with which to feed her children; also the forbidden secret place, in front.

For of this place, the elders had taught him, he must show no interest until he reached puberty. This, considered Ubara, was probably why he had recently been beaten with a whip by Boss Man; because he had stayed out swimming in the bay, his body yearning for the women of his clan on Flinders Island. Yet in his heart Ubara knew that the whiskered elders of his tribe, being long on wisdom but short on erections, doubtless had need of him to procreate children; virile young men being necessary to prevent the tribe from extinction.

At the moment, however, he thought it strange as Moll came and stood before him in laughter (so close that he could have touched her) that his loins did not rise to her as had happened on many occasions during the dreamtime of sleep, when ghostly Aboriginal women came and caressed him. This, Ubara assumed, was probably because she was not of his kind. For the loins of a young hunter do not erect to the nearness of a female turtle, she who lays her

213

eggs in the dunes at dusk: nor do big things rise to the sight of a mother wallaby, she who carries her young in a pouch; or to the smell of a girl *bettong*, or even a lady *potoroo*.

What kind of a hunter would he be, for instance, were he to lust after the clucking of a hen? No, thought Ubara; no indeed. This white one is not for me, nor am I for her; we are of different kind. I have no need of her, neither has she need of me.

'How do you do?' he asked, now giving the greeting he had been taught by the mission.

'I am well, thank you,' replied Moll, and straightened a little as Ubara, seeing cuts and bruises upon her body reached out and touched one which was purpling upon her breast.

'Are they beating you also, Miss Lady?'

'They are not beating me, Ubara. I fell.'

'I am sorry. It must have been a big fall for you to suffer so much. You are crying, Miss Lady?'

'I am not crying, Ubara,' and taking the wig from his hand, Moll left him without a backward glance.

No doubt boss man considers her desirable, thought Ubara, but for my part I cannot think why. Her breasts are too full and her bottom too big. Further, how can a man treat seriously a woman of any colour who carries her hair in her hand? Also, she possesses front teeth – enough to deter the loins of the most unworthy hunter.

Because of all this, Ubara rejected her; yet knew pity that her body had cuts and bruises, as his.

Clearly, the boss man up at Duna had been beating her; he had often heard them quarrelling. Had she, Ubara wondered, also been staying out on the sea too long?

Later, while Moll was lying in her chaise longue, on the verandah, Ubara came to her.

'You are there, Miss Lady?'

The darkness of the banksia around the verandah made massive shapes in flowers and foliage, for convolvulus grew here also; the moon was shy.

'I am here, Ubara,' answered Moll.

'May I come, Miss Lady?'

Rising, Moll beckoned, and Ubara's black face appeared between rails of the verandah, and his eyes, large and startled, rolled in his cheeks; lightly he sprang then, like a young antelope, and landed before Moll on the boards, saying breathlessly:

'Today you spoke with me. You will talk again?'

'I will,' and the boy said:

'Two days before this, boss man brought his big boat, and I saw it. Since I am not able to return to my people on Flinders Island, would not big boss take me there?'

'Big boss does not sail his boat to Flinders.'

'That is so, for dreamtime told me. The spirits said that the boat will only go to Oyster Bay, above Eaglehawk. But if boss man will take me across the sea to the land above the eagle and the hawk, I can go walkabout to Banks Strait, and from there paddle a canoe to Flinders.'

He knelt before Moll's chair now, his hands together, his eyes pleading. 'Miss Lady, my body says I must go to Flinders, you understand? I am happy here with you, but my body longs for Flinders . . .'

'Why so much hurry, Ubara?'

Moll knew the reason, but such was his charm and earnestness that she heard his husky intonation with pleasure: nor did he speak as is related here, but in the manner of the Aborigine. Ubara said:

'You do not know of us, the Stoney Creek people? But many years back the boss governor drew a black line on the land with his stick and sent all my people to Flinders Island, though some did stay in Oyster Cove, and if we did not go, fired guns at us and killed us. My

215

grandfather died, also my father, but my mother still lives on Flinders and she calls to me in dreamtime, to come and fill a wife.'

'What is dreamtime?'

Ubara contemplated this, then said, 'Long ago, many Aborigines lived here in Tasmania in the world of dreaming, and none died, but lived on as spirits, you understand?' His eyes begged. 'So, although we are all dead, we are also alive, being together. For to die is to live and to live is to die – therefore, it is necessary for me to know manhood and take wives and bring forth children for the tribe. Please ask the boss man to take me to Oyster Cove, for there is dingo madness near Eaglehawk.'

'Dingo madness?'

'The dingo is an Aboriginal dog. The white men's dogs on Eaglehawk Neck have bitten them, and given to them the madness. Now they run, these dingoes, in packs across Forestier, and it is dangerous. Better to go by boat to Oyster Cove . . .'

'What is this madness, Ubara?'

'Big boss has a word for it that I do not know. Those who are bitten howl like dogs, and are afraid of water.'

Moll rose, saying, 'I will ask him for you. Go now, Ubara.'

Twenty-seven

Moll, arranging flowers she had picked from the garden, did not notice the *Sea Witch* being moored beneath its rattan canopy down at Duna Wharf. Such was the intensity of her plans for Richard these days, that Zachary had the uncanny ability to appear when she least expected him. Now he entered the kitchen and threw off his sou'wester, clapping his hands with his usual gregarious gusto at the food.

'You are late,' said Moll, glancing at the clock.

'Aye, girl. I took a Roarin' Forty off Maria Island and had to run for shelter, so I hung about until it dropped. I could do with a hand on the fores'il when the weather's thick, ye know. She's a dumb little bitch in a squall.'

'Any time you wish,' answered Moll and took the flowers and vase into the dining room. 'I get bored with doing nothing.'

'Right! Tomorrow we'll go out into the bay and I'll teach you to box a compass.'

'You 'ave got trouble coming my friend! What is a compass?'

'Nothing like the trouble Captain Booth's in!' Zachary filled a tumbler to the rim with whisky and drank in gasps. 'He's got the prison inspectorate comin' out from London.' He settled himself in a cane chair on the verandah and stared with frowning hostility.

'Is he important?'

'Could be – interfering bastard! You try running a penal colony with those sods on your back. Reform, reform

217

– that's all we ever hear from them.' He drank again. 'What's more, he's arrivin' in time for the governor's party.'

Moll said with measured intent, 'Is it not time some questions were asked about this terrible place . . .?'

It instantly raised his temper. 'Is that a fact? It's grandmas like you who stand on the sidelines shouting, "Hey, hey!" every time Booth slaps a convict's wrist . . . If I had my way I'd flog every one – ten a day, on routine. They're the scum o' the earth and deserve all they get, every man jack!'

Moll said with equanimity, 'When I met Captain Booth in Port Arthur, I 'eard a man screaming.'

Zachary rose. 'Ach, balls! You've only got to show 'em the cat and they bawl their heads off. If you'd been alongside the filth as long as me, you'd land 'em fifty without even looking at their charge sheets. I've flogged 'em aboard in batches, the swabs, and I'd do so ag'in,' and Moll answered:

'It plays the role of a paradise, this place, but it is a hell on earth. My heart bleeds for them, men, women, yes and children.'

Zachary, already within a haze of whisky on an empty stomach, drained his glass and shouted, red-faced, 'You've got the bloody gall to stand there lecturing me on the ethics o' crime and punishment? Jesus, woman!' He flourished a big fist before her. 'You damned frogs are all the same – you conveniently forget your Devil's Island and the thousands you butchered during your bloody Revolution.'

'A very different situation, Zachary, and I am not a frog. Liberty, equality, fraternity, and if you put that fist any closer I will 'ave a knife between your ribs.' She started to lay the table.

One moment domestic serenity, next a political scene; it was like that these days – hair and insults flying when

218

Zachary couldn't win the arguments. Six months after they had arrived at Duna, the flaring quarrels came and went with routine regularity – the onset of growing dislike and hostility; Zachary, Moll claimed, always fractious changed his mood as a chameleon changed its colour: he in response called her frigid. And, as the initial kindness in him died, so his lovemaking changed from wooing to an assault.

But now, this immediate passion ended, both sat quietly at the table, Moll eating with comparative delicacy, Zachary with his usual belligerent lust. As an ape feeds, thought Moll; or a pig at swill.

'What is dog madness?' she asked then, to break the silence, and he stared at her with cold dislike, replying:

'A disease that comes with the bite of a rabid dog. There's a bit of it around here at the moment.'

Moll sipped her wine. 'In Cascades?'

'Well, not actually on the peninsula, but a lot up on Forestier, above Eaglehawk.'

'That is what Ubara said.'

Lifting the bottle he refilled his wine glass. 'What's it to him, for God's sake?'

'He just happened to mention it.'

'You'd be wise to keep that young fella at arm's length.'

'I 'ave to speak to someone; it is lonely 'ere.'

He shrugged with his usual surly disregard for her private circumstance. 'What's up with him this time, anyway?'

'He wants to go home, Zach.'

'Three meals a day – what more does he need?'

'His tribe is on Flinders and he is a child no longer. It is necessary that he should return to his people.'

Zachary chuckled evilly. 'Feelin' his feet, is he?'

'It is perfectly natural, is it not?'

He rose, scraping back his chair contemptuously. 'Like the randy old Spaniards – all desires arrive from their

219

balls – don't blame us Spaniards!' He crossed the room unsteadily, glass in hand. 'Next he'll be gettin' ideas about you.'

'Do not be silly, Zach. His mother is on Flinders and he wants to go 'ome, that is all.'

'I bet.'

The moon, a yellow orb after the day of storm, sat on a misted sea; Sirius, thought Moll, watching, was surely making the sign of the Cross? Soon Richard would come. Soon too, if all went as she had planned it – and this business of Ubara was the last problem to be resolved – Zachary would be but a distasteful memory.

'Will you take him, Zach?'

'The Aborigine? Where? Take him where?'

'I've just told you. He wants to go to Flinders . . .'

'Not bloody likely. It's way off my route.'

'Couldn't you drop him off next time you load provisions at St Mary's? He could then make his own way.'

'I could, but I won't.'

Moll said quietly, 'Like the rest of his kind, he was brought here to the mission against his will. We 'ave driven his people north of the black line . . . be generous, Zach. Do this for me . . .?'

It intrigued him, and he leaned towards her, grinning wide.

'You don't need him here?'

'Not any more,' Moll replied automatically, as a woman does when her soul is otherwise engaged, for this was one of the last debts to be paid. She would miss the company of the young and ebullient Ubara . . . but it was the boats she needed most; more than anything in the world at the moment, she needed the *Sea Witch* and its tender. Zachary invaded her secrecy:

'So ye want me to start the little sod on his way to Flinders?' His brow, Moll noticed, was heavily furrowed in the light of the lamp. He moved his big shoulders as one petrified by his strength; a bear feasting.

'Yes.'

He winked at her. 'It'll cost ye, Frenchy.'

'Somehow, I thought it might.'

'One good turn deserves another, don't it? And I've just remembered – the governor's party is landing at St Mary's. I'll fix it that the black fella's aboard with us.' He rose. 'So now, after the bargin' and windin' I've had today, I think I'll take an early night with me lover – how about that?'

'As you wish,' said Moll, and thought: one day, when this lustful pig is off his guard . . . one day when he least expects it, I will bring a knife from the kitchen and fasten it between his shoulder blades. One day, Zachary . . . and she said:

'Coming, my love, coming . . .'

Moll could not sleep because of pain; this, the culmination of Zachary's sexual violence, found her wandering down the empty corridors of Duna. In her nightgown she went accompanied, as are so many women, by that dark maiden of the night called Scald.

Mrs Scald went with her hand in hand; she who laid siege to a million amphitheatres and the gladiatorial combat that some men call love: no time for wooing Lotharios, this one, but companion of the fist and phallus . . . to compound the injury to a woman's dignity by an assault upon her loins with a branding pain.

And so Moll went, in company with a world of sisters . . . Mrs Scald leading the way to toilet; she who gave the blessing of copulation and childbirth to generations of her sex as yet unborn.

Holding herself, moaning a little, Moll swayed along in agony while Zachary, her once impotent lover (but an hour back hell-bent on the ravishing) lay spread-eagled on his bed.

Sitting on the balcony now, rocking herself . . . Moll wept.

It was cool on the balcony of Duna; a little wind kissed Moll's sweating face, and she raised it to the moon and a calling night bird. Nothing stirred. It was as if the hand of God had laid gentleness on the sea; even the wind was perfumed. Then something moved; some indefinable disturbance from the sands below where bloomed the heart berry, golden guinea flower and lilac bells . . . a tiger or copperhead snake, perhaps? A possum or Tasmanian devil which ranged in their thousands over the island . . .?

Silence again, a dark secretive silence. And to Moll's astonishment, the figure of a man emerged from the flowering rock orchid, its yellow blossom spilling over the burned-out patches of an earlier winter.

Moll stared in disbelief, for now the moon painted the intruder with revealing clarity . . . the yellow and black uniform of the time-serving convict. Next moment she raised her hands to her mouth to stifle her cry.

The intruder, unmistakably, was Richard.

The sight of him spurred Moll into activity, and seeing a movement on the balcony, Richard came swiftly out of the foliage surrounding the house; and stood there, looking up.

Now, yards apart when Moll reached the garden, they stared momentarily; he with uncertainty, Moll with disbelief, and their greeting was brief.

'For God's sake!' And Moll dragged him into the cover of the banksia. 'What are you doing here?'

'That's a good one – what are you?'

His usual, laid back demeanour steadied her. Speechless with pleasure, Moll stared up at him, seeing only the whiteness of his face. His hair was black with curls, upon his chin was a stubbled growth of beard; this had already left faint pink scratches upon her cheek . . . scratches which, in the morning, would turn red . . .

The moon showed the face of the man above her: older, much older; the travail of his hardships etching up his features to thirty . . . and then he smiled, and he was Richard. Moll whispered in anguish, staring about her:

'We can't stay here . . .!'

'Why not? Won't your old man like it?'

'Oh, this is madness – do not be ridiculous!'

'I'm being perfectly natural. Back home it was twice a week!'

'My God,' Moll whispered, 'you never change, any of you! Where 'ave you come from – Impression Bay?'

'That's right.'

'How did you get out?'

'Schoolboy stuff – pillows and a blanket. The lads are covering for me.'

'Until when?' she demanded.

'Until the dawn whistle. It isn't a rest camp, you know.'

Gripping his shoulders, Moll shook him. 'I do not know. I do not know anything, except that you are 'ere and you are being a stupid damned Englishman. This is not a game. They will flog you if they find you 'ere, and if Zachary sees us together he will shoot you.'

'Jesus, that's a bit steep. I haven't even met him.'

Moll said levelly, her voice quieter, 'I am in pain. I am in great pain, you 'ear me? Later I will explain, but not now. Now I will tell you only this – so take your hands off me and listen. . . .'

And she drew him deeper into the foliage.

Twenty-eight

Weeping winter, lovely sister to the Van Diemen summer, put on an extra coloured petticoat and tiptoed over the land: cooler winds swept over the mountains, the valleys flourished in hues of golden guinea and gentian; Christmas bells mingled with the state flower, the beautiful blue gum; flying duck orchids and heart berry mated in the silent places of their riotous habitat.

From the dew-sated land strange snares of perfume were flung up, not from the flowers, but from the pure-sweet bones of black ancestors who had inhabited Tasman since the world was ice, a pristine scenting of the wind.

The *Eliza,* under the command of Captain Hurburgh, initially built for transporting the Peninsula's settlers, had recently become the governor's yacht. In this capacity it was host to the impending party; and Moll, enchanting in pink and a white hat, walked on the arm of Zachary up its gangplank to the consternation of upstaged wives and the unbridled admiration of their husbands. At the rail both were greeted by Captain Booth with salute and handshake, and escorted aboard to their stateroom. Ubara followed with their luggage for the weekend stay.

'You,' he was commanded by Captain Hurburgh, 'put those away and then make aft. The bosun knows about you; get in the lifeboat – out of sight, understand?'

'Yes, boss,' and Ubara with an appealing look at Moll, betokened his goodbye.

★ ★ ★

It was a glittering assembly of outstation superintendents, overseers and station commanders; officials from the Boys' Prison at Point Puer, to the senior staff of the Subaltern's House and epauletted officers of Military Security.

Chaplain and deacons chatted amiably with settlement constables, while their cosseted and corseted wives competed for ascendancy's favour.

It was a galaxy of ceremonial colour and distinction. Many were here only for the initial sherry reception, the more important, mainly military, staying for the sail north to St Mary's, the nearest town of importance on a route which, if continued, would have taken the *Eliza* as far north as the Roaring Forties. Now Captain Booth's voice cut through the buzz of animated talk.

'Ladies and gentlemen, may I present a new couple, Captain Zachary, our provisioning administrator, and his wife.' All heads turned to Zachary's bow and Moll's curtsy. 'Many here will remember Zach as captain of the *Lady Juliana*.' He continued, 'one responsible for bringing thousands of unwelcome females to our shores, but who is now safely confined to the conjugal pleasures of Cascades with this delightful example – and who can blame him?'

Laughter at this and a surge of tinkling glass; guffaws from the men and soprano ejaculations behind fluttering fans, for the heat of the crowded saloon was oppressive.

Booth added, 'We now await the arrival of the governor, his lady, and their distinguished guest, the Inspector General of Prisons . . .' and he added with unveiled cynicism, 'Who, as you are aware, is gracing us not only with his presence, but with the intention – if yesterday was an example – of telling us how to run the bloody place.'

'God!' whispered Zachary. 'He doesn't wrap it up!'

'It is too 'ot in 'ere. I am going outside,' and Moll led the way up the companionway steps to the deck above.

★ ★ ★

Here under the dying sun shone the substantial stone buildings and cottages of Port Arthur, the luxurious gardens of the commandant which turned the bestial into the enchanting. Someone had said of it: 'The port who looks like a beautiful woman, but who, at heart, is a whore.'

Even the elegant steeple of the church, reaching skyward in the reddening light, had known the suicide of its builder: down whose aisles shuffled the leg-ironed convicts, many the heroes of their generations . . . standing within sight of the Quiet Cells, Booth's Silent System with its single ticket journey to the nearby asylum.

Moll said, shading her face from the sunset, 'Whatever Booth says – and you, too, Zachary – this place could do with outside inquiries. I am glad the inspector is coming.'

'Here's your chance to tell him so,' came the reply.

Along the cobbled quay where the *Eliza* was moored came the governor's coach and pair, a postilions in front and a footman behind arrayed in their baubles of pomp. Standing aft, with the companionway obliterating her view of the gangplank, Moll commanded the sight of Sir John Franklin and his lady descending.

From the far door of the coach emerged another . . .

Moll's hand went to her throat.

'In the name of the holy saints,' she whispered.

'Francesca, what's wrong?' Zachary now, alternately staring down at her and peering at the coach.

'Oh my God, it *cannot* be!' Moll said softly.

'Jesus woman, what you on about?'

Now Captain Booth was hurrying to the gangplank and Moll shrank back behind the companionway entrance: almost immediately the governor and his party were aboard.

Moll, meanwhile, her face ashen, was staring like a woman petrified. Zachary said, 'Pull ye'self together. Are ye ill, or summat?'

She whispered, clutching him, 'Let's get away. Zachary, for God's sake get me away!'

Realization dawned upon him. 'Do ye know that fella?'

Sweat flooded to Moll's face. 'The inspector general – it is Bosanky!'

'Who?'

'Justice Bosanky, the circuit judge!'

Zachary lowered his voice. 'Christ almighty!'

'There's still time!' said Moll. 'Come on – get ashore!'

'Too late. The gangplank's jammed with people.'

'It's our only chance . . .!'

He smiled down nonchalantly. 'Not a cat in hell's chance, for here they come. And this is your pigeon, remember, not mine. You've landed yourself in this; I'm havin' no part of it.'

Sir John Franklin and Bosanky, having finished shaking hands with departing shore guests, turned indecisively. Moll whispered urgently:

'There is still time, look!'

'Aye look,' came Zachary's reply, 'they're coming over. Face it out, ye hear me? Act normally . . .'

'I can't – Richard is in this, too.'

'And so am I! You've made your bed, you lie on it. I'm in the clear, and that's all that counts with me.'

Nearer they came now, nearer; idly wandering towards them in a group, with Captain Booth leading them.

Zachary said softly, his face wreathing false smiles:

'Don't speak – understand? Whatever he says to you, don't talk . . . the voice . . .' and Booth, closing upon them, cried affably:

'Yes, I agree, Mrs Zachary – it is stiflingly hot downstairs,' and he bowed to them, the essence of grace and elegance. 'Sir John – Captain Zach you already know, of course. May I present to you his wife, Mrs Zachary?'

Moll fighting the weakness of her trembling knees, curtsied to the governor and his wife, her dress outspread, her face low: and rising, looked straight into the blunted features of Justice Bosanky.

Into an expressionless face she looked, seeing nothing but vacuity; the cold eyes she knew so well: not a hint of recognition moved upon his face.

Booth spoke his name and, bowing, he took Moll's gloved hand, and kissed it.

'I am charmed, to be sure, Mrs Zachary,' and straightened, returning Zachary's happy smile of greeting.

'Ah now, sir,' said Booth. 'Although I do not recommend it in this heat, we'll have to go below to meet the others.'

The sweat was cold upon Moll's forehead and she shivered with alarm now; it rose from her legs, slowly enveloping her.

'For Christ's sake get a hold o' yourself,' said Zachary softly. 'He wouldn't recognize you in a month o' Sundays. Do ye think you're the only lay he's got on his conscience?'

'He recognized me all right.'

The *Eliza*'s deck trembled beneath them. The engine revolutions increased; the little white yacht, now under a good head of steam, moved slowly away from the quay. Commands were shouted, ropes splashed. The rowing barge – a tender being towed behind to take guests ashore in shallow waters – took the strain.

'One thing's sure, we've burned our boats,' said Zachary.

Now the *Eliza* left in her wake the gravestones of the Isle of the Dead and turned east for Cape Pillar; a floating palace of light moving on a dusking sea.

'We'd best get below with the rest of 'em,' suggested Zachary.

'That is asking for trouble.'

'It'll come a lot quicker skulking up here.'

Music began from below, growing in volume as, arm

in arm, they descended to the saloon. Here, people were chatting amiably in groups, the men resplendent in evening dress, military scarlet or naval blue, their women beautiful in off-the-shoulder gowns. Remote in a corner a spinet accompanied a violin . . . some plaintive air that reminded Moll of home.

Inwardly consumed with dread she fought for outward calmness, knowing that one as observant as Bosanky would discern the slightest apprehension. Through a clutch of drinking men (as she made polite conversation with a passing acquaintance) Moll saw him clearly. Were his eyes upon her already, she wondered, or was it supposition? Then through a gap of passing bodies, she saw his sudden, riveted attention.

White-coated waiters, preceded by trays, were angling lithely across the crowded floor; the music rose to a higher note.

Zachary suddenly at her elbow, said:

'Watch yourself. He's coming over.'

Disengaging himself from the governor's party, Bosanky, glass in hand, wandered through the guests. Reaching Moll and Zachary, he bowed with old world charm, saying:

'Captain, forgive my presumption and I will forgive yours. Do you realize you're hogging the company of the most beautiful woman in the room?' And Zachary replied assertively:

'Be God, sir, ye'll get your eyes scratched out!'

'Yes, won't I?' Bosanky's bland face smiled into Moll's. 'Presumably, one has to do the Grand Tour in order to capture such loveliness?'

'They breed 'em rare in France, mind,' cried Zachary, and Moll silently cursed him.

'Yes, don't they?' Bosanky sipped his wine. 'From what region, may I ask, Mrs Zachary?' His eyes moved over hers.

'I am from Paris, sir.'

'You met there?'

'On the Seine in springtime.' And she added, 'Spring-time in Paris is a rendezvous of many lovers, *monsieur.*' Moll's heart was thudding against her dress in wild disorder. She said vaguely, '*C'est international!*'

'You have been here long?'

'Nearly two years. We came straight here from Paris,' said Zachary.

'But I understand that you commanded the *Lady Juliana,* Captain . . .'

Zachary emptied his hands with fine nautical grace. 'From Portsmouth, though I caught the filly first, ye understand – after having me pick of a couple o' hundred charmers.'

'Charmers indeed,' said Bosanky facetiously, adding quietly, 'It astonishes me that a woman should pick a convict settlement to begin her married life. If I had any option in the matter, you'd not see me within a thousand miles of this accursed place. It is intolerably hot and its's Australian, which is enough to turn the stomach of all but the least discerning Englishmen . . .' and here he bowed to Moll again. 'Though its disadvantages are outweighed by the company of such ladies . . . of whom, even at my great age, I am very fond!' He smiled. 'An incurable romantic, ma'am, for which I can only apologize. Would it be too great an impertinence, to ask you to take a turn around the deck?' And here he bowed to Zachary with exaggerated pomp. 'Sir, I should perhaps address the request to you, but suffice to say that I am now beyond the charms of women, so your lady will be safe,' and he offered Moll his arm.

There was little to be done about it. Nodding a gracious acceptance, Moll took it, leaving a look of dread at Zachary over her shoulder in the moment before Captain Booth came up.

230

'*Arrah*! What's happening? Watch it, Zachary!' He threw up his hands in mock horror.

'The fella's got her – I've little option!'

'Let's hope so. Women and wine! He's been here scarce an hour, and he's evaporated nigh a bottle o' whisky.'

'You've already lost her, Captain Zach,' said the old Governor, joining them.'

'Och, she's French, Sir John, she can take care of herself,' said Zachary.

The *Eliza,* with the graceful deportment that told her pedigree, glowed like a diadem on the placid sea; her red and green navigation lights wounding the shark-infested waters as she rounded Cape Pillar. With white floods of tiny crustaceans creaming her prow, she left in her foaming wake flocks of harsh-voiced gulls who wailed above her sparkling phosphorescence.

With sounds of the social activity dying behind them, Moll and Bosanky walked arm in arm along the silent deck; Moll's revulsion at his closeness being dominated by a growing dread: one moment wondering, in the desperation of her hopes, at Richard's safety if this man had already recognized her . . . or if, by some miracle, the sight and sounds of her had passed from his tortured mind.

After all, she told herself, Bosanky had grown prematurely old . . . so many of her kind had passed through his hands for punishment; his memory was bound to be impaired . . . Yet now it seemed that he was already guiding her, as one human guides another, to her and Richard's inevitable destruction.

Reaching the stern, Bosanky released her. Momentarily, unspeaking, they leaned against the boat's rail looking at the wake.

Moll saw his face as a ghost of her past; the brows heavily

shadowed, the jowls hanging purpled upon his pin-bone cheeks. And the moonlight played strange tricks with his countenance: his fleshy lips, drawn back over prominent teeth, giving him kinship with the wolf.

'You are cold, Mrs Zachary?'

Moll pulled her satin wrap closer about her shoulders. 'I am not cold, *monsieur* – it is delightful here.'

Bosanky said, 'Then the night is improving for me, *madame*, for this is the first moment I have enjoyed since my arrival. Few civil servants relish the prospect of the role of a prison visitor; least of all a downgrading, even to a high post in the Prison Inspectorate . . . can you hear me above the sea?'

'Yes, sir.'

He gulped at his whisky and put the glass on the rail. 'Our government inspectorate, you see, is a sort of receptacle into which Ministers pour all the ingredients of failure – sick officers, malcontents from the Eastern stations, and the general unwanted riffraff of public service – people with cans on their tails or possessing adverse confidential reports. I am now looked upon as one of these . . . do I bore you?'

'Not in the least.'

Picking up his glass, he held it up to the moon, slanting the whisky. 'Also, I drink too much, as you have probably already noticed . . . the outcome, dear French lady, of a career that ended in absolute and total failure.' And Moll interjected swiftly:

'Would it not be better, perhaps . . .' She looked uncertainly about her, and he added to her words:

'Better to return to the party, were you going to say? Oh, please, *madame*, I beg you to listen. In this life there are so few to whom one can honestly confide.' Bosanky took a long breath, looking away.

'I have a family at home, you know, but nobody to whom a man can confess misfortune . . .' and he touched

Moll's hand. 'My wife is a fool. All such intimacies end, with her, in lame and impotent conclusion. For this is a world, Mrs Zachary, where only success is welcomed; in failure one flounders in a morass of loneliness and perdition . . . I was once a judge, you know.'

Moll closed her eyes. 'I . . . I did not know . . .'

The deck suddenly slanted beneath them; both held the rail.

'Oh yes, Mrs Zachary, I was a judge – a circuit judge, I'll have you know – and with a name feared and respected throughout the north-west of Britain. Indeed, in the Inns of Court the Judiciary considered me to be in the ascendancy. I was destined for high office – a knighthood, a peerage, even. Indeed, with honours conferred upon one who had served his country honourably and well, I might even have been appointed the Lord Chief Justice!'

To escape Bosanky's penetrating gaze, Moll looked at the sky, and was astounded to see the face of Ubara peering down at her from the prow of the aft lifeboat. But the man was speaking again, drawing the bonds of her captivity tighter about her.

'But then, at the apex of my success, came disaster.' Bosanky shrugged with empty resignation. 'A woman, of course – who else? – the root of all catastrophe . . . Overnight, my prospects vanished.'

Moll said, amazed at the serenity of her voice, 'Why are you telling me all this, Mr Bosanky?' And he straightened, drained his glass, flung it overboard, and said:

'By God, if you don't know, you bitch, there's nobody who does. Because you are the incarnate of my presence here!' His voice rose. 'You it was, with your accursed accomplice, who have brought me to this disgrace – debarred from my profession, rejected by my kind!' He began uncontrollably to shake now, and reaching out tried to snatch at her wig, crying, 'Even that betrays you. D'ye think I don't know the colour of your hair? But no man,

233

woman or child escapes Bosanky, and if it is my last act on earth I will see you hang for it – you and your damned Richard Carling. A retrial, both of you, and publicly hanged in this Colony before I leave here, by God!'

Moll was now retreating before him as his aggression forced her along the rail. Tripping over the towrope, she momentarily floundered about, clutching at the rail to save herself falling, and Bosanky, his face convulsed, cried:

'The fates have brought us together, Moll Walbee, or whatever you call yourself now – the fates and natural justice. So go back to the man who owns a slut and tell him that, like you, he can only guess at the moment when the warders will come – yes, for him, too, for he has compounded the felony and is equally guilty. Tomorrow, might it be? The day after we return to port? Or now, perhaps, the moment I lift a finger . . .?'

Moll slipped away from him. 'Do as you like!'

Motionless, they stared at one another in the intensity of their hatred, and the gulls, wheeling above them, seemed to shriek the discord as the engine of the *Eliza* quickened in the eddying tide-race; Moll braced herself to the slant of the deck, and left him.

'*Man overboard! Man overboard!*' The bosun, running aft, cried, 'It's the inspector, sir – I saw him fall . . .'

'Who?'

'Mr Bosanky – I saw him splash in – I was at the stern porthole! It's Mr Bosanky.'

'God almighty!' said Zachary.

Now there was a scurrying rush to the boat's rail; men and women streamed up in panic from the saloon; crew members darted from all directions, carrying life-belts.

'Man overboard!' The cry was taken up in a chorus of shouts:

Captain Booth heard it at the bar downstairs, dropped his glass and raced up the companionway steps; the

234

governor heard it and stood rigidly, his arms around his wife. Captain Hurburgh on the bridge heard it, too, and shouted commands. The *Eliza*'s engines belled and slowed. Racing hand over hand up the mast a sailor curled himself around the ratlines and yelled down:

'Man's fallin' astern, cap'n!' And he peered into the yacht's wake where a head, rapidly receding, bobbed black against the churning foam. 'A hundred yards on starboard,' he cried. 'Get about, sir, get about!'

And Zachary, unmoving, stared accusingly into Moll's face and said above the hubbub:

'Ye *lifted* him! God's blood . . . ye lifted him!'

'I did not lay a finger on 'im'

'Did anyone see you aft together?'

Moll shook her head.

'Did anyone see ye go with him – apart from me?'

She said, 'Nobody. Listen to me! He said he recognized me, that the police would come for us – at any time they would come, he said. But I did not touch 'im, Zachary – I swear to you, I did not touch 'im!'

Now the *Eliza*'s prow swung about; the rowing barge, still tethered behind, was invaded by shouting sailors, their oars waving high as it cast off to join the search. A man's voice wailed above the commotion:

'The rail's open here, ye know . . .!'

'What?' And another:

'As he went by he hit his head on the jolly.'

'The tow rail's open – he must have fell against it!'

Captain Booth came striding aft, Moll and Zachary following him. In a commotion of jabbering voices and commands, somebody slammed the aft rail shut.

'Look sir, he fell through the rail!'

'My God,' said Booth, 'this is going to open a stinking can of worms. Search all night, Captain Hurburgh, then get us back to Port Arthur!'

'He was drinking very heavily, mind you,' said the governor.

And Ubara, still unnoticed in the aft lifeboat listened: then, before men came to lower it, climbed out of it and down on to the deck. Finding Moll, he said:

'We go back now? We do not go to Oyster Cove, Miss Lady?'

'Perhaps, Ubara, I do not know.'

'Now that man is dead, we return to Port Arthur?'

'Later, for heaven's sake, boy, later . . .!' She pushed him impatiently away. Ubara said:

'Now I will never go to Flinders, will I?'

Moll followed him, at first with her eyes; then caught his shoulder, turning him.

'How do you know the man is dead, Ubara?'

'He is dead – the sharks.'

Moll closed her eyes. He said, 'He was going to catch you, even to kill you, he said. You have been good to me. Never again will people harm you.'

Moll stared at him with incredulity; Ubara added:

'But if I had known we would go back to Port Arthur, I would not have killed him now, but later. You are crying, for I have done wrong? I am sorry, Miss Lady.'

Rooted in disbelief, Moll still stared at him.

'Did he see anything?' asked Captain Booth, in passing.

'Nothing,' Moll answered with an effort. 'I have just been questioning him. He was asleep in the lifeboat, where Captain Hurburgh sent him.'

'We'll put this one down to whisky,' said Booth, 'but thank God I'm not the governor,' and he left them.

Twenty-nine

'Whisky,' cried Zachary, a week later, 'has a hundred different powers, but has never learned how to swim,' and he braced his legs to the roll of the *Sea Witch* and tipped up a bottle to his mouth. Moll shouted above the wind:

'Can you swim, Zach?'

'Not a stroke.' He stooped to the tiller of the little sloop and took her expertly into the tack: the south wind caught her, slanting her against the tide.

Moll, kneeling in the thwarts, braced herself against the tugging foresail; the rigging sang; the burgee on the mast-top flapped merrily; loving it, the boat now ran goose-winged and free, wallowing in deep troughs.

'Stand by to go about!' bawled Zachary, and Moll, under his instructions, slackened off the sheet, leaped over to port and took up the strain; the *Sea Witch* swung, her prow storming water, and took the new bearing. Later, under foresail only, with the going quieter, Moll said:

'I thought all sailors could swim.'

Zachary drained the bottle and tossed it overboard. 'Not the sensible ones. Nobody's having me gurgling and splashing, doin' the bloody breaststroke with fifty miles to go. Down deep into Davey Jones's locker like a stone, that's me.'

Moll thought: one push, when he is least expecting it, and the torment would be over . . . a push, a splash . . . another drowning . . .

'What you lookin' at?' Zachary brushed spindrift from his beard.

'Just thinking.'

'Then stop thinkin' and come and sail the thing. After that I'll teach ye how to lay a compass bearing.'

Moll joined him in the stern. 'Lay a bearing?'

'In case you ever got lost out here on your own – steer the right course on a compass bearing, me darlin', and it'll land ye home as straight at the crow flies, to Duna or anywhere else in the world.'

'I would like to learn about the compass,' said Moll.

Within the course of a month, Moll had crewed for Zachary on the *Sea Witch* to Oyster Cove and back. Sailing together, loading and unloading, they had provisioned Bruny Island and as far north-east as Maria, which was forty miles south of Oyster Cove the farthermost outstation of Zachary's provisioning runs.

Oyster Cove!

The name beat in Moll's head; she had been there twice to date.

But, sometimes on Moll's suggestion, when the weather was calm and the sea-run short, Zachary sailed alone, as now, away from Duna on the first day of August (a planned rendezvous date with Richard). Fate had indeed been kind.

'I'll be getting along then,' announced Zachary.

'Hurry, or you'll miss the tide,' said Moll.

'You're a mite anxious to get me away, aren't you? I missed me sailor's farewell last night, an' all.'

'You were too drunk. Make up for it when you come home,' and Moll stood on the wharf beneath the little rattan awning where they kept the *Sea Witch* moored, chained and padlocked to a sea-bolt when not in use, and she watched until the little sloop was a dot on the horizon.

Richard, as planned, with Zachary absent, came at midnight.

★　★　★

He did not come alone, but with another, a man of great size and strength called Mike Flynn; one who stood in the foliage of the banksia while Richard climbed up to the first floor of the house, the way he had come before. Opening the balcony doors, Moll ran into his arms and they fought in whispers, gasps and kisses.

'You have been ill again?'

'Yes, but I am better now.'

'You are sure?'

'I am quite sure.'

And Moll saw through the window the hills of Sorell and beyond them the gentle slopes of Mount Wellington frowning over the sea. In a sky emblazoned by stars she saw this, and in Richard's lovemaking again knew pain; but the pain was as nothing to her amid the joy of his possession.

And so she lay within his arms, and their breathing was as one and there was no sound in the room save the calling of night birds from the sands and the thudding of the breakers. No other sound they heard except the nothingness which only lovers hear.

In this warmth, which was of one giving to the other, Moll touched Richard, renewing his desire, and drew him into her again. Now there was no longer pent breathing but a strange gentleness in the oneness.

The touch of her in the dark stilled Richard in the loving, so that they lay side by side without words: no words estranged them, night and sound obliterated.

How could it be, thought Moll, as she held him, to walk at home in *la belle France* with this man who, for money, I once betrayed? How wonderful it would be to go hand in hand with him down the lanes of Avesnes le Compte, within the calling of the wind!

As the wild bird makes a nest for its young; as the little fishes mate above the high waterfalls . . . how good it would be to make his child, to share with him the light as well as darkness! How beautiful would be the child that I would make for him!

A fire and a cooking-pot is all I ask. To live without plan or design – to eat and sleep with him, make sport in wickedness, go to bed, and church; laugh, weep with him without arrogance or dependence!

Richard said, 'I can hear my heart beating.'

'It is not your heart, it is mine . . .'

Here we lie, she thought, this man and I, within the threat of death! And what is this small ecstasy but the entry of one stupid body into another?

Yet here, God granting, we may make new life . . . Knowing this, remembering it, she knew the scent of flowers within the strength of Richard's kisses . . . the little bells of blue and gold that grew along the lanes of childhood. Oh God, she thought, do not end this pain in me. Do not take away the hurt of my chastisement . . . this expiation of the love that I was offered. Break me in this man's hands if it brings me defilement: of lust or sanctity, I care not which.

And knowing her again in a young man's intrusion, Richard paused, hearing a quick inrush of her breath.

'You are in pain?' he asked.

'I am not.'

'Come now, have I hurt you?'

Moll did not reply; no man in the world, be it Zachary or Richard, she thought, is going to have me as cruelly as this again.

'Do not worry, my darling,' and she lay as in a fraud of death, eyes clenched.

The man called Mike Flynn, Richard's companion hiding below in the foliage of the banksia, cocked an eye up at the balcony window, and called, 'By all the saints, what's happenin' up there?'

'Coming any minute!' A whispered reply.

240

'About time too.'

And, had one been watching, he would have seen being lowered from the balcony on a rope a sack containing the contents of Duna's larder: fresh roo meat, dried fish, tins of beef and mutton, wheaten bread and a cask of goat's milk, and Mike Flynn went back to Impression Bay with a sack of food for his comrades.

Now Moll gave to Richard a suit of civilian clothes she had cut down from Zachary's size; Richard dressed himself in these. Then they knelt together on the balcony, facing each other, and Moll smeared upon Richard's face burned cork, so that his whiteness would not be seen by the soldiers patrolling Forestier: and in this service to him there grew between them a new understanding. For this, to Moll, was the culmination of all she had planned; this hiding of his identity was the essence of their intimacy, now grown from the body to the heart.

'You are risking your life, you realize this?' Richard asked.

'Do not worry, I tell you. I am the cat with nine lives.'

'If Bosanky had not fallen overboard, for instance, you would not be here, but in Paramatta.'

'Then good for him that he fell overboard,' said Moll. 'All is written in the stars, is it not?'

'Not in my book.'

'But it is in mine. Many women believe this; it is a bond that binds us to our lovers. The stars tell the fate of all women.'

'Rubbish – that is gypsy and bangle-earring stuff!'

'No, it is true,' said Moll. 'If it is willed in the stars that we are going to die, nothing can change it.'

'Meanwhile, you are risking your life for me at every moment.'

Moll opened her hands at him. 'Of what use will my life be, if I do not share it with you?' and Richard answered:

'After I am gone they will ask questions. Even if they kill me, what will be your excuse with the *Sea Witch* tender gone and you have stolen the key? Of course they will know my identity, and then yours; they will put two and two together, and know that you helped me escape. They may even accuse you of Bosanky's death, and the punishment for that will be hanging.'

His eyes were good in the moonlight.

Moll said, 'I love you now in the measure of a lover. Perhaps I have loved you all my life, and have not known it. If it means that we will die, then so be it.'

'There is an excellent chance of it.'

'Then let it be one for the other; together, you in my arms, which is the way of true lovers.'

With a finger Richard traced the curve of her breast. In the blackness of his hair Moll saw the greying at his temple. His breathing chastened her, an absolution of his caring; therefore the night was new again in the cherishing, their whispers and kisses. And Richard bared his body to her again in a new loving, and strangely there was for her no pain. Reaching up Moll covered his mouth with kisses.

Ubara, now standing alone beneath a distant tree, watched their empty window and understood; knowing that soon, when he was back with his clan on Flinders, he would take a woman and love her under the moon, as this; two women perhaps; even three.

And when the loving was over and the window lightened, Ubara turned and ran down the beach, knowing that soon Miss Lady and her new man would come.

Outside Sunset Cave, Ubara, breathless, squatted on the sand.

'This,' said Moll to Richard, 'is Ubara,' and the Aborigine rose, bowing.

Moll added, 'Ubara wishes to go to Flinders Island. Further, he is used to the sea, and knows the tracks on Forestier. He will accompany you.'

'You didn't mention him before,' commented Richard.

'In case you would not agree to him accompanying you. Now you have no option. It is sensible; it is safe. The way through the scrub is difficult for whites. I do not think you could find your way alone.'

'The tracks to Oyster Cove are on the back of my hand,' said Ubara.

'He can be trusted?' asked Richard.

'You will never guess how much. Come,' said Moll, and led them into the cave.

Here, in the Sunset Cave neither moon nor sea made entry. Richard and Ubara followed Moll in the darkness until they came to an iron door sealed in the rock face. Feeling with a key, Moll found the lock; the door swung back in noisy rasps. Entering a narrow compartment, she lit the stub of a candle; light glowed, exposing the prow of a rowing boat, one similar to a two-man canoe.

'Good God!' said Richard.

Moll said, 'It is the tender of the *Sea Witch*, Zachary's provisioning canoe. Sometimes it is carried aboard for unloading provisions from shallow water.' Moll lifted it by the prow. 'Look, it is very light.'

She unfolded a little map on the tender's prow, they crouched over it like felons over a bomb.

'This,' said Moll, 'is a map of the Tasman Peninsula. We are 'ere, at Cascades. The Forestier Peninsula is about 'alf a mile away, but to cross the sea there would be madness – Eaglehawk Neck is too close and it is heavily guarded.

'Sharks?' asked Richard, and saw blunted features in the light of the candle. Ubara said:

'Sharks are plenty, boss man, but not so many in the shallows near Eaglehawk.'

'Then we will cross there.'

'You will not,' interjected Moll. 'There, where the estuary is only a hundred yards wide, a man could swim across to Forestier; but in the sea are iron rods and wire that catch him by the legs. The longest way is quicker.'

'Between Woody Island and Norfolk?' asked Ubara.

Richard said, 'Back in the camp they say that nobody on a raft has succeeded in crossing the estuary there.'

Replied Moll, 'But you have a boat – though it means you will 'ave to carry it.'

'I have carried heavier things lately.'

Moll examined his face in the flickering light. Recently, she had known him only as a lover in the night, in moonlight, or in darkness. But now she could see that the forced labour of the chain gangs had stolen his youth. No longer was he the debonair dandy of the highway to whom life and death was an ironic joke. Suffering had brought to his eyes an elemental sadness. His voice raked her back to reality.

'What happens when we get to Forestier?'

'Sink the tender in deep water when you reach shore, first taking out the food I 'ave stored in the prow. If you are seen by the patrols, the semaphore stations will signal, and many soldiers will come out from Woody and Eaglehawk. Ubara knows a cave. Hide in that for a day. After that, travel by night, overland to Oyster Cove.'

'A compass . . .?'

'Ubara is the compass,' and the Aboriginal said:

'I knows the sea also.'

'How far to Oyster?'

Ubara rolled his eyes. 'Thirty mile?'

'And you will be waiting for us at Oyster Cove, Francesca?'

Moll nodded. 'Tomorrow I travel down to Port Arthur on the railway – Zachary is now picking up provisions there from the Commissariat Stores. I am to meet 'im on the quay. At midday tomorrow, we sail the *Sea Witch* north. First stop is Arthur's Peak, to feed the signallers; then we go to Fortesque and Waterfall, to provision the guards. After that we sail to Eaglehawk, where, no doubt, they will tell us of your escape.'

'And after that?'

'Then we sail to Maria Island, look 'ere it is,' and she stabbed a finger at her little map. 'Take this with you. The boat will be moored alongside a wharf, Ubara knows it.'

'And Zachary?' asked Richard. 'How to get rid of him?'

'Zachary will be drinking with the superintendent in his hut on the Maria wharf.'

'So close? That's asking for it!'

'It is not. The safest place is right on top of them. Then, alone, I will take the boat to Oyster Cove, and when you and Ubara come aboard there we sail for Flinders.'

Moll snuffed out the candle and they pulled the canoe out on to the sand; in darkness she shut the door and locked it.

Now they stood together on the foreshore; Moll was shivering. Ubara said:

'It is time to go, Miss Lady, so here is my gift to you,' and he took from his loin cloth a little string of sharks' teeth and put it around Moll's neck, then elbowed Richard in passing, saying:

'You come now, big boss, and I will take you to the home of my people.'

Moll tried to kiss Ubara as they stood in the tide-swim, but he pushed her away.

'God go with you,' she said to Richard, and stood watching until the tender, with both men paddling, was a dot on the moonlit sea.

Then dropping to her knees in the sand, Moll said:

'Holy Mary, Mother of God . . .' and for the second time in months, told her beads.

Thirty

Richard and Ubara (with a short thick club beside him) paddled the tender slowly, awaiting a dulling of the moon; always near midnight the sea mist rolled in from the Forestier Peninsula, lasted but an hour or two, then cleared. Working to the west of Woody Island, it was necessary to clear the signal station without even a crescent moon showing. Already, from the east came the distant barking of the Eaglehawk Neck guard dogs, and as Richard paddled he saw the moonlight shining on the sweat of Ubara's ebony shoulders, which was not with the effort, but was the sweat of fear.

'Woody flags, big boss,' whispered Ubara, and Richard saw through the sea mist the first faint outline of the signalling station which transmitted messages on the flags by day – hilltop to hilltop; by night speaking with the tongues of lanterns – the colours of green and red; green for all clear; red for escape. Now the all-clear message spoke from the dark, said Ubara, and Richard told him to stop talking and paddle.

This was shark water, and Richard knew it. So voracious were the Bass Strait sharks, he had learned, that one, caught and gutted from a bay trawler and thrown back into the sea as offal, swam under the boat and consumed its own entrails. Farther east, near Eaglehawk, they were not so prevalent, but there the under-sea wire made a crossing more hazardous and prisoners caught in the wire were pot-shot targets for delighted redcoats ranging the shore. Now the limp flags of Woody Island were directly above them, and the tide, eddying around the rocky promontory, caught the tender and swirled it easily around the headland. From somewhere above in the blackness a man was singing, his voice bass and pure in places where the wind held sound.

'We wait, big boss?' whispered Ubara, for the canoe was suddenly caught in the glow of the lantern's beam.

'Go on,' commanded Richard, and a few silent strokes left the lantern glow behind.

Now the clouds relented and the crescent moon, manufactured for Turkish harems, stood brittle and cold in an azure sky of brilliant stars. Richard paddled with slow, deft strokes, awaiting the hue and cry from the observation sentry, and the smack of the musket ball between his shoulders, then she lowered her veil, did this coquettish moon, and covered the world in blackness.

Moll in her bed in Duna, tossed and turned in an agony of apprehension, awaiting, with tingling ears, the first distant siren that warned of an escape . . . the first inarticulate cry that would turn into a hullabaloo of discord, command, and action. For escape, the essence of all criminality on the peninsula, was not to be tolerated and recaptured escapees were subjected to public floggings which left them more dead than alive.

And now the accursed moon, though a crescent, beamed over Duna with wilful, evil design, lighting every cranny of its hummocked disorder, filling her room with a baleful light; and the distant breakers surged and spent themselves in thumping speculation. When the clock downstairs struck two a.m. Moll gave up sleep; rose, washed, dressed, then waited in fevered anticipation for time to pass before walking over the sands to the head of the Convict Railway.

Given Lady Luck, Moll reflected, Richard and Ubara

would, by now, be safely on the shore of the Forestier Peninsula.

It was while within sight of the railway platform that she heard the wailing of distant sirens, the signalling of an escape.

God, perhaps, had sent the sea mist, thought Richard, and blanketed this accursed moon.

The waters of the estuary, in the vacuum between tides, lapped gently against the hull of the tender as they paddled it north. Nothing else moved in the ebony blackness; no sounds but the sea and the crying of distant gulls. And then, suddenly about them, the breaking dawn turned blood-red in the lights of the semaphore stations behind them, and faintly sounded a distant siren. The light and sounds quickened them. Now paddling furiously, as men defiant of detection, they raced for the Forestier shore. The prow of the canoe rasped on sand, and Ubara was first out. Crouching, with the boat upon their backs, they ran for cover as the first grey hands of dawn touched the eastern sky.

The convicts hauling the railway wagon were restless; staring about them with frightened eyes as they laid their weight on the ropes; the men in front casting apprehensive glances over their shoulders: at times, on the downhill, the wagon careered, its half-filled load of station officials and school children hanging on with false abandon, for all about them wailed the escape sirens.

They wailed from passing stations, from the roofs of isolated constable huts, from the police stations and wayside working chain gangs who straightened from stone-breaking to see the wagon fly past. Braced on the bogies, front and back, the hauliers whispered agitatedly among themselves, their eyes watching their masters, the javelins, and the pointed sticks.

248

But Moll sat up with a relaxed, almost apathetical surveillance of the scene coming up before her, the Port Arthur harbour with its wharf and Commissariat Stores where the *Sea Witch* was finishing her loading. And still the sirens wailed, an tuneless orchestral accompaniment to the clanging wheels. But one thing she realized: all the time they wailed, Richard was safe; it was when they stopped that she had to worry.

Now she was on the waterfront, and the *Sea Witch* made shape among the cluttered jetsam of the blue-sheen harbour with its white balconied buildings. Zachary rose from amidships. With him, to Moll's surprise, was Captain Booth.

'Good morning, Mrs Zach!' His greeting was gregarious and affable.

'Bonjour, Captain Booth,' Moll replied with an amity she did not feel.

Jumping ashore from the boat, he surveyed her crying, 'You know, Zach, you amaze me! If I kennelled such a filly at home, ye'd ne'er find me using her as ship's ballast, for she looks like a bright spring day! God alive, man, you've a convict to handle such chores!' He took Moll's hand. 'Sure, if you belonged to me you'd do a mite better than with this old sea gypsy!'

'It is the luck of the draw, as you say, Captain Booth. What is all the noise?'

'Have ye not heard the escape sirens before?'

'Never like this.'

Booth said with fine Celtic charm, 'Don't ye bother your pretty head about such things, but just one kindness I'd ask of ye. Will ye make sure you're back here for the inquest on Mr Bosanky in three days' time?'

'An inquest?'

'Mrs Zach, it's nothin'! But since you were the last to be seen with him, your presence has been requested.'

'That's what the captain came to inform me,' added

Zachary tonelessly.

'But I can tell you nothing!' Moll answered, and Booth spread his hands.

'Now isn't that what I told them? But its officialdom, I fear, so will ye be here just the same? Ten o' the clock on Friday morning in my office?' – and he turned to Zachary, who replied:

'On the dot, sir, never fear,' and Booth added:

'You see there's a wee point come up that needs an answer, Mrs Zach. It appears that Mr Bosanky told Captain Hurburgh – in the course o' conversation, ye know – that he could swear he'd met ye before . . .'

Moll felt cold air touch her face. 'But that is ridiculous. I mean . . . I would 'ave known him immediately!'

Booth smiled. 'That's what I told the unofficial inquiry, but the coroner wants a statement.' His tone was now terse.

'Zachary said, 'I hope there's not the slightest inference . . .?'

'That someone gave him a push? Of course not!' Booth patted Moll's arm. 'Just a denial that you knew him, ma'am, and that will be the end of it. The poor old fella was under the bottle, remember?' And with a salute he strode away.

With a racing heart, Moll went aboard the *Sea Witch*.

'It strikes me, they're on to ye,' said Zachary. Naked, but for his shorts, with his bright hair and beard glistening in the sun, he looked like Atlas who had just put down the world; enormous, supportive, yet strangely insubstantial, and he added:

'You're bad news, woman, so if you breathe a word incriminatin' me I'll take me fists to you again, ye hear me? You're on your own, Moll Walbee.'

'I 'ave been on my own ever since I met you, you pig', she said, and she pushed past him into the cabin.

★ ★ ★

250

Having reached Forestier, Richard and Ubara were resting deep within a cave two miles north of Eaglehawk, one of many that stretched inland along the foreshore. There they watched the day brighten over its entrance. Soon, said Ubara, the tide would come in and fill the cave almost to the roof; here would be safety despite the surge of the sea, for they could sit in the boat till the tide receded, and wait for darkness before going on.

'How far to Oyster Cove, you say?' asked Richard.

'Thirty mile, perhaps. I told you.'

'God we're going to have to move!'

'There is time; it is good,' said Ubara. 'Two days running – there will be time.'

The barking of the Eaglehawk guard dogs rose to a new crescendo.

'If they don't winkle us out before. Just listen to that racket!'

'It is the dog patrols.'

'Won't they smell us?'

'The sea will not allow it.'

Ubara, naked but for a loin cloth, showed neither fatigue nor cold. Richard, shivering with the dawn cold, said:

'Won't they see our tracks in the shore?'

'The sea is kind. Already our feet marks are dying.'

'The sea comes in here you say?'

'Nearly up to the roof.'

'Jesus!'

'It is safe – no need to call on Jesus,' said Ubara. 'We sit in the boat to breathe. He calls the sea in, He will take it back. And when it goes home again, then we will travel. Only if things go bad must you call on Jesus.'

Richard could not see his face; only the white roll of his eyes.

'Indeed,' added the lad, 'later we will pray, but not now. Now is the time to sleep. You will pray with me, big boss?'

251

'Any time you like,' said Richard, as the barking of the dogs came closer, and suddenly Ubara sniffed the air and said:

'It is strange. The dogs are outside, yet I can smell them in here.'

'Perhaps they have been here when searching earlier,' suggested Richard.

'That is possible,' and Ubara sniffed the air of the cave again, not seeing the eyes of the dog watching them from a ledge up near the roof; she, a dingo of the swamps of Forestier, having just given birth to a litter, nosed the air of the cave also and snuggled closer about her hour-old pups, for she smelled the danger, too – that of humans.

Apprehension had been upon the dingo from the moment these two enemies had arrived. Until now she had hunted the swamps for carrion, and then, having mated with a chained dog on Eaglehawk neck two miles to the south, she had returned to her lair to give birth. Also, since it was necessary for a milking mother to feed, she would have to descend to the floor of the cave to hunt when the water receded.

There was a faintness in the dingo which she did not understand; a sickness that brought her to the vomit even while her cubs were feeding. Going for the hunt would mean passing the humans down on the floor. The dingo slept, but with one eye open, knowing the sickness of the milk fever, and the mouths of her pups were painful upon her teats. Soon, she thought, she would die; meanwhile, until that happened, it was necessary for her to hunt and make milk, in that order, so she could feed her young.

When the tide began to enter the cave, Richard and Ubara got into the canoe, and it rose, with the rise of the sea, nearly up to the roof.

'Another six inches and we've bloody had it,' observed Richard.

252

'Another six inches and it will go down, and please do not swear, big boss; the mission lady will be displeased.'

'I beg her pardon,' said Richard.

Moll meanwhile, was crewing for Zachary on the *Sea Witch*: he having signed for her cargo provisions for the outstations, and having taken her away from the Port Arthur wharf, now tacked for the open sea.

It was a morning of bright sunlight, the sea crested with foam-topped waves once clear of the harbour; the wind sang merrily in the rigging; the little sloop heeled with spindrift in her sails. Moll was at the wheel while Zachary, below, was hauling provisions top side for the second stop in Fortesque Bay.

As they neared the settlement on a starboard run, the sirens wailed across the sea, greeting them like dying gulls, and the flag semaphore was on full duty. Zachary came aft and stood there with Moll, reading the signals aloud with his eye to a telescope:

'Convict absconded. Impression Bay. Crossing to Forestier believed. Alert all stations: Saltwater River, Sloping Island, Norfolk Bay, Hobart.'

'Impression, eh? That's only just up the road from us!'

Zachary grunted, 'But he doesn't seem to be bound our way, thank God.'

'Hobart?' asked Moll innocently. 'What chance of escape is there from Hobart?'

'Every chance. They stow away on anything.'

'But first they have to cross to Forestier?'

'Aye, if they can't get boats the silly beggars make rafts – from logs, tin cans, anythin' that floats, and propel them along by swimming. Then the sharks come in and take 'em by the legs.'

'How terrible!'

'For the sharks, perhaps. Most of the samples I've seen

wouldn't make a decent meal,' and he suddenly added, 'By the way where's that black fella?'

'Who?'

'You know who I mean. The Aborigine.'

'Back in Duna – where do you think?'

The wind took Moll's hair, whirling it about her head; the wig was a curse at times like this, but she dared not discard it within telescopic sight of land; now she fought it, tying it down beneath her sou'wester hat.

Zachary asked, 'Incidentally, when did you last see the tender to this thing?'

'The tender?' Fixing her hair still, Moll played for time.

'The rowing boat. Come on woman, wake up!'

'Oh, the lifeboat. Not since you last took it out.'

'Then it's still under lock and key in Sunset?'

'Unless you've had it out.'

'There'd be hell to pay if anyone got their hands on it.'

'Steal it from the cave? It's an armour plated door!'

'Where's the keys?'

'On your key ring.' Moll laughed. 'You're jumpy all of a sudden, aren't you?'

'I've only just remembered the bloody thing. Where is the key ring then?'

'In your jacket pocket.'

As in a panic he ran below, and came back holding up the key.

'Thank God for that, too,' said he.

Yes indeed, thought Moll; thank God.

And closed her eyes to a cold wind on her sweating face.

They did not speak more because the little wharf in Fortescue Bay was coming up; two redcoats were waiting on it for the rations.

Zachary shouted, as he flung the mooring ropes:

'Have they got that convict yet?'

One redcoat was covering them with his musket; the other, a man of surly countenance, regarded Zachary with open contempt, replying:

'Not yet.'

'Do they know who he is?'

Moll held her breath.

'Some bastard out of Impression, that's all. I 'ope I gets a turn on the cat when they finds him. We been up since the crack o' dawn.'

'They'll find him all right, they always do,' said Zachary.

With the provisions unloaded there, Zachary took the *Sea Witch* north up the coast of the Peninsula to Waterfall and Tasman's Arch, and provisioned the garrisons there. Then, running before a gusty westerly, they made for Eaglehawk Neck.

Now the sun was setting over the rim of the world, sinking like a ball of liquid fire into distant horizons where, thought Moll, the octopus and manta ray went and sea horses danced . . . in the paradise that the world could be away from this crucifying anxiety.

Reaching Eaglehawk amid the furious howling and yelping of the chained guard dogs, Zachary bawled through cupped hands to the sentry on the wharf.

'Have they got that convict?'

'No.'

'Out of Impression, ain't he?'

'Chain-gang convict, that's all we know.'

The *Sea Witch* moved closer to the wharf; ropes were flung, splashing in the sea.

Zachary looked at the sky before tying up.

'Bad weather comin' up.'

'It's only a blow,' said Moll abstractedly.

'It'll be worse father north, up at Oyster – there you're on the edge of the roaring forties, remember.'

She straightened from the ropes. 'We'll just do Oyster Cove, then a quick run for home.'

Zachary grumbled in his beard. 'It might be wise to do the Oyster Cove rations next week. Give 'em a chance to collect this convict fella . . . anyway, the weather . . .'

Moll laughed aloud. 'Admit it, Zach – bad weather? You've got the English wind up! I will handle the convict. Leave him to me!'

He thumbed his massive chest. 'Me scared o' those weedy beggars? God give me strength!' And he added, 'You talk too much – get below and haul those boxes up!'

Thirty-one

The dingo was hungry.

All that morning the cubs had been feeding, draining her of strength; and while she did not fear for her own survival, it was necessary that her offspring should live to perpetuate future generations of dingoes.

Therefore, in her lair at the top of the cave roof, she glared down at the humans, one black and one white, who obstructed her way to the hunt. And with the coming of the dusk, she rose in the lair and, shivering, stared down at their sleeping forms. Side by side they lay; the white one with a naked leg outflung, among puddles left by the receding tide.

With the cubs nuzzling for her, the dingo pushed them away and, salivating badly, left them and crept down, from rock to rock, to the cave floor. Because her pupils were dilating and there was a sickness in her for the vomit, the dingo saw the humans in waves of nausea. And as she crept up to pass the sleeping men one moved and his outstretched leg barred her way.

Infuriated, the dingo leaped, fastened her teeth in the impeding leg and bit deep. Richard shouted, fought away sleep and struck her with his fist, but the dingo came again, biting at the same wound. And Ubara, a second too late, struck down with his club.

The mother dingo, her skull smashed, died between them.

★ ★ ★

257

Now, at the cave entrance, in the thickening dusk, Ubara examined the wound on the inside of Richard's right thigh.

'It is nothing,' said Richard.

'Of course not,' replied Ubara. 'But because it is nothing we will wash it with sea water; the salt will cleanse it,' and saying this he splashed water from the cave floor on to the wound, which was but three small teeth marks welling a little blood.

'Forget it,' said Richard, 'the poor bitch. See, she's in milk,' and he painted up at the cave roof. 'There must be cubs there.'

Ubara brought out a knife, saying, 'Lie still and I will cut away the bite . . .' and bent to the wound.

'Hold it!' protested Richard. 'We've got miles to walk – *hold it!*'

Ubara paused, the knife suspended. 'The bite may not be clean.'

That's a chance I take. I need this leg.'

'Big boss, I need it also, for you are too big to carry. But if the dingo is dirty, you will soon have much pain.'

'Meanwhile, I've got two legs and I'm sticking to them. Do what you like to me when we get to Oyster Cove.' And they went together into the early dark, leaving the body of the dead dingo stretched out at the cave entrance, and the pups in the cave roof starved.

Now the sea was choppy and excited, as if in greeting to a storm being born. The prevailing westerly on the fortieth parallel blew hard down the Bass Strait and over the island of Flinders, and the breakers rolled in from the Tasman Sea, gathering themselves in great green billows that crashed along the rocky shores of Clarke and Cane Barren, spraying high in foam and thunder. The morning darkened. Cold, smouldering clouds, purple with anger, barged across the caverns of the sky as if in haste to drown the earth.

Zachary looked up and spat over the side of the *Sea Witch*.

'All this for a few rations up at Oyster Cove! We're in for a blow, and you won't like it. But this is what ye wanted, so now you'll bloody get it.'

'One thing's sure, we 'ave left the convict behind!' Moll laughed at his discomfiture.

Yet within the lee of Maria Island, the storm abated; and as if in expiation, the sun came out to warm a happy day; so they anchored and watched the shore patrols of redcoats outlined against the sky. And while Zachary slept on the deck, Moll went below, and for another rare occasion in her life, told her beads, saying:

'Holy Mary, Mother of God, pray for us . . .' In French she said this, it being her mother tongue, keeping the beads secreted. Zachary stirred on the deck above, yawning vulgarly at the sun; and still Moll told her beads in a gentle incantation: hearing this, Zachary, soft-footed, came to the cabin door.

'What the hell is happenin'?'

Surprised by his sudden entry, Moll answered, 'I . . . I was talking to myself.'

'You wasn't, you bitch, you were tellin' the beads. From Naples to Peru I've sailed, and I've heard that racket before.'

Moll said, 'If you want to know, I was praying for my sister.'

'Is that a fact? Your goose is cooked, missus. You'll need prayers right enough when Booth gets his hands on you. The matron of Paramatta sells her best ones to the Hobart brothels. And there's some tough old Toms, Dicks 'an Harrys holed up in those bordellos!'

Moll sat, eyes closed, and continued to tell her beads, and Zachary shouted:

'Ye get the riffraff o' the docks, ye know; the drunks and the bobtails, from the taverns o' the clod-hoppers to the pot-wallopers outta the gaols. Beggars, bushrangers and beachcombers – all wi' a bob in their hands queuing up for you, me darlin!' And he tipped a bottle to his mouth and gasped, wiping the top. 'Ye know somethin', Frenchy? – You'll be in great demand, and for the first time in your life you'll earn your keep!'

Moll thought: follow him up on deck; one push and he'd be over. Follow him, follow him . . . one push . . . and fend him away with the boat-hook. Nobody would miss such evil, nobody would know. But the beads were still in her fingers and the Cross was lying silver and gold, in the palm of her hand, glinting in the weak sun. She bowed her head, needing God more than at any moment of her life; needing answers of forgiveness with greater necessity; not for her soul, but to stay alive for Richard.

Frantically now, her mood changed, she wondered at his progress towards Oyster Cove. Ubara would guide him, all would be well because of Ubara. And then the thought struck her that perhaps the black boy had actually been sent to her, to help her to pay this debt to another human. This brought a brief, stimulating relief . . . a scintillating hope suddenly possessing her being. And even as she rose and went to the cabin door, in time to see Zachary staggering drunkenly about the deck with his bottle waving, Moll remembered Ubara, and held the rosary against her face.

And then, remembering that she only ever prayed when she wanted something, her mood changed yet again, and she sank to her knees. It was there that Zachary again confronted her.

'By God,' he said, and flung the empty bottle overboard, 'you'll be on your knees, Frenchy, before I'm done wi' you,' and he hauled her to her feet. 'Stand by the fores'il, we're on our way to Maria!'

And Moll saw a single shaft of sunlight beaming down upon the sea.

Richard and Ubara, at that moment, were into bush country, a mile inland from the sea, and going north as the crow flies.

With Ubara leading, they went in a loping, swaying trot, in a wilderness where everything was excessive – endless plain, mosquitoes, a flat panorama of rough scrub. Stripped to the waist Richard went now, furiously lashing at the pestering flies that followed their bodies in buzzing swarms. On their right lay the storm-tossed vista of the Tasman Sea; behind them, in front of them, embracing them in its arms of utter sterility, lay the bush: Tasmanian devils started up at their approach; lizards, petrified by the heat, clawed at the sun.

Here the deserted savanna grasslands, forest clumps and empty moorlands told their story of an Aboriginal habitation for the past 10,000 years; the low cairns and caves being dotted with stone arrangements, the fires of their lowly civilization before the coming of the murdering White Man.

Here, thought Richard, as he loped along in pursuit of the tireless Ubara, the Tasmanian Aborigines continued to farm their land in ever decreasing acres as it was inexorably stolen from them by the invading Europeans: and prehistoric clans existed for 10,000 years before that, weathered the heat of summers and a glacial cold; time after time, Richard swerved in his run to avoid the remains of their little charcoal fires, tokens of Europe's eternal shame for which forgiveness, Ubara told him, could never be given.

'So now,' said he, 'my people have been driven back to Flinders Island, living out the lives of hunters on the muttonbirds and seals of the Bass Strait; and some of my clan have not yet gone there, but live near Oyster Cove.

It is good that Miss Lady is going to meet us there.'

'It is excellent,' replied Richard, speaking his language of precise mission English.

'And better still that you will come to live with me on Flinders. There my elders will care for you. You will not be harmed.'

'Anywhere away from Van Diemen's Land.'

'You will marry Miss Lady, when you get to Flinders?'

'With her permission.'

'That is good. And perhaps you will not beat her as the white boss used to beat her while she was at Duna?'

Richard raised his sweating face at this. 'He beat her?'

'Many times, for I saw the hurting on her,' and he held up a fist before his face. 'With this he beat her. Perhaps when I marry my wives, I will beat them too, mostly upon the head; but he is not her husband, for I heard them talking.'

'No wife should be beaten,' said Richard, 'except with a stick no thicker that a man's thumb–' "The Rule of Thumb" – that is our law.'

Ubara added, 'Had I stayed at Duna, and she also, and big boss beat her again, I would have killed him. Miss Lady was kind to me. Later, if you beat her, either with a fist or a stick, I will kill you also.'

'It is good to know where one stands.'

Ubara straightened on his haunches and looked at the sky. 'Now the world comes lighter, so we will find another cave, and rest. In darkness tonight, we will go walkabout again, up to Oyster – Ubara, he will guide you.'

'Thank you.'

'Do not thank me. I do it only for Miss Lady.'

During the day five redcoats, searching, came within sight of the new cave they had found: Ubara saw them, and watched; Richard did not see them, for he was sleeping.

★ ★ ★

262

The *Sea Witch* was dipping her nose into westerly breakers, the result of a big sea building up before the roaring
forty winds; but Zachary held her steady on the tack until
they slid up to the loading wharf on Maria Island, some
fifteen miles north of Eaglehawk Garrison, and this before
the fall of darkness.

A door on the wharf opened and a big, white-haired
fellow, the island superintendent (one new to Moll) came
out, his arms wide open to Zachary in greeting.

'An old friend?' asked she.

'Bill Billock,' answered Zachary. 'We sailed as ship-
mates, shared the same roof, sparked the same women,'
and he pushed past her on the deck. 'A friendship women
don't understand. Tonight we will get drunk together.'

'And what of the escaped convict?'

Zachary flung a mooring rope and the superintendent
caught it.

'You have a musket, haven't you? After he's had the best
of you, blow his head off. I'll see you in the mornin'.' And
he leaped ashore, gripped his friend's hand, and followed
him into the garrison hut. A soldier then emerged and
with a pipe cocked up in his mouth, began to patrol the
wharf in idle speculation.

Meanwhile the wind was rising to a fury and the little
sloop, though within the shelter of the cove, rolled and
dipped at its moorings; poor weather in which to sail to
Flinders.

Zachary might have conveniently left her, but this
rising storm was now another crucial problem.

Surrounded by what was left of the provisions, she sat
watching the hands of the bulkhead clock.

Sitting there, Moll wondered where Richard and Ubara
were. If good fortune served them, they would soon be
at Oyster Cove, she thought – some twenty miles to the
north. And to achieve the rendezvous with them, she

would have to sail the sloop single-handed. Then, after picking them up, sail onward north to Flinders Island. But then, she acknowledged gratefully, she would have the assistance of Ubara, who knew of the sea.

Meanwhile, in lulls of the wind and the thundering of the sea behind her, she could hear the siren wailing faintly from Eaglehawk: signal lights were playing their indecipherable messages on the porthole glass.

Now, on deck again, Moll slackened off the fore and aft mooring ropes, ready for a quick shove-off into the darkness the moment danger threatened. The redcoat momentarily stared at her as he patrolled the wharf.

Darkness fell suddenly, like the spread of a witch's cape. The hands of the bulkhead clock glistened dull gold in the light of the cabin lamp. Faintly Moll heard sounds of carousing coming from the wharf hut; bawdy sailor's songs sullied the night. Rising, she pored over the chart table, found Oyster Cove . . . and traced the route to it with a finger. Yes, it was a twenty-mile run from here, and the trick was so to judge it that she got there when Richard and Ubara arrived at midnight. In this sea, she reflected, it would take longer, so best to leave now . . .?

Crouching on deck, Moll watched the sentry, his face averted against the wind, stumble off into the darkness of his beat.

Slipping off the mooring ropes, she raised the foresail; instantly it billowed in the westerly, turning the little craft to face a white-topped sea. In a sudden flash of the moon she saw the ocean, its breakers rising and falling; heard its thunder growing as she ran the sloop before the wind. Within seconds, the loading wharf of Maria Island was far behind her, and she was alone with the sea and the roaring forties.

Thirty-two

Zachary and Billock, the Maria Island superintendent, were finishing their third bottle of whisky when the message arrived.

The signaller entered the wharf hut and put the signal on the desk. In a haze of stupidity, Superintendent Billock read the message aloud:

> Escaped convict identified as Richard Carling of Impression Bay chain gang. Prisoner used tender of Duna's *Sea Witch* to cross channel to Forestier. Captain Zachary and woman now known as Mrs Zachary believed implicated. Arrest both. Impound boat. Stations Eaglehawk and Maria Island now alerted. Acknowledge. Report Captain Booth

Zachary started across the table as the Superintendent lowered the paper.

'The bitch,' whispered Zachary. 'She deserves all she gets.'

Billock rose, sweeping aside the fumes of whisky. 'You know what this means?'

'It means I been took,' said Zachary, and thumbed his face in the meaningless effort of the near dead-drunk. 'The damned bitch!'

And Billock, reaching for a handbell, rang it furiously, shouting to the signaller:

'Acknowledge signal, and add these words: "Captain Zachary here in custody. *Sea Witch* being impounded and woman aboard arrested." Send it quickly!'

265

And still ringing the handbell, he left Zachary and ran out on to the wharf.

But the *Sea Witch* had gone; the loading wharf was empty.

'Holy Mary, Mother o' God,' said Superintendent Billock, and slipped down upon his knees. With an empty bottle of whisky hugged against him he stared out into the sea darkness, shouting, 'Sentry, *sentry!*'

The soldier came running, his musket at the ready, his face a puddle of wetness in the spitting wind. Billock yelled:

'The boat – the provisioning boat, you fool! Where is it?'

'Jesus, she were there a minute back!'

'By heaven, you'll be flogged for this,' cried Billock, and scrambling to his feet, shouted to the assembling soldiers:

'After her, ye hear me? Get to the boats. After her!'

'In this sea?' cried Zachary, coming up. 'Just look at it!'

'Arrest him. Chain him!' Billock's white hair was now standing on end. 'Booth will hang the lot of us if the woman gets away!'

'But she won't get away,' said Zachary, as the soldiers seized him. 'In a sea like that she won't last an hour, and neither will your boats.'

'What then?'

'Signal Eaglehawk garrison, tell them to get horsemen out and ride north for Oyster Cove.'

'Why Oyster Cove?'

'Because that's where she's picking up Carling – I'll lay ten to one on it!'

'There's storm flash floods reported between here and Oyster! God, man she may be sailing south for Hobart, for all we know. And why should I believe you, anyway? According to Booth you're in on this escape!'

'Bill, I swear to you . . .'

'Swear away,' shouted Billock. 'Off to the cells with him – you've done enough damage for one night, my friend.'

'My friend?' asked Zachary, throwing the soldiers off, and Billock smiled, saying:

'Nobody's got a friend when Booth is on the warpath,' and he tossed away the empty bottle. 'Inside with him and chain him, and I'll have him up before the commandant.'

Zachary cried, 'I know nothing of this escape, ye hear me? *Nothing!*'

'Tell that to Captain O'Hara Booth, my lad,' said Billock.

The sea was mountainous north of Maria Island; the gale blowing wave crests into noisy spindrift that lashed Moll's face as she took the *Sea Witch* into a slanting, heaving tack. And the moon, storm-tossed above the sudden tempestuous night, floated in a baleful silence over the wasteful Tasman Sea. Now Moll crouched with the wind of the forties roaring behind her; pursuit by the Maria Island boats would be difficult, so she was safe on that score. But the danger lay in dragoons galloping from Eaglehawk along the coast to the north.

Now the wind rose to a higher note and the mast of the *Sea Witch* swung across a leaden sky. Somewhere out in the bay a light, storm-tossed, was winking and flashing like a beacon of hope, and the little sloop floundered towards it; one moment floating high on wave-crest and spume; next second wallowing down into deep lacy troughs; and the wind was standing on the tails of ten thousand cats, thought Moll, as she fought to stay on an even course, with the land rapidly disappearing behind her.

But – and this Moll knew – to simply run before the wind to escape pursuit was impotent madness; soon, like it or not, she would have to turn north and seek the coast. And so, in a brief lull, she swung the wheel and went about into the teeth of the wind; like an animal trapped, the sloop held quiet in less agitated water, and in this calm Moll strapped the wheel and half furled the mainsail; the craft instantly swung, seeking a tack, and quietened further, heading back to shore. Moll now took her reluctantly into the teeth of the gale. With the starboard deck awash she took her in a mad escapade of wind and falling water: soaked, averting her face from the driving rain, Moll stood square on in the way Zachary had taught her. And the moon, as if in admiration of her seamanship, flooded the sea with silver light.

Shivering, her teeth chattering, and bracing her body to each new deluge of water, Moll lashed herself to the wheel; even finding time to get a compass bearing from the binnacle, and sailed true north on a long, plunging tack up the Tasman coast for Oyster Cove.

Ubara guided Richard along the foreshore when once they got clear of the telescopes of the Eaglehawk garrison: by walking and running with naked feet in the tide-swim, their footprints were instantly washed out and their scent killed to pursuing dogs, these being kept half starved at Eaglehawk Neck for the pursuit of escaping convicts; the gallows taking over after the dogs had finished their rip and claw.

'Soon we rest again,' said Ubara, looking up at the sun, which told of midday.

'About time too,' said Richard, who could not explain his early exhaustion.

The years of chain-gang working, the log felling and hauling had hardened his body to the consistency of teak; and while the food was mainly skilly – a thin, watery soup in which red globules of salted pork floated sickeningly –

the diet sufficed him. But now, most strangely to him, Richard found the pace of Ubara's stride wearisome. Sweat began to run in hot flushes down his naked chest to soak the waistband of his trousers; his breathing became gasps.

So now, in a quiet inlet in the foreshore rocks, he flung himself down gratefully into the hot sand while Ubara, his breathing composed, squatted nearby.

'You are hungry, big boss?'

'No, Ubara.'

'Then we go on, I think.'

'We do not go on. We stay while I take a breather.'

Ubara said, squinting at the sun, 'When we left the dingo cave, I heard the Tasmanian devils.'

'I heard them also.'

'They screamed to say they know of us, and I heard them talking. "One black man and one white man," the devils said. "They have come to kill wallabies and bandicoots and take the food from our mouths." You understand me, big boss?'

'I understand, but do not believe,' said Richard. 'If you can understand what the Tasmanian devils say, you are a magician, not a bloody Aborigine.'

'You call me fool, big boss?'

'No. I am the fool for allowing us to get us into this stupid predicament.'

'Now I do not understand. Your leg hurts?'

Richard pulled down his trousers and the place where the dingo's teeth had bitten was purpled and swollen. Ubara said:

'Did I not tell you? Even now it would be better to cut it.'

'Perhaps, but when we get to Oyster Cove. How far?'

'As the fallow deer runs – six hours.'

'Then we had best get on. Listen!' Richard put up a finger. Ubara shrugged, saying:

'It is the Eaglehawk dogs; their voices sing on the wind.'

'Bloodhounds?'

'Perhaps, but a dog runs only as quickly as the man holding it, and we will run faster.'

'Speak for yourself,' said Richard, and gritted his teeth to the pain of the dingo's bite, and wondered about this, not knowing that she, the dingo, was rabid.

With the dim outline of Maria Island forming in the east, they ran on, splashing in the tide-swill. The foam was cool about their ankles, but did not reach the inside of Richard's thigh where the poison of the dog madness had already begun moving. For whereas this madness takes a week or more to show in the human, the running was quickening its evil. The poison was beginning to burn.

That dusk a storm began to gather on the Tasman Sea; in place of the beauty of sparkling water, there came a satanic darkness, as if the earth itself had begun to shake. And so the earth shook, said Ubara, and the sea splashed and thundered, sending foaming breakers crashing down on to the shore where they ran together. The Aborigine went in long, antelope strides; Richard followed in his tracks, not leaping obstructing boulders as did Ubara, but trotting around them, to save his strength.

The poison of the dingo spread ever more quickly through his veins and, arriving in his head, caused Richard dizziness: and so, because the sickness was in his throat already, Richard stopped in Ubara's tracks; and with the storm crashing water about him, turned slowly on the balls of his feet like a man shot in the head and, face down, fell.

'Big boss!' cried Ubara and, turning, ran back to him.

There was a place of shelter in the beach rocks and into this place Ubara dragged Richard, who was too heavy

270

for him to lift. Ubara pulled down Richard's trousers to expose the bite, which was now a mound of swelling like a purple tangerine on the velvet of the thigh.

First, Ubara made fire by rubbing sticks together, and fed the fire with dry eucalyptus leaves; then, taking his skinning knife from his loin cloth, he first held the blade in the flame, then cooled it in water. Going to Richard, he knelt and cut neatly into the wound. The poison leaped up in a little fountain of blood and puss. Washing the wound with clean spring water cupped in his hands, Ubara then washed clean his own loin cloth and, naked now, tore off a strip. Then Ubara sucked at the wound; sucked out the poison, first from the wound, then from the artery that was poisoned by the wound . . . draining the veins that led to the brain. And Richard, the fever relenting, opened his eyes.

'What the hell's going on?' He struggled upright, but fell back.

'It is necessary,' said Ubara, as he bound Richard's thigh. 'I told you, but you would not listen. The dingo was sick with the dog madness and she has made you ill.'

'That's all I need,' said Richard. 'Thank you, Ubara,' and leaning on the Aborigine's shoulder, stood upright. And Ubara said:

'I do not do these things for you, big boss. I do it for Miss Lady.'

Richard wiped sweat from his face. 'So you keep telling me. It is good that we understand one another. Now we rest, eh?'

'Only until you are strong; then we go on.'

It was a world of scrubland; a lunar landscape of crippled trees and thickets where little creatures walked in moonlight.

Here, in this wilderness of nothingness, wild pigs roamed, preying on the little rat kangaroos: here goes the platypus and the spiny anteater, the echidna, Australia's hedgehog. Rabbits run in droves here; hares snitch the wind; snakes swerve and wriggle – the tiger up to six feet long, and his brother, the smaller copperhead, both with venomous bites. Scorpions crawl beside the jackjumper ant; here the trap-door spider has been known to kill, and his sister, the tarantula can prove more than disagreeable. All of whom, with the exception of their poison sacks, were delectable to Ubara, who fried them on hot stones and ate his fill: for Richard, however, he went back to the shore and found six whelks, some sea snails and a handful of cockles for his supper; these Richard ate raw with the last of Moll's bread.

'You like Aboriginal food?' asked Ubara happily.

'Not a lot.'

'The seafood I got for you – you liked that better?'

'It filled my belly, and I am grateful.'

Ubara began, 'You understand, Big Boss . . .'

'That you did it for Miss Lady, not for me. I take the point.'

'It is true I did it for her, for you mean nothing to me. But now it is dark again. You are ready to go on? Go now, and we will reach Oyster Cove at midnight, where Miss Lady will be waiting for me.'

With Ubara leading they went off again in the early moonlight; Ubara with his long, loping stride; Richard behind him, his splayed feet slipping and sliding in the sand. And as they ran, the wind beat about them in blustering squalls and rain.

As Richard ran, there came from his lips strange sounds now, which were not the sounds of a human running . . . but of those Ubara had often heard before.

Thirty-three

Midnight. The wind had quietened, and the stars, their faces washed clean, glimmered above a threatening sea: a broken saucer of a moon hung wounded and alone in victim silence. Nothing stirred; God's hand had banished the tumult.

Riding on a puff of wind, Moll took the *Sea Witch* straight on to the beach of Oyster Cove, as she had seen Zachary do before. And Richard, leaning heavily on Ubara, came from the shelter of vetch grass, the hair of the sands, and ran in hopping, stumbling strides through the rippling tide.

'*Moll!*'

'*Richard!*'

She threw down the rope ladder to them and they hauled themselves aboard.

'Look!' cried Ubara, and pointed.

On the moonlit skyline a troop of horsemen made shape: momentarily pausing, they suddenly broke formation, turned and galloped in a follow-the-leader down to the sea.

Richard shouted:

'The dragoons out of Eaglehawk. *Come on!*' And as Moll hauled up the mainsail, he leaped to the wheel, while Ubara, jumping overboard again, laid his weight against the bow. The sloop floated, made way seaward, her foresail flapping in moody discontent. Slowly, the distance between boat and shore widened, and little billows of sea mist, like ghosts shepherded by an anxious moon, closed ranks behind them. Then something cracked over the mast and a single musket ball, as if in official protest, whined its way into the mist to plop unseen into distant water.

'Now for Flinders Island,' said Moll, and took the wheel.

But even as she said this, thunder, aloof and threatening, barked and snapped on the rim of the world.

'The storm, he come back?' asked Ubara, and Moll replied:

'If it does, and it's anything like I've been 'aving, we will never reach Flinders.'

'But we must go there, Miss Lady. You promised.' Ubara's white eyes rolled in his face.

'If the wind will let me.'

Richard, tightened the foresheets and joined them at the wheel; peering down as the binnacle, he said, 'The glass is falling,' and he tapped it. 'If the westerly comes again, it'll blow us out to sea.'

'If it does that, we will return,' said Moll, and Ubara added:

'Of course we must go to Flinders, for my people will be waiting. Yesterday, on the walkabout, I did speak to them. To the old man I spoke, the elders . . .'

The sloop was now making good speed north, the wind playing tonic-solfa in her sails.

'Over a distance of two hundred miles, you spoke to your elders?' Richard made a wry face.

Ubara drew himself up. 'This is dreamtime, and white people do not understand. I spoke to the bald elders, I tell you, and they are making ready with a feast for us. The only thing that may stop me going home is the dog madness; this I told them also.'

'The dog madness?' Moll, steadying the wheel, looked up at this.

'Big boss has been bitten.'

'Bitten?'

'It is nothing,' answered Richard, and explained it.

But even before he had finished, the sky darkened; clouds shouldered their way across the dale of the sky; a single vivid lightning flash forked down in strickening brilliance, and thunder crashed and reverberated.

The wind of the roaring forties had returned.

Within moments the sea was a pluming waste of white water. Like a cockleshell the *Sea Witch* spun about and ran before it, goose-winged in billowing sails. And before the night was done and morning came in a sky of dripping gold, the sloop was a hundred miles east of Flinders Island, and Ubara was weeping.

'Now I will never see my people,' said he, and the tears welled and rolled down his black bulging cheeks, filling his tribal scars. 'It is necessary that I take wives, and no wives live here, except for the shark and turtle,' and Moll said in consolation:

'Once we find land we can rest. Then we will try again to go to Flinders,' but Richard, while Ubara was at the wheel, said to her in the cabin:

'Land? What land? There is nothing between us and New Zealand. Twelve hundred miles eastward on the fortieth parallel.'

'You know these waters?'

'No, but I can read a chart,' and he unrolled one and spread it out on the table. 'Look, only Lord Howe Island is up in the north, and that's British – as bad as the place we've come from.'

Moll said, 'Somehow, we've got to get back; if we can sail west again we will strike the Australian mainland.'

'One thing's for sure – Flinders isn't worth having, anyway. We're in this, too, you know, whatever you've promised Ubara. They'd have us in the bag a day after we landed there.'

'It is above the black line, remember . . . Aboriginal country.'

'Be your age! The blacks can't protect us – they can't even protect themselves!'

There was about Richard a sort of haggard petulance, as if he had left his charm in the chain gangs of Impression Bay. Gone were his fine good looks; his hair, once lustrous black and reaching to his shoulders, was now tinged with gray; and his eyes, once so bright, were now shadowed, set deep in his high-boned cheeks, for the sun was pitiless.

This, thought Moll, was one of Britain's modern specimens; the chain gang fugitive who had lost his identity under the whip and was now but the husk of the man she knew.

For him she had risked her life. Perhaps all males began all right, but ended in husks, in the manner of Zachary and Jean Pierre.

At that moment, Richard, as if reading her mind, turned and faced her, and she saw his eyes. They were shining with an unusual light, one she had seen before in the faces of the caged lunatics of the Paris streets whom the populace jeered at and taunted as the carts went by: and then the face before her smiled, and it was Richard again.

He said softly, 'If the wind changes, we'll try to get back to Flinders and drop the lad off; then north, I say – true north, up and along the Australian mainland – for they'll pick us off these local islands like a pair of flies.' Taking Moll into his arms, he kissed her, and she felt the thinness of his body and the trembling in him that was, unknown to her, the onset of his fever.

'This bite. Show me,' said Moll.

'Oh no you don't – it's in a queer old place!' He laughed with boyish suddenness; she thought his mood strange.

'Come on, *come on!*'

He teased her now, kissing her face, her hair; dark hair, for the fair wig had gone with the first run from Maria.

The boat heaved gently on a sullen sea; a burnished sun, the colour of brass, flung its heat about on a light summering wind.

'Ubara says it could lead to madness because the dog was ill.'

'Ubara is a Job's Comforter. True I was poisoned, but now the wound is clean, for he incised it. Some lad, your Ubara – I wouldn't be here but for him. But if it really turns to hydrophobia, I'll be the first to know.'

'Hydrophobia? What is that?'

Richard removed his trousers now. Moll took off the bloodstained bandage and examined the wound; much of the anguish of the flesh had vanished; the incision of the knife looked clean.

'Fear of water,' said Richard.

'What do you mean?'

'What I say. Ubara calls it dog madness, its real name is rabies, or hydrophobia, and once you get it, you're usually a gonna. But whether my dingo was mad or not, I haven't got it, thanks to Ubara. So tie me up again and let's get back to the business in hand – a route to somewhere, before we die in this heat.'

Ubara suddenly appeared in the cabin doorway, saying, expressionlessly, 'I lick the poison out . . . like this, you understand . . .?' And he made sucking noises with his thick lips. 'So big boss will not bark like a dog.'

'Bark like a dog?'

'That's what happens if you catch hydrophobia,' added Richard, 'so if you hear me howling like a dingo, throw me overboard.'

Moll closed her eyes. 'Oh God, how terrible!'

'This,' said Richard, bending over the chart again, 'is what I suggest we do . . .'

★　★　★

On the evening of the third day at sea, with the big westerly relenting (but still driving them eastward) they were aware that they were being escorted.

Although people talked of sharks in the Tasman Sea – the disappearance of Bosanky's body was put down to these – few had actually seen any. Richard said, indicating dorsal fins carving the sea astern:

'Pike whales, those, and harmless; but at dawn this morning I saw three sharks alongside.'

'Is that bad?'

'It could be if you fall overboard,' and Ubara cried, coming up from the prow:

'Look, last night I caught these!' and he held up a string upon which were hooked flounder and cod fish by the gills. 'Also sharks I see plenty, following the boat for a death.'

'You're a happy soul,' said Richard, and took the fish, holding them up to the sun. 'But we do not need these yet, Ubara. With half a ton of provisions aboard, we can eat ourselves silly.'

'But always I catch fish for Miss Lady – these are for her, not you.'

'I see.' Richard fluttered a wink at Moll. 'Meanwhile, you'd do better to make a bowl to catch water next time it rains, for salt fish makes you thirsty. There's scarcely a pint of fresh water left aboard.'

'I will do this,' said Ubara, and left them, and Richard said contemplatively:

'I wouldn't say he exactly loves me.'

'He is only a child,' answered Moll.

'He is not. He is seventeen years old and he's got hair on his chest.'

'Then a man with a child's mind.'

'With that knife he's a man, and don't you forget it!' His mood was again belligerent. 'More, he's got a keen eye for you.'

278

'Do not be ridiculous!'

Richard's eyes moved over her: the shirt and knee-length skirt Moll wore were already stained and torn. Her hair was tousled and blowing about her shoulders; she looked like some sea sprite tossed up from fathomless depths of coral. Take off your clothes, thought he, give you a silver tail and you would become a mermaid; one most beautifully and classically formed.

Her face, he saw, was tanned deep brown by the sun and wind: the rents in her clothes betrayed the light brown of her body, which had come through surf bathing at Duna. And standing there, Moll, as he, knew a wanting that was not desire, but the necessity of communion with another human . . . the need of support in the face of common danger. And even as Richard briefly put his arms about her and held her against him, Moll saw the darting dorsal fins of following sharks; but this, most strangely, did not epitomize her growing apprehension.

Ubara came from the prow with a breadth of canvas and, kneeling, began to arrange this around the tabernacle of the mast to catch rain. And seeing his quick upward glance of disapproval, Moll knew the truth of it: that there was a greater danger here than sharks. Then, Richard, releasing her, held her away, and, with Ubara watching, deliberately reached out and did up the top button of her ragged shirt, whispering:

'Two men and one woman adrift on a boat: one black, one white and one brown. The trouble is, my beauty you are becoming blacker every minute.'

On the fifth day at sea, the westerly blew up again, and despite all efforts to tack into it on a battering, stormy course, the attempt failed, and the blow, prevailing from the west, turned the *Sea Witch* in a welter of rolling breakers; hurling her eastward with the threat to dismast her if she persisted. And when, with nightfall, the conditions relented, Richard led Moll and Ubara into the cabin, and said, stabbing a finger at the chart:

'It is not possible, Ubara. You have seen our attempts to sail against the wind to Flinders.'

'I have seen,' said the Aborigine.

'Now we have only one alternative if we want to stay alive – run before the wind to the first land. Always when at sea, if you persist upon a single course, you strike land. Do you understand?'

'I understand,' said Ubara, weeping.

'Where will we land?' asked Moll.

'New Zealand bars the way eastward. The course is ninety degrees. If we can keep on that course we will come to land.'

'What is New Zealand?' asked Ubara.

'It is a country. I have never been there, neither has Miss Lady but we will live if we reach it; if we do not reach it, we will die.'

Ubara said, 'My tribe is waiting for me on Flinders, also some wives, for I am ready to marry. Will there be wives in the new country?'

'Thousands!' said Richard happily.

'But not of my people?'

'They call themselves Maoris,' said Moll.

'They are black?'

'They are white.'

'Is there no sun there, then?'

'Sun in plenty,' said Richard. 'It is a beautiful land, but better if we can reach it – it is now about nine hundred miles away.'

'But no black wives?'

'Does it matter if a wife is black, or white?' asked Moll, and Ubara, his tears suddenly dry, answered:

'In the dreamtime it mattered greatly, but this is today. Also, I have remembered a woman of our clan who married a whitey, and the children of her belly were the colour of gold,' and he suddenly clapped his hands together to an inner delight adding, 'Perhaps I cannot go to my tribe, but there is no need to be without a wife.' He patted Richard's shoulder in a new companionship. 'One between two is better than no wife at all; even my elders would agree with that,' and he peered at Moll. 'You would be agreeable, Miss Lady?'

Moll caught Richard's swift assenting nod.

'I will give it some thought, Ubara,' said she, and Richard added:

'When we reach New Zealand, of course. It is ridiculous to consider marriage at a time like this; first it is necessary to stay alive.'

'We will all stay alive,' replied Ubara. 'I will pray to the gods. Already they have told me that I will live to see dreamtime.' Then with a gesture of contentment with this agreement, Ubara rose and went up on to the deck, and Richard said:

'Jesus, as if we hadn't enough to contend with!'

Moll said, 'He possesses a knife.'

'I have already tasted it,' said Richard. 'Dear God, we could do without adolescents, wedding bells, and conjugal rights.'

'I can handle him.'

'Let's hope you can, for I don't feel up to it.' Richard passed a hand across his face.

'You feel worse?'

'Of course not. A little dog bite? What do you take me for?' And he glared at Moll with strangely malevolent anger.

On the night of the sixth day on the eastward run, becalmed in night mist, Moll awoke in her bunk. The sloop was plunging and rolling in a blanket of fog; Richard, asleep opposite, was grumbling like a man in an approaching delirium. And above his stuttering gasps

281

came a voice, a faint whisper on the sea face like one from another world:

'*Sea Witch, Sea Witch!* Are you there?'

Rushing up on to deck, Moll saw Ubara about to call a reply, and clapped her hand over his mouth.

'No, Ubara. *No!*'

In her embrace the black stood motionless, and the warmth of her was against him, for the moon was cold. Now the voice came again, fainter still, calling dolefully:

'*Sea Witch, Sea Witch* . . . reply if you
can hear me . . .'

Suddenly Richard appeared beside Moll, his finger up for silence. The voice spoke again, then drifted into silence; the three crouched together amid the slapping of water and creak of rigging, under the obliterated stars.

Richard said later, staring down at the chart:

'God help us. I thought we were at least two hundred miles east of Hobart, where she's stationed . . .'

'The *Eliza*? You're sure it was the *Eliza*?'

'Who else? She can steam while we're becalmed. And if this mist lifts before the wind comes again, she'll find us and tow us back to port. I never dreamed she'd search so far.'

'Clearly we're very important people,' said Moll lightly, and this stilled Richard so that he turned and stared at her in the lamplight; and his eyes, in that eerie light, were shining strangely. He said softly:

'For Christ's sake, don't you take anything seriously? This mad devil here, this stupid voyage – don't you know what will happen if they catch us?' And he gripped her shoulders and shook her violently, 'What kind of woman are you, for God's sake?'

'One who is going to get you to New Zealand; meanwhile you are 'urting, so you are ill,' but Richard

282

did not release her. Ubara, reaching out, pulled his hands away.

'Do not touch her! You understand, big boss?' he said softly. 'Hurt her like that again and Ubara will kill you.'

Moll said, in the quiet, soft-voiced sunset of the ocean, 'Two places only I 'ave loved in this world, only two: but this new world I love best of all, because I am sharing it with you.'

'It is sufficient that we are together,' said Richard.

Moll pulled up her feet and put her arms about her brown legs. 'The first world I loved was Avenses le Compte, the little French village where I was born, before my father took us to Paris . . .'

'Tell me of this place.'

'It was shot with sun, my village; with avenues of Spanish siesta trees, an *estaminet* for the wine-tasters, also a clattering pump where you could drink from your cupped hands pure spring water . . .' Moll signed in pleasurable contemplation.

'When I was four years old I started in the kindergarten in St Joseph's, the village school. Always, men 'ave been after me, and it was the same then. "Francesca le Roy," said one young lover – he was aged six, if I recall – "what is the colour of the drawers you are wearing?" At which I was very shocked, and answered, "please go away, you 'orrid boy."'

Richard laughed, following the fleeting expressions of Moll's face. 'Tell me more!'

'Well it appeared that the practice of those small boys was to bet on the colour of the drawers the new girls were wearing, and, if they did not show them, they would gather at the stile that led to the school gate and lie there, these horrors, while the new girls climbed over it, going home.

'Now this village stile became famous in Avenses le

Compte. To this very day, assignations are made there, marriages proposed, and all because of me . . .'

'Go on, I'll buy it!'

'But so determined was I that nobody would see my drawers, that I took them off before going home.'

'*No*! I don't believe it!'

'It is true. Removing them, I put them in my little school bag, and with all those 'orrible boys lying on their backs waiting to look up my dress, I lifted my petticoat, climbed that stile and sailed home without a backward glance.

'Which put an end to the colour of my drawers, for they lay dumbstruck, their mouths gaping. They'd never seen anything like it before.'

'I well believe it!'

'I tell you, every small boy was discussing the phenomenon . . . and I created a legend. Thereafter if you made an assignation with a lover, the official place to meet was at Francesca's stile.'

Bending, Richard kissed her. Ubara, at the wheel, saw the kiss and narrowed his eyes.

'One day,' said Richard, 'I will meet you there and make love to you. But first, I will lie upon my back at the stile and you will climb over it with the greatest possible dignity.'

'For you, beloved,' answered Moll, 'it would be a pleasure; meanwhile – but do not tell anyone – I am again without my drawers . . .'

'Get rid of Ubara and I will see what can be done about that,' said Richard.

The next day, drifting eastward on a zephyr of a breeze, Moll said:

'After my experiences with Zachary, I think I am going to insist upon a legal marriage before anyone again makes love to me.'

They were lying outstretched on the sun-baked fore-deck, and despite the presence of a watchful Ubara, the sun was very nearly their undoing. Richard answered:

'If you insist upon it, but remember, if you marry me, you will be marrying a pauper.'

'That is not so, my darling,' and Moll went into the cabin, rummaged in a secret place there, and returned with her little bag of jewels. These she emptied out upon the deck.

It was as if the lid of a treasure chest had been opened; the sun blazed light upon their faces.

Richard picked some up, saying, 'Emeralds, rubies, diamonds – a *fortune*. You did better than me when it came to highway robbery.'

'Let's us give a prayer for the one who saved them for us.'

At this Richard looked at her, his expression querulous. 'A compatriot at the Old Three Pigeons?'

'No, somebody better; one honourable and kind.'

'I bet it was a man!'

Moll nodded distantly.

'His name?' said Richard. 'To complete the green of my jealousy, at least you should give him a name.'

'Tom Sprogg,' replied Moll. 'But do not ask more – leave it at that,' and she stared at the sea.

Ubara, again at the wheel, turned his ear to the wind, and listened, and watched.

Thirty-four

Now the world awoke in regal beauty, and the *Sea Witch*, riding the swell, ran briskly before the roaring forties, which blew as the cormorant goes. Over a white-painted, choppy sea she went, with Moll at the wheel, Ubara asleep in a rope coil and Richard in the cabin. Simultaneously, as Ubara relieved her and took the wheel for the morning watch, so the cabin door opened; Richard beckoned, and she joined him.

'Shut the door,' said he.

This man, Moll thought, is but the reflection of the one I knew. His stubbled growth of beard enhanced the pale disfigurement of his face in the onslaught of serious illness: this, a ragged scarecrow of forgotten gaiety. Yet still he owned his elegance and dignity.

He said, 'It would be easy to ignore my situation, but I owe it to you to explain what will happen.'

Richard's eyes, disordered with heightening fever, glowed. Moll sat down; the sloop, suddenly alive, leaped beneath them. She said:

'I know what you are going to tell me.'

'You think you do, but I have seen this thing before,' and he wiped his sweating face. 'When I was a child we went to Brixham. I watched the herring trawlers coming into harbour, and saw one, the smallest there, anchored far out in the bay . . .' He took a deep breath. 'My father, wondering why this was, rowed me out to her. I was six years old, I remember. What I saw that day has stayed with me since.

286

'On the lugger's deck, tied naked to the mast, was a wizened old man, and the crew were throwing buckets of water over him. The boat's captain, seeing us approach, told us to keep away. The old man, said he, had got hydrophobia, which is a disease that brings fear of water, yet sea water, my father learned when we got back ashore, is the only hope of a cure.' He touched Moll's hand. 'Better for you to know what to expect – the howls and the barking . . .'

Moll covered her face.

'Listen,' Richard continued. 'It comes in two kinds, this disease – the *dumb* and the *furia*: I have the latter, I know. Already I am suffering the torture of the sea. . . It will be necessary, when I get worse, to tie me down lest I injure you. If you want me to live, douse me constantly with sea water – make me drink it, if you can. Ubara must help. And one thing more. If the bite upon my leg becomes ulcerated, then you must do as the lugger's crew did to that old man.' He stared at her in dim light. 'You must incise the ulcer and fill the wound with gunpowder – there is plenty of this aboard . . . fill the wound and set light to the powder, and this will cauterize it – my only chance of survival.'

'Oh God, how terrible!'

He said, gripping Moll, 'If I can stand it, so must you,' and he suddenly rose, pacing about. 'To go overboard would be easy, but that is the coward's way; also, Ubara is here and I do not trust him. God knows what will become of you if I leave you alone with the Aborigine . . .' He added, 'Remember, he has a knife.'

'He had a knife, but not now,' said Moll. 'I lifted it.'

'Good. You have it safe?'

'Somewhere where Ubara will not find it,' and Moll rose and wiggled her hips.

Said Richard, 'You can joke at a time like this?' And at this Moll's voice rose in sudden anger:

'Can a woman do otherwise? I am sitting in the middle of the Tasman Sea, and do not know where I am. My man 'as caught the rabies. There is an Aborigine at the wheel who wants to bed me, and men searching the sea to take me back and 'ang me. Is that not the best joke you 'ave 'eard in a month of Sundays, like you damn English say?'

The wind rose again, which it always did with nightfall, and Moll, helped by Ubara, shortened the mainsail and tightened up the jib. And Richard, lying on his back on the roof of the sloop's cabin, with his hands and feet tied, stared up at the timeless stars.

With his arms and legs outstretched like a man prepared for sacrifice, his wrists and ankles were lashed to the roof hand-rails, while Ubara threw buckets of sea water over him to cool his fever. And when the Aborigine tired, he took over the wheel from Moll and she continued the drenching; trailing a canvas bucket on a rope to fill it from the sea, then tipping it over Richard's fevered body.

And when the cooler dusk came, with the sloop bucking precariously, Moll crept out under the pale moon and lay beside Richard to give him her warmth under his blankets, but, with the first warmer fingers of dawn staining the eastern sky, she rose and began again the business of the dousing buckets.

In this manner, with the *Sea Witch* racing eastward in the belly of the wind, or at other times becalmed, the treatment continued; one moment soaked, next moment Richard's body steamed dry.

On the ninth day at sea the rains came.

They came not in pattering comfort, but in tub-washing gushes of water from leaden skies; it rained, but it did not rain; water fell in an unending deluge that beat down upon Moll's near nakedness as she fought to protect

Richard on the cabin roof, And even while she held him, whispering words he did not heed, he cursed her in his madness with filthy epithets, arching and bucking his body in attempt to throw her off. And when exhausted by her efforts, Moll tried to make him drink, he, red-eyed and foaming at the mouth in his terror of water, spat it back into her face . . . She consoled him, not in English, but in her mother tongue; and then began again the lifting and throwing, bucket after bucket through each splintering day, while Ubara, half asleep at the wheel, watched the procession of her agony: the bucket down now, haul it up, lift and pour it over the now apparently lifeless form spread-eagled on the roof.

Moll sank to her knees and held herself, and with Richard's wasting body outstretched before her, looked about her at the glassy waste of the Tasman Sea: suddenly aware, more by instinct than his sudden appearance, of the black legs of Ubara braced on the roof nearby; and raised her face to his: a face, crowned with a mass of crinkled fuzz called hair, that broke into a grin.

'He dies soon, Miss Lady . . .?'

Moll drew her rags closer about her, for Ubara had seen the curve of her breast: clearly the sight was now of interest to him.

He said, 'Do not hide yourself from me, Miss Lady. I saw you before, remember?' And moved red-palmed hands at her, and they shone in the rays of the sun.

'Please, Miss Lady. I cannot wait for dreamtime. Also big boss cannot serve you as a husband.' And he untied the piece of sheet he had been using as a loin-cloth, dropped it at his feet, and stood there smiling at her in an obscene and primitive beauty. 'But look I can now serve you as a husband, for the sun made you red, then golden, then brown; soon you will be the colour of an Aboriginal girl. Therefore, the wish is now upon me to take you as wife.'

As he approached, so Moll retreated, sliding off the roof, until she was pressing against the cabin wall. She heard herself say:

'Do this, Ubara, and you will never be able to return to Flinders.'

'Yes, you are right, Miss Lady. I will never return now; the big wind tells me this. So in the new country we will make children, you and me. Only one wife I will have – for this, I know, is your custom.'

The knife, which Moll had taken from him earlier, was now in the hand behind her back, and clearly he assumed this attitude to be submissive; reaching out, he unbuttoned the neck of her shirt, then unfastened her skirt so that she was as naked as he.

'Please, Ubara . . . not here. Perhaps big boss will see us.'

This was an error, for it added anger to his lust. Moll fought her repugnance. The smell of him was in her nostrils, his hands, now upon her breasts, nauseated her. But the image of Richard's helplessness was before her. She could hear him moving feebly on the cabin roof. And as Ubara's appetite increased and he mistook her resignation for acceptance, she knew that time was not her ally; after he had possessed her, surely he would kill Richard as a rival. But for this, she would have submitted to save Richard's life; but with her knowledge of this new danger came guile. Pushing Ubara away with one hand, she shouted into his face:

'Leave me! Now is not the time! If I do this without the permission of big boss, he will kill me – you, too!' And the effect came instantly.

Ubara leaped on to the cabin roof and, reaching Richard, he attacked him, his hands clutching for a hold.

Moll's reaction was automatic: the knife shot like an arrow and trembled in the Aborigine's chest.

Ubara rose, a man appalled, his eyes rolling. Momentarily, he staggered, staring in Moll's direction, then swung about and fell across the sloop's rail. Feet waving, he disappeared into the sea. Now a brief turmoil of flashing white, entangling limbs, and a blood-stained wake: all in hours, all in seconds.

Gripping the stern rail, Moll stared at a white-foamed, empty sea broken only by a medley of cutting fins, the sharks.

Richard gasped. Returning to him she knelt, lifting him against her. But now the wheel was spinning as the sloop answered to the sea, and she returned to it, slowly hauling the *Sea Witch* back on course.

Standing there, she knew no emotion save that of self-preservation; an urge to be obeyed for one reason only – to save the scarecrow of a man moving feebly on the cabin roof.

Through the succeeding days and nights of the second week at sea, the days were reborn in elegiac beauty.

In a calm of summer wind and cloudless skies, the little sloop carved the waves with shoals of fish curving at her prow, and the sharks and porpoises fed until the sea was crimson.

Then, on the sixteenth day at sea, with a strange and balmy perfume scenting the breeze, a storm, renewed and violent, swept down from the west in a new blast of wind and water. Moll, lying exhausted at the wheel, listened to the rising gale, and above the wind heard an eerie, canine yelping coming from the cabin where Richard, now salivating badly, lay as in a fraud of death.

Earlier, with a last despairing effort she had wiped the froth from his mouth; while howling, he did his best to bite her; and managed to haul him into the starboard bunk, there to tie him so that he could not fall out.

Now, as the *Sea Witch* pitched and wallowed in the new threat, there came from the cabin only silence; it seemed to betoken the arrival of death. Not daring to leave the wheel to go to him, Moll lashed herself to it; drenched she clung on, keeping the sloop's stern on to the spume-crested rollers plundering in twenty feet high from the darkening sea behind her.

With night the storm relented and a pale, opal moon stared mistily down upon the scene: in this lull Moll crawled on hands and knees to the cabin where Richard lay.

First, she lashed his body more securely in the bunk; then, exposing him, she raised the lamp and examined his swollen thigh. Where the dingo had bitten, the flesh was filled with poison; more, the bite had ulcerated, heaping proud, discoloured.

Moll knew that Richard would die if she did not cauterize the wound as he had bidden her.

Unconscious now, his lips protesting feebly, Richard lay still as she bathed the wound. Going to the stores, she found a gunpowder flask and, filling a teaspoon with the powder, trickled it on to the wound; it mounded, standing like a little pyramid of blackness against the stark whiteness of his thigh.

Bent above him now, fighting her growing sickness, Moll struck the tinder box, lit a taper, took a deep breath and applied it to the gunpowder. It flared light and black smoke, and Richard screamed. Flinging himself against the ropes that held him, he screamed and screamed. And Moll, hauling open the cabin door, ran out, slammed it shut and leaned against it while the screams went on behind her; covering her ears, she slid slowly down to the deck and sat there, rocking herself in tears. Suddenly the screaming stopped.

Like the cut of a knife, it stopped, leaving nothing but the sighing of the wind.

Returning to Richard's side, Moll swabbed away the burned powder, and with infinite care dressed the wound and covered him gently with the blankets: bending, she kissed his white face.

'I love you,' she said. 'I love you.'

Preceded by lightning and detonating thunder, the storm returned on the twentieth day, rising to an even higher note. Gone were the soft-footed sunsets of earlier days. In a procession of vagrant fury, the breakers of the forties built up, tossing the boat high one moment, then sucking her down into green-water scoops.

In quickening buffets of the wind the sloop was swept along in boisterous disorder, a turbulence greater than anything Moll had yet experienced. It was if the elements were combining to destroy her in a final rampage: thunderous in majesty under a sky of purple cats' paws, the storm was instantly cyclonic; it inundated everything: water was three feet deep in the cabin, and swilling down the thwarts. The waves were actually scouring the sea bottom, bringing up the shingle of shallowed water, while the wind shrieked accompaniment; like the voices, thought Moll, of reincarnated sailors.

But the little craft was equally defiant. Struggling on, digging her prow into the waves, she shook herself anew to the buffeting. Now scudding to port, now floundering to starboard, she somehow rode the gale. And Moll, pelted at the wheel with stair-rod rain, hung on. With the mainsail furled tight and the jib threatening tatters, she braced herself, staring eastward above the heaving roof of the cabin, always eastward.

The tempest increased. A new body of water, building up from the north, came thundering down to merge in cross-currents, hurling the *Sea Witch* high, deluging her; sucking at her with an undertow that came full tide, spinning her about, tearing away her jib. There was a crack: looking up, Moll saw the mast snap like a match in the storm's fingers, and she crouched against the binnacle as wood, ropes and cleats came crashing down.

Dismasted, the boat momentarily paused on a wave crest as if shocked at the injury, then leaped a cable's length as the wind shifted – to a new blast coming from the south. And the woman beside the wheel, streaming foam, suddenly rose like an avenging spirit. With one hand gripping the wheel and her hair flying, she made a fist and shook it at the sky, shouting in French:

'You are not going to have 'im! You 'ear me? You are not going to have 'im!'

The wind snatched at her words, obliterating them; most strangely then, as if listening, the tumult momentarily abated, and there beamed down upon the storm-tossed ocean a light of singular beauty, joining a galaxy of light coming up from the east. Seeing it Moll felt the *Sea Witch* buck high beneath her, sending her reeling along the deck; there to crash headlong against the companionway, and go tumbling down its steps. And the sloop, spinning madly, was lifted up and channelled through an outcrop of foreshore rocks: to come crashing down in splintering wood into the lacy tide-swill of a foreign shore. While all about her, dredged up from the ocean's depths by the storm lay tumbled horse skulls, the mares and stallions drowned in an ancient time; white-nosed, hollow-eyed, indestructible.

Moll opened her eyes to the dawn's redness.

Aware of gentle wave–lap, she lay face down on the hot sand in a vacuum of returning awareness. Trickling water, she heard, the ear always being the first to serve. Then, above a gentle pattering about her, her eyes focused in her returning consciousness on the white breast of an inquiring gull . . . his yellow feet moved before her, a ghost of white and yellow.

294

When the vision opened its beak and cried stridently, Moll moved a hand out for the bird. Instantly it sprang aloft and beat about her in frightening wings and shrieks. Hauling herself up, screwing up her face to the aches of her racked body, Moll stared about her.

'Richard . . .?'

The seagull had gone: nothing now moved in this new world of heat and silence. The yellow sands, the promontory of rocks jutting up about her; and beyond it the glittering Tasman Sea.

'*Richard!*'

Up upon her knees now, in growing agitation Moll rose, swaying upon splayed feet, her clothes, ripped away, were dangling about her in tatters.

And she saw, in growing panic, the smashed hull of the *Sea Witch* lying upright in sand in hundred yards away: the faithful and prim little sloop, now flung like a child's toy high up on the foreshore.

'Richard, *Richard!*'

With awareness came terror that she might have lost him, and Moll began a stumbling, staggering run towards the wreck.

Reaching the splintered debris, she hauled herself up its thwarts, crawling painfully on skinned knees to the cabin door; this, burst open, exposed the water-logged shambles within, a mess of floating receptacles and discarded food. Her movement, as she waded fearfully inside, lapped the flood water almost up to Richard's face. For he lay there as she had left him, still covered with the blankets, still lashed to the bunk.

'*Richard!*'

As if expecting her, he opened his eyes. She kissed his face, his hands, his hair in a fumble of tears. The fever had left him; but as a man in a terminal illness he lay shivering, his eyes sunken, the flesh sagging on his shrunken body; an epitome of death, but *alive*.

To Moll's astonishment he moved a hand, took a strand of her hair and held it before her in his fingers.

'Your hair has gone white, Francesca,' he said.

'It does not matter. Nothing matters,' she said, 'except that you are *free*!'

Book IV

1848–FRANCE

Thirty-five

In the month of October, years after Francesca was wrecked with Richard on New Zealand's shores, Chantelle Le Roy, now aged sixteen, took her school pupils in Avesnes le Compte to see the swallows fly away.

This necessitated climbing what was known locally as Francesca's Stile, a legendary structure standing near the post office kept by Madame Campion, a woman of grace and plenty: plenty when it came to proportions, grace when it came to lovers, said the village gossip.

'Chantelle le Roy!'

Chantelle, about to mount Francesca's Stile with a snake of toddlers waiting behind her, turned to see the postmistress bearing down upon her: panting, flushed with her efforts in whalebone stays, Madame Campion was waving an envelope.

'A letter, *ma chérie!* Look, a letter!', and Chantelle took it.

'You will open it now?' Madame Campion's lost beauty contrived to sully the October morning; autumn having reluctantly died in the arms of winter.

Chantelle answered, 'With your permission, Madame Campion, I will open it later.'

'No doubt it is from your sister Francesca?'

'Probably.'

'The postmark,' said Madame Campion, 'is illegible.'

'All to the good, but I know where she is, *madame.* Now, if you will excuse me . . .?' But a hand restrained Chantelle.

At this, the children, aware of adult hostility, hoped for a violent outcome, it being known that Teacher wasn't as soft as she looked: also Madame, who was not popular, kept a cane on the counter for the chastisement of innocent comrades.

'It could be important that you read it now, Chantelle,' said Madame Campion. 'Your poor Francesca might even have been left a widow.'

'Or a fortune,' added Chantelle, and shaking away the restraining hand, led the children on.

The postmistress's nosiness was not the sole reason for her delaying. She was reliving past incidents. Life, thought she, had bequeathed to the female le Roys both charm and beauty: first the elegant mother, Madame le Roy, who as a serving maid in the count's mansion had been advanced in dignity to the head of his table. Francesca came next, a peacock of beauty but a wicked bare-legged crow of a child within – showing her bottom to the boys at the age of six. And now Chantelle – butter wouldn't melt in her mouth, but *oh là là* – no young woman had the right to own such loveliness. Madame Campion cried after Chantelle and the children:

'One thing's for sure, *mademoiselle* – she writes a lot, your devoted sister, but she's a long time coming to let you share her good fortune. Married to a rich Englishman, is she? I'll believe that when I see 'im.'

Chantelle, pointing out the swallows gathering in the sky, did not answer.

In her school cottage, sitting by the window of her bedroom, which overlooked the lane leading to Francesca's Stile, Chantelle opened the letter and read it.

Hamilton Bank Chambers,
Hamilton, New Zealand.

9th July 1848

My dear Chantelle,

I am a stranger to you, except for Francesca's reference to me in her letters. And I have the sad task to inform you that your beloved sister died at the above address two months ago. I could not tell you this before, because the only address available to me was the Lannes Boulevard in Paris; I didn't know your address in France until I recently discovered Francesca's last letter to you, one unposted, among her private papers. This letter is scarcely decipherable, for she was ill when writing it, so I have copied it out for you, and repeat it here:

My darling Chantelle,

Today is your sixteenth birthday! Imagine it, and consider how old I am becoming!

Forgive me for not writing lately, but for a long time I have not been myself, having contracted an illness during a rather uncomfortable sea voyage, and from which, say these pestilential doctors, my chest has not completely recovered. But be assured that soon Richard and I will come and bring you to the wonderful land we have discovered.

My hair, once black, like yours, is now snow white – can you believe it? Once the gay Francesca (whose activities had to be seen to be believed) I am now one of the local hags. Give me a broom and I'd be up and around the chimneys. Now my lost beauty shall lie in you, my sweet, so we will come to fetch you soon and show you off to the neighbours.

Richard has never looked better. I swear he is more handsome than ever, and still devoted to his poor old Moll, as he calls me; and although many visit us these days, I know that all his friendships are absolutely platonic, bless him. More, he has proved a Midas. Everything he touches turns to gold. We were never short of ready capital, as you know, so we opened our own bank here . . . (trading under another name you will notice). Running a business in the way Richard does is like having a key to the bank of England! Yet always he seeks to make more and more!

And now to my secret surprise. Confined to a wheelchair these past four years, I have taken up writing. And for the *cause célèbre* of your birthday I have composed this poem for you:

> Oh, Sister mine, whose future is my prayer,
> May thou be richly blessed with just of care
> Sufficient to enoble and refine
> The character, the sweetness that is thine.
> May purity and love in thee abide . . .
> Patience and gentleness . . .

Here the poem became indecipherable and Richard continued with his own letter, saying:

At this point, I am afraid, the letter was ended by Francesca's death.

Now, Chantelle, she was much worried about your financial situation, and during her last illness begged me to travel to Avesnes to discover your circumstances.

Therefore I will sail for France in January, when, given fair wind, I should reach you with the coming of spring.

It being necessary, said Francesca, to avoid prying eyes (Avesnes, she told me, is the most dreadful place for gossip) she suggested that our first meeting should

take place at a legendary spot called Francesca's Stile
– oh yes I know all about it! – thus it will not be
necessary for us to wear white carnations.

On my arrival in *pas de Calais* I will write to you
again; meanwhile, my condolences in your grief:
only those who knew and loved your sister suffer
the enormity of the loss.

Meanwhile, be assured of my respect until we
meet.

Your affectionate brother-in-law,
Richard Denning.

PS   The change of name will need little explanation.
When you reply, please use it, and not the name of
Carling . . .

The following April, Chantelle led her school pupils down
the lane to the big field to see the swallows arrive.

Spring was bursting out all over, she told them, and
soon the air would be filled with metallic twittering songs;
soon, too, she said, with the whole world falling in love,
the barns would be alive with chattering nests of mud,
feathers, and white brown-spotted eggs.

In a snake went the children over Francesca's Stile,
and returning with Chantelle at their head, again met
the postmistress.

'Another letter for you, *mademoiselle!*' said Madame
Campion flourishing it.

Chantelle read a second letter from Richard, telling of his
arrival in Europe; he said he would come to Avesnes the
following Saturday and asked if she would book him into
an hotel for the night.

On the day he was due, Chantelle put on her prettiest
spring frock, combed out her dark hair to her waist and tied

it with red ribbon. She put on the only hat she possessed, which was white and summery: this she wore at a jaunty angle. And on her way to meet Richard at Francesca's Stile, she encountered the postmistress yet again.

'They tell me there is handsome gentleman waiting at the stile,' said Madame Campion. 'Could it be that the last letter was from him, and that your Prince Charming has come at last?'

'If I answer that, *madame*,' replied Chantelle, 'you will be as wise as me,' and walked on.

Seeing Richard more clearly as she approached, she stared in disbelief.

Until then, Chantelle had built in her mind an image of an older man: but not only was Francesca's husband still quite young, he was incredibly handsome.

Richard, for his part, saw not the child Chantelle standing there – the little sister of Francesca's dreams – but a child of womanhood, one instantly adorned in beauty. Dressed in an embroidered white bodice was she; a white skirt she wore to her ankles; around her throat was a band of black velvet; she held herself with a fine maturity.

'Mademoiselle le Roy?'

Chantelle graciously inclined her head in assent, replying:

'Sir Richard Carling, I presume – but travelling incognito?'

With a smile, Richard bowed, took the gloved hand before him and raised it to his lips; seeing, in the moment he rose, a nearby assembly of gaping villagers – farmers with their stringy wives, comely daughters and elderly matrons (and Madame Campion was among them) – nudging and elbowing each other in growing expectation, he said:

'We are not alone!' whispered Richard.

'Yes, I know,' answered Chantelle. 'This, you see, is a most romantic village. Births, deaths and weddings are all they 'ave to discuss. And so, brother-in-law, if you lift me over, not only will it delight them, but will give them something to talk about.'

'Lift you over?' Richard was nonplussed.

'Over the stile, *monsieur*. If I climb it – and I must do this without showing an inch of petticoat – they will be disappointed; but if you lift me over it, they will assume that we will soon be lovers.'

'What delightful folklore!'

'Like your kissing gates back home in England, *monsieur*? – a kiss before you can pass?'

Chuckling, Richard lifted Chantelle over the stile, momentarily holding her against him as a burst of applause came from the villagers. But, as he gently lowered her to her feet, Chantelle did an astonishing thing: putting her arms around his neck she kissed him on the mouth, and what began in sisterly affection ended in quickened breathing. Now, standing before him, the colour rose to Chantelle's cheeks, and she lowered her face, saying:

'*Monsieur*, that was unforgivable. But do you know . . .' and here she raised her blushing face . . . 'that is the first kiss I 'ave given to any man?'

'Unkissed? At the age of sixteen?' Richard laughed, waving to the villagers, who, now contented, were returning to the village.

Thought Richard: this is the image of Francesca, beautiful, alluring, provocative. But, there was also about her a simple goodness, a nun-like virtue that Moll had never possessed . . .

Yet the idea, suggested by Francesca, of bringing her home to New Zealand was clearly out of the question. Such unsophistication would bring her isolation among the emancipated circles in which he now walked, and he

305

could never afford the gossip. Also, and this was important to him, although he was obeying Moll's wishes in coming to discover her sister's circumstances, he didn't intend to sacrifice any of his new-found freedom after four years of domestic affliction with Moll and her confounded wheelchair. My God, *no.*

But more – much more. With counterfeiters working in the basement of his bank chambers, valuable insider dealing in the Bourse de Commerce in Paris, and five thousand pipes of opium being smuggled into Shanghai, New Zealand could well proved a hazard, and he didn't want a child hanging on to his coat-tails should it prove necessary to bunk.

Better to open a small bank account for her in Arras, and call the visit a day, for she was clearly living on life's bare necessities: such a girl, surely, would not demand a lot . . .

'Well now,' said Richard, 'are we ready?'

'For what, *monsieur*?' Chantelle, still embarrassed by her recent behaviour, raised starry eyes.

Richard was surprised that she had not yet even mentioned her sister. He asked:

'Are we not ready to go to the hotel?'

'There is no 'otel in Avesnes, *monsieur*. The nearest is at Arras. Anyway, 'ow could I let my sister's 'usband stay in a cold hotel? Therefore I 'ave changed and aired my bed, so you can sleep in comfort.'

'But what about you?'

'The schoolmaster's wife says I can sleep at the school 'ouse.'

The villagers watched as Chantelle and Richard entered the school cottage.

'This,' exclaimed Richard, 'is marvellous! Here you have everything for your convenience!'

'Except the money,' answered Chantelle. 'Schoolteachers in France 'ave to eat also, like the birds.'

'Times are thin?' he laughed at the ceiling. 'Not by the look of this table!'

'This table is special. For weeks I 'ave been saving . . .'

Richard was not jocular now. 'Don't tell me you are short of money!' He stared askance at her. 'Francesca gave me to understand you were well off!'

'*Non.*'

'But the jewels she sent you!'

'Yes, but not to me – to Uncle Maurice, for my keep.'

Richard drank, watching her; this was coming as a disappointment. He said suavely, 'But, when Uncle Maurice died, did he not leave you money?'

'*Non.* He 'ad many children of 'is own.'

Richard filled his glass and swallowed noisily. This was now a shock to his system. He had sailed over ten thousands miles in the hope of discovering wealth in abundance, and had found only a pauper. Controlling his voice, he asked calmly:

'Will . . . will you tell me how much you've got in the bank?'

'I 'ave no bank account.'

'God Almighty!'

Chantelle added, 'I . . . I 'ave got a hundred francs saved, in the Post Office . . .' and Richard's anger showed; he replied:

'That won't get you very far, will it!' Rising from the table he momentarily paced the room. The girl said:

'You come only because you thought I was rich, monsieur . . .?' Tears filled her eyes and she bowed her head.

'Of course not, child, don't be ridiculous!' At which, unaccountably, Chantelle perceptably brightened.

Now they ate in the silence of unspoken questions: for Richard, the realization of his wild goose journey had now divorced him from amiable conversation: but more, he was astonished by Chantelle's physical likeness to Francesca; the girl's exquisite beauty reached out to him over the white cloth between them. Even her voice . . . But . . . and this he noted, too . . . her eyes, bright blue, held a wondrous quality of innocence which Moll, for all her charms, could scarcely be said to possess: so the situation, thought he, may yet be handled to a wise man's advantage . . .

Yet there also existed within Chantelle's smile, a small, almost malevolent threat; it induced in Richard a faint foreboding which he could not distil into recognition. It was as if he had been under her quiet assessment from the moment he had entered the cottage. And this portent increased with Chantelle's continued silence: her smile was constant, but only upon her mouth . . . and to break the embarrassment of the quiet, he said, the meal over:

'I . . . I have been wondering what is best for you, Chantelle, and have come to this conclusion. I shall open a small bank account in your name – with a deposit of a few hundred francs – an amount which could be subsidised should you need more eventually. You understand me?'

'Perfectly.'

Richard drank more wine: his confidence grew.

'Had your sister been alive, it would have been possible for you to return with me to New Zealand – indeed, that was originally our intention, but the situation has changed somewhat . . . Francesca's death, I mean . . .'

There was not a flicker of expression in the eyes across the table. Faltering a little, Richard continued:

'My . . . my bachelorhood would . . . would be compromised by having so young a female in the house – but one old enough, you understand, to raise local gossip.'

What he actually meant was that with Moll sitting for years in a wheelchair, he had been given the run of the local fillies and a female resident would immediately engage their interest: further, he had recently made the acquaintance of a mature woman of beauty and social standing, one his senior by many years whom, he hoped, would not make too many physical demands upon him after his life of dissolution. Virility, he was fast discovering, was an expendable commodity. Take this young temptress back to New Zealand and he could be dead in under a year. But further – pleasant visions comforted him these days, of slippers and feet up by the fire of a rich and pleasant lady. Coming out of his reverie, Richard heard himself say:

'The amount would not be ungenerous. I am not a rich man, but . . .'

''Ow much?'

'How much?'

''Ow much you put in my account?' asked Chantelle.

'Oh, I don't know – let's say five hundred?'

Deliberately she lifted her wine, drank, and said:

'Ce n'est pas possible.'

'Not possible? What is not possible? I think it is very generous!'

She gestured graceful futility. 'Not since the *gendarmes* come.'

'The *gendarmes*?'

'The police three times they come, looking for Moll.'

'Looking for Francesca? But why?' And Chantelle said, slanting her eyes in memory:

'For the murder of Jean Pierre. But now they say the English also want her for killing a judge on a ship . . .'

Richard made to interject, but she silenced him with a finger, adding, 'Also, for assisting the escape of a prisoner.'

'A prisoner? What prisoner?'

She shrugged with noncommittal indifference. 'Oh, I forget. An English prisoner somewhere in Australia, I think.'

309

A silence came, one broken only by Richard's breathing.

Chantelle continued, 'And so, since the *gendarmes* will *certainement* come back and question me more, it would be safer for me to go with you to New Zealand.' She paused, adding:

'You see, we le Roys 'ave a family motto, *Diex lo volt* – "God wills it" – and He has willed that people like you, brother-in-law, are born to keep people like us in luxury – first Moll, and now me. And, if you prove reluctant, we are given a little stick with which to beat you . . .' and she smiled, fluffed up her hair and winked. 'My little stick is a whisper into the ear of the *gendarmes* next time they come . . . they are tryin' so 'ard to discover your address . . .'

'Blackmail!'

The effect of this was appalling to Chantelle, for she rose in anger, crying:

'Damn pig, you Englishman, for calling me that! Always Chantelle 'as been honest, that is why Moll was a banker's wife, and I only a poor schoolteacher!' And she wandered the room in tears, picking up things and slapping them down, clearly upset. Now it was Richard's turn to ask:

'How much?'

''Ow much?'

Chantelle, childlike, put a finger in her mouth and smiled at the ceiling, saying: 'The same as Moll got – 'alf of everything, and while you are thinking that over, *monsieur*, may I leave you for a little minute . . .?'

The little *bitch*!

Moll was a saint compared with her.

And while he had no wish to become involved again with the female le Roys, there seemed little alternative: in the words of men in spittoon taverns, he thought, she's got me by the short and curlies.

310

Nevertheless, he reasoned, it might be best to promise everything now, and then offload her on to an unsuspecting suitor in New Zealand at the first opportunity.

For visions of his dissolute past now began to assail Richard like processional phantasmagoria: the entire cast of the Old Three Pigeons he saw, led by a weeping Biddy; the astonished face of Judge Bosanky as he entered the Shrewsbury lock-up rose in the mist of wine, and he heard again the clanking of his chain-gang fetters as he laboured on Van Diemen's shore: then a hangman's rope descended from the ceiling of his imagination, and he heard the roar of the crowd. For hang he would, most certainly, if the vixen in the next room got the ear of the *gendarmes* . . . extradited from France to die like a dog in England.

But there was one consolation . . . Of love and life he had taken his fill of the loyal Moll Walbee, and of one thing he was sure – at least the sprite in the room next door was virtuous. If stained by greed in Montmarte, Chantelle (one could actually see it in her face) was an innocent when it came to sexuality. Still a child in years, she was yet untutored in sensual pleasure. Perhaps thought Richard, I might be able to build with this child a father and daughter relationship, an affinity uncluttered by vulgar physical demands. But at that very moment the bedroom door opened and Chantelle came through it as bare as an egg.

Crossing the room while Richard stared at her in disbelief, she began to undo the buttons of his waistcoat, meanwhile whispering huskily into his ear:

'Forget the 'orrid old money for a bit, *monsieur*, let's get down to the real business,' and, leading him by the hand, took him into the bedroom, put him on the bed and paraded around like Delilah did to Samson before the roof fell in, saying:

'Come, brother-in-law, don't you think Chantelle is hot enough to become the second Moll Walbee?'

★ ★ ★

311

When, within minutes, the bedroom lamp went out, Madame Campion, the postmistress, elbowed her neighbours, nodded at the darkened window, and said:

'There now – see what I mean? Someone ought to tell the poor soul. He's the third this week, and it's only Tuesday.'